M   04

HANGMAN'S
HOUSE

Though she had not dared hope to win Ireland's biggest flat race, she disconsolately saw the second, third, and fourth places captured by any but Joyzelle

HANGMAN'S HOUSE

BY
DONN BYRNE

Author of "Messer Marco Polo," "O'Malley
of Shanganagh," "The Wind Bloweth," etc.

ILLUSTRATED BY
JOHN RICHARD FLANAGAN

THE CENTURY CO.
New York & London

Copyright, 1925, 1926, by
THE PICTORIAL REVIEW COMPANY

Copyright, 1926, by
THE CENTURY CO.

———

First printing, March, 1926

PRINTED IN U. S. A.

82
B9963
XHa

Coriner 5.16 3-15-65

60419

A FOREWORD TO FOREIGNERS

My people, messieurs 'dames, for all their romance, are a practical nation.   A national novelist, to them, is not a figure to be placed in an
academy in a gold-laced coat, as the French is,
or compelled to wear a beard and act like a person in a play, as German and Austrian novelists,
or a fellow to be ever on your guard against, to
admire very slightly, very grudgingly, to be con-
temptuously patronizing toward, as is the English
novelist to the modern Englishman.   An Irish
novelist gets from the Irish people a certain reverence, a good measure of kindliness, considerable
latitude in conduct and thought: in fine he gets his
due from a God-fearing people.   But he must not
forget that his first duty is homeward.

Granuaile is quite properly a jealous lady.
The poet in verse or prose who prefers the
foreigner is quite welcome to the foreigner—and
be damned to him and them! as we say in the
Gaelic.   If you want to parade before foreigners,
you can have the foreigner's praise, and no more.
You will never know that love that Thomas

v

Moore knew, or Charles Lever, or Miss Edith
Somerville and "Martin Ross." The poet William Yeats might not be forgiven for introducing
the nine bean-rows of English suburbanity (as
of Kingston-on-Thames or Sunbury, God knoweth!) into the eagle-haunted heather of Innisfree
had he not written that "Ballad of Father Gilligan" that is like a violin bow across our heart-
strings. And that Mister Synge, who gained so
many plaudits abroad some years past, had never
a "God bless the work!" from home because he
would not, or could not, write an Irish play for
Irish men.

The most marked difference to be found between the civilization of the city of the excellent
Timothy Healy (whom God preserve!) and the
civilization of the city of Pericles is this: that
where the Athenian sought something intellectually new, the Dubliner, and the Galwegian and
the Corkonian also, require something of proven
value. The proper subject of conversation for
an Irishman, you may have noticed, is Ireland.
Where your average Englishman thinks that Jack
Cade was a heavy-weight boxer of the reign of
Henry VI, and the Wars of the Roses something
like the *bataille des fleurs* at Nice, we know every
man and every engagement in every Irish war.
Our legendary heroes are household words with

us, even those whom the disciples of the English poet William Morris and the German musician Richard Wagner have fashioned for us; our babes lisp their names between debates as to the relative value of dominion and republican governments.

But apart from the population of Ireland, there are Irishmen everywhere. In New York, in the West Indies, in Monte Carlo of course, in Cairo, in Seville, yes, in Jerusalem's self I have met them, and their question to me has always been the question of General Napper Tandy to the author of "The Wearing of the Green." I don't suppose that down in their heart of hearts anybody cares a tinker's curse about politics, barring politicians. Give us good racing, cheaper cigarettes, and civil policemen, and your Lordships may sleep better of nights. . . . But back of the question of "How is old Ireland?" there is this: "Tell us, is Three-Rock Mountain as purple as ever? And are the three-year-olds as wonderful as ever as they charge up the Curragh Mile? Are there swans on the Liffey? Are the fields still green? Tell me, does the Irish wind whisper gently among the Irish trees, or was it only a dream of exile?" I can remember many years ago in Bermuda being shown the tamarisk (or was it some other sort of tree? I have forgotten) under which Thomas Moore, our poet,

used sit. Those with me were thinking of the
pleasant picture of a poet sitting under the sway-
ing branches, dreaming out some precious phrase.
But from that tree I could see a greenness of
fields, a billowing of land I could duplicate in
many a spot in Leinster. So like Ireland it was
that there was a wringing of my own heart, and
I thought: this, and "At The Mid Hour of
Night" are Moore's greatest poems, and of the
tears near my eyes I was not ashamed. I hope
this little bit of understanding will weigh on the
day when I shall have to answer for many cruel-
ties, against my gibes at his facile rhymes. . . .
I have a journeyman's smattering of many liter-
atures, but nothing touches me so much as the
cry of the Irish captain grown gray and old
in Tangier in the days when Charles II was king:

*Dha waughee areesh may a gyart-lore mech gheena
Dyim hoghee an eesh dyeem is veng areesh ogg.*

[If I were set once more in the midst of my people,
decay would go from me, and again I 'd be young.]

I am certain that no race has for its home the
intense love we Irish have for Ireland. It is more
than love. It is a passion. We make no secret
of it, and people gibe at us, saying, with a sneer
that does not speak well of their manners, "Why
don't you go back to Ireland?" Which is not

merited, for every one must know the intricate prison this life is, and how this friendship, that grave, and even the unutterable vulgarity of money matters tie us to an alien land. So that to many a million of us, and a million's sons and daughters, Ireland must be a land of dreams. We are like the children who listen about a nursery fire to a tale out of Grimm or Hans Andersen. But the children grow up, and they know—God help them!—that there was never a Cinderella, who had a magic coach, or king's daughters who danced away their slippers among enchanted trees, but our Ireland, we know, did and does live. Gentle and simple, we have all our memories, the hunt ball or the cross-roads dance. Surely there was never such gaiety, such music.

It happened that I returned to Ireland after the German War, in a period very unsettling for all countries and for ours particularly so. Many native precious things were gone. A new era has always a new civilization, perhaps better, perhaps not. Whatever remains, the old fashion of Irish novels is dead as Pharaoh. And to myself, the last traditional Irish novelist (the last, living masters, because the youngest: I have only begun my six and thirtieth year), the work of writing the last traditional Irish novel has fallen. We shall always—please God!—have Irish writ-

ers, but their models will be Scandinavian or
American. Our young men have seen terrible
realities, and in the Ireland of the future you
must be efficient in order to live. So the school
of Goldsmith and Sterne will pass, and the author
will appeal to the brain instead of the heart,
which is perhaps as it should be—and perhaps
not. But coming home to Ireland at that time,
it seemed to me that I was like some young poet
of Carthage who was returning to find great
Dido in her tomb, and whose work it was to set
down, for men and men's sons to remember, the
shining beauty of her face.

They are not in Grafton Street any more, those
girls whose faces, whose silvery voices made a
fair day fairer. London and Deauville and
New York are the gainers. But I can remember
going from College to Stephen's Greens, and seeing that street like a garden, so much of beauty
did it hold. And those old men, soldiers who
conquered and statesmen who ruled the world—
the black years have swallowed them. Where is
Parnell's brother, who was daily a pillar to be
seen? and that great Greek scholar, the friend of
continental kings? and poor Endymion, with his
umbrellas and his swords? Have I heard the
last ballad-singer, his come-all-you splitting the
air? I fear I have. Soon, I suppose, even I

shall forget. When I was a boy, Sir Daniel Donelly, the great boxer, was still a memory of living men. And I can remember when Orby won the Derby stakes for Ireland, beating Woolwinder and the gallant Slieve Gallion by a length and a length and a half. Will ever another Derby winner be foaled and trained in Ireland? And will there ever be another winner of the Waterloo Cup like Lord Lurgan's great hound Master McGrath? And I can remember when looking forward we saw revolution as a gallant, chivalrous adventure, in our foolish romantic hearts. Already those great Irish regiments are being forgotten, the Inniskillen Dragoons and the Connaught Rangers. They are disbanded now, whose colors were glorious on all fields of battle. Surely it is better. They were never meant for apothecaries' wars.

So that, before all this is forgotten, I have written a book of Ireland for Irishmen. Some phrase, some name in it may conjure up the world they knew as children. . . . I shall never write a "Vicar of Wakefield" or draw an Uncle Toby or Corporal Trim, but in my own way—myself, the poorest perhaps, the humblest certainly of the hierarchy of Irish novelists—I may have the privilege of doing something for my people. The knowledge of that is sufficient reward, and if there is added to it, from the reader, a blessing on the hand that writes, I am so much the richer.

DONN BYRNE.

Saint Lucy's Day, 1925.

ILLUSTRATIONS

ILLUSTRATIONS

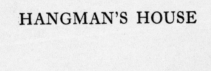

HANGMAN'S HOUSE

HANGMAN'S HOUSE

I

§ 1

ONCE more had come now the miracle of the Irish June. Yellow of gorse; red of clover; purple of the Dublin Mountains. Everywhere the white of the hawthorn; there would be a hard winter coming, the gloomy farmers said, so much of it there was. And wherever a clump of trees were, there grew great crops of bluebells. And the primrose lingered, who should have been gone three weeks and more. And over the white roads the trees met, elm and ash and sturdy horse-chestnut, making cool green tunnels, like some property out of a fairy story. And where there were dock-leaves by the roadside the golden snail crept, with his long sensitive eyes, his little house on his back—*sheleg-a-bookie*, the Irish children call him affectionately, snail of the hump—the golden snail with his mottled house, who leaves a band of silver on the green leaf.

Once more had come now the miracle of the Irish June. Westward the sun drove, like some majestic bird, and the rays, yellow as yellow wine, cleared the purple peaks and slopes, the peaks of the Sugar Loaves, the Big and the Little; the Scalp; and Katie Gallagher's and Two-Rock Mountain; and Three-Rock Mountain, that in Irish is called *Slieve Roe,* the Red Hill. But in the valleys and lowlands the foggy dew still rested, so that the kine and horses were breast-deep in it, as in a sea of silver. And from the mountains there blew a little breeze cool as cool water. All the population of the trees was busy. There sounded the passionate note of the wood-dove. The cheery blackbird sang, and the thrush whistled. There arose the little piping of the finches. The lark mounted into the high air, and the kingfisher skimmed the river in search of the golden speckled trout.

Once more had come now the miracle of the Irish June, recking nothing of revolts or reprisals, riot or civil commotion, or that humorous alien phrase about treason against our Sovereign Lord the King, His Crown and Dignity. Somewhence south she had come, out of some secret hiding-place of Africa, and coming high over the Mediterranean she had touched the harsh highlands of

Spain, and, smiling on France, she had come straight as a pigeon to her kingdom. Now there was nothing north of her but the grim and silent Pole, so here she must stay. All the trees nodded to her, all the flowers waved, the rivers sang and the salmon leaped high from his pool. The little people of the hills and the strange creatures of the mist yielded her precedence, retiring some secret whither, the fairy pipers who pipe by the fairy forts, and the little cobbling leprecauns who own each of them a crock of gold, and the Women of the Shee who wail in the mists of winter when great men die, the Naked Hangman with his gibbet, and the great horse-like *pooka,* snorting fire, who covers Ireland in three bounds. All these were gone, doing her reverence. She came with the silver of the foggy dew about her feet, and the sun in her hair, yellow as yellow wine, and about her was a garment of apple green, and the coolness of her hands was the coolness of the singing rivers. And the ripple of the grass and the winds perfumed with clover were her heralds, so that the poacher of the hills, and the fishermen of Aran and the peasant tilling his acre stopped for a moment to say, "God is good!" Once more now had come the miracle of the Irish June.

§ 2

If you were to ask all over the County of Dublin which was the most pleasant homestead there, you would invariably elicit the answer: "Begor, that's a hard question to put on a man, and devil a bit of me knows, barring it's the McDermots' place at Dermotstown." And if you were to go thither, winding through the green lanes and over the little clear streams that nestle under Three Rock Mountain, you would probably be disappointed, for all you would see at first would be the fields of grass, bluish-green like untroubled sea-water, and acres of oats, ripening gently as a child breathes, and paddocks where colts gamboled while their staid mothers moved from tuft to tuft of the green pasture. There were no intricate iron gates, only an ivy-covered lodge half concealing an avenue leading toward a group of ancient trees. And feeling you had lost your way, you would inquire at the lodge. A very old, very healthy man, with shrewd eyes and gnarled hands and bent back, would appear.

"Could you tell me, please, where Dermotstown is?"

"And where would it be," he would answer heatedly, "but where you 're standing?"

"But I don't see the house."

"And how could you see the house with the trees that are in it?"

"Is herself" (or "the woman of the house," you will say, because Irish people loathe that strange word "Mrs.") "is herself at home, do you know?"

"And sure how would I know, whether it 's at home she is, or not at home? Sure, I can't stir from this one place."

"Or young Mr. McDermot?"

"Is it Master Dermot? And sure when was he ever known to be at home, barring when all was over for the night, between hunting and coursing, and troubling the men at work in the fields with his new ideas of agriculture—"

"Ah, sure, my God! your Honor, is it listening to that queer old man you are?" and his red-faced daughter would hustle out. "And am n't I the, unfortunate woman to be handed such a father? Go on right up, your Honor; sure they 're all at home, and well he knows it, too, for a bird can't light on the lawn so, without his seeing it, but he 's the queer arguing old man!"

The drive dodges, shifts, and winds to avoid

old oak-trees that must have been old when the
Druids were young—in Ireland no Irishman will
cut down a live tree—and suddenly, in the midst
of the grove, you come on the house, solid, dignified, cheerful.   The lawn in front of it is like
a bowling-green, and everywhere around it is a
riot of flowers.   Back of it gardens extend,
clipped yews, and queer gnarled apple-trees,
and yellow hives of straw for the brown bees.
And suddenly there is the joyous clamor of
dogs.

To the right you can see the sweet purple out-
line of the Wicklow hills; Bray Head, like the
head of some monstrous sea-animal, the silver
edges of the Irish Sea.   There at your feet is the
oval of the Leopardstown race-course, none
sweeter in the world.   There to the left down the
slopes of the hills lies Dublin City—the green of
great Phœnix Park, where the deer are grazing,
soft Anna Liffey flowing beside it to the sea.
There is the sun glistening on the great copper
dome of the Four Courts; there the gray spires of
the churches; there the sands of Ringsend, where
Essex, Queen Elizabeth's darling, landed to conquer Ireland, and where he left, to lose his head.
All around is eternity and beauty, nothing ugly,
nothing new, unless you except the house in the
distance that Mr. Richard Croker, the American

millionaire-statesman, is having built for himself.

Outside was beauty and eternity. Within there was peace. This was no Norman tower built by men in armor from overseas. Nor was it a wild fortress once the pride of the clans of the hills, O'Byrnes and O'Moores. There was about this place the spirit of the age, but not of an age of battle and rapine. Here was a homestead such as was loved in the days when the Peers and Commons of Ireland gathered in College Green, and Grattan thundered against Castlereagh, and Curran made the Four Courts ring with the greatest eloquence since Cicero. Here in those strenuous days was peace, while in Dublin Tiger Roche the duelist and Major Kilkelly roamed, seeking a fight as an appetizer for breakfast.

And here was peace still. In peace the brown bees made their golden honey. The dogs chased one another in the grass. The trees murmured under the wind with a gentle sound as of a wave curling and breaking on a calm beach. Here old servants lived happily. Here was hospitality. Bees sang in the clover, swallows darted to and from the eaves. In the evening the luck-bringing crickets chirruped. Here was what the old Irish mystics called *"Kewn Kreestha,"* the Quiet of Christ.

§ 3

The ancient lodge-keeper had caught an unfortunate under-gardener in his toils and was discussing with him the tragedy of existence.

"You're a young lad, and they beat you. You're a fine man, and they persecute you. You're an ancient man, and they bury you." He took a pinch of snuff, solemn as a cardinal. "That's all I see in life. Now, tell me, did you ever see any good in it?"

"Oh now and again, Neddy Joe. An odd glass o' whisky, a piece of pig's cheek, or a horse coming in at three to one itself—"

"And the odd glass only makes you want a gallon, and the pig as likely as not as tough as a tree, and the money a bookie gives you is only lent to you. My boy, my boy, as Tom Moore said, it's all vanity and the affliction of spirits." His ear caught the stretching gallop of a great horse down the road, and he turned to the under-gardener. "Let you get to work, young man," he snubbed him, "and not be taking up my time with your empty conversation."

"Well, the devil scald you for an old—"

"Away and chase your snails, you tinker.

Here's the young master. You and your pig's
cheek, and your glass o' whisky!"

The big black gelding slowed down to a trot, to
a walk, entering the avenue. The lodge-keeper
raised his ancient voice.

"Isn't it the queer shame for you, Master Dermot, to be taking the best horse in the stables and
you only down to see the men working in the
fields? And wouldn't Minnie-Louishe, the bay
mare, have done you just as well? Or your two
fine legs itself?"

Very slight, very young,—not twenty-five yet,
—very dark in the hair, very gray in the eye, reg-
ular in the features as a girl, the young McDermot might have seemed effeminate but for a certain fixed set to the mouth, a little gravish look
of responsibility. A horseman would note, too,
his light firm seat, and sense the fineness of his
hands on the mount's mouth. There was something familiar about the type of face; one
couldn't place it somehow—the fixed gray eyes,
the steady forward look. And then suddenly you
remembered. Put away the tweed cap, and the
riding-stock. Let the black hair roll in ringlets
to the shoulders. Let there be a slight mustache.
And you have the type you see in old paintings
in Irish and Scottish and English houses, of cavaliers who fought Cromwell, and men who went

with Sarsfield, Earl of Lucan, to battle for France at Ramillies and Fontenoy, and men who stood by the old Pretender, and fought with Prince Charles, the men of Fifteen and the Forty-five. The Wild Geese of Ireland.

"You didn't see your cousin John, and you out riding did you, Master Dermot?"

"My cousin John? What cousin John?"

"Your cousin John D'Arcy, and who else?"

"You're losing your mind, Neddy Joe. John D'Arcy's in Russia."

"Well, if Russia's three miles off, he's there. But if it's not, he's not there. And there's no man can be in two places at the one time, barring he was a bird of the air. I tell you, Master Dermot, your cousin John D'Arcy's back."

"Where is he?"

"He's at Jimmy the Hangman's."

"Damn it, Neddy Joe! Stop calling him that name. He's Lord Glenmalure."

"He may be Lord O'Brien of Glenmalure to you, Master Dermot, but to me and mine and the country at large he's Jimmy the Hangman, for there was never a Lord Chief Justice of Ireland," said he, "has stretched more necks in his day than the same James O'Brien, and stretched the necks of the fine Fenian fellows, my own son among them. So I'll call him Jimmy the Hangman, as is my right, Master Dermot."

"Did you see John D'Arcy?"

"I did. And you'd hardly know him, so."

"Is he changed so much?"

"Devil a change. Barring he's grown to be a grand robust man. And a big brown beard on him, down to his watch-chain. If I did n't know him for the twister he is, I'd say he was the grand lad entirely."

"I wonder why he came so quietly," young Dermot puzzled. "And what's he doing at James O'Brien's?"

"He came quietly for the usual reason, I suppose, and the reason of many a better man—that the police were after him. Where else would he go, but here or there, and you know the welcome your mother would put before him, and she knowing the crookedness that's in him."

Young Dermot gathered the horse to go forward.

"Ah, well! what does it matter?"

"And as to what he's come for—"

"Oh, we don't know." The horse was moving.

"'T is what I heard say," old Neddy Joe cried,

"that there was hope in him to marry Miss Connaught."

He turned to find his red-cheeked daughter furious with him.

"And are n't you the dirty devil of an old man to be saying that to the lad! And why did you?"

"To give him a hint to be getting a move on himself I did it."

"And did you think that little Miss Connaught would marry a twister like John D'Arcy?"

"And don't good women always marry twisters? And by the same token don't good men always marry cantankerous women? Did n't I marry your mother?"

"And so you think so little of women—"

"I do so. Mind me now, until I tell you what y' are! You 're thick in the body but you 're thicker in the head. Away with you, you tinker's biddy! What do you know about women? You 're only a woman yourself."

§ 4

His mother was in the rose garden, watching the coming of the great blooms of June. A very sweet-faced woman, who had seen much tragedy,

and whom tragedy had only made sweeter.
There were shadows around her brown eyes, and
in her brown hair were veins of silver. Her
voice had still the soft Philadelphian accent it
spoke when the elder McDermot had come to
America with Meagher of the Sword and flung
himself into the Civil War. Her husband had
been dead now these twenty years, and her first
son lay somewhere on an African veldt, dead with
the dead of the Munster Fusiliers, and Kathleen
her little daughter slept in Kill of the Grange.
There was only Dermot now. She watched him
come to her through the orchard, striding over
the dappled grass. Always she watched him with
a little grave smile. He had never been a child:
he had always been a grave boy—ever since he
was three years old. Always the same quiet direct way about him. He had been closer to her
than her first-born, the gallant Fusilier who was
dead outside Ladysmith, or even the little fair
daughter who had gone away. Desmond had
been dashing and romantic, like his father, and
Kathleen had begun to show the beauty of her
Irish grandmother who had set all London by the
ears, but Dermot was grave, courteous, direct,
like her own Quaker folk in Pennsylvania. He
never laughed as his father and brother and sister had done so generously, but his face would

light with a smile like yellow sunshine. At other
times there was a little frown of puzzled concentration on his face. She saw it had deepened this
morning, as he came toward her among her roses.

"Well, Dermot, my son?"

"Mother, where is John D'Arcy our cousin?"

"Isn't he in Russia, or with the Russians, fighting the Japanese?"

"Neddy Joe says he is at Glenmalure's."

"I shouldn't be surprised, my son. If the Russians are losing, John D'Arcy wouldn't stay with
them long."

"Neddy Joe says he has grown a big beard."

"That's funny." His mother paused. "He
was always so proud of his features. Funny!"

"Mother!"

"Yes, Dermot."

"Would Glenmalure give him Connaught to
marry?"

"I don't see why he wouldn't, my son. If
John D'Arcy settles down, he's the sort of son-in-
law James O'Brien would like. He's a keen politician. He's unscrupulous. He's like O'Brien
himself."

"But O'Brien wouldn't like rebels."

"There are rebels and rebels. There are very
brave hearts and very black ones. There are

men who rebel so that they can be bought into
loyalty at a high price. O'Brien himself, Dermot. James O'Brien, the rebel poet at twenty-
five writing the 'Song of Defeat' and forty years
later Baron O'Brien of Glenmalure, known
through the country as Jimmy the Hangman."

"Is John D'Arcy like that, Mother?"

"Yes, son."

He took a few steps down the garden path,
slapped at a bee buzzing close to him, came back.

"Mother—" he looked at her steadily—"am
I too young to marry?"

Her heart sank. For an instant it ceased being flesh and blood and became lead. Her throat
contracted. Then she smiled.

"Of course not, Dermot."

"Would you mind very much, Mother, if I
brought a wife to our house?"

"No, Dermot. Of course not, my son. Is it
Connaught?" she asked.

"Yes, Mother."

"And she has—"

"No, not yet, Mother. But I'm going to see
now."

And he went from her, in his grave direct way,
out of the rose garden, through the orchard,
across the dappled grass.

§ 5

Of course she would mind.   A mist came into
her eyes, now he was gone, and no longer were the
firm buds of the roses visible to her, but a vague
cloud of red and white color before her.   Of
course she would mind.   And she had thought to
herself often, as mothers will, that Dermot would
be one of those men who would not marry, but
would remain with her, unshared, unspoiled, and
close her eyes in sleep, and then, the house being
so lonely after her, would take some grave sweet
woman for a wife, now she was gone.   He was
so grave, so like a man almost, that she could not
imagine him wooing.   But it had to come.

"Thee is a very selfish woman, Anne," she told
herself.

But if it were Connaught it would n't be bad at
all, she told herself now.   Connaught would be
like a daughter in the place.   Who better than
Connaught would like the beehives, and the yew-
trees groomed like horses, and the old apple-trees,
ancient friends?   And the dogs would all welcome
her, and the horses whinny at her coming.   And
the house, so sweet and ordered now, would become pleasantly rumpled, with vitality in it.   The

great piano, on which she played the romantic Chopin of her youth and the sugared Italian melody of her married life, would awake to the harmony and rhythm of newer music. And again there would be babies in the old house.

Again there would be babies in the old house. She had forgotten that. Again there would be work for her. For years and years now she had felt idle, unnecessary. Though she had had three children, for years now she had seemed like an old maid, looking after the house, making a hobby of her flowers. Desmond the soldier had been so long from home before the Boer sniper had caught him; and Kathleen—it was so long since she died, poor lamb; and Dermot had always been such an independent lad and needed no mothering. But babies to grandmother and to guide —and Connaught to take care of, too, for Connaught's mother had died when she was a child! Connaught would need her with her babies, her babies and Dermot's.

"I am a selfish old woman," the mother said again and smiled.

And one thing more. Dermot would be more happy. He was n't happy now. He had always been such a reserved boy, and had never told her much, but she knew. Always the sea was bothering him, ever since he had been a boy of seven.

It had been the dream of his childhood to join a
navy, the American preferably, and rise as Irish
sailors had risen before, as John Paul Jones had
risen, and Commodore Jack Barry. The Irish
tradition of the sea was dying. The great names
were setting, like old St. Brendan's, greatest of
prehistoric mariners, and the Macnamaras of
Clare—hounds of the sea, their names meant—
who had harried Africa, and that dim brave Galway figure who had been Columbus's pilot. But
Desmond, instead of remaining at home as the
elder son should, had gone for a soldier, and until
he would return, Dermot was chained to the land.
And Desmond never returned.

Not only was he chained to the land but he was
chained to the name. Gone are the kings of Ireland, the High King and the Kings of the Five
Provinces; gone the marquisates and the counties
palatine; gone the gallowglasses with their pikes
and shields. The old castles are gone, and the
rushes that strewed the floor of them, and the
great wolf-dogs that drowsed before the bog-oak
fires. The old harpists are gone, with their harps
of booming applewood, and of them hardly even
a little tune remains. But over the country there
are still great names, titles old as time. The O
Morchoe, Chief of the Sept; Fitzjohn Fitzgerald,
Knight of Glyn; the MacGillicuddy of the Reeks.

They remain, like mountain peaks of some continent sunk beneath the ocean. They remain as a testimony—and as a danger. And chief among them McDermot's own name stood. A kinsman of his still held the title of Prince of Coolavin, and though he had sons, yet to Dermot the title might come. There are always fire, storm, civil riot, and commotion, as the law phrase goes. There is always the Act of God. There are always those very vague but evidently dangerous people called the King's Enemies.

For these old chiefs, knights, princes, there is no pomp or ceremony, no parades cock-a-hoop or heralds blowing silver trumpets. There is only loyalty in people's hearts, and a great tradition. There is in the Gaelic Revelation talk of a day when the Boar will rise in the Valley of the Black Pig, and the Red Militia will hold Ireland for three years and three days. And to Louth will come a Miller without Thumbs, and his mill-race will run red with blood, and the chiefs of Ireland will gather in a high place and proclaim a queen. What this old mysticism means, no man knows. Nothing, perhaps, but the cry of a crazed monk on an island in the Atlantic, but in Ireland it clings. Ask any of the old Irish families about it; they will laugh but look embarrassed. If you were to suggest a hundred years ago, fifty years ago, yes, and in some cases even now, the exchange of one of these Irish titles for an earldom or a duchy, if you were n't a very good shot with a pistol you were a dead man.

Anne McDermot smiled. She had slipped very easily into this atmosphere. The heart of her own Western people is not very different from the heart of the Gael. And she had been so long in the magic land that this tapestry of an old chivalry was clear to her. In front of it she could see her handsome disappointed lad, who would have loved to roam the wide seas over, from the heroic ice of Baffin's Bay to the perfumed islands of the South, and follow the sun as it went westward from China to Panama, and who cared more for one sweet breeze at sea than all the miracles of the land. But who had remained at home, taking care of her and of Dermotstown and its farms, and standing by for Clan Dermot in case he was needed.

And she thought: "After all, he can't go away. And he knows it. This land of his father's and grandfather's must n't pass into unkindly alien hands. The bigger the man and the name, the bigger the duty. And perhaps," she thought, "the dream will pass, and he will be happy here. A young bride he would love, and a young son, and a little daughter. Abhorred duty becomes a pleasure. Many a girl is wild in her mind, dreaming heroic passionate dreams, and she marries and the children come, and she is happy as a cricket. And perhaps with men that comes, too," she said, "though men are more difficult to settle than women. If Connaught married him he would be happy. How else, with Connaught, could a person be but happy and proud?"

But could Connaught marry him? It rested not with her but with her father. In Ireland love is a queer occult sacrament. Love-making there is plenty, which means nothing, but love itself is a wild and shy thing, which alights only when people are men and women in thought and feeling. So that a girl's parents decide for her, knowing a life of which she knows nothing. And often with the blind obstinacy of the old they decide wrongly, and console themselves by saying it was the Will of God.

If Connaught married him, thought his mother, she would have work to do, in guiding the young pair in tactful unseen ways, in spoiling their babies, she smiled. And if Connaught did n't marry him, or, rather, Glenmalure had other plans for her, then also she would have work to do, for he would no longer be a calm grave young lad, but only a stricken boy, her own big stricken boy.

ALL Connaught's looks, her coloring came from her mother's family. Her small stature, her soft black hair, reddish black, with purple lights in it. Her light-brown eyes—sherry-colored, honey-colored—what you will; dark orange specks in them, like the specks you see on a trout. Her nose a little tilted, her mouth a little too wide for beauty, but for honesty and sincerity not one millimeter. The width of mouth and the lovely shaped, too-large hands were the only defects in her perfection, but the hands were firm and cold, and the mouth was firm and warm. With loveliness you had health. And none ever thought of the over-large hands, the over-wide mouth, while looking at the reddish-black hair, the orange-flecked hazel eyes. Of her father, Glenmalure, either the young James O'Brien, the rebel poet, with curly black hair and gray eyes and face lean as a hound's, or the old hanging judge with a jowl like iron, and twisted mouth, and knife-like suspicious eyes—of her father, Glenmalure, there was nothing in her.

There seemed to be two Connaught O'Briens. One the world saw usually, the trim debonair little horsewoman, in habit and boots and mannish hat, striding around with a cigarette in her mouth, testing curb and girth before being tossed into the saddle,—a strange little imp who seemed fifteen instead of twenty-one, and who appeared dressed for a masquerade rather than for some of the stiffest hunting country in Ireland,—and then there was the Connaught in slim frock, and with her hair done in the Irish manner, the white division down the center of the head. The lovely mass sweeping in a sweet line to the great knot at the nape of the neck, that was lissome and slender, like the stalk of some great flower. And this Connaught's eyes were not keen and direct, but shy and dreaming. And this Connaught seemed taller than she actually was, as the first Connaught seemed less tall.

The first Connaught was content with the line of the mountains; was keen for the sharp mountain air. Loved the plains of Meath where the stag was hunted, and the gorse of Kildare where the red fox hid, and the rocky slopes of Bray where they chased with harriers. The roar on the Irish race-courses before the tapes went up;

the keen competition of the Horse Show; the rain
in her face; the sharp frost under white winter
moons, the Northern Lights at the coming of
spring—these the first Connaught loved.   But
the second, the dreaming Connaught, looked
through the mountains into strange foreign lands;
looked westward the hundred odd miles toward
Galway of the Tribes, and between Galway and
the New World there was only the Atlantic Ocean
—"a sup of water," an old man once said to her,
"and if it was n't for the unnatural breadth of it,
sure you could see the quick American people, and
them arguing on the sidewalks of New York!"
Eastward was France, and the light of the boulevards, and the gay handsome Latins at the opera;
and Switzerland, where were ice sports, skating
and skiing and great mountains to climb, and always people.   And Monte Carlo of the gambling,
and the gayest world of all the world; and Spain,
where they danced strange staccato dances; and
Portugal, where there were dead stuffed kings in
glass cases, so she had heard.   And Egypt, where
the Sphinx was, and the pyramids, and dahabiyehs
(was n't that the word?) going up the lovely
moonlit Nile.   All those strange beautiful places,
all those new interesting people!   Ah! in the
phrase of her country, she did be thinking long!
   At five her father, who was James O'Brien,

Queen's Counsel then, had put her in a convent at Drogheda, so as to have his hands free for his political and legal career. And there she stayed while he fought his way to be attorney-general, then Lord Justice O'Brien, then Lord Chief Justice of Ireland—the harshest judge Ireland had known since Norbury hanged poor Robert Emmet. They had been very kind to her, very sweet, the sisters, in spite of her alien faith, and she had loved the sweet clean rooms, the gardens, and the nuns' graveyard, as peaceful as a small lake island at sunset. Then, as brusquely as he had put her in, her father took her out.

Why, God alone knows. He paid her as little attention at sixteen as he did at five. To the new house at Glenmalure came only old officials, members of Parliament; army officers, none below the rank and corresponding age of colonel; members of royal commissions. Came also their women folk, who had learned to hold their tongues early in married life. Quite early in the evening, Glenmalure would take out his watch, look at it seriously: "Half-past nine o'clock, Conn. Go to bed!"

Four or five times he took her to London, forgot her in hotels, and kept her with him sometimes while he talked to his friends until two in the morning, while she went to sleep where she

sat.   Once a Member of Parliament took pity on
her, and proceeded to give her a holiday.   He
took her to the Tower to see the crown jewels.
Returning, he stopped at Whitehall, showed her
the statue of Charles I, and discoursed solemnly
for forty minutes on the iniquities of the Stuarts,
his main theme being that though he demanded
respectability in his private life of no king, yet he
demanded, in the name of the Commons of the
country, such outward similitude of good repute
as would redound to the credit of the nation in
foreign lands.   He then brought her to the Wax-
works and showed her a startling likeness of that
Doctor Crippen who murdered and boned his
wife.   He gave her an immense meal at one of
the more reputable restaurants, and took down
the date of her birthday in a small book.   She
was seventeen at the time and thanked him gravely
for the outing.   He is dead now.   God rest him!
he meant well.

At eighteen her father sent for her and told
her that she was rich.   Her grandfather, her
mother's father, had left her a fortune hewn from
the marble quarries of Connemara.   It did n't
seem to move her.

"Well, well?   Can't you say something?
Well?"

"Is it a lot of money?"

"Yes. As much as you 'll ever need. Don't you want to do something with it?"

"I 'd like a couple of horses," she said.

"You 've got a hunter and you 've got a hack."

"I 'd like to buy a couple of colts and race them!"

"Well, it 's your money."

She could see the disgust in his face, for it had suddenly occurred to him with a shock that the child of his generating was a fool and, what was worse, a female fool. But when two years later Miss Connaught O'Brien's Irish Dusk won the Phœnix Plate against a field of crack two-year-olds, he reserved decision, and when a year later, at Leopardstown, the sweet filly Lady of Lyons (by Lionheart out of Arabian Lady) romped home for the Grand Prize in front of the Prince of Wales's fine entry, he gave her all the credit she deserved. He took it for granted that her Bard of Armagh, with a gentleman rider up,— young Mr. Dermot McDermot,—would win the Conyngham Cup on the fearsome course at Punchestown, and the gallant old Bard and his jockey did.

If she had asked at this time to be allowed to travel he might have consented, within reasonable limits. With a disagreeable chaperon, an efficient courier, a flock of guide-books, and a medicine-chest, she would have been sent to take homeopathic doses of scenery and monuments through Europe, a feminine and effeminate version of the grand tour of fifty years before. On the other hand, he might have raged, enlarging on a favorite theme of his; to wit, that all Latins were immoral and, worse than immoral, unwashed. That the Alps were vulgarized by tourists, while MacGillicuddy's Reeks were majestic and exclusive. As to culture, in literature what could reach the sublime lyrics of Thomas Moore? (Possibly Alfred, Lord Tennyson, in spots, but none else.) In the field of fiction, could Thackeray touch Oliver Goldsmith's "Vicar of Wakefield"? He was damned if he could! What on the stage could rival those Irish classics, "She Stoops to Conquer" and "The Rivals"? No literature, he felt justified in stating, had produced masterpieces comparable to these. Music. Was there not Balfe's "Bohemian Girl" and Mr. Wallace of Waterford's exquisite "Maritana"? Then why travel? These arguments, it may be pointed out, are difficult to answer with less than a butcher's cleaver.

In his old age, his comparative old age, his mind that had wandered so far in devious currents of politics and loyalties was turning to the beloved isle. He urged Connaught to take an interest in the racing greyhound. It would be a splendid thing to win the Waterloo Cup for coursing to Ireland—a triumph for Irish sport.

"We have accomplished a lot for Ireland, Conn. Your mother's family have been identified for generations with what is admittedly one of the greatest infantry regiments in the world, the Connaught Rangers. You, in the realm of the turf, have done much to raise the prestige of the Irish horse. While for myself I can undoubtedly aver that no justice, no Lord Justice, no Lord Chief Justice of Ireland has insisted with more determination than I on having observed that supreme law which is the well-being of the people. *Salus populi suprema lex!*" Thus Jimmy the Hangman.

But he wasn't destined to do much more good (or evil, as your politics may be) for the people. Stricken with sickness on his bench, he was induced to retire, and his grateful queen created him Baron O'Brien of Glenmalure. All he needed was a rest, he said. But how long a rest he never suspected. All his life he had worked, fought, schemed. The machine he had driven so mercilessly had broken down. His mind was still trenchant, his will keen, but he would never again be a central figure in politics. He had to be content with advising, analyzing. Suddenly

one day he felt worse. A great Dublin doctor
came.

"Well, man, well!" O'Brien barked.

"My lord," the doctor said, "I regret to tell
you you are mortally ill."

"I am going to die?"

"Yes, my lord."

"You damned fool!",he swore. "Get back to
your pills. People like me don't die, not before
they are ninety. No. Not a word!" He rang
for his secretary. "Bring me another doctor,"
he ordered. "This one's cracked." The second man confirmed the diagnosis. He had him
all but thrown out of the house. Specialists were
telegraphed for to London. They came, one in
silk hat and silky Vandyke beard, and frock-coat.
The other was a red-faced, cheery man in tweeds
and a bowler hat. The frock-coat made a solemn examination. He turned to the man in
tweeds deferentially.

"Would you care to make an examination, Sir
William?"

"Ah, no," said Tweeds, "I don't have to."

"Then I'm all right?" Glenmalure laughed.

"I don't know what you call all right—" the
red-faced specialist looked straight at him—"but
you'll be dead in a month."

Glenmalure grinned.   Sir William spoke a language he understood.

"A month?"

"I'll tell you what, O'Brien.   I'll give you
five weeks, not a day less, not a day more."

"It's enough," the old judge grinned bravely.
When they were gone he sent for Connaught.

"I was right," he told her, "there's nothing
wrong with me.   Conn, never have a Dublin doctor."

"Are you sure you're all right, Father?"

"How often do I have to say it?   Perfectly
right."

"I'm so glad," she said simply.   "I was very
much afraid."

"Conn!"

"Yes, sir."

"Conn, did you ever think of getting married?"

"Of course, I did," she laughed.

"Damn it, girl!   Concretely.   I mean concretely."

"I—I don't think so."

Outside an infatuation for a fat Italian tenor, at
fifteen, whom she had only seen and heard once,
she had never been disturbed.   She had been
made love to, as girls are in Dublin, on the tongue
and as a game, and she had answered on the

tongue and as a game.   And once, coming from a
dance, a subaltern had kissed her, as was his duty,
and she had asked herself surprisedly: Was that
all there was to it?   And what was all the fuss
about?

"Has anybody asked you to marry him?"

"Oh, yes!" she smiled.   "There was a lieutenant in a militia regiment—"

"Oh, pshaw!"

"And the curate at Monkstown—"

"Damned impertinence!"

"And Adams, the English bookie, but he was
more in love with the stable than with me."

"Conn," he said coldly, "is there anybody you
know you would care to marry?"

"There's none I know, except young Dermot—"

"A farmer!"

"The best gentleman rider in Ireland!"

"Is that enough for a man?"

"No, I suppose not."

"Then there's nobody?"

"Nobody, sir, and I'm not keen on marrying.
And you're making me very uncomfortable.
Please, Father, when I want to get married I'll
tell you and until then, please— Are you sure
you're all right, sir?"

"Quite all right, Conn."

He lay for a while looking out at the soft dusk.
The bees were home, and the daisies had covered
their pert faces for the night. And now the
cricket began its soft song, and the bats flitted
through the gloaming. He pulled at his immense
jowl, called for candles and pens and paper.

"Would n't it be better now, your Lordship, if
I was to call the secretary, and let your Lordship
be telling him what 's on your mind and him to be
writing it down?" old Murphy, his valet, who had
been his tipstaff, protested.

"No! Damn the secretary! Do what I tell
you."

"Well, I don't know what the doctors would
say if they knew, but sure you 'll have to have
your own way, as always."

Very laboriously the old baron wrote page
after page, addressed the envelope himself and
sealed it.

"Murphy! Blast your eyes, Murphy, where
are you? Here! Post this letter to-night."

"And why could n't it go in the morning's mail-
bag, your Lordship?"

"It could n't."

"Well, if it could n't, it could n't—" he went off
—"but for a matter of twelve or fourteen hours
itself, begor if I can see the hurry," he grumbled,
"for there 's never anything in a letter but bad

news, in my experience. There, Mike O'Hara!
Blast your eyes, Mike O'Hara, where are you?
Here! Saddle a horse and post this letter to-
night."

"And why could n't it go in the morning's mail-
bag, Mr. Murphy, sir?"

"It just could n't," Murphy answered with
severity.

Off the letter went that night, and within two
weeks, tired from traveling across Europe night
and day—not from St. Petersburg but from
Vienna—there appeared at Glenmalure John
D'Arcy, son of the baron's old schoolfellow and
faithful follower, who when in life had been the
Right Honorable Michael D'Arcy, Judge, of Her
Majesty's Most Honorable Privy Council in
Ireland, but better known by the Irish voter and
taxpayer, as "Tricky Mick."

§ 2

Connaught had never seen John D'Arcy before
he turned up unexpectedly at Glenmalure. He
had gone on his travels before she had left her
convent, and on the rare occasions when he visited
Dublin he never came to Glenmalure. Her father

ous haggard man, lithe, with pale face and long hair, with an exalted expression and a flow of hardly coherent speech, so much would his spirit be perturbed.   She had expected the revolutionary of the stage, the young Nihilist of Russian melodrama.   She saw a suave burly man, with a great reddish-brown beard, such as a Romanoff archduke might wear, or a German admiral, or a Magyar count.   His conversation was not of politics and military affairs, but of Monte Carlo and the Riviera, of Paris when dawn crept over the Sacré Cœur at Montmartre, and the great bustle of the halls began; of Cairo and Shepheard's Hotel, of dahabiyehs going up the green Nile, past cotton-fields where bullocks drew water from sluices, keeping time to the monotonous chant of the sakiyeh; of frozen Russian Petersburg, where the boatmen drove rafts in spring, singing the saddest of all songs, and Moscow where all the bells are, and Yard's where the gipsies sing the wildest chants in the world.

"And you have come home for good now?" she asked.   "You are going to settle down?"

"Yes."

"And you will never see all those sweet places any more?"

"Nearly all those places are within a few days of London.   I shall see them every year."

"John," she asked, "what exactly are you going to do?"

"Didn't your father say anything to you of my plans?"

"No. Why should he?"

D'Arcy looked at her in surprise for a moment.

"Well, I'm going in for Parliament, Conn. Your father is going to use his influence to have me nominated for a safe seat."

"And when Parliament isn't sitting you're going to holiday in Paris and Moscow and Prague and Seville? Are you going to have a place in Ireland?"

"Yes, Conn. I think so." His smile was very agreeable.

"John, are you going to race horses?"

"Yes, Conn."

"But won't that all take a lot of money? I thought—you don't mind my saying it, do you? —that you weren't very well off."

"I'll manage." The smile had become a grin.

"John, you must let me help you about the racing, advise you—and that."

"I shall, Conn." He was all but laughing now.

"But I suppose," she grumbled, "that one of these days you'll be getting married, and your wife won't like a strange female around the stables."

"Conn, are you sure your father said nothing to you about his plans—my plans?"

"No. Why should he?"

"No reason at all, but— No; none at all."

§ 3

It took her a little while to get over the immensity of beard. It seemed to her that a man should be old before he grew to such dignity. And it was with a shock that she was convinced, by his eyes, by his words, that he was a young man. He played tennis magnificently. And the beard did n't seem the least out of place with the white flannels. He played much better than she ever could, beating her hollow.

"Of course in Ireland you have n't much chance to play a first-class game. Now, in the Riviera—"

It was a surprise to her that anywhere in the world was sport of a higher class than in Ireland. But when they went out riding, she had plenty to criticize. His seat was all right; his hands were poor—but, then, he could n't be blamed for that, good hands being the gift of God. But he rode in a finicky style she despised. His toes were in

the stirrups instead of thrust home in the Irish
manner. He negotiated fences in a clever but
careful way.

"That won't do for an Irish hunting-field,
John."

"My dear girl, what do you think the style of
these people would look like in the Bois de Bou-
logne or Rotten Row?" There was a good deal
to that. She felt properly abashed.

When they stood looking down at Dublin, he
was like a picture on the white horse, big, straight.
His great rufous beard moved gently by the
breeze. He was like some archduke casting an
eye over a future battle-field. She felt awed.

But the great beard was not to last. Her father, in his brusque, judicial way, suddenly decided against it.

"John," he barked, "take those damned things
off."

"What, sir?"

"Those whiskers. They look like a disguise."

"But, sir—"

"Take them off, I said. Damn it! you look
like a painter. What Irish constituency would
elect you with that handicap?"

"But I rather like it, sir!"

"Take it off!"

"I 'll compromise, sir. Leave it to me."

"You 're strangely obstinate about it. However, look human, not like a beach-comber."

He did compromise. He appeared after a visit to Dublin in a neat Vandyke beard, which made him look very subtle, very polished, like an English baronet of the more serious turns of thought. Connaught was the first to see him.

"Oh, John," she cried, "what have you done to your beard? And I was beginning to like it so much!"

"Am I changed?"

"Immensely. You looked leonine with the other, lovely, splendid. Now you are so clever-looking, so man-of-the-world. You have changed.

"I say, John!"

"Yes, Conn."

"I wonder what you look like clean-shaven. Have n't you a photograph of yourself?"

"No."

"But somebody must have. Some of your friends?"

"No, not one."

"No photographs at all. Is n't that strange! Are you sure?"

"Absolutely sure."

§ 4

When, after dinner, he stood and talked to her father and herself in the long drawing-room of Glenmalure, Connaught thought that she had never seen so fine a figure. His evening things fitted him with a grace rare in England or Ireland. His sleek pointed beard removed any suspicion of effeminacy about him.

There was about him, she thought as she leaned forward listening to him discuss with her father the fate of Arabi Pasha,—that great old rebel!—there was about him a dignified grandeur. Out of each place he had been he had taken something, the grace of Paris, the polished courtesy of Vienna, the subtlety of Egypt, and something a little exotic—not Oriental. Had he got that from Russia? What an addition he would make to a House of Parliament, the calm subtle speech, the Irish eloquence! Oh, he would make his figure in the world!

She loved, too, that incident in his history where he had plotted with compatriots in Paris to set Ireland free. There is nothing the Irish are more proud of than their tradition of great rebels, Shane O'Neill and Hugh the younger,

Silken Thomas, Earl of Desmond; Wolfe Tone and Napper Tandy; Lord Edward Fitzgerald, poor Pamela's husband, and Robert Emmet whom Sarah Curran loved; Michael O'Dwyer of the Glen—their names are legion. By some unknown law of periodicity a magic is flung on the country and the sanest men go rebellious. The young men see visions and the old men dream dreams. The ghostly tramp of the Boys of Wexford is heard in historic streets, and on the hills the Jackets Green of Sarsfield's troopers are sensed under the west wind. And a madness comes on the people, and once more there are green jackets and green banners and the moonlight glinting on pikes. An orderly movement of trained soldiery, the work of artillery, and if that fails a trick of political passe-passe—and all is over but the hangings. And people smile, thinking how futile, how crazy it has all been, but as they smile there are tears in their eyes and a lump in their throats.

And even the English grow sorry, so that many come over and learn to speak Gaelic, which they will call Erse, with a Cockney accent, and wear kilts which the Irish discarded many centuries ago. It is as though a foreigner, enamored of the American spirit and culture, were to adopt the buffalo robe and feathered head-dress of Lo, the poor Indian, and stalk with stoical dignity down Broadway to Bowling Green. But it is very complimentary.

And about the men who have plotted and fought, and who have escaped the hanging and the transportation, there remains always a sense of dignity and heroism, so that boys raise their caps as they pass. It is like the halo of a military saint, if such there be. And their wives are proud forever.

She would be a lucky girl, Connaught thought, who would marry D'Arcy. She would have a husband with an assured and great future, and a past romantic as old chivalry. Handsome, graceful, dignified, and with a very sweet courtesy. And all the world he could show her, the great capitals of Europe he knew so well; they would go through them like two lovers. And the pride this woman would feel as her husband rose to address the hushed House! "D'Arcy, the Irish Member, speaking!" And if he went in for racing, the thrill to be beside him as the blurred brown field turned the rails into the last few furlongs; the hunched gaily clad jockeys; the horses stretching like elastic, the thump of hooves on turf. Lucky girl!

And "Oh, damn!" Connaught thought, she sup-

posed he 'd have to marry some dowdy old frump
for her money!

§ 5

The old baron sat and watched him as he talked
of Arabi Pasha, smoked his long panatela; listened very little and thought a lot.

D'Arcy was n't much of a man, he decided.
The old Lord Chief Justice had looked too many
murderers and felons in the eye not to know a
man when he saw one. No, you could n't call
D'Arcy a hefty man, but he would make a fine
son-in-law.

He remembered with a touch of disgust a conversation with him that afternoon.

"John," he had asked, "about this Paris business: were you in very deep?"

"Oh, no, sir. Not very."

"Have they anything on you?"

Had the old judge's eyes been sharp he would
have noticed D'Arcy become white and uncomfortable. But his eyes were n't sharp. It was
only his mind.

"Damn it, man, you know what I mean. You

know from the Paris end, don't you, that there
has nearly been a revolution at this moment? If
the Russians had won and gone south to India,
and England declared war, Ireland would have
been up and in arms. As a matter of fact, here
and there the poor fools did collect and are only
dispersing now. Their officers will have trouble
sending them home," he mused. "But you know
all this," he presumed. "The question is only:
have they any evidence against you of connection
with this?"

"How, sir?"

"Any signed oaths; anything of that kind?"

"No, sir." D'Arcy laughed relievedly. "I
only flirted with it."

"Hungh!" the old man grunted. "Any of the
old crowd in Paris when you were there? Old
Dinny Hogan?"

"Hogan's dead, sir."

"Is he, now? A queer hating old man, I mind
him well. He has a son."

"Patrice Hogan. He's a commandant of cavalry, in Algiers, I think."

"Isn't he the lad that went through Cochin
China for the French Government, disguised as
a native, and wrote a book about it? A great
job, that! Is that he?"

"I—I think it is, sir."

"If he's anything like his father he'll be a bad enemy." D'Arcy went white as a sheet. "And his daughter—what's her name?"

"Maeve."

"Is n't she a roaring beauty, and a great singer? I heard she was in all the operas of France."

"She's very good-looking. But not opera, sir; a singer of vaudeville."

"Ah, sure, what's the difference? Singing's singing! Where's she now?"

"I—I—I'm sure I don't know, sir. She went to Russia—"

"Were you ever taken with this girl, if she's such a roaring beauty, and a grand singer?"

A pity your eyes are bad, Lord Justice! A pity your eyes are bad!

"No, sir. That is, a little, perhaps—but if anybody says I was, it's a lie."

He is trembling now. There are beads of sweat on his forehead.

"Sure, there's nothing to get angry about. What matter if you were head over heels itself?"

"But why do you ask, sir?"

"Old Dinny was a friend o' mine. We took the Fenian Oath together in the mad days. That's the only reason I ask, my boy. But you're through with it all now, John?"

"As I said, sir, I only touched the fringe, flirted with it."

Hungh! the old judge snorted. So that was the way of the young nowadays. Flirted with treason; "a little taken" with a rebel beauty. "By the living God!" the old judge swore, "when I was a rebel, I was in it up to the ears. I had my pike and pistols and uniform, and was ready to fight until I saw there was no chance of success. And if they'd ever caught me it would have been a well-soaped rope, and a ten-feet drop. Until I made my peace and my bargain. Sure isn't my 'Song of Defeat' still quoted in the Fenian sheets?" And a little taken with Hogan's sweet daughter! Was that what young men had come to? In his young days and he a rebel, was there a maid or a matron in Cork or Kerry he hadn't made love to? "Sure wasn't it enough to ruin a woman's character if she were seen talking to me in the street itself?" he chuckled. And then the serious things of life had demanded a hearing, fame and position and money, and he had put away love and rebellion as one puts away a pierrot's dress after carnival. Eh! but he had been a man!

D'Arcy would never be a man, as men of a rougher, more passionate age measured virility, but, as he thought before, he would make a fine

son-in-law. He was very clever, Glenmalure decided, and he was unscrupulous. He would make
his way in politics, trimming his sails to whatever
breeze there blew. And when it was necessary
for him to desert a cause and go to the opposite
camp, he would act with a show of brave emotion
and conscience, and the people would believe him,
for the people are always fools. *Populus vult
decipi,* did n't an ancient statesman say? A country is disappointed if it is n't betrayed. Yes.
D'Arcy would worm his way forward from seat
to seat and post to post, now by lies, now by black-
mail, until he ended up in the odor of sanctity
and the House of Lords. And probably, the old
baron chuckled, they would call him in all sincerity "Honest John"! It is to be feared that politics make a man cynical.

Crooked, in the country phrase, as a dog's hind
leg, where politics were concerned, he would be
straight in marriage and straight where money
was concerned, because of that most contemptible
of all truths, honesty is the best policy. He
was n't the sort of man to risk his position for a
pair of roving eyes, and because his place and his
income depended on his wife, he would be very
courteous, kind, attentive to her. He would be
a very good son-in-law.

And what if D'Arcy were n't in love with her,

or she with him? He had n't been in love with
Connaught's mother when he married her, and yet
he had been a good husband to her. He had admired her, respected her, so that when she died
there had been such a void in his life that he could
not understand it. Nor could he marry again,
though advantageous alliances were open. There
was one spot in the iron heart that was warm; the
love before marriage might be a delusion, but the
love that came after marriage flourished like the
green bay-tree. The thing to do was to arrange
it suitably.

He had arranged it suitably. Were Connaught a weak, very feminine, silly sort of girl,
he would have got a strong husband. Like—oh
let him see!—like young McDermot, were he
older. He liked that lad's firm gray eye, his firm
jaw. He had very gentle hands for a horse, but
he had wrists like steel when occasion rose. And
how those horsemen handled a mount was how
they would handle a woman. If Connaught had
been different, though she was only twenty-one
and he twenty-five—ah, you could n't change her,
and he would n't want her changed! It was better as it was, the sincere and straight and strong
Connaught and the very clever and agreeable
weakling D'Arcy. She would have independence
and comfort and glory, his little girl.

He did love the child, though he had never said much about it. He could n't, somehow; in that one thing he was inarticulate. But he thought: "If I could have evinced fondness and uttered vocal affection, I would have been a sloppy fool like this D'Arcy, and not the grim Lord Chief Justice of Ireland." "Jimmy the Hangman" a periodical had once called him, he remembered with a chuckle. But this love was not the less real for being dumb.

There was only one thing he regretted, and that was that the queen had not made him an earl instead of a baron, and Miss Connaught would have been the Lady Connaught O'Brien, and how sweetly that name would have gone with her Irish beauty, her calm dignity, her orange-flecked eyes and soft black hair. And indeed damned well the old queen might have done that thing, he thought, seeing that if it had n't been for him and a few like him she would have had no Ireland at all. The loyalty of loyal Irish is toward the crown of England, not toward the sovereign, so he damned her with no feeling of treason, cursing her solid German virtues, her too-obvious respectability. Sure, what could you expect of an old one, he grumbled, who had shown interest in only one piece of music in her life, and it was discovered that the name of that tune was "Come where the booze is cheaper!"

This new man who was coming to the throne, this—what do you call him?—this Edward, begor, he might be induced to make a good job of it. He was a good sportsman, so people said. It was an idea now, and D'Arcy could be jammed into a militia commission somehow—Captain and Lady Connaught D'Arcy.

"I tell you what, O'Brien," he remembered a voice saying, "I'll give you five weeks, not a day less, not a day more."

And that was over two weeks ago. Oh, begob, 't was too late now.

III

§ 1

"WELL, Dermot, my lad, I suppose it's your cousin John you've come to see? He and Connaught are off to Baldoyle Races. I'm surprised you're not there, yourself."

"It's you I wanted to see, sir."

"Well, it must be something very important if it keeps you at home on a day like this."

"It is, sir, very important."

Without, the June sun had mounted high and the silent summer midday reigned. Kine were knee-deep in the mountain streams, and the horses sought the shelter of the elm-trees. Even the birds were still. The organ-note of the bees had become a soft drowsiness. Outside the library windows the voice of the groom who was holding young Dermot's mount broke the silence.

"Wo! Wo! Would you be easy, now? Begor, is it my ear you're after, you cannibal of the world——"

Within the library was coolness and dignity, and shade. On the shelves the great tomes of calf-skin slept, old men's wisdom, and old men's reminiscences and old men's love. Before the great littered table Glenmalure worked, peering through a single eyeglass at a letter written by as old and as frail a man as himself. There was so much to be done, so many letters to be read and written, and so little time! If he had n't liked young Dermot so much, he would n't have even seen him for a minute. But he was glad he did now. All the old frailty of him rejoiced in the young suppleness in boots and riding-breeches standing by the fern-filled hearth. The black hair, the serious gray eyes, the firm stand—what a lad to have for a son! the old baron thought. But as a son-in-law—

"Sir," Dermot spoke, "may I marry Connaught?"

A little pause. "Does Connaught know you 're asking me this?"

"No, sir."

"Are you in love with her, as they say?"

"I don't know, sir. It's a very large word. I suppose I am."

"And she?"

"Connaught is fond of me, sir. We 've known each other since we were children. We 've been always good friends.

"Believe me, sir," he broke out. "We 'd be happy. I 'd take good care of her."

"You'd take very good care of her, Dermot. But would you be happy?"

"Why not, sir?"

"Dermot," the old man asked, "would you think of a public career, politics, Parliament?"

"No, sir. I'm no good at making speeches, and I think politics is not clean sport."

"You wouldn't live in London?"

"How could I, sir? There's Dermotstown to be taken care of. And besides, what could I do in London?"

"You see, you're tied. And is that fair to Connaught?"

"How, sir?"

"Don't you think that Connaught wants life, glory, a big career for her husband? Dances and theaters, the big world, adulation, position, glamour?"

"Does she, sir? I didn't know."

"Every young woman does, Dermot. And Connaught with her beauty and her money, and with such claims on influence as my services warrant, is entitled to this. Connaught's husband, Dermot, will go far."

"Then you think it would be unfair to Connaught were I to ask her to marry me?"

"I'm sure of it, boy, unless——"

"Unless what, sir?"

"Unless you sell Dermotstown, and jump in for politics."

"I won't, sir."

"If you were very much in love with her, you would. So you see, you can't be, Dermot."

"That's got nothing to do with it, sir. Dermotstown is my father's and my grandfather's trust to me. And Connaught would be the first to despise me if I threw over a trust for love of her, and it would be nothing to how I'd despise myself. I think I'll be running along, sir."

"Dermot," the old baron said uneasily, "Connaught will marry John D'Arcy. Say it, damn it!" he roared. "Say it!"

"There's nothing to say, sir, but this: I hope she'll be happy every day, every hour, every minute of her life."

"Boy," Glenmalure said, "your father was in many ways a damned fool, but all in all he was a very gallant Irish gentleman."

"Thanks, sir!"

"And you are no fool, and you are like your father. Will you remain friends with Connaught?"

"Yes."

"Will you be a friend to her, if she needs you? Will you promise?"

"Of course, sir. There's no need to ask. I

would anyway. And do you mind if I run along, sir?" And he was gone.

Glenmalure could hear the firm voice outside. "All right, Callahan, thanks. Let go his head."

"There," thought the old baron, "there goes a man!" A sudden impulse brought him to his feet. He moved painfully toward the tapestried bell-pull by the mantel. But his wiser self objected.

"Let you sit down now, James O'Brien, let you sit down now. And let you not be making a damned fool of yourself at your time of life!"

And Glenmalure sat down.

§ 2

Anne McDermot heard the clatter of her son's mount in the stable-yard. Waited. Moved toward the great window that opened on the orchard. Waited. There were no hasting footsteps toward her. Then she knew.

Outside in the golden afternoon, there was the white twinkle of butterflies. Toward the yellow straw hives laden bees flew like bullets. Swallows whipped like arrows. The last of the apple-blossoms gave a fragrance like wild honey.

There was the swish of a scythe. One of the men
was cutting the hay in the orchard. His voice
rose in an old Donegal love-song:

"As I rode out very early, to view the green meadows in
    Spring;
It was down by the side of a river, I spied a fair maid—
    She did sing.
I stood in my silent amazement to gaze on that creature
    so fair.
She seemed to be brighter than Venus, the maid with the
    bonny black hair."

Now her son's steps were in the house. She
could hear him coming slowly. That was the
sound of cap and riding-crop being thrown down.
The singer whetted the blade of the scythe with
his stone. Again the crude folk-song:

"Her skin was as white as a lily and her cheeks like the
    red rose in June.
Her eyes they did sparkle like diamonds, and her breath
    it did bear a perfume.
And a dress of the bright shining velvet was the dress
    that this maiden did wear,
And chains of pure gold and bright silver were bound in
    her bonny black hair."

She did not move as he entered the room and
came toward her. She was afraid of the change
that might be in his face. If his heart was stricken

too sorely, could hers bear it? He came forward and stood by her and her hand blindly sought his.

"For a long time we wandered together without naming
    a due wedding day.
One day when conversing together, very kindly to me
    she did say—"

"We are to be alone here, little mother, you and I." His voice was firm.

" 'It 's I have another more kindly my land and my
    fortune to share,
So farewell to you now and forever,' said the maid with
    the bonny black hair."

"She 's to marry John D'Arcy, Mother." She ventured a swift glance at his eyes. There were no tears there, but, she felt, there were tears in his heart.

"As I walked down by the harbour I saw a ship for the
    proud land of Spain
They were singing and dancing with pleasure—"

The singer's scythe caught in a root. "Well, bad luck to you for an old apple-tree!" he swore cheerfully.

"Dermot, little son," Anne's soft Quaker voice spoke at last," "would thee like to go away for a while? Go and see thy uncles in America? Go on a ship, dearest, for a while—"

"No, little mother," he said. "I 'll stick by my job."

She looked at him. She looked at him with surprise. He had changed. In three hours he had changed. He had galloped away from her that morning a mannish boy, but a boy all the same, and he had ridden back a man full-grown.

IV

§ 1

INTO Fifth Avenue, this May afternoon, spring had leaped like a dancer. The little trees on the sidewalks were inhaling it, as a convalescent would take drafts of fresh air, after the imprisonment of winter. Southward, a few blocks away in Madison Square, the grass was green again, and a bird was singing high above the rumble of wagons and the *plod-plod* of horses' hooves. The morning had had a golden smile, the noontide a sweet drowsiness, and now the sun was going westward. Soon would be blue shadows, and a sunset that would prophesy as happy a morrow.

But the three men in a sitting-room of the Holland House were not happy. The very old man with the thick white hair, and the lined face and the fingers gnarled from prison toil, had despair in his haggard, washed-out eyes. The kindly gray-haired and somewhat shabby priest had a drooping resignation in his face. The square-built stocky soldier in civilian's clothes gnawed the edge of his mustache, and his dark eyes smoldered.

"So it 's all over," said the soldier.

" 'T is the will of God!" said the priest. The old man leaped with sudden fire.

"How can it be the will of God," he burst out savagely, "that little yellow men should be brave, and great hulking white men cowards? For twenty years in prison I heard about the will of God. Look at my hair, my face. Look at my hands, look at my back bent from sewing postbags. The will of God, me, I 'm sick of it!"

"Hush now, O'Sullivan More. No matter what load is on you, let you not say that," the old priest pleaded.

"Everything in their hands, the big fat fools," the old rebel stormed; "the little islanders gone, and they could have passed into India like a river. China was theirs. Australia caught like a hare in a corner. And England would have had to fight. This time we 'd have pulled it off," he said, "and Ireland would have been free.

"Oh, 'the Bear that walks like a Man'!" he sneered. "The bear that runs like a kicked cur!"

They sat silent for a little while. Into the

conventional sitting-room of the hotel where they
had plotted the downfall of great nations, all the
humdrum noise of the day filtered with utter cal-
lousness, as though to tell them that no matter
what high treason was plotted, what dynasties
fell, what nations lost their banner, life must go
fermenting on. The rumble of traffic below, the
metallic larrup of the elevated train in Sixth
Avenue, the crash of a street organ into a ballad
of the day:

East Side! West Side! all around the town!
Ring-a-ring of roses! London Bridge is falling down!
Boys and girls together, me and Mamie O'Rourke,
When we danced the light fantastic on the sidewalks of
    New York.

Eh, what did the world care what battles were
lost, what hearts broken, so long as men had work
to do, and there was dancing in the evenings!

"So it's all over," again said the soldier.

"No, my God! No!" O'Sullivan pleaded.
"General, Father, let me go across. The boys
are ready. They're keen to go out. Just one
blow for the *Shan Van Voght,* the Poor Old
Woman—"

"No!" The soldier shook his head. "No!"

"Ah, Jer, we could n't," the old priest said.

"Sure, you wouldn't send all those lads to their death, without some hope of victory. It would be madness."

"And, sure, what did me and my friends care about death—" the old man's eyes flashed—"or victory itself," he said, "so long as the heart of the country beat, and there would be examples to rouse it in the dark days? And didn't we go through worse than death, me and my four friends, that spent twenty years in prison, in the same tier of cells, without ever passing a word to one another? And the bread and water, and the hard work, and the cold and the rats, and the water oozing through the walls. So that when the time was up, one of us was dead, and the other three went from the prison to the madhouse. And when I came out, I was only an old man, and my green fields were in the hands of the grabber, and my little sister deep in her grave. Put me on the hills again, Father," he pleaded, "with the Green Flag over me and let me strike one blow for the bitter, bitter years!"

"Ah, sure, it wasn't only you that saw tragic days, Jer." The priest smiled sadly. "I was a little lad," he said, "in the days of the famine, when the white potatoes turned into black slime, and the smell of death was in the land. And on the roads great powerful men dropped and died with the hunger. And wee children—ah, 't would break your heart! In our own small cabin, Jer, as you know, my five wee brothers and sisters died of the hunger. My father, a big red man— there was no work for him anywhere. And when he saw the wee ones dying, he went out of his mind. There was an Englishman had sheep on the mountains, and my father thought that a drop of broth and a bit of meal would keep the life in the children and the neighbors until the relief ships came from America. So he went out and stole a sheep. But he was a poor thief, my father, and they caught him, bringing the dead sheep down the mountainside in the starlight and he wet with the sweat of weakness. So they took him to prison, Jer, and my five wee brothers and sisters died. And the morning they hanged him for stealing the sheep we nor he had neither bite nor sup of. My mother turned her face to the wall and died. She thought I was dead too, with the rest of them, or she would n't have gone. And I lay there with the five wee dead ones, and my mother who was dead, until the Quaker people found me and took me away.

"And so I always thought, Jer, that maybe we 'd do better running Ireland ourselves, than to let little children die of hunger while foreigners fattened sheep for the buying men."

§ 2

"The question now," said the soldier, "is, which one of this council is to.go over and stop things?" The white-headed old rebel rose from the table and went toward the window. "Which of us has most influence?"

"Jer." The priest nodded toward the old man at the window. "But we couldn't trust him," he whispered, "he'd have the boys out in a week."

"How about you, Father?"

"They'd listen kindly to me, and kneel down for my blessing, and they'd go home and put an extra edge on the pike, and say: 'Isn't it a queer thing how mild Father Dan has grown! A saint out of heaven he is, but, saint or no saint, devil a stop he'll put on this party.'"

"Then how about me?"

"Ah, sure, General dear, what use would you be stopping a revolution? You're only a soldier. The orators would make mince-meat out of you."

"Is there any one, then?"

"There's the Citizen."

"The Commandant Hogan? He's in Africa with his regiment."

"Devil an Africa. He's on leave in Europe.

There was some trouble on with little Maeve, the sister—"

"The singer?"

"The same. He came back to look after her. And even if he was in Africa, he'd get leave to come and help Ireland."

"Would they mind him?"

"They would. They would so. Besides his great name as a fighter, he's the son of old Dinny Hogan, the Irreconcilable. And he's got a way with him, even with orators."

"All right then, the Citizen goes."

"Jer," the priest called softly to O'Sullivan More. "Jer, we're sending the Citizen to Ireland to make the boys go home."

The old man by the window merely bowed his back a little more. All the fire and spring had gone from him. He was once more the convict in the prison yard.

"Jer," the priest called gently, "there'll be another day."

"And if there is," the old man answered brokenly, "what is that to me? I'll be in the cold ground. Isn't it worse that way, to think of fighting, and one not there? And a great winning maybe, and me and my four friends to know nothing of it. Ah, Dan, it's hard!"

"And how do you know you won't be there?"

the old priest said gently, "though it 's dead itself you are. Do you think so little of the Man above that He 'd hold us back when the pikes are gathering at the rising of the moon. Ah, no, Jer, 't is not that sort He is. We 'll be marching with the men, and when they 're pressed maybe, and their hearts failing with the great odds against them, a power will come to us to seem what we were below. And they 'll say: 'Do you see the Gray Men in the line of battle?' they 'll ask. ' 'T is Father Dan and O'Sullivan More are in it, two great old rebels, come back from the Land of Ghosts.' And a carnage and madness of fighting will come on them, so that nothing can stand in their way.

"I 'll promise you that, Jer; I 'll promise you that to-day, in the hour of defeat and in the land of the stranger. When the time comes we 'll be there, you and I. The Man above will not refuse me that kindness for me and my friend. For all my life," he said, "I 've been a good priest of His, Jer; I have so."

V

§ 1

FOR a week or more now Connaught had been feeling neglected. To Glenmalure there had been coming shrewd hard-faced political men who were holding long conferences with her father and John D'Arcy. At all times of the day she could hear their clipped voices in the library, her father's booming note coming in now and then, and all through the conversation the suavity of D'Arcy's tones. She knew very well what was afoot: the launching of D'Arcy into political life. But she was very much surprised to find so many obstacles raised. If it were n't for her father's mighty influence he would n't have had a poodle's chance with a sow badger. And this surprised her. For she thought that none would have been so valuable an acquisition to a party as he, with his suave manner and his great cleverness. It was queer how they fought shy of him. They distrusted polish, her people; perhaps that was it. Even the servants of the house distrusted him, it would seem, for they were meticulously

polite to him. He was always "Mr. John, sir";
never, as young Dermot was, "your Honor's
Lordship, my dear son." All this enmity and
distance she felt in the air made her very strongly
partizan of him. She spoke of him to the weaz-
ened "boy" of fifty-six who rolled the tennis-
courts.

"Mr. John is a great player."

"Ma'am, Miss Connaught, do you tell me so?"

"Do I tell you so? The devil strike a hump
on you, Jameen! can't you see it with your own
two eyes?"

"Maybe I can, now, and maybe I can't."

"Jameen," she wheedled, "why don't you like
him?"

"Ma'am, Miss Connaught, I 'll tell you——" he
stopped and straightened his aged back——"and I
won't tell you a word of a lie. 'T is this: that
you can't feel at home with him. He never lets
out a good hearty curse at you."

"Is that anything against him?"

"Oh, 't is! 'T is indeed. A horse without a
kick in him, a man without a curse, and an egg
without salt—the back o' my hand to all three!"

No tennis these days with John D'Arcy.
There were too many political conferences. Her
father was driving him as he had driven himself
in the ancient national battles of years before.

Her father, she thought, was working as though he were working against time, and she did n't like it. His face was gray. His hands shook. She must speak to him about it soon. Though he was all right in health—had n't the London specialists told him so?—yet even for John D'Arcy he must not work so hard.

Days were dull. Inexplicably Dermot eluded her. Every summer before, when he could spare time from the farms, he would take her sailing in the big sloop in the Irish Sea, teaching her the feel of a tiller, the setting of sails, the steering that leaves a long straight wake behind, and none of your amateurish snaky trails. Once he had brought her all the way to Holyhead in Wales, and sent her home in the mail-boat. The bright effervescing sea, the wind coming down from the mountains, the blue hills dropping westward! There was something so clean, so fast about a boat. It was the only thing in the world, she thought, that could compare to the sight and spirit of the two-year-olds tearing along the five furlong course toward the post. Every year she had looked forward to this sailing on the sea with Dermot. And this year he was eluding her. She wondered if he had tired of taking her, and she felt sad and hurt.

And every evening now, when dinner was over,

she would go into the drawing-room, leaving her father and John D'Arcy and the guests—for there were always guests, these days, political men—to the coffee and decanters. And there she would wait for them, smoking a cigarette and playing the great piano. And from the dining-room would come the voices of the guests raised in the thunder of political *clichés*:

"The more I live and the more I see the more convinced I am that there is no limit to the development of the Irish people." Or:

"In my opinion no country has risen to international eminence without the aid of the military genius of the Irish race." And much more in this tenor.

And she would rise from where she was, and catching sight of herself in a glass, would look for a minute, and seeing the sweet hood of her black hair, her honey-colored eyes, her heart-shaped face, the flowing line of neck and arm, the frock she had chosen with great care for the evening, she would address herself ludicrously with a smile:

"And isn't it yourself is the fool of the world, Connaught O'Brien, to be grooming yourself like a racing mare, and not a man to tell you you're the fine elegant woman!" And she would wander out, picking up a wrap, into the gardens of Glen-

malure. To-night the June moon was nearing
the full, and had risen a little way over the Irish
Sea, and back of her the Wicklow Mountains had
become mysterious blue spears. The smell of the
hawthorn was out in the little wind, and the scent
of the roses and the lingering scent of apple-
blossoms—all in the air like a delicate wine.
And afar off whitewashed cottages drowsed like
drowsing cattle, and great white roads wove their
ribbons over the brown shoulders of the mountains. The moon glinted on the Irish Sea.
Somewhere a man was playing a dance tune on a
melodeon, and somewhere else a dog barked into
the stillness of the night, a queer eerie sound. In
the grass beside her padded one of the house dogs,
a Scottish terrier, heavy with dignity.

Afar off on the Irish Sea she could see the lights
of the mail-boat pulling out for Holyhead sixty
miles away, and she could imagine the singing sea
beside it, and the pleasantness of the white decks
in this moonlit hour. Aboard it were people going everywhither: to England, to Scotland, to
France; to the quaint towns of North Germany,
where the streets were narrow and cobbled; to
Liverpool to catch the America boat—the long
adventurous week at sea, and then Sandy Hook
rising out of the Western waves—was n't it Sandy
Hook? It was there that Lipton was going to

race for the cup, and the jolly old merchant had
invited Dermot to accompany him. She could
see the tall white pyramid of the *Shamrock* lying
over as it cut through the waves like a knife, hear
the thunder of the mainsail as they came about.
. . . Everybody was going somewhere except herself. Only that morning in Dublin, a battalion of
the Munster Fusiliers had marched along the
quays from Broadstone to North Wall, on their
way to India. They had swung past in a cheery
river, officers proudly at the head, the band crashing into the traditional marching tune:

"Oh, the girls of France are fair and free,
    And Flemish maids are willing—"

The sight of the big drummer was with her
still, as he swung his sticks like Indian clubs. All
seemed so cheerful, so gay. They were going
somewhere. And she thought of them in India—
the great cool temples with immense brazen
gongs; the copper population of little slim people;
the bullock-carts, creaking through crowded ka-
leidoscopic bazaars; great snakes being tamed
by shriveled men playing little music in reed pipes;
and the tall handsome Irish soldiers smiling at
the pretty native women of the place, and caring
very little about the girls they 'd left behind them.

A bar of the music came into her head, and un-

der the moon in the garden she began to dance little rhythmical steps to and fro to the imagined
tune, while the little badger dog looked on, sitting
on his stern and cocking his head now on one side,
now on the other, after the manner of all Scottish
terriers since the deluge, his brown eye alight with
curiosity.   A great fleece of island cloud swept
over the moon, covering it with a bronze-edged
veil, and Connaught suddenly remembered the
empty drawing-room.

"They'll be in now," she said.

But they were n't.   They still held the dining-
room.   The soft buttery voice of a Nationalist
Member was extolling his countrymen.

"And when I say that the Irish people comprise
the finest peasantry on any sod—"

Connaught opened the door, and looked in.

"Listen!" she said.   "Damn the Irish people.
Good night!"   And so to bed!

§ 2

Indeed and indeed, now, these were the dull
and disappointing days!   She had to go alone to
the Curragh races, for John was off to some political meeting in Waterford for the day, and her

father had correspondence to do, he said, that could not wait. Sure, couldn't it wait until to-morrow? Connaught asked. And he had an-swered with amazing softness: "No, child. Go off, now, and don't be bothering me—and good luck attend you." She had tried the McDermots, but Anne McDermot had traveled North, and Dermot, the steward told her, had gone to Cork to look after a mowing-machine that had landed there from Chicago, and of which there was no sign. "And devil a see of it he'll ever see, for they're the rare thieving geniuses, the same Cork-onians. They'd steal the cross from the shoul-ders of Christ to fire a potheen still. Be damned but they would!"

"Do you tell me so?" said Connaught. "My father's from there."

Fine racing at the Curragh. A fast field and a sweet wind blowing over the plains of Kildare. But she didn't enjoy herself, for it is a queer thing how little you like a place unless there is some one with you you care for. And one thinks how this friend or that lover would like the day, the scene, the town. And there is a great pity in one that they are absent. And this day will never re-peat itself, and they are not here. The finer the day, the scene, the town, the sharper the little pang of sadness, when one is alone. She had a sweet chestnut filly entered for the Irish Derby, Joyzelle, a daughter of Belfast Belle by that fine sire Patrick Joyce, and though she had not dared hope to win Ireland's biggest flat race, yet she was disappointed to see the pretty lady "down the field," as the backers describe it. She stood in the members' inclosure, a cigarette in her mouth giving her for a moment the look of a boy of nineteen, while she disconsolately saw the second, third, and fourth places captured by any but Joyzelle. And the filly had started at a good inside price, five to one.

"I might have had a place or show," she grumbled to Sir Miler Reilly.

"Indeed you might, Connaught. You might that," the burly Galway baronet agreed. "I saw your entry before the race, and devil a prettier head, not even barring your own, was on this course to-day. She looked strong and staying, and the great strain she has in her. And Barney Riordan gave her a grand ride. I wonder now," he puzzled, "if it is that she has n't the speed."

"It might be that," Connaught smiled.

She went home alone from the Curragh to Dublin, alone from Dublin to Glenmalure. The late hazy June twilight was in it, colored like an almond-blossom. When she arrived John had returned from Waterford, and he had brought a bishop with him, and they two and her father talked about school grants from Parliament, as though such a thing as the Irish Derby never existed. It was her father who alluded to it at last. She wished it had been John.

"Connaught," he asked at dinner, "how did your horse make out?"

"She was nowhere."

"Miss Connaught—" the bishop was unctuously shocked—"were you gambling on a horse?"

"Yes, I own horses and race them and gamble on them." She smiled frigidly. "Also I play cards, smoke cigarettes, and can swear like a trooper. Would your Grace care to hear me?"

"Connaught!" her father thundered. But John was smiling, and in the end she had to smile too.

In the morning the quiet accustomed round of life began anew. Very little to do and nothing happening. She took out a couple of foxhound puppies she was walking for the hunt. They trotted after her complacently—their long ears, their grotesque sterns—such hobbledehoys. At a bend of the road she met Neddy Joe, the lodge-keeper of Dermotstown.

"Is it yourself is in it, Neddy Joe?"

"Begor, ma'am, Miss Connaught," he said,

" 't is well you might ask that, and 't is well you
might be surprised to see me at all, what with the
weight of age that 's on me, and the trials I 've
seen in my life. In answer to your Ladyship's
question, as to whether it 's myself that 's in it,
I 'll say, it is."

"Sure you 're fine, Neddy Joe, as supple as a
two-year-old. Tell me, where is that young devil
of a chief of yours?"

"Is it Master Dermot? Begor, ma'am, Miss
Connaught, 't is gone crazy he is. Working from
morning till night, and not only working himself
but drives the honest workmen the like of slaves.
Such a thing was never heard before.

"Do you know what my opinion is, Miss Connaught, my child? Crazy with love, he is."

"But that would only make him dreamy."

" 'T is a different way it takes different people.
There 's some goes in for the drink, thinking that
the mildness of liquor will take off the sharp
edges of love. And I knew a lad once in the
Barony of Forth, in the County of Wexford, and
when the madness of love for some girl come on
him he would go out and pick a fight with some
strapping agricultural fellow who would be twice
his size, and begor, he 'd get the head knocked off
him. He claimed it steadied him. Oh, divers
ways it takes divers people."

"And whom would your Master Dermot be in love with?"

"Would it be yourself, now, Miss Connaught, my dear?"

"It would not," she laughed. "If it were myself, he'd tell me, wouldn't he?"

"He would—and he wouldn't. There's queer people in the world," he said, "and the world itself," he went on, adroitly shifting to his favorite topic: that all flesh was grass, "is the queer hard place. Trouble and discontent, and nothing in the latter end!"

"And how about heaven, Neddy Joe?"

"A true word you said there, Miss Connaught; how about it? Will there be dogs coursing after hounds there? Will there be a good make of cutty pipe, and Gallagher's cut plug to be filling it with? Will there be the racing of horses, and e'er a chance of doing a bookie in the eye on a twenty-to-one shot coming home? A drinking-place or two where you can have fine sharp arguments about Home Rule, or a game of spoil five in the evenings, and a nice stake in the outcome? And a ballad-singer without and him giving you 'Rise up, Willie Reilly,' or a man with a melodeon, playing 'The High Caul Cap.' A fight now and then to clear the air, the way lightning does be making the summer wholesome. Or the grandest sport of all, a rounded widow woman to be talking about love with!

"Begor, miss my dear," he went on, "I once had a talk with a clergyman the time I was tottering on the cobblestones o' death. And from his talk I made out that heaven was like a meeting in church or chapel, day in, day out, week in, week out, and all the days from year to year. And sure that was cold comfort to me that could never put a foot inside a religious house on account of the lugubrious faces of the people. Be damned to that, I say!"

" 'T is a poor end, Neddy Joe," and Connaught felt utterly downcast.

"And when you think of the hard days that go before it!"

"And the days they are so long, Neddy Joe."

" 'T is a wonder to me," the old man said, "that you, and all the money that you have, Miss Connaught, never thought of treating yourself to some fine able husband."

"Neddy Joe!"

" 'T is a coarse taste. 'T is a coarse taste, I 'll admit. Ah, but it does be grand for passing the time!"

She moved away, laughing, from the sad old pagan, the puppies following her, and as she went she could hear him muttering to himself aloud:

" 'T is a queer and dirty trick a man's mother plays on him, the day she brings him into the meager world!"

§ 3

"Miss Connaught," Murphy the valet told her, "your father would like to be having a word with you."

"Where is he, Murphy?"

"He is within, in the library."

Now the definite heat of the summer day was done. Though not for hours would sunset be, there was now coolness in the gardens, and once more the small music of the birds, thrush and blackbird, the little family of the finches, the *tweet* of the swallow, the pompous note of the dove. Now were the trees quiet, the ash and elm, the gnarled kindly apple-trees, the copper beeches like ancient forests, the proud horse-chestnuts. The grass awaited patiently the coming of the dew, and the flowers were beginning to close now that the day was all but a few hours done. The blue mountains wore great clusters of gold, and the top of Three-Rock was touched with fire. Now was the hour when nuns walked in their gardens, as the Lord God did in His once at the close of day. The weary bees came droning toward their hives.

She left the flash of the swallow's wings, to go into the library, and on the threshold of it it seemed to her she was stepping into another world, or into some dark chamber of the under-world, so alien was the atmosphere to the drows-ing vitality without. There was only thought in here and thought was so meager compared with life. The calf-bound books were so ugly; the flowers of the earth had life in every leaf, and these were mouldering as were the men who wrote them. Their sonorous sentences were inconse-quential in comparison with the droning of the bees. Outside, the oaks had seen five centuries, and were only in their prime, while here the figure of the Lord Chief Justice who had had power over life and death, property and institutions was stricken when he was hardly passed three score of years. A swift pity fluttered in her heart for him, for he seemed so tired, so worn. Haggard-ness was written in his massive face, and there was weariness in the boarhound's jowl. And he worked still at his littered table, while the eternal mountains slept under the purple mantle of the setting sun. She went swiftly to his side.

"Childeen—" he looked up at her—"do you know how fond of you I am?"

She bent down and kissed the wrinkled forehead that was pitiably worn now, and had once been so terrible under the great wig of the chief judge, when the red robes of high justice were about his shoulders. The Right Honorable the Lord Chief Justice of Ireland, Jimmy the Hangman, Baron O'Brien of Glenmalure—and he was only a worn old man now, her father.

"Childeen," he spoke again, "when I think of things for you, I only think for your own good."

"Sir—" there were smarting tears in her eyes— "dear sir, what can I say but that I know that?"

"Sit you down, Connaught. Sit you down, then, little daughter, opposite me. I have something to tell you.

"Do you remember some time ago I asked you if you had any thought of marrying, if you had any one in your head?"

"I do, sir."

"And you said you had not."

"Yes."

"Connaught, I want you to marry. And I want you to marry John D'Arcy."

She thought for a little while. Then she raised her head.

"Would he have me, sir?"

"Yes, Connaught. He will be happy and proud to have you."

"I don't know, of course." She was flushed and embarrassed. "But I suppose it is all right. This is rather unexpected—" she laughed nervously—"is n't it?"

"Connaught, if we were to look for a hundred years, we could n't find a better match for you. John has got brains and ambition. There is no limit to what he can do with the start I can give him in politics and your money, my dear. He will end up with an earldom. Earl Glenmalure, and you will be Countess Glenmalure, my little daughter, and you will carry on the work your father began. Your poor old father, Connaught, is only a life peer, after all, and your mother's people are only honest soldiering folk, for all their knighthoods, their decorations. You will be the founder of a noble house."

"John!"

"Not John—you, Connaught. Without your money and your character, and your father, John's success would be only mediocre. Without John you would be nowhere.

"Besides, Connaught, as far as the personal end goes, he 's handsome, distinguished, polished. You 'll be happy with him, my dear. The great world is before you. Connaught, shall we say yes?"

"I suppose so, Father." She blushed. "Yes."

"And now, Connaught, I want this marriage to be very soon."

"How soon, sir?"

"Very soon. Listen, child. John will contest the first safe Northern seat open, and will win. I 've seen to that. This will be in November. There will be months of work before that. Also a house in London to prepare. So you see."

"But that would mean at once, sir."

"Yes, Connaught."

"But, Father, I don't know John D'Arcy. I must have time. I—I don't love him, sir. I know he 's everything you say, but— Do you see, this marriage and love are so new to me—"

"Now, my dear, listen to me. This talk of love is the last thing I should have expected from you. Of course you 'll love John D'Arcy. But you won't love him until you 're married to him and have been married for some time. One does n't marry for love, my dear; one marries for companionship, for interest, for the foundations of family. Given the companionship, the love will come. This marriage for love and passion is a morbid thing. It passes like summer thunderstorms. And a woman is left in a house with a man whom she has loved and does n't like. Connaught, your mother was n't in love with me when we married, nor I with her, and yet it was n't very long until we cared for each other, so that when she died—" he paused.

"I know, sir, I've heard."

"So you see . . . Connaught, I want you to be married this week and privately."

"Dear God, sir, no! I can't." She started up in protest. "I—I hardly know the man."

"You know him well enough, Connaught."

"But, sir, don't you see how much it entails? It's impossible. It's absurd. You could n't ask me to. I am to be intimate with this man, possibly have children—I hardly know him. Oh, sir, you can't ask me!"

All the color had left her face. From its white mask her tawny eyes looked forth with affright. She was poised on the balls of her feet as though to run, as an alarmed doe might run. Her father's voice came gentle and solemn:

"Little Connaught, of all these things there is too much made. All these dreams of young women, all this life one makes in one's head, it lasts only for a little, and if reality does not come it turns morbid and sour. The fairy palaces are damp and drafty, and the young prince out of the West is discovered to be an effeminate egotist, and in the end a woman wants a secure and warm home, and a masculine and human husband. . . . Why must you be afraid? Is John not a gentleman? Will you be bothered, offended, insulted? I think not. Even, if you like, my dear, you can be the same as here, in my house."

"But, even so, why must everything be private, underhand? Why so soon? Father, I am being married as though I were some housemaid who had been foolish. Why can't everything wait until a fitting time? until John is elected and ready?"

"Because that would take so long, Connaught, a year and more. And then when he is just in, could he leave the beginnings of a career, the House eager to see what he 's made of, to go and marry a wife? There will be debates until dawn in Parliament, hard-fought battles. A young man must not be hampered by a brand-new wife.

"And there is another reason, little Connaught. I don't know why, but of late I have felt often that I was nearing my end. At times it seemed that the angel of death was beside me, so close that I could almost hear the beating of his wings—"

"Sir! sir!"

"It may be my fancy, little daughter, but— And if it happened, I would go to a place, as I think, where there is nothing, not knowing you were safe, your life provided for; you would be at the mercy of the world, in which, as I have

"Connaught, I want you to be married this week, and privately"

seen it, there is little mercy. And if there is a fair country, and I meet your mother, how should I answer her when she asks of you? 'And how is our daughter, James O'Brien? Has she any children at her house? And is there a little girl who is like me?' And I should have to say, 'Madam, there are no children, nor any husband.' And what would she say, who always trusted me?"

Connaught came around to him swiftly, put her young arm about his shoulder.

"Very well, sir," she whispered.

"Then it's to be this week?"

"Yes. But—I don't know—" She saw the great jaw sag again, the eyes grow dull. And very bravely she drew herself up and spoke up:

"I can be ready this week."

He took her warm white hand in his great gray talons that were like the talons of some immense hawk of the air.

"If It, then, be anything, may It bless you and keep you forever, my little daughter."

He rang the bell firmly for Murphy.

"Mr. John is somewhere about the house." His voice was crisp again. "Find him and send him here."

VI

§ 1

SHE had gone over to Dermotstown for dinner, inviting herself, and when the time came to return she had said she would like to walk back in the cool of the evening, if Dermot would accompany her.

They left the white low house, and the moon, that was waning now, had risen and was glowing low in the east, with a great atmosphere of dignity. Everywhere was peace, the white thatched cottages showed under the moon, and from their windows golden lights shone, peaceful as the sound of a little bell. And somewhere was the eternal, half-alarmed, half-joyous barking of a dog. A coolness was on the land after the heat of the day, and the scents of summer were in the air, soft hawthorn and shrill wild rose, and the pleasant savor of new-mown grass. They passed along the white road silently, as friends do. A disturbed corn-crake somewhere filled the land with strange harmonious discordance. But Connaught paid no attention. She was looking down

at the road beneath her, engrossed, thinking.
They crossed a bridge over a little stream where
the water warbled like birds over the loose round
stones. Farther down, in a pool of the willow
branches, there was the splash of an otter or a
stoat seeking trout. They went on.

"Oh, Dermot," she said slowly, "I am going
to be married."

"Yes, Connaught."

"To John D'Arcy, Dermot, your cousin."

"I hope you will be very happy, Connaught," he
said after a pause. "I hope he will make you
very happy."

"Oh, Dermot, is this a good thing, or is it
not?" she asked suddenly. "I have promised to
marry him, and will. But I know so little about
it and him, and it all has been so unexpected.
Dermot, you and I have been so much together,
known each other so well, for so long! What
do you think, Dermot? What do you say?"

"I think it's all right, Connaught," he said.
"John is very clever. He'll do well. And I
think he's all right, Conn. You remember there
was something against him? Well that was only
shifty politics, and there was nothing in that to
bother you. And he knows the world so well.
You'll have a very good time."

"But this worries me, do you see, Dermot?

That I don't love him. My father says that is all right, will come right."

"If your father says it will be all right, it will, Conn," he answered bravely. "I suppose it's enough that a man loves a woman. The woman then loves him, when they're married; do you see? That's the way of it."

"Do you thing it's all right, Dermot?"

"I do, Conn." She glanced at him.

"Dermot, you look ghastly in the moonlight. Are you not feeling well, lad?"

"I haven't been feeling up to much lately, Conn. It's nothing, though."

"Was that why you didn't come to the Curragh to see Joyzelle run?"

"Yes," he answered. "I went down to Cork for a rest."

"Boy," she pleaded, "you must take care of yourself."

They had come to the little village of Five Houses. The moonlight made day of the one broad street. As they turned into it, they could hear a lad's shrill voice raised in the rebel song of Ninety-eight—The *Shan Van Voght*, the Poor Old Woman.

> "Oh, the French are on the say,
> Says the *Shan Van Voght.*

Oh the French are on the say,
    Says the *Shan Van Voght.*
The French are on the say,
They 'll be here by break of day
And the Rose will decay,
    Says the *Shan Van Voght.*"

"Right outside the new Resident Magistrate's house, too," Dermot said. "He 'll be out."

    "And the English will decay,
        Says the *Shan Van Voght.*"

In the moonlight, bright as day, they could see the singer, a lanky red-headed lad of barely fourteen, with a swinging step of the mountainy people, a cap thrust back on his head, an ash sapling in his hand. The rebel ballad rang out like a challenge, and surely enough, as Dermot had prophesied, it had brought the new Resident out. He was a small elderly military man, with a face baked to a terra-cotta color by the Indian sun, and a white cropped mustache. And his features showed a grotesque dismay.

"God bless my soul!" he said. "Come here, little boy."

The little boy came over and stood by him, overtopping him by a couple of inches.

"What an extraordinary song for you to sing, little boy!"

" 'T is an old song of my grandfather's, Major," the lad said, "that was out in the Sixty-seven and was transported to Van Dieman's Land."

"But you didn't learn that from your grandfather!"

"I did not, Major, for my grandfather died before I was born, in the transportation amongst the Australian blacks."

"Then where did you get it, boy?"

" 'T is this way, Major. 'T was a day or so ago I was driving the goats up the mountain, and singing to myself a song I had picked up in Cabinteely, and 'Good-bye, Dolly Grey,' was the name that was on it. And I met this man and him coming down the mountain—"

"What man?"

"This man that gave me the song, Major. He stops and looks at me. 'Are you Irish?' he says. 'I am, your Honor,' says I. 'Well,' he said, 'for one pin I'd lift you with my boot into the next county, for singing a foolish song the likes of that.' 'Is there e'er a better one in it, your Honor?' 'There is,' say he. And he up and gives a tune out of him, and 't was my grandfather's old song. 'Let you be singing that, now,' said he, and he gives me a clip on the ear and goes his way."

"What sort of a man was this, my boy?"

"A fine figure of a man, Major; a gentleman like yourself, begging his pardon; a grand suit of clothes on him, and him the trim of a fighting-man."

"Did the man tell you his name, little boy?"

"He did not, Major, but he said when I'd called him 'your Honor' two or three times, that there was a better name to call him by, and that was 'Citizen.'"

"Now, my boy—" the Major pulled out a large silver coin—"I'm going to teach you a better song."

"A better one than the fighting-man's, Major?"

"Much better. Now listen and repeat:

"I thank the Goodness and the Grace
    That on my birth have smiled,"

"I thank the Goodness and the Grace
    That on my birth have smiled, major—"

"And made me in these Christian days—"

"And made me in these—what days did you say, major? —ay, Christian days—"

"A happy English child!"

The lad handed the big silver coin back with dignity.

"'T is a nice song, Major, and grand rhymes

to it, and 't is a lot of money you offered me to
learn it, and I 'm very thankful to you, but if it 's
equal to you, Major, I 'd liefer have the song the
Citizen taught me, though all I got for learning
it was a clout on the ear."

§ 2

And now Five Houses was far behind them,
and out of the road, white as an egg, they had
turned into the green tunnel of chestnut-trees that
led to Glenmalure. The moon was high now,
and the mountains were faint blue peaks, the sea
a soft silver mist. Over Dublin City a great halo
of light rose, and the watch-tower on Howth
winked like some gigantic star. But one by one
the lights of the little cottages snuffed out, because the country folk must arise betimes in summer, for the cutting of hay, and the pulling of flax,
and the milking of the heavy-uddered kine. Soon
even the great houses would be dark and the
lights of Dublin fade, and all the country would
sleep as now the birds slept, and under the moon
Ireland would smile in its dreams.

And Connaught said: "All my life," she said,
"I 've been dreaming of far countries. Of Paris

and its flood of lights, of the Thames slowly flowing past the Parliament House, and Brussels where there is so much gaiety, and Monte Carlo where people gamble as even we don't gamble. I've been thinking long for those places. And now when the time comes to leave for them, Dermot, I am becoming homesick. The blue peaks of the Sugar Loaves, Dermot—" she looked at them—"are piercing my heart."

"But you will always be coming back, Connaught," he told her. "Much of your time will be spent here."

"I don't know, Dermot. I notice," she said, "when an Irishman is elected to Parliament, he spends all the time he can in England. He says he is an exile there and weeps for his country, but he can only be dragged back for a general election. It's a strange thing," she smiled.

"You'll be back, Connaught."

"Yes, but only as a visitor, and in England I'll be a stranger and sojourner. Dermot, I'm bothersome to-night."

"Conn," he told her, "you're going to have a splendid time there. Think of the racing, the Derby and the Oaks and the Thousand Guineas. And the hunting in Yorkshire."

"And my heart will be with the Irish two-year-olds tearing up the five-furlong course at Leop-

ardstown, and I 'll miss the voice of Mickey
Swain, bawling the odds, when I 'm among the
calm fashionable English people. And the hunting of Yorkshire won't make up for the Ward
Union, and the hounds after the stag, and the
horses going hell-for-leather at Fairyhouse River.

"Dermot—" she turned to him—"do you know
that this is the last time we meet as the friends we
are? When next you see me it will be at my wedding."

"But, Conn," he said, and he knew he was
wrong, "we 'll always be friends."

"Yes," she answered, "old friends. But
there 'll always be something in the atmosphere.
We will never again be free. We will never go
sailing alone past Ireland's Eye, and Lambay
Island. You will never give me a leg-up into the
saddle in the old way; there will be always some
politeness and ceremony. And you will never
curse me as when we went out fishing: 'Damn you,
Conn, be quiet or go home.' Do you see,
Dermot?

"Oh, Dermot, why could n't it have been you
who were going to be a great man and rule the
country! Then we could have been lovers and
marry. And all this would have been an adventure then, and not a business."

"I could not be clever enough for a great man,

Conn," he said. His voice was queer and muffled. "And I'd be ridiculous away from my own Irish place—except at sea. Go off, Conn, and be a great lady. And in years to come when you are the rage of London, and ruling the Cabinet, I shall come and see you, a red-faced man in tweeds, half farmer and half fisherman, and you will explain me as one of the friends of your youth."

"I shall jump up and kiss you wherever I am— if I were sitting on the king's knees itself," she laughed, "and you will bring the woman you marry."

"I am not the marrying kind, Conn," he said.

They were at the great doors of Glenmalure.

"Come in, Dermot," she said, "but good-by my friend."

"Good-by—" he understood— "Connaught, my dear."

She looked at him for an instant, put her arm round his shoulder, and kissed him, then pushed open the great hall door. In the antlered lobby, John D'Arcy stood before the fire of sea-coal. There he stood, elegant as an actor.

"Hello, Connaught!" he smiled. And "Oh, hello, Dermot," he drawled.

"How do you do?" Dermot all but snarled.

"John, do you know, the funniest thing!" Connaught smiled. "When were passing Five

Houses, the new Resident Magistrate came out of his place to stop a boy singing. You ought to have seen him—funny little Indian officer! The boy was singing the *Shan Van Voght,* and nothing would do Major Grantham but to find out who taught it him. The boy said a man on the moun--tain—"

"A man on the mountain taught him the *Shan Van Voght?*"

"Yes, a stranger. 'A gentleman like yourself, sir,' he told the major, 'in a grand suit of clothes, and the trim of a fighting-man.' "

John had suddenly gone white. He leaned forward. His eyes were shining in a sort of excitement.

"Was he a fair man? Did he look foreign?"

"The boy did n't say, John. But when the major wanted to teach him 'A Happy English Child'—"

"But the man, Conn. Did the boy give his name? Did he say why he was singing this?"

"He said the man's name was the Citizen, but about why he was singing it he did n't say a word. And when the major—" she smiled.

With a faint excuse D'Arcy moved away on sagging knees. He left them for the dining-room. From the open door could be heard the *glug* of a decanter.

JOHN HAD SUDDENLY GONE WHITE. HE LEANED
FORWARD. HIS EYES WERE SHINING IN A SORT OF EX-
CITEMENT

"What's wrong with him?" Conn asked. "Why does he look so white? What's he taking a drink for?"

"Must have a sort of chill," Dermot said.

VII

§ 1

OUT of some ancient Druidic faith, unconsciously, the folk of Glenmalure had decorated the long drawing-room with great sprays
of flowers, tall ferns, and little branches of green
trees. And the high French windows were open
on the riotous gardens, so that everywhere was
golden sunshine and tall stately trees. In the
distance were the mountains like aloof magnificent gods. The song of the thrush and the
hoarse passion of the wood-dove were audible,
and into the long room came now a straying brown
bee, and now a quivering dancing butterfly,
primrose-colored but for round black dots on the
wings, as though they wished to see who were this
couple who had strayed from the human habit of
marrying in gloomy churches.

But for all the sunshine, and for all the flowers,
there was about nearly all the actors of this marriage an air of strange tenseness. There was
Connaught, in her heather-colored tweed suit, her
face white as a white flower, her hands, her knees,

all her body, trembling with the tenseness of defense. There was D'Arcy beside her, and a sidelong look in his eye, as though he would rather have his glance on the door than on the celebrant. Tall and burly in his blue clothes, with his poised head, his neat beard, he would be a fine man but for the cowardice under his brow at this moment. There behind him stood Dermot, his mouth grim as though he were going into battle, beside a fluttering excited bridesmaid whose appearance was not familiar to him, and whose name he had hardly caught. On a great high-backed chair sat the old baron, his face gray as a gray sky, and about him some strange feeling that he was holding himself together with a last reserve of strength. Of all there, only the celebrant and his clerk and the blushing bridesmaid seemed normal to a wedding ceremony. Afar off, near the door, was a ruck of house servants, gardeners, grooms.

Because D'Arcy was of an elder faith, a minister of his own church had been requisitioned, a tall young monk in white habit with black hood, a face clean-cut as the face of some ancient Greek, somber eyes, and a head of golden curls but for the circle where a black cap covered the tonsure. He was like some mystic out of a medieval cloister. Beside him stood his clerk, a gray-eyed, redheaded Irish boy, in black cassock and white sur-

plice, holding a vessel of blessed water, his face
stupid with wonder.

"*Ego conjungo vos in matrimonium,*" the Dominican blessed them. "I join you together in
marriage, in the name of Our Father . . ."

He took the wedding symbol and laid it on the
black cover of his missal. With a sprig of yew
he sprinkled it with blessed water.

"*Benedic, Domine, annulum hunc:* Bless, O
Lord, this ring which we bless in Thy name, that
she who shall wear it, keeping true faith unto her,
may ever abide in peace."

Now, according to the ritual, was she wed with
the ring, endowed with gold and silver, in the
name of the Trinity. The priest spoke in soft
Italianate Latin:

"*Confirma hoc, Deus, quod operatus es:* Con-
firm, O God, that which Thou hast wrought in us.

"From Thy holy Temple which is in Jerusalem.

"Kyrie eleison!" came the crisp Greek. "Lord
have mercy!"

The sonorous periods of the Latin prayer
rolled out, drowning the bourdon of the bees, and
silencing the voices of the birds, thrush and blackbird and cooing wood-pigeon. "*Fidelis et casta
nubat in Christo,*" he prayed. "May she marry in
Christ faithful and chaste, and remain a follower
of holy women: may she be amiable to her hus-

band like Rachel, wise like Rebecca, long-lived and
faithful like Sarah . . . *muniat infirmitatem
suam robore disciplinae:* may she fortify her weakness by the strength of discipline; may she be in
shamefacedness grave, in modesty venerable, in
heavenly doctrines learned . . ."

His voice rose suddenly: *"Deus Abraham,
Deus Isaac, Deus Jacob sit vobiscum:* may the
God of Abraham, the God of Isaac, and the God
of Jacob be with you, and Himself fulfil His blessing upon you: that you may see your children's
children unto the third and fourth generation
. . . *per omnia saecula saeculorum,* world without end, Amen."

He closed the missal gently, kissed and handed
it to the little clerk, thrust his hands up the wide
white sleeves of his habit.

And so Connaught O'Brien was married!

§ 2

She went to her father immediately, seeing how
ill-looking he was, how gray in the face. And
there were tears in his eyes, which touched her to
the heart. She knelt beside him.

"Oh, sir," she said, "you're looking very

ill! I can't go away and leave you like this."

"Yes, you can, little Connaught." His gray
hand was on her shoulder. "I am all right. I
am all right now. I am just a little tired," he
said; "and when you are gone, Conn, I am going
to rest, to rest for a long time. Little daughter,
you 've made me very happy, and at peace."

"Have I, sir? I 'm glad. But Father, are
you sure you 'll be all right?"

"Perfectly, Conn. I 'll get young Dermot to
come around and see me." He looked to where
Dermot was speaking to D'Arcy in a corner of
the room. "Conn," he said, "be always nice to
young Dermot, all the days of your life."

"I will, sir," she said simply. "I—I 'm very
fond of Dermot."

D'Arcy had brought him aside, out of ear-shot
of every one. There was agitation on the elder
man's face.

"You have n't heard of anybody around," he
said, "singing the *Shan Van Voght,* and looking
foreign?"

"Nothing except from the mountainy lad the
night before last," Dermot answered curtly.

"Anything of a foreigner, army officer
French?"

"No. Look here, D'Arcy, what are you afraid
of?"

"Nothing. But if such a man turned up," he went on, "and asked for me, would you mind saying that I'd gone to South America? He's a simple sort of fellow and would believe that. And if he asks, would you suggest that Connaught's husband was not John D'Arcy but James D'Arcy? It's nothing of importance," he added weakly, "but I don't want to be bothered with the man."

"Do you mean would I tell lies for you?"

"That's a hard way to talk of a simple favor."

"Let me tell you, D'Arcy, I won't. Get out of your own messes your own way. And look here: if you mix up Connaught in any of your rotten political intrigues, and bring her into any trouble or scandal, so help me God, John D'Arcy, I'll break every bone in your crooked body."

"Oh, ho! I suppose you'd have liked to marry her yourself."

"Did Lord Glenmalure say that to you?"

"No. But it's pretty evident now."

"Well, it's not only evident but true, do you see? So remember what I tell you."

Connaught came over to them.

"Shall we go now, John?" she asked quietly. To Dermot she gave a haggard little smile.

"Yes, Conn," he said. "Good-by, Cousin Der-

mot," he smiled, and somehow his words and his
smile were insulting.

And so Connaught O'Brien left home.

§ 3

So rapidly had all this happened—the return
of John, his own interview with Glenmalure, the
marriage of Connaught—that Dermot had not yet
grasped it entirely. It might all have happened
in a play of the theater, so unreal did it appear in
his life. Ten days ago there had been Connaught, with no thought of anything but the racing of horses, the hunting of foxes, the tending of
gardens. There she might have been for years,
forever indeed, just Connaught. And here to-
day was no Connaught, and John D'Arcy's wife
had left Glenmalure and the sweet blue mountains,
left the red fox in the covert and the sleek fine
horses in the paddock, and withdrawn from the
blooming gardens, to go and be a great lady in
London town; and neither Glenmalure nor the
country-side would ever again be the same without her. It would be like a house whose owner
had gone away.

It was a queer thing, but when his sister, little

Kathleen, had died, there had come a sharp pang of sorrow and then peace. She had been such a young merry thing about the house, like a gentle bird, and there was such promise in her of becoming beautiful. All the child's life had been happy, and when she left them she had gone so quickly, so peacefully, it was as though she were being translated into some sweet invisible state of being. She was forever with the Lord, at Kill o' the Grange it was written, and Dermot believed that. Behind her she left a beautiful memory, like the scent of verbena. And his mother's face had grown sweeter, and there were more gray hairs. . . . Where Desmond had fallen, a little stone marked the brown African veldt, and on it was carved, for the colonists of coming times to read: "Here sleep some Irish soldiers and their officer." Under the immense Southern stars, he kept sentry there. And Dermot could only be proud that a brother of his had been admitted to the testimony of the race whose fighting-men had died in all quarters of the globe: in North and South Africa, in China where the Boxers rose; in France and in the High and Low Germanies; in Russia and Sweden and Italy; in South America under Blacklock and under O'Higgins, Captain-General of Chili; at Bunker Hill and the Wilderness in America of the North—nowhere but is hallowed by

Gaelic blood. Here sleep some Irish soldiers and their officer!

Both these departures were fitting: the child who was too merry and beautiful for this world, where tragedy is and unbeauty, and was more fitting to adorn some bright island of the moon. And the soldier who had died in the hour of victory. But the going of Connaught, even though she were alive—there was no sharp pang to that, only a dull ache. And there was no peace, only disquietude. What he felt now was the void he had felt when, Desmond being gone, his dream of the sea was over. Others would plow the green billows, and go down to battle in the dawn, some new Copenhagen or Cape Trafalgar, and he would not be there. And still the sea sang upon the shore, and was lashed into gray-faced fury under the equinoctial gales or smiled beneath the friendly moon. He understood he was in love with the sea, and wedded by Fate to the land. And now he was in love too with Connaught O'Brien, and she had been wedded by Destiny to John D'Arcy.

He said to himself simply that cleverness of brain must be an extraordinary gift, when so much can be won by it: a wife like Connaught, a place in the councils of the nation, money, titles. And John was n't even honest; he knew that. He

would change his convictions, if convictions they
could be called, as easily as he would change his
coat. It was a queer thing, Dermot thought,
that honesty and loyalty were so little, compared
with the quick head, the facile gesture. And
kindly men were often poor, and cruel men rich.
'T was all a matter of brains, he thought. Well,
he had none of them. At school when other boys
were being given medals for their knowledge of
Cicero and Herodotus, all he knew was how to
cast a dry fly in a stream, and that got you nowhere. At the university the only distinction he
had achieved was of being sent down for riding
in, and winning, a point-to-point race on a borrowed hunter, when he should have been mugging
up in conic sections. What gifts he had were use-
less in a world of thought. The knowledge of
boats, and the tricky winds of the Irish Sea—
that might win a cup but never a seat in Parliament. He had a healing hand with dogs and cattle, and that might win a dog's heart but never
fame. And over the sticks there was no better
rider of his weight, professionals not excepted,
and that might gain him some decent country girl,
but never a woman of quality. "I am kin to
wind and fish and horse and dog," he said, "because there must be a lot of the animal in me."
So simple were his thoughts. "And that is why

I am glad Anne my mother is away during this, for, like the animal, I must be alone when hurt."

Last night, because it was the eve of Connaught's wedding, he had roamed the mountain and the shore, and he had awakened the hare in the long grass, and the grouse and plover in the heather, and afar off a fox had barked at him. And coming down to the shore, the gulls had resented his intrusion, with sharp querulous cries, and the cormorants had flapped their black wings at him, and the sandpipers fled at his approach. The only human thing he saw was an encampment of tinkers, as the Irish call their gipsies, by a road of Wicklow. Two brace of them there were, men and women. He noticed their faces as they slept by one another, man tinker and woman tinker, in the lush grass. They had strong aquiline features and lank black hair. And he remembered never to have seen any soft Irish face among them anywhere. Like marries like, he thought, tinkerman to tinkerwoman. What is in the head and what is in the mind counts, he puzzled, for wealth is only a matter of a few coins more or less on one side or the other, and rank means nothing, men and women being the same under ermine as under rags. But the head is all. And he thought of Connaught, with her love of travel and bright places, and D'Arcy,

skilled, polished. They both had minds and ambitions that soared above the ken of the like of
him. Kingfisher to Kingfisher will wed, he told
himself, and never to the sad osprey like himself.
For him there is only his own gray bird, if he
wants her. "I have no brains," he thought, "but
I am becoming over-wise before my time."

The very short summer night was over. At
ten of the evening the light had hardly died, and
now at two of the morning the dawn was beginning. "Weeping may endure for a night," he remembered a text from college chapel, "but joy
cometh in the morning." And he thought of the
many that had been speciously comforted by it.
And the night he had passed, he grimaced, and
this morning Connaught was to be married!

§ 4

They would be nearing Waterford now, Dermot thought, D'Arcy and Connaught D'Arcy, and
to-night would take the boat to Fishguard, and
from Fishguard go to Devon and Cornwall,
through the wild hills of Wales where the rough
sure-footed Welsh ponies grazed under gnarled
Druidic oaks, and thence into the sweet West Eng-

lish country, where the folk were not English at
all, but Celt and Spaniard, and the last of the
English fairies lived, and Arthur and the Knights
of his Round Table arose from sunken Lyonesse
beneath Atlantic waters and galloped through the
Cornish and Devon dusk. And to-morrow night
the moon would rise over the land of cream and
apples, the moon of honey.

And Dermot remembered that there was another as lonely as himself, the old baron. How
ill he had looked to-day! With Connaught gone
there would be none to feel kindly toward him.
It occurred to Dermot that Connaught would be
grateful if he rode over and asked was there anything he could do for the old man. Whether
Connaught was gone or not, whether or not the
baron had refused him his daughter, there was no
reason for leaving a neighbor in his loneliness.
He had the mare put in the dog-cart, and spun
over.

The groom who took the mare's head at Glenmalure seemed strained. And Murphy, the old
valet, had been crying. Dermot wondered was it
after Connaught.

"Is himself within?"

"He is, Master Dermot, but he won't be for
long."

"Is he going away?"

"He 's going on a long and bitter journey, your young Honor, a dark and secret journey, and all alone he 's going." The old valet's voice came in shuddering sobs, "and leaving me that 's been with him this forty year. Ah, Master Dermot, 't is in my heart to be looking for some kindly tree."

But Dermot had gone inside quickly and was mounting the wide stairs. He knocked at a great oaken door, opened it.

In the light summer dusk he could see two people inside. There was Glenmalure lying, not on his bed, canopied like a seat of justice, but on a huge couch near a window. About him was a red silken dressing-gown that seemed like a robe of office. By another window stood the young monk who had celebrated the marriage in the morning. Above the red robe, the old justice's white head and great jaw had assumed an immense power and dignity. Above the white habit and black hood, the young priest's ascetic face was taut with effort and pain.

"Come in, Dermot, come in," Glenmalure called, as Dermot hesitated.

"Murphy, poor Murphy," the baron smiled, "insisted on bringing his Reverence here." A long wave of weakness passed over his face, and then came a false strength again. "I am dying, Dermot," he said.

"Sir, is there anything I can do? Anything you 've forgotten?"

"There is Murphy, poor Murphy," he pondered. "He is well taken care of in my will, but, lad, he won't be happy here with John. Could you get him a corner somewhere?"

"I 'll take him to Dermotstown, sir. Anything else?"

"Dermot—" his face was pathetic in doubt— "did I do right to-day? Our little Connaught— will she be happy?"

"She will, sir," Dermot answered him; "she will be happy as the day is long. She will be a great lady and a great power."

"Perhaps I was wrong," the old man wondered, "to send you away."

"Ah no, sir! Connaught is not for a stay-at-home like me. She would have eaten her heart out here. You were right, sir."

The young monk thought this all trivial on the brink of death. "Sir," he protested, "leave these worldly things be—"

"Dermot—" the old baron smiled—"his Reverence, here, tells me that in a few minutes I must face a tribunal greater than ever my own was. I had only power of life and death, but here is power of damnation and eternal hell-fire. How of the forms of legal precedence, priest?" he jeered. "What of a jury of my peers? What evidence is admitted, what thrown out? How of motives, premeditation, the exact degrees of guilt? Does this God of yours fill all offices himself—justiciary, jury, witness, counsel for and against—"

"God," the young monk chided terribly, "God is not mocked!"

All life seemed to have left the old baron. His face was white. There seemed no breathing. Dermot rose.

"Is he gone?"

"No," said the priest.

They stood watching the still face, and suddenly from the lips came a voice that was not the voice of the Lord Chief Justice, but the voice of a young passionate man.

"Where is Wolfe Tone?" it asked. "He lies in his prison cell, his throat mangled, his life mangled; of him nothing is left but honor. And Emmet—a hireling judge of England's has lopped that young brave life. Martyred is Lord Edward Fitzgerald. And Napper Tandy, the shrewd Northern man—the cold mists of exile have swallowed him up. The red battalion of aggression

rolls over our green land, but a lion is in the way."
It warned. "There is a lion in the streets."

And the tones suddenly broke into passionate
verse:

> "Through the snow and the sleet,
>   And the black bog mire
> Broken we crawl to your feet,
>   Quenched our fire.
> But another day will come,
>   With a brighter sun.
> And you 'll hear the throb of the drum,
>   The crack of the gun.
> Another day, O Mother Eire!"

The monk looked questioningly at Dermot.
He had never heard of the great justice's rebel
youth or of the "Song of Defeat."

"Quick, priest! How shall I plead?" The
old man had come to for a moment.

"My lord, His Mercy endureth forever!"

But a crooked set came to the old fighter's jaw
and for the last time his great voice sang out in
challenge:

"Not guilty!"

The Dominican dropped to his knees.

"Requiem æternam dona ei, Domine," he
prayed. "Eternal rest vouchsafe to him, O
Lord."

Dermot moved toward the window. A telegram must be sent to Waterford to catch Connaught and her husband. Eh, what a wedding-night! And he thought, better not send it; but then she would never forgive him, nor herself. He pondered what he should say.

Below suddenly all the dogs began to howl, and the birds disturbed in the trees set up a shrill twitter of alarm. A servant shrieked piercingly, and ran across the gardens to something pitiably limp that was hanging from a tree. Dermot interposed himself quickly between the young priest's eyes and the garden.

For poor Murphy needed now no corner in Dermotstown. He had sneaked away with his master. There was a witness for the defense.

VIII

§ 1

GONE now were June and July, the pleasant sisters; gone August, warm, mature; gone September, the frail nostalgic month; gone October of the turning leaves, the light night frosts; and the paw of winter showed like the paw of a bear. Westward the Atlantic rose to sullenness, gray the waves, bearded, cold, they broke on the sands of Kerry with a snarling roar, they slapped the cliffs of Connacht tauntingly. No longer were glorious dawns and sunsets of fairy-land. Eastward the sun rose in red anger and westward dropped like a plummet, suddenly, violently, in mid-ocean. And the rains of November came, gray swathing sheets, and the winds of November, cold with the cold of mountaintops.

Now were the major songsters gone, blackbirds and thrush and lark. Gone the swallows. The kingfisher was invisible and the voice of the wood-pigeon was not heard in the land. But the wren, the wren, the king of all birds, was here now, and the robin redbreast of the brown eye. High over the marshes the jack-snipe flew his tricky swerving course, and the golden plover winged. And came the wild duck southward and the barnacle-goose, and distantly on the breeze came the deep brazen note of the wild swan, distantly showed the high white triangle. And the eagle barked at the coming snow.

And now was hunting of foxes.

There is something eerie about the hunting of foxes that obtains in no other chase. There is nothing of food in them, as there is in the hare, the deer, the game-birds. There is a majesty in hunting the deer with dogs, on his native heath— not in the urban device of enlarging him, as they will call kicking him out of a baker's cart, chasing him over safe country, and capturing him, to be chased another day. O good Saint Hubert! And there is a keen dash about coursing the flying hare with greyhounds. But about the chase of the fox there is a mysticism, a fragment of ancient wisdom and ritual whose real meaning has been lost down the ages.

For of all animals the fox is the most cunning, most mysterious. His small, not unhuman face, his little body, his great red brush. He is nonchalant, seldom afraid. He knows the winds, he knows the country, not with the instinctive small knowledge of ordinary game, but with the strategy of a field-marshal. He lays out a line to follow, giving himself most advantage, toward an earth perhaps twenty miles away. Against him are the trained swiftness and scent of the hounds, the experience of, the huntsman, the science of the master, and his haunts stopped by the hunt servants. Against him all this and yet often as not he gets away safely. There is no doubt about it, he reasons cleverly as man. And none of the animals of the field will have aught to do with him, so strange is he, barring the moody badger, lonely as himself, who accords him the occasional hospitality of its burrow.

There is something gay and nonchalant about Dan Russel, the reddish mister, as Chaucer named him. There is a gallantry about his descent on a barn-yard in the dusk or on a moonlit night. The barn-yard dog has few terrors for him. And he has been known to lift a goose even while he is being hunted with the pack, and trot ahead, carrying it in his saturnine grinning mouth. This, it has been argued, was to show his contempt of the whole ceremony of hunting him with hounds and horses and horn.

If this were all, his intelligence and his gallantry, he might indeed be killed as a gentleman is killed in Ireland, with a gun. For to leave him unmolested is impossible, so great are his depredations. But about him the most important thing is yet to be told. There is a mystery and terror surrounding him, as in Japan, where there is a very sinister and evil dance done by artists, called the Dance of the Fox; Michio Itow has it. And in China witches turn into foxes and roam the country of nights, as indeed they do in parts of Ireland. And women who have beautiful mask-shaped faces are avoided because of some ancient wisdom that has been forgotten.

And stranger than all this fancy is fact. There is a title and estate in Ireland called Gormans-town, very ancient, a viscounty of 1478. And when a Viscount Gormanstown is dying, so it is known and so it has been twice authenticated by many living men, there gathers on the lawn of Gormanstown in the dusk, a great population of foxes. Whence they came none know. On the lawn they sit, quiet as statuary, their green eyes are luminous, the heavy scent of them is in the air. And through the long night they are there. There is heard their soft padding, their sniffing at the doors. They are not seen in the day, but every dusk they come and every night they stay, until the dead viscount is laid to rest. They go then, none know whither.

There is a very ancient Irish title, The Fox (*A' Sionnach* it is in Gaelic, which leaves no doubt

that fox is meant), which is borne by a living man,
but what its origin is I have never heard.

Such is the fox. Cunning, jovial, saturnine,
mysterious, abhorred of animals, friend of the
friendless badger, a being out of the fringe of
some mysterious dim world. There is in the Irish
consciousness a tendency to treat him not as an
animal, but as some droll spirit out of a state
where the werwolf and the *pooka* dwell. For
him is no simple death like that of a slug and a
palmful of gunpowder. There must be hounds,
the ritual of the chase, a horn such as the Druids
of old used, clothes that have the red of the ceremonial garments of some sacrificial priest, out of
some ancient Celtic wisdom. We are a very
superstitious people? Very well, we are a superstitious people. What of it? Such is the fox.

§ 2

To Ballydavid on a soft November morning
came the Tara Hunt. Moisture of rain in the
air, mist upon the ditches, the rolling plains, the
heavy turf. There in the village street, near Barney McGuigan's Public House, they gathered,
with the rotund Barney himself ("Mine Host of

the Tara Arms," the journalists call him) and his
four stout serving-maids bringing out drinks to
the thirsty hunters. There gathered some of the
finest horses in Ireland, Miles the Slasher, Mr.
P. Brady's horse, that was to contest the Grand
National in March; Up, Garryowen!—the huge
black gelding belonging to Prince Nugent of Austria; Papal Zouave, Joe Moloney's great-hearted
boy; Old Acquaintance, the winner at the Dublin
Horse Show; and the sweet little mare so curiously named, Italian Indecency (by Casanova out
of Billingsgate Jennie), who was to break her
heart in spring at the Irish bank at Punchestown.
Came some of the greatest horses in the world
there; came strong farmers' horses ridden by
sporting sons; came hacks ridden by army officers;
came polo ponies mounted by boys.

Sedate, business-like, keen, rolled the sea of
hounds, one of the most famous packs in Ireland.
About them a great tradition had grown. With
their predecessors in pre-Union days a bailiff had
been hunted. But that was in the time of Sir
Simon De Courcy. Here were hounds with pedi-
grees longer than the horses, longer even than the
majority of the riders to hounds. Bess and Ivy
and Iolanthe, of the best breeding in Yorkshire,
and Pocahontas and Eva from the Virginia strain,
and Negress and Venus and Granuaile from

the famous family of the Antrim Rapparee. And
Millie (for Melpomene,) who had hunted and
killed a fox all by herself after a fifteen-mile run;
and the gentle Maggie Murphy, about whom was
the tradition that she had brought home a nice fat
peasant child for her puppies' supper. Ah, but
that was in the County of Cork! . . . There they
were, under the eye of the huntsman whose wife
had left him because he had no time or love for
her, so much did he lavish on his hounds. There
they were, two and forty couple of them, a-
wagging of their sterns.

And to the Tara Hunt now came all the folk
of adjacent counties, and came the people of Dublin. Eugénie, Empress of the French, had driven
to it, and another empress, she of Austria, had
ridden to hounds with it with her *bel ami*. And
Garibaldi had created no small sensation there
with his black theatrical charger, his red theatrical shirt. Thither on this November day had
ridden the master, the Baron de Spoer, his features Dutch, or those of his ancestor who had
fought with William at the Boyne. Thither came
his five big sons, Giles de Spoer, Geoffrey de
Spoer, Jean, St. Edmond, and Ulick. Thither
came the Earl of Connemara, a boy of nineteen.
Thither came the Duc d' O'Hanlon, who claimed
seventy years of age and was nearer ninety.

Thither came Sir Valentine de Lacy, whose patent of nobility was of October, 1611; and thither came Sir Jonathan Small, whose patent was of October last.

Thither came Murphy of Ennisbeg, the perhaps richest commoner in the Three Kingdoms. Thither came Bohun de Trelli, the poorest nobleman in the world. His ancestors had come to England with the Conqueror, and fought in Palestine, and he, poor gentleman—his horse was borrowed, his saddle borrowed, breakfast he had had little or none. Thither came Eleanor, Dowager Countess of Cooley, who swore mightily, drank deeply, and had impoverished herself giving to the poor. Thither drove Mr. Richard Croker, the American millionaire-statesman, prim as a bishop.

Thither came Œnone Maturin, dainty, fragile even, and than that same woman there was not a greater scoundrel in all horse-dealing. Thither came General Sir Clunie Campbell, the dour Scot who commanded her Majesty's forces in Ireland, and thither Conor O'Kelly, who had been condemned to be hanged, drawn, and quartered for treason against her same Majesty, and who had protested that the sentence seemed rather severe and couldn't they leave the hanging out? Later he had been reprieved and liberated as a political gesture. Thither came the Reverend Abraham Ferrers in seemly black, which was the only seemly thing about him. Thither came the Bird Corrigan, so called because when his creditors sought him, the bird had flown. He was later to marry a wealthy woman and live unhappily ever after, the joyous hazards of life being gone. Thither came the Toucher Hennessy, whose sobriquet needs no elucidation.

Thither came Connaught D'Arcy, white, thin, reserved, riding Bard of Armagh. Thither came John D'Arcy, on a stuffy close-coupled fencer. He had allowed his beard to grow full again, and that above the red hunting-coat gave him the appearance of a sporting-print of thirty years before. Very prosperous he seemed in white breeches and gleaming boots and hat, but his eyes were seedy. Thither came Dermot McDermot on Thruster, that excellent horse, thinner, paler than usual, with shadows about his eyes. Thither came a stranger on a big hired hunter, a smiling foreign-looking military man, who seemed to enjoy himself whole-heartedly, and whom nobody knew.

Now the village was full, what with hounds and riders, carriages, dog-carts, bicycles. Men left their work in the fields, dropping the spade from their hands, to follow the hunt, a strange excitement seething in them to see the fox streaking away in a flash of brownish red, the hounds pouring after him, the full cry, the horn winding, the scarlet riders pushing their mounts at the fences. And men left the counters of shops, saying: "Am I to follow this mean small trade, and the great excitement there's in the fields. Sack me or not, mister. I'm off on my two legs to let a shout out of me when I see the red one go by." And the schoolmaster wondered not where all his pupils had gone, and old men whom doctors had told they were on the point of death, were hoisted into dog-carts so they could hear once more the sweet music of the hounds. And tinkers had turned up from all parts to see the fine horses, and in the village one blind man with two women followers played a tin whistle, and another blind man, who had a little boy, played on the Irish pipes a queer haunting melody of Carolan's.

A wizened earth-stopper, like a troll or gnome, appeared at the master's bridle.

"Have you them all covered up now, badgers' holes and drains and everything, Macgilligan?"

"Your Honor, I wouldn't tell you a word o' lie, but all around the country the earth is corked as tight as a bottle o' whisky in the parlors o' heaven."

"Begor, if it isn't, I won't lay an inch of your back sound—"

"And who'd blame you, your Honor, it would n't be me. Listen, now, sir: if forty hares was to be hunted by forty hounds, there 's not one would find e'er a shelter in the Province o'Meath this day."

A shrill yelp came from a hound kicked by some unfortunate's horse, and the master turned to implore that fire from heaven and timely eruption from hell should meet to blast and wither the owner of the spavined ring-boned whistler that 's after kicking the beautiful hounds. The hunt moved on toward the first covert.

As they moved forward, half walking, half trotting, Dermot drew near D'Arcy's wife, and on her white face there dawned for a minute the wringing ghost of a smile. "Hello, Dermot!" was all she said, and "Hello, Conn!" his answer. For a month now he had n't seen her, nor she him, and even those few weeks had changed her. He could remember May and June, and the Connaught of early summer, and the Connaught of gray November was so different. Then the boyish laughing girl, now a hard woman. The golden eyes that once were like sunshine, and now like challenging metal. And all the softness of the mouth had gone and it was now grim. Her chin was higher. On her white face was a contemptuous virginal look that made her seem aloof,

inviolate. Where was the placidity of the matron, the melting quality of the spouse? If he
had not himself heard the Dominican preach the
words of union between D'Arcy and herself, he
would have said, "Here is no wife, only an embit-
tered girl."

And D'Arcy—he had changed, too. There
was something soft about him, something crumbling. There are tales told of men going to pieces
on Pacific shores, on the magic islands of the
South. In the magic of the North, men can go
to pieces, too. Always is there whisky, and always sport, and an air of fairy-land, and one puts
off from one day to the next the harsh business of
life, so that unless one has got fire and hardness—

A grouse whirred out of the covert. A rabbit
scuttled off under the tolerant noses of the hounds.
"Leu in, leu in!" came the voice of the huntsman.
"Diana, Venus, Negress, Mag! Find him, girls,
find him! Leu in!" And he pushed on after
them on his little black mare.

"Sure, there 's no fox in it at all!" the master
complained.

"If there is n't, your honor," an earth-stopper
spoke up, " 't is myself that 's blind, me that has
the finest eyesight in all Ireland. For 't is not
one fox is in it but three, and only early this morn-

ing and the waning moon in it I saw them, and
them dancing ring-a-ring-rosies just like Christian
people."

"'T was too much drink you had taken!"

"For the love of God, is it me to have drink
taken, that got the pledge from Father Matthew,
and that nearing sixty year ago—"

"Gone away!" some one called.

In the distance a red streak was moving cunningly along a ditch. Came a whimper from the
covert. Came suddenly the loud music of a
hound.

"My jewel, Negress."

The red streak began to stretch, crossed the
ditch, settled down for a long run, the brush up
like a banner. Hounds became silent, got down
on the scent, moved along like a river. The master's mount broke into an easy gallop, the huntsman skimmed along on the little black mare.
Back of them rode a hundred and fifty men
and women. Hounds in full cry and galloping
horsemen, and a little red flash hardly visible in
the brown fields. Gone away!

As Dermot settled down on Thruster he found
himself riding neck and neck with the stranger
whom none knew. He recognized the horse, a
great saffron-colored brute, as the bane of Regan's
livery-stable, a horse that had killed two men, but

that Regan would not get rid of, so valuable did he deem it and such hopes he had it would one day settle down and be no longer a rogue. It was all right as long as it was going, but at the check its rider must be cautious. They rose to the first fence, and landed neatly. Dermot was interested in the man's riding, so strange did it appear on an Irish or even on an English field. Straight as an arrow, and yet not tight, he sat the great saffron-colored horse. Immobile he took the ditches. There was about him the air of some cavalry commander of a finished school, riding at a review. His red hunting-coat had the sleek appearance of uniform. Some English lancer? No, the way he held his reins, left hand with the right lapping over for leverage—something foreign about that. And yet the man was Irish, Dermot was certain, the clean-cut features, the deep-gray eyes, the curly black head. Some stranger Regan had stuck with that awful brute.

"Better mind that yellow devil of yours," he called.

"I hear he's a handful," the man laughed. The cadence of his sentence was Irish.

Now of the one hundred and fifty starters there were barely forty left. The others had cracked under the first burst of speed, and the ditches had been too much for some, so that they must seek a

friendly gate, or a low place in the bank. Afar
off they straggled, red and drab and tweed coats,
and alongside of them and in advance of them
swept the foot followers, country boys, laborers,
tinkers, what not. Connaught was still in the
first flight, on the great old steeplechaser, but
D'Arcy had dropped out. Dermot could see her
off to the right, near a clump of whins. The
hounds were no longer a flying streak but a troubled milling mass. They had lost the red fox.

They sat, breathing their horses. Thruster
easy with the sense of a long chase before him.
Dermot's stranger loosed the reins. He was
flushed with enjoyment.

> "Oh, the French are on the say,
>   Says the *Shan Van Voght,*"

he sang lowly

> "Oh, the French are on the say,
>   Says the *Shan Van Voght* . . ."

He dropped the reins on the horse's neck, took
out a cigarette case, offered it to Dermot with
lifted eyebrows, lit one himself, was throwing the
match away.

And suddenly the great yellow brute reared.

It rose up terribly, like some horror in a dream,
pawing the air with its great front hooves, an

SUDDENLY THE GREAT YELLOW BRUTE REARED, PAWING
THE AIR WITH ITS GREAT FRONT HOOVES

immense leaning tower of maniacal yellow
strength. The rider shifted forward gently as
though nothing were happening. As it came
down on its fore feet again with a thud, there
came the crack of the crop on its neck. It
wrenched its head down, and rose again, scream-
ing, a tearing obscenity of sound. It pivoted
around on its hindquarters, the stranger in red not
clinging but balancing to it, like some trick of
vaudeville.

"Look out, he's going over," Dermot called.

But the rider had slipped off gently, and with a
terrific pull had brought the brute to its feet. As
it bared the terrible yellow teeth, every centi-
meter of breath in the slim rider's body was blown
by him up the mount's quivering nostrils. The
man-killer stood still, trembling. The rider
slipped into the saddle again, and, hunched forward like a jockey, began stroking with his fingers,
caressing, massaging, all around the horse's ears.

> "The French are on the say,
> They'll be here by break of day,"

he crooned. There was something wonderfully
soothing about his voice. It was like some little
lullaby.

> "And the Rose will decay,"

he sang to the horse

> "Says the *Shan Van Voght*.
> The English will decay,
> Says the *Shan Van Voght*."

Whatever magic was in his fingers, or whatever miraculous soothing tunes were in the croon, the big yellow brute stood gentle as a lamb. "It's all a matter of confidence," the rider in red told Dermot, "confidence and kindness. He's not a bad horse, at all."

§ 3

And then from a clump of gorse the fox stole away cautiously, all but invisibly, down wind. But the eyes of some small red-headed boy were too keen for him. The childish scream of triumph split the air.

"Is it the fox is in it, wee lad?"

" 'T is the King of the Foxes himself is in it, and him the size of a donkey!"

Now hounds had picked up the scent, and settled down for a long swinging run. What with the wind was in it and the country bare but for small timber and easy ditches, and not even a drain itself, he would make, the huntsman figured,

for Kill of the Downs graveyard, where foxes often refuged themselves in vaults. A long seven
miles, anyway, and he settled down on the little
black mare. Ahead of him the hounds drove like
a mottled cloud. Beside him the master galloped
easily, and back of him thundered the first flight of
the hunt—young McDermot, and the stranger on
the saffron horse, and Connaught D'Arcy and
Œnone Maturin, and four of the baron's sons,
and ten or twelve others. Fields slipped past in
a slow panorama, ditch and copse and covert of
gorse. Young cattle scampered out of the way,
and a donkey ran with them a little distance, and
brayed pitiably when it was left behind at the first
big fence.

And Connaught being all but beside him now,
Dermot was thinking of the happenings since
Glenmalure died. She had come back with
D'Arcy that same day, and, very quiet and white
and dignified, had seen all that was mortal of the
great justice put away. "Man that is born of a
woman is of few days, and full of trouble.
He cometh forth like a flower . . . and continu-
eth not." His robes and title and wealth were
as nothing in the democracy of death. The poor
man of the roadside was better off, perhaps, for
after him he left friends, and sweet memories, and
reverence. But Glenmalure had left only bit-

terness and hatred.   Even his name, Glenmalure,
was forgotten and his daughter did not hear it.
Only his house was left and his fearful sobriquet
—Jimmy the Hangman's House, his one monument, the great place of Glenmalure was now
called.   And it hurt Connaught to the heart to see
now how little political friendships counted; they
were no friendships at all, but only alliances of
force, and now that the great man was dead, and
could no longer rule in the Privy Council with his
great jaw, and had no longer the ear of the tem-
poral powers, every jackal in the country thought
it safe to despise him.   Connaught did n't mind
the country people's dislike of him, for, after all,
the red-robed hanging judge had smashed them in
the time of the rising, but his associates and those
who had professed friendship she did mind.   It
seemed to her she was the only person who had
cared for him, she and the poor valet Murphy.

"He was not a bad man, Dermot."   It was the
first time he had ever seen tears in her eyes.   "He
was good to me, and he was so good to old Murphy that he would not stay alive after him, and he
was very good to my mother, so I have always
heard."

"He was only a little hard, Conn.   The law
makes people hard."

"He was a good friend to many people, and

now he is dead they have not a good word for him. Me, I 'm learning, Dermot, I 'm learning hard."

D'Arcy could not have been very kindly in those days; perhaps he did n't understand how grieved his wife was in her loss, and perhaps in manner he may have shown he was glad the Lord Chief Justice was gone, for he was not a little afraid of the man, as who was not? This was no time for love-making, either, and perhaps he had disregarded that, but from the funeral of Glenmalure, then had dated the coldness which had grown into something like enmity. In late July or early August had arisen the question of Parliament, and the men who had promised their aid to Glenmalure now hemmed and hawed when it came to fulfilling their promise. How did they know that D'Arcy would be amenable to party discipline, strict as the discipline of an army? And had n't he once been mixed up in revolutionary politics? People looked askance at that. All these matters had been gone into carefully by Glenmalure, but his arguments and guarantees were forgotten now, and, at that, valueless. The more suave D'Arcy became, the more suspicious grew the leaders. He asked Connaught to speak to them, and for her they might have done a lot. Her word they trusted. But Connaught would n't interfere; perhaps she was angry at their having

gone back on their word to her father, and was
too contemptuous to sue to them. Perhaps she
did n't care enough as to whether or not D'Arcy
ever got a seat.

The full truth of the matter Connaught never
knew, for it was not in D'Arcy to tell her of an
occurrence in which he finished decidedly the
worse. He had gone to the offices of the nationalist party at the request of the political leader,
and there he had met the suave member for Ossory, the diplomat of the party, and a few of the
Northern men for whose constituency he was intended to stand.

"Mr. D'Arcy," purred the member for Ossory,
"we regret that in view of the troubled state of
the country, and of the rumor of, as it were, revolutionary activities in various districts, we don't
feel justified in risking the seat, so—shall we de-
fer your candidature?"

"But your promises to Baron Glenmalure?"
John reddened.

"Our promises to the late Lord Glenmalure,"
Ossory explained, "were given for a definite *quid
pro quo,* certain influences in the Privy Council.
But Lord Glenmalure is dead."

"The truth of the matter is, mister," a Northerner broke in, "we don't want you."

"I don't understand," John fumed.

"Well, I'll tell you. Were you in with the Hogan gang in Paris?"

"I knew them casually."

"Ay, you knew them casually. You were n't man enough to risk your neck, or your skin in the hills. Tell me, were you ever in Russia?"

"As a tourist."

"Were you ever fighting the Japanese?"

"Never."

"Well, mister, you took the credit for it, and you took the credit for being a great rebel. I know you, mister; you 're Tricky Mick's son all through."

"I object to this."

"Object and be damned, mister. If my opinion were asked, it was n't after Hogan's politics you were hanging, but after Hogan's good-looking daughter," he added coarsely. But his shot must have been nearer the mark than he knew, for John turned white. He rose with dignity.

"I don't think I should care to be affiliated with a party whose promises are so easily broken—"

"Gorra! is it Tricky Mick's son I hear talking?" the Northerner jeered.

"Or with men whose manners are of the gutter—"

"I 'll put them red whiskers of yours in the gutter," the Northerner screeched, "if you 'll step outside and put up your hands."

"Gentlemen! gentlemen!" the member for Ossory implored. "Will you shut up, Pat McQuerney!" he ordered.

"So that I shall confine my activities, for the present," said John, "to the sphere of sport." He carried the scene off well, but in his heart he knew he had been bested. He knew that without the iron Glenmalure behind him these men would never countenance him. Ah, well he had a pleasant home and money.

Came September and they were still at Glenmalure. In revolt from the Parliamentary folk, D'Arcy began to surround himself with the cheaper type of racing-man and with journalists, pleasant cynical folk with whom he drank, and drank too much, at Jammet's and "The Dolphin." To them he talked of the glamour of European capitals and of amourettes with exotic foreign women. He seemed to have grown all of a sudden shallow, and rather cheap. There was even talk of his paying attention to some dancer of revue, which Dermot could not credit, so recently was the man married, and to Conn, too, whose beauty was so noted. How could he turn from the purple-black hair and golden eyes

to some over-perfumed vulgar dancing-woman?
Ah, no, there was no truth in that, Dermot
thought, but it would be good for her to go away.
He rode up to Glenmalure. There was an air of
mourning about the great house. How much the
old man had filled it with his stern vitality!

Connaught was white-faced but more beautiful
than before. The soft girlishness had gone from
her features and they had taken on a tragic noble
firmness. There was now a challenge in her eyes.
"Well, Dermot?" she smiled.

"Conn, is John up for Parliament this autumn?"

"No, Dermot."

"Then, Conn, why don't you get away for a
while? What's the use of sticking around in
Ireland? It's sad here with your father gone."

"Where should I go, Dermot?"

"Go to Paris, to Rome, to Egypt, all the places
you wanted to see. Conn, my dear, you used
dream of these places. What's come over you,
little friend?"

"With whom should I go, Dermot?"

"With your husband, of course. Does n't he
want to take you?"

"Yes, of course. But Dermot, I don't know
him well enough to go off to a strange place with
him, do you see?" Her rare little low laughter

came. I was hardly married before this business
of my poor father came up, and since then I 've
been too bothered to improve the acquaintance.
Dermot, don't worry about me, will you not,
please. Please, Dermot."

"All right, Conn, but—"

"Dermot, please."

"Very well." Ah, how she had changed!
Where was the softness, the dreaming, the merriment now?

Himself, too, had changed, he knew and felt.
Physically his body had grown a little heavier, his
face leaner, and in his hair, at twenty-six, were
strands of gray, but that meant nothing. In Ireland people's hair grew gray early and they young
as the birds. But a strange change had come over
the way he thought and felt, and the only way he
could describe that was, it seemed a longer, more
settled rhythm. He had grown into the habit of
sitting up late, reading,—a thing he had never
done before,—when Anne his mother and all the
household were in their beds. The pleasant fire
of coals clinked and crackled, and the golden
light of the lamps shone, and on a chair opposite
him in the pleasant drawing-room a spaniel slumbered, while in front of the fire a red setter and a
deerhound drowsed. That was the wisest thing
about his mother: she never minded the dogs; and

many a woman, he knew, would object to his dogs in her drawing-room, be they ever so clean. And from the shelves he had selected queer books: "The Vicissitudes of Families," those strange volumes by Sir Bernard Burke, the Ulster King-of-Arms, and Mr. Fitzpatrick's "Secret Service under Pitt." There were also the novels of Hall Caine, whose people he could understand, they being Celts too, and just over the water, in the Isle of Man; and there was Tennyson's "In Memoriam," and "Maud," of which there was an echo in his heart. The bells of Dublin would ring midnight and then one of the morning and the book would slip from his hands, and the pipe grow cold in his fingers and he would sit looking into the fire while the dogs slept on.

It was as though he had discovered some new and startling accomplishment, so strange did connected thought appear to him. By such devious little paths and tunnels of suggestion did it wind and turn, so that one moment one would be thinking of tennis-courts and from that one would end up at the age of the Emperor of China. And it was queer to hunt the thought back, from its ending to its starting-point. One began to notice so much. It was only a day or so ago Neddy Joe the lodge-keeper had mentioned his age, ninety-one, "a great time I was born in, the great Bony-

parte playing ducks and drakes with the kings of
Europe, by God! and never dreaming that there
was a fellow born in Merrison Square in the City
of Dublin, Arthur Wellesley, that was afterward
Th' Ironjook, would knock the devil out of him at
his own game o' war. Do I mind O'Connell,
Jasus, I do. He said that all the liberty in the
world was n't worth a drop of human blood.
Would you say that was a brave man?

"Do you know what I mind, Master Dermot,
avick? I mind your great grandfather, the oldest man in Connaught, him over a hundred and
ten, and bright as be damned. 'T was at Coolavin. (My occupation there, is it? Oh, general. Cleaning dishes in the kitchen, exercising
race-horses on the track, and filling your granny's
snuff-boxes in the drawing-room.) Do you know,
your great grandfather had no Irish, and his wife
had no English, so they had to talk in French.
Fine strapping children they had, so that French
must be a grand language entirely. But I heard
the old prince talk and me a lad, and he remembered George the First coming to England and
not a word of English at him, but only the German tongue, and two old biddies with him you
would n't be seen talking to on a dark road, and
him mad in love with the pair of them, and one of

them shaking with fat, and the other with as little meat on her as the stick in my hand.

"And the old one said this, too: that he minded his grandfather talking about the fighting against Cromwell at Drogheda, and that Cromwell was a thick-set ignorant sort of man, with a wart on his chin. And the Irish fought with bows and arrows against him.

"Is n't that a forbye thing, that I can mind a man that minded a man who had fought against Cromwell with bows and arrows!"

Yes, it was a strange "forbye" thing, Dermot thought. Only two lives between him and the men who fought against Cromwell; a generation or so more would have looked on the sweet treacherous face of the Queen of Scots, and every man thought his life so important, his space so great. Were n't human beings overrating themselves, rather? And was it underrating themselves or was it the chain that was important? At any rate, it was too deep for him.

It was too deep for him, but out of this struggling darkness of thought he was learning proportion. Already the old ambitions and ideals were falling from him. His old love for the sea—examining it, he found it wanting in something. Was it enough for a life to go down in ships of

battle, ambling from port to port, fêted here,
fêted there? And perhaps one day in the century
would come a great battle. And the life one had
lived in preparation would be crowned by a few
hours of belching guns and struck flags. And
then quietness and a pension and an old choleric
naval officer complaining to his juniors that everything glorious passes away. Now it seemed a
selfish life lying in wait for glory or lazily passing
a mechanical existence. In his own life now on
land were everyday problems of importance. He
had an idea in his mind of improving Glen Farm
by removing the hawthorn hedges, and making the
divisions good for tillage. And that had never
been done before, and how to do it? That was
a matter of farm economics. And there was also
the question of trees that ought to be removed and
trees that ought to stay. Some trees seemed to
have a right to be there, though they interfered
with agriculture. And what trees to leave and
what to remove, and on what basis, beyond that
of feeling? Didn't Henry Grattan move his
house rather than cut down an encroaching great
tree? And quaint though that may seem, there
was a great deal in it, Dermot felt. There was a
feeling that God had to do with trees, and to interfere with His work seemed irreverence. And
a tree appealed to you with the dignity of a horse

or a great dog. Also, what of the birds of the
air, their little homes? Nature had its economics, too. And how far could one trespass? In
some countries, he had heard, all the trees were
down and no birds gave music any more. And
had the population gained by the sale of timber
what they had lost with the birds? A bird's song
is such a heartening thing.

Also were other problems. There was the
matter of plowing the land, of mowing the hay.
There were now produced great mechanical engines for that. But what of the people? How
of the plowmen who could steer a line straight as
that drawn by a rule, proud of their horses as of a
sweetheart? How of the tanned mowers, the
timing of their swinging scythes as accurate as the
timing of a golf swing? They made good money;
their families were decently raised; they were
proud of their craft. And one must send them
away. And in America or Australia or the towns
of England they did n't do well. They were no
longer skilled workers. They huddled in slums
and decency gave way to degradation. And drink
and consumption began their inroads upon them.
The children brought up in mean streets. Eh, it
was hard! And yet, this damned progress must
go on and men must die by it.

And why the progress? he thought. What

would it avail him to put in mechanical plows and
reapers and binders? It would put more money
in his pocket. But he didn't want more money:
he had enough. Then don't use them. But
everybody else did, and if he didn't, in a little
while the place would take on a quaint proportion
of a thatched cottage at a centennial exposition.
One didn't want to look like a soft fool!

Oh, be damned to it all!

He would rise, knocking out his pipe, and knowing well that he would have a solution of each
problem in the morning. The dogs would be
hurried out through the great windows to the ken-
nels in the courtyard. And he would stop for a
minute, looking at the night, whether a moon was
in the sky or a great blaze of stars, or the soft
Irish rain. And night after night his eyes and his
heart would go toward Glenmalure. . . .

Only a few months and such a change in her.
All her sweet girlishness gone, her soft color
ousted by tragic pallor. She was like a woman
apart on a mountaintop, who but recently had
been the spirit of smiling gardens. Once she had
been one with all the sweet landscape about her,
field and tree and garden and sweet slope of mountain. And now she rose above them. Against
the background of the Wicklow Mountains she
was like some tragic queen of the theater. And

he, too—he was not what he had been. He seemed to have grown ten years in a few months.

They had been like Adam and Eve in the ancient garden, happy, friendly, taking each other for granted. And now they were like Adam and Eve after the fall, knowing good and evil, he aware of her as never in his life had he been aware of person before, though she might not think twice of him. And there had been no apple from the Tree of Knowledge eaten, unless it were a sort of instinctive knowledge that the world was not a happy garden. And there had been no serpent to disturb them, unless it were John D'Arcy. A poor analogy, he thought.

§ 4

But the fox had changed his mind about Kill o' the Downs, distrusting the protection of the dead who slept there. And, taking a wide sweep to the right, he was making for Ballydruid, whence the hunt had started. Some burrow or cromlech of a dead Druid king would afford him shelter, and when he went to earth in the Firbolg burial-mounds no hunt terrier could ever dig him out. The hounds were splashed with mud. Only the gallant strain of the horses kept them up. All

the first flight were still to the fore, the master
and four of his sons, the stranger on the saffron
brute, who was riding beside Œnone Maturin
now, Connaught and Dermot, and a dozen others.
Now came a crumbling stone ditch which the
horses took in their stride like hurdles. Now a
bank on both sides of which were little dikes for
drainage of water, and on top of this the horses
sprang, neatly as cats, changed feet, jumped forward to the ground again. Now was a blackthorn hedge that must be crashed through, riders
guarding their faces with their right arms. The
thud-thud of hooves, fields away the cry of the
hounds. The ammoniacal scent of horses and
leather. Somewhere in the distance the muddy
red fox, invisible in the autumn tints of the fields.
At the Rathdown road came a check.

They stood around, breathing their horses,
waiting for the first whimper that would give notice that the scent was found again. Down the
road came riding the stragglers who had eschewed
the fields, hoping to pick up the hunt at some distant point. Came the toucher Hennessy, with a
victim in tow, some week-end visitor of the major's. Came ladies on hacks, came a dog-cart,
came Scott the horse-dealer, came John D'Arcy.

Dermot was talking to Connaught when her
husband came up, speaking of old hunts with the

Ward Union. As D'Arcy rode forward she greeted him with cold politeness.

"You were lucky to find us."

He muttered some monosyllable, glared at Dermot, and looked around the field with that arrogant insulting glance of his. With his shining hat and great reddish beard, now they were standing, he was the most notable figure at the check. Œnone Maturin was evidently pointing out the people of interest to the stranger. She pointed out the old Baron de Spoer; the toucher Hennessy, who, it was claimed, had touched the Pope for his car fare home to Ireland; she pointed out Dermot. The stranger had an air of smiling gallantry.

She pointed out the horse-dealer Scott, who had recently drunk a Belgian remount officer blind and while in that state had sold him thirty mules as sixty cavalry horses. She pointed out Mick Lacey the farmer, whose daughter had married an Italian prince. She pointed out Mrs. Wylie-Wylie, who said she never felt normal until she had three whiskies and sodas under her stays. The stranger laughed.

She pointed out D'Arcy, and the smile on the stranger's face might have been wiped off with a sponge, so suddenly did it change. It became a white grim threat. Without a word he left the girl in mid-sentence, and pushed the yellow brute

across the throng of riders toward D'Arcy. He
reined in in front of him.

"Are you by any chance," he asked in a cold
hard voice, "the D'Arcy who was in Paris in
ninety-five?"

Let this be said for John: that now when faced
with the menace of those hard white features,
those angry eyes, whatever the menace was, he
never flinched or changed color. He might
blanch in prospect, but in actuality he had the
seeming of bravery.

"Never was in Paris in my life," he growled
surlily. "Who the devil are you?"

"I'm sorry, sir." The tension passed from the
rider's face. "I made a mistake, for which I
hope you'll pardon me—and you, madame."
He bowed to Connaught. "And the man I'm
looking for would be rather younger than you,
sir, and clean-shaven. I am very stupid. Again,
apologies." And he raised his hat and rode
away. "Agh!" growled D'Arcy.

Connaught was looking at her husband with
cold disapproving eyes.

"Why did you lie to that man, John?" she
asked coldly.

"Because I don't want to be bothered with
damned foreigners."

Came a whimper from Negress. Venus lumbered forward, snouting the ground. Her clear ringing note smote the air like a bell. The horn winded, calling the scattered hounds. "Hounds, please. Hounds, damn you! please!" The master held the riders back. The mottled stream swept forward on the found line. The huntsman's black mare broke into her beautiful quick canter. Horses shuffled, trotted, stretched into a gallop. In a green field a stone's throw away a reddish-brown quarry moved. "Gone away!" some one shouted. "Tally-up! Tally-up!" Horses fought for their heads. The hunt thundered toward the first fence. The mounts rose from the ground like swallows.

The ground slid past beneath them, the greenish brown of old bronze. It slid beneath them as though they were riding clouds instead of horses. The remaining weeds of the fields shook with the thunder of the horses' feet, thistle and ragroot and clump of rushes. Beneath them flew patches of black dog water, little banks of gorse, turf, ditches where the horses laid never an iron. A flash of timber and a crash. Some one was down. Hard luck! Who was it? Don't know.

And now suddenly a mania of the chase took every one, hounds and horses and riders. A few fields away the fox dragged his heavy brush, and lumbered on. The Red Man was beaten and he

knew it, and the hounds, sensing it, put out their
reserve for the kill.   And now their voices rose in
loud clamor, and now were silent.   And the fury
of the chase captured the wise horses and they
fought for their heads like fiends; their necks
stretched, their nostrils quivered.   And out of
the fields arose the birds of winter and wailed
in the gray air, mottled magpie and glossy
crow.

The hunt thundered on after the hounds.   The
huntsman's little black mare flew like some skim-
ming bird.   The master's huge gray threw great
divots of turf behind him.   The stranger's saffron
brute went forward in great tigerish bounds.   A
scramble and thud as a horse made a mistake at
a jump and came down badly, pitching his rider.
And the rider lay there, his collar-bone broken,
or his neck broken, who knows?   Onward the
hunt.

Dermot threw a look aside to see was Connaught there.   She was safe.   Her hat had gone,
and about her head her glossy hair was like a
hood, and into her cheeks a sweet wild-rose color
had come, with the excitement of the hunt.   Her
lips were parted, her eyes shone. . . . They
topped another fence, and they were in the field
with the hounds.   But the hounds were chasing
no longer.   They were swarming, snarling, and

something reddish brown, and limp, was being bandied among them like a football.

For Dan Russel, the Red Man—his days were done. And very gallantly and very ceremonially had he died, with a hundred horses and a hundred hounds chasing him, and folk in red coats and black-velvet caps and high silk hats. And he had been hunted by men of ancient chivalric lineage and ladies, as the song has it, of high degree. Not for him death in a poacher's trap or from a peasant's shot-gun, but elaborate, expensive, ceremonial. And to-night the sullen badger would miss his only friend, the arrogant walk, the coarse scent of him. And to-night a lonely vixen would bark complainingly at the silent moon. And no rabbit would scream in the glades of bracken as he padded softly along, the triangular mask, the green gleaming eyes, the russet fell, the brush flaunted like a banner. And the birds would be quiet in the trees.

He had gone now, Reynard, the sly one, to the dim occult paradise of beasts, where dwells the lumbering uncouth *pooka,* and where the seals go, who have brown eyes like women's, and where dance the fairies who are like beautiful minute human beings but have no souls. And where the gnomes live, surly and grimy as smiths. And little dead-born babies laugh at their antics there.

And in that world are the dead harmless empty
people whom we call mad. And are other
strange and piteous things the reason for whose
making only God knoweth. . . . Ended were the
days of Dan Russel the Fox.

§ 5

And so the hunt was ended, the brush given to
Œnone Maturin, and the master clambered into
a dog-cart, leaving his horse with a groom. And
the huntsman started to collect his hounds. And,
out of nowhere seemingly, came a small breathless
boy who caught the stranger's stirrup-leather and
spoke hurriedly to him; and the stranger, turning
in his saddle, surveyed the country keenly, and,
with a smile and a lift of his hat to all, left, put the
yellow horse at a ditch, and started cantering
across country. And Dermot and Connaught
started back to Ballydruid through the lanes soft
with winter. There was still the remnant of the
flush in her cheek.

"You are looking well to-day, Conn."

"Am I, Dermot?" she smiled. "Do you know,
for a little while there, in the last rush, I felt I
was young again. And my father alive. And
no trouble in the world."

"Conn," he said, "you must try to be like that more. I—all your friends, Conn, are heart-broken to see you sad. You must cheer up, be yourself again, for their, for our sake."

"Yes, Dermot," she said half meekly, "I must."

And then she said: "Perhaps things are not as black as they seem. Aren't a lot of things just imagination and strangeness, Dermot? One gets accustomed in time. What I mean," she said quickly, "is my father being gone."

They had come in the main road to Ballydruid. A patrol of constabulary was thrown across the road. There was something very business-like about their green uniforms, the black of their rifle barrels. A sergeant with a full mustache saluted.

"Asking your pardon, sir and ma'am," he broke into a thick Roscommon accent, "did you see any-thing of a foreign man at the hunt, and him on Regan's big, yellow, man-eating horse?"

"I did," Dermot answered, "and a grand horse-man he is."

"And sure why wouldn't he be," the sergeant demanded, "and him commander of a regiment of horses in the French Army? Would you tell me now, your Honor, which way did he go when the hunt was ended?"

"Is it for stealing the horse you're after him?"

"It is not," the sergeant replied importantly,

"but this: that this commander is an enemy to Her Majesty, and a Fenian man. I'll tell you what's in it," he whispered loudly: "revolution!"

"You're crazy," Dermot laughed. "There hasn't been a revolution for thirty years."

"And it's on account of us nobbling fellows like that, your Honor, that the country's at peace. And from information received to-day, this fellow's the most dangerous of the lot."

"Information received. I suppose the Bird Corrigan has been playing a joke on you, and he leaping with liquor."

"'Twas not the Bird Corrigan, so, and him in the mystery of drink told us, but her Ladyship's husband," he looked at Connaught, "and him white as a sheet and shaking like the leaves of Christmas. A great name for daring he put on this fellow, so that we brought out the guns.

"Oh, begor, your Ladyship, 'twas none other than himself."

Her face was not white, but gray now, so deathly did it appear. The lips blue; the eyes were like some strange fancy painted on gray linen.

"If this gentleman is taken," she asked, and seemed to enunciate with difficulty, "will he be imprisoned?"

"Oh, begor, he will, ma'am! And if what

your Ladyship's husband says is true, 't will be a matter for twenty years or life itself."

She pushed past the sergeant suddenly, saying no more. And Dermot, touching Thruster with the spur, came up quickly beside her. Her head was bowed, and down her cheeks great pitiable tears were rolling. The fingers of her right hand fumbled on the Bard's mane.

"I knew he was bad, Dermot," she said, and a gulp of a sob wrenched her throat, "I knew he was crooked, Dermot, but I never knew he would tell the police on a hunted man. Your little friend Connaught, Dermot—she will be known soon as D'Arcy the Informer's wife."

He could say nothing, but rode ahead, his face grim. Beside him he could hear her soft low sobbing. He ground his teeth in an anguish of rage. "By God! John D'Arcy, some day you 'll answer to me for this," he promised himself. Back down the road came the thunder of a horse's hooves. Connaught turned her mount.

"Oh, Dermot," she said, "they have him!"

It was Regan's yellow horse, for a surety, but the rider was not the red-coated cavalry officer. A countryman sat loosely in the saddle, with long tweed trousers and flannel coat and black slouch hat. And before him on the pommel were the gay red coat and gay white breeches and shining

boots. The loud challenge of the sergeant
brought the horse to a standstill.

"Easy, now; easy, now, my lad. Tell me
where did you get this horse and them clothes.
Out with it, now, and remember that anything you
say," he warned magnificently, "will be used
against you."

"Sergeant honey," the countryman was answer-
ing, " 't was to yourself I was coming to tell all
about it.

" 'T was this way, sergeant," he began. "This
gentleman came up to my wee house after the
hunt, and he let a screech out of him. 'My good
man,' says he, 'have you a suit of clothes you could
sell?' 'I have,' says I, 'if there 's a good price on
them.' 'The price,' says he, 'is no object at all.'
Do you follow me, Sergeant?"

"I do. I do."

" 'The truth is,' says he, 'a great disgust has
come over me with my way of life,' says he, 'hunting foxes and drinking whisky and courting women
night and day,' says he, 'so I 'm off to America.
And let you take the horse and clothes,' says he,
'and give them to the first decent man you meet.'
'This man,' says I to myself, 'is mad, and I must
humor him. I 'll bring the horse and the queer
clothes to Sergeant Patsy Brannagan,' says I.
'Do,' says he, 'begor, do. I always had a great

liking for Patsy,' says he, 'and his ould mother.' "

"I have no ould mother," said the sergeant.

"Oh, my poor fellow, do you tell me so! Well, this man gets into my Sunday suit, and 'Is it far from here to the Cove of Cork?' says he. ' 'T is,' says I. 'How far?' says he. 'One hundred and sixty miles,' says I. 'In what direction?' says he. 'South,' says I——"

"My man," the sergeant asked coldly, "are n't you the lad that 's known as the Fenian O'Leary?"

"Well, now, Sergeant dear, 't is only a joke of the boys, that same name——"

"My impression is——" the sergeant eyed him askance——"that the information you 're giving me is information to mislead. And what is more, my lad, I 've got an idea that you 're holding me here in conversation while the man gets away."

"Oh, if that 's the way you feel, Sergeant——" the countryman descended from the horse dejectedly——"if that 's what you think, let you throw your leg over the yellow fellow and chase the man. I hope you find him," he laughed. "I do so. Put the red coat on, mister dear," he wheedled. "The way you 'll look and you on the horse, like the Duke of Wellington at Waterloo. 'T is a great pity," he mourned, "that I dropped the castor hat and me galloping to find you. It would have gone grand with your mustachios."

IX

§ 1

ALL that Dermot remembered of D'Arcy or had heard of him contrasted strangely with the man as he now was. He had thought of him as a pleasant, tricky, smooth fellow, the sort who is Mamma's darling in the home, Teacher's pet at school, hard unscrupulous worker at the university, paying all attention to books and none to athletics. Men of this type marry early and marry well, as far as material fortune is concerned. They go along a swift pathway of success, liked only by those men whose policy accords with theirs. Open vices they have none. But they are always the secret drinkers, the folk who elope with their best friend's wife. They are the devourers of widow's houses, the trustee bankers who abscond with the money of orphans. And sometimes one of them, who has done all these things, and by accident or the trickery of law escaped, dies in full honor and a white choker, and a bishop in lawn sleeves mourns over his bier, and to him is erected a marble monument, and one wonders in a weak moment where is the tremendous justice of God. To this type Dermot would have assigned John D'Arcy.

But the man had changed. He had become nearly strong. A weak and purring politician could have devised some way of making the Northerners keep to their promise. And besides, it was n't like the old John D'Arcy to be keeping foolish company around the bars of Dublin. The other would have been too much afraid of what the City would think of him. The new man threw his respectability to the winds.

Also, the old John D'Arcy would not have been as strong a villain as to set the police on the stranger horseman at Tara. He would have found some other way of accomplishing his end. Something of the old graceful twisting. Now from a delicate, sly crook, D'Arcy had changed into a fine robust figure of melodrama, as he had changed from a pale-faced youth into a burly reddish-brown bearded man, the antithetical appearance of dishonesty. A fat man might be a fool, but who had ever heard of a fat villain? Dermot thought. Ah well, fat or no, Dermot insisted to himself, a villain his cousin John decidedly was.

He puzzled with himself what this matter of fear hanging over John was. What had the

French officer to do with it? A matter of politics, he doubted it. Whatever John had been doing in Paris, it was hardly possible that he was in the very inner circles of revolution. The men in that combination, so he had heard, were hard-bitten secretive men who were planning more the escapes of their friends from jail than on landing armadas on the shores of Ireland; dynamiting prison walls, and hiring whalers to make raids in Australia to get the old felons away, if there were any left. Actual revolutions, he had heard, were plotted in America, but sure there had n't been one for the third of a century! No, he felt with common sense, these men would not admit a light-weight like D'Arcy into their councils. So there would be little chance that there was any matter of a broken oath. If D'Arcy knew the revolutionaries at all, it was only in the casual pleasant café life. What John had done, most probably, in Paris was to use his Irish descent and nationality as a lever for introduction into French society, into that royalist circle that is the most exclusive of all circles, where the officers of the old Irish Brigade had cut such a dash, the men of Lord Clare's regiment of dragoons, and the old Earls of Lucan, and this Jacobite marquis and that Galway prince. In that circle D'Arcy had probably ruffled like the greatest noble of them all.

Then what, he reasoned, would the quarrel of the French officer of the latest school of refugees have to do with it? Son of any fighter of Fenian days, he would have little interest in royalist circles, such intense republicans the Fenians were. Could John have said anything about the new school, and been promptly challenged to a duel, and as promptly run away?

Or could it be some question of money?

That was the more probable, because it was not likely, John having run away, that an army officer would follow him, in the hope of persuading him to fight. If John's modest income had been realized on, and squandered, surely he had achieved the end of his kind, a rich marriage. But would Connaught hand over her money and property to John? If she were in love with him, yes. But she was n't. Then she would do little beyond giving him enough to keep him quiet. In Glenmalure things were not going well, he knew. He had heard— as how could he help hearing in a country whose acoustics are so perfect?—that there were guests now in the Lord Justice's house whom the old baron would have turned out of the doors had he been alive. Thither now to dinner came bookmakers, Mickey Regan in particular, a shifty bird who had started on his career with three-cardmonte at fairs, and who had bribed more jockeys

and doped more horses than all the book-makers
of his time put together. It was this Regan who,
when watched so closely that traditional methods
of throwing a race could not be employed, devised
the scheme of small pieces of sponge stuffed up
his horse's nostrils. He lost the race and won
thousands. Doctor de Lacy, that sporting medi-
cal man whose name was never mentioned in any
reputable place, brought thither his bloated face,
his suave manners. Thither came Mrs. Dolly
Ryan, that bold handsome widow, against whom
nothing could be said, but a tremendous amount
suspected. Thither came Miss Cholmondly-
Williams, the keenest card-player in Ireland.
And after dinner, in the card-room where Glenmalure and his cronies had played at chess and
smoked long churchwarden pipes, or played whist
and compounded a punch cunningly with potheen
of the mountains, and sugar from Jamaica, and
lemons of the Mediterranean, and Indian nut-
megs; their heads massive with knowledge of law
and life, their exquisite hands, their measured dignified words—in that room now gathered this unseemly rout of new and vulgar people, with
loud laughter and loud jokes, and loud ultra-
fashionable clothes, with small roulette tables and
dice. And when they played cards they played

baccarat. And champagne was their drink, and often they laced it with brandy.

Connaught, Dermot knew, hardly spoke to her husband now, beyond ordinary frigidly polite words, and always there was some woman of her mother's people staying with her: some tan-faced woman from Galway who rode to hounds with the Blazers, and scrambled in rocky Connacht streams fishing for salmon, and spent the evenings reading George Eliot and Charlotte Brontë by the light of wax candles; or some thin exquisite Englishwoman keen on the brasses of old cathedrals and on stamping out slums. During dinner John's guests would be self-conscious and overpolite, and when after dinner Connaught and her eternal relative withdrew on the plea of a nightly headache, there would be a general sigh of relief.

And then in a minute or so would come the clamor in the card-room.

" 'T is queer doings these days at Jimmy the Hangman's house, Master Dermot," old Neddy Joe gabbled to him. "The beardy fellow, your cousin John, winning a mint of money from crooked Mickey Regan, and them nearly hitting each other over saying which was the biggest scoundrel. And a woman there going screeching mad with the drink."

"Why the hell don't you mind your own damned business?" Dermot shouted.

"Your Honor, sir, anything connected with Jimmy the Hangman, with him or his, is business of mine," Neddy Joe replied with dignity. "For didn't he stretch the neck of my own fine boy in the troubled times? I hated him alive and I hate him dead, but ah, Master Dermot, isn't it queer and hard to see the jackdaws hopping where once a great eagle flew?

"And did you hear, your Honor, that little Miss Connaught has turned over her horses to Robinson to train?"

Thank God for that! Dermot thought. There was one thing the crew couldn't get their rotten hands on. Robinson with the cold eye, the hat on the side of his head, the match between his teeth, was one person that couldn't be bribed or talked over. He took orders from the owner and nobody else. John D'Arcy couldn't work him. And down in his heart Dermot had been afraid that crooked John might get his hands on the horses too. And Connaught's reputation, which was that of as straight an owner as ever sent a horse to the post, would be no longer safe. It would have been a heartbreaking thing to hear the crowds ask, as the green-and-gold-colors cantered down, "Is he out to win or out for the exercise?"

John was going around now, open and brazen. Whatever danger he had scented from the French officer, he evidently thought was past. The warning to the police, John had figured, had made him clear the country. But that he was still in the country Dermot knew.

Dermot had been down at a coursing meeting in North Louth. Nearly everything in farm work was snugged down for the winter, and time had been lying heavily on his hands. He had a nomination for the meet, and had entered a dog of one of his gardeners', a keen young puppy over whom the country-side was excited, taking odds now that she would be in the finals of the Irish Cup. She was a well-boned intelligent lady of about sixty pounds' weight, and she might well be a world-beater. So he went down North to see.

There is something in coursing that suits the season, gray land with the grass crisp with frost, rolling dunes, stunted wintry hedges, and here and there a high bank, and somewhere a little brook running, lazy with winter, the scum of ice in its edges. The men and women huddled in great-coats and mufflers and stamping for warmth on the hard soil. High muscular dogs swathed like horses. The book-makers with their bags of coins.

And then a hare ("Puss," as he is called in the cant of the sport) is started. And the slipper, with the great hounds in couples, jockies the dogs into position, and suddenly unleashes them. And then is incredible swiftness. As fast as the eye can follow them they traverse the frozen grass, brown Puss ahead, his body an arc of speed, behind him the greyhounds with their diminutive pounding as of horses. And Puss seems to stand still on his funny little hind paws and turn like a boat coming about to the tiller, and he is off on a new tack while the dogs hurl past him, unable to check their speed, and Puss has gained a hundred yards and is in full speed before they are ready to begin again. And often Puss escapes, and tells his midnight sweethearts of the imminent deadly hounds and how he tricked them, and forgets the farmer's traps with their cruel serrated edges, where he lies in agony the lonely night with never a dog to put him out of misery. And often he is more fortunate and the foremost dog bowls him over with a quick snap of teeth. The judges ponder while the red-faced men offer one another the silver flask of whisky on account of the cold and for their stomach's sake and their often infirmities. And Paddy Swayne the bookie opens his satchel and his throat of brass:

"I'll pay now on Tetrarch's Daughter."

Ah, it's very pleasant, the coursing!

A very pretty little pup, Silver Birch, had tempted Dermot with its long lines, its promise of weight and intelligence, and he bought her and was bringing her into Dundalk from Crannoge in the cold evening when before him on the road he heard a man's deep voice singing:

> "And what will the Orangemen do?
> Says the *Shan Van Voght*.
> And what will the Orangemen do?
> Says the *Shan Van Voght*.
> What would the Orangemen do,
> But throw off their red and blue—"

Dermot was coming up a little side road, with a great cross road intersecting it, the long road into Ulster through the Gap of the North, as it is called. A little way past Dundalk the road would go through Lurgan Green, pass the little Quaker village of Ravensdale, skirt the edge of Slievegullion, broadest and most legendary of Irish Mountains; thence a man could go onward to Lough Neagh, the great lake, and winding past the town of Ballymena, come to the Glens of Antrim. It is a great, fair, and lonely road.

> "And swear that they'll be true,
> To the *Shan Van Voght*.

> That they'll be forever true,
> Says the *Shan Van Voght.*"

The song rang out in the silvery gray winter evening like a challenge, and Dermot wondered whether it was becoming a popular ballad once more, so often did it seem to him he had heard it of late: the little red-headed boy singing it in the village of Five Houses, the army man from France humming it in the hunting-field, and now this man, whoever he was, singing it as a marching song on the great Ulster road.

As Dermot came out of the little side road he saw the singer.

It seemed to be a monk in the brown habit of the Franciscan friar, the loose shapeless robe with the brown cowl hanging behind, like the hood of a woman's cape, and bound with a great white cord. But the skirt of the robe was lifted up around his middle, and the monk's hands in the pockets of his black trousers; a fat Turkish cigarette was in a corner of the Franciscan's mouth, and he sang as he walked. For a moment Dermot felt like laughing loudly. And then a quick wave of pity and apprehension swept over him. The poor man was drunk. He thought quickly that he ought to do something, and not let him stumble into the nearest town to be made fun of or to be

X

§ 1

SLIPPED the short winter days by: now wanly smiling in distant sunshine; now crisp and frosty, the black roads gleaming like pewter, the bushes a tracery of rime; now gray with rain, gray and mournful. And the fox was hunted, and the hare coursed, and the surly badger drawn by powerful dogs. And the country people drank too much whisky and played too much cards, and the men in the towns clustered around bars at nightfall and consumed incredible amounts of black foaming porter, and told stories of great sporting events gone by, of how Cooper the Englishman was beaten for the boxing championship by Dan Donelly at the Curragh of Kildare, and because he won that fight he got a gold belt "and they made a Lord of him, by God!" Which was in a measure true, for he was knighted by a drunken viceroy. And the talk would turn on badgers and fighting-dogs, and some one would tell the story of the Great Pig Pape:

"There was a sea-captain of Donegal trading

in America, and he had a dog he was proud and fond of, and there was a fellow from the Bowery, begor! and he had a dog was the champion dog of America. And they made a match between them, and the sea-captain's dog got killed. 'That's queer!' says the sea-captain. 'Your dog was no good,' says the Bowery fellow. 'Is that so?' says the sea-captain. ' 'T is your dog is no good, a pig could beat him.' And everybody laughed. 'Do you doubt me?' the sea-captain lets a screech out of him with rage and sorrow. 'Well, here's my ship, and all its cargo of tobacco and spirit,' says he, 'and I've got a house in the County of Donegal, and a slate roof on it, and a bath in it, and mirrors round the bath, and a matter of a thousand dollars in the bank' says he, 'and as fine a young plump wife as you ever laid your eyes on, and I'll bet them all,' says he, 'that I'll bring a pig will eat him. And if your dog loses you come with me to the County of Donegal, and you do the dirtiest of work on the farm, and every morning I'll kick you to put myself in good humor, and every night I'll kick you to ease my feelings and me going to my bed.' 'Bring on your pig' says the Bowery fellow, for he wasn't a bad lad and just wanted to get rid of the poor sea-captain quietly. Begor, what does my captain do but the next time he's in South he brings north

with him one of the Brazilian pigs, peccary is the
name is on them, lean as greyhounds, teeth like
razors, and the serpent of the jungle is their
evening meal. So there was no fight in it at all.
One minute the Bowery fellow's dog was the
grandest bulldog you ever laid your eyes on, and
the next he was food for the crows. 'Well, captain,' says the Bowery fellow, and he picks up his
dead dog, 'I 'm ready to go with you, but would
you give me time to bury my poor dog? And you
can stay with me to see I don't get away.' 'Give
me your hand,' says the sea-captain. 'Give me
your hand, decent fellow. 'T is ashamed I am of
myself this day.' "

And other will tell of an event that happened no
less recently than a week ago in Belfast, when Pat
Hennessy the policeman, the wrestling champion
of Ireland, was suspicious of a small "black man"
near the docks. "He was n't a black black man,
but a browny sort of fellow."

"Here, what are you?" says Pat.

"I 'm a wrestler," says the wee fellow.

"Ho, ho!" says Pat. "You 're a wrestler.
Are you?"

And he makes a pass at him in fun.

And the wee fellow takes him by the hand, and
be damned if he does n't lay him on his back!

And Pat at him with a rush, and with a turn the

wee fellow trips him.   And it happens three times
running.   "I 've seen it myself."

"He had the Black Art," says one.

Probably some traveling Japanese sailor, who
gave wrestling exhibitions in ju-jitsu.   But:

"It might be the Black One himself."

"God between us and all harm!" and each one
blesses himself.   And there will grow up a legend
in the North of how Pat Hennessy wrestled Satan
on the docks of Belfast, and Satan was in the guise
of a little black man.   And in the end Pat Hennessy will have won by uttering in awed accents
some sacred name, whereupon the champion of
The Place Under Our Feet, as the Omeath people
call it, will have disappeared with a blinding flash
and an evil odor.   And the cause of religion will
be advanced in these evil days.

But in the cottages of Donegal and Connemara
is no drinking, and no stories of sport.   The turf
fire glints on the whitewashed walls and the gleaming crockery of the dresser.   And an old lady
with a spotless white cap and with no English is
making lace that will appear after many hands
and many profits in Fifth Avenue drawing-rooms.
And if her eyes are very old there is maybe a rush-
light for her.   And the talk is of the American letter that came to Paddy's Mary's Kate from Pitts-
burgh last week, and of the tram-cars of New

York, where the son of the house is working. And some old man by the fire will tell of the cities he has seen and he a quartermaster at the wheel of some sailing-ship: of Savannah where there are only black men, God help us; of the China ports, where he once saw a man from Aran he knew, in the streets of Hongkong, but could n't get speech with him, on account of the throng of people. "In China, now—would you believe it?—they use men for horses, drawing the carriages of the quality people. With my own eyes I saw them, and I would n't tell a lie. A man in a carriage and a man drawing him. Not once but a thousand times. A queer backward country, China." "Is it a sickly people, Dickeen, that the Chinese are, to have to be drawn in carriages?" "Well, now, I would n't say that." "'T is a lazy people they are so?" "Well, I would n't say that, either, for they 're the tireless workers. Just a queer obscure people, on the edge of the world!"

And if the children are still up, there is always a story. The story of the Naked Hangman, for instance. Or some wonder of Harry Stattle, the great magician—the Aristotle of the professors. Or the tale of Dermot and Granya, or that story of the two lovers who were buried in graves far apart, and on certain nights a moonbow, which is a rainbow caused by the moon, joins the parted graves.

But the children are more often asleep, or are supposed to be, in the adjoining room, and the barefooted mother pads in gently.

"Is n't there sleep on you, white child?"

"Thinking of Christmas I was and I lying here. How many days are there now, little mother?"

"*Trideog, ceathairdeog, cuigdeog*—thirteen, fourteen, fifteen. Fifteen until the Christmas."

"Will there be a present for me, mother of the heart?"

"There will be a present for you, white love. A ribbon for your hair, and little knitting-needles, all of your own, and a book with pictures in it, all the way from America. Go in your sleep now.

Say your prayer! *Crios Bhrighde—*"

"Crios Bhrighde, faoi mo lor!
Brat Mhuire faoi mo cheann!
Tar, a Mhichil oig, agus glac mo lamh!"

"The girdle of Brigid about me!
The cloak of Mary under my head!
Come, young Michael, the Archangel, and take my
    hand!"

§ 2

In Dublin, during this month of waiting, Christmas is not thought of with the enthusiasm devoted to the following day, the twenty-sixth. For piety may be a good thing, but sport is better. And on St. Stephen's day carnival begins. In country districts boys parade with a wren on a ribboned stick and chant loudly:—

"The wren, the wren, the king of all birds
St. Stephen's Day he was caught in the furze!
His size is little. His power is great.
Put your hand in your pocket and stand us a treat."

And on that night, other things being equal, the fight for the heavy-weight championship of Ireland is fought. And the great theatrical revue of the year is opened. But on the afternoon of that day the Hannastown races are held, and in motors and on side cars, and in pony-traps and donkey-carts and on foot itself, all the County of Dublin turns out. The first big steeplechase of the sporting year is run then, and often the winner of that is later the winner of the Grand National. And for a month before, the entries are discussed: the weights, though these are of little significance; the weather, which means much. And betting begins long weeks ahead. There comes news that a certain jockey has been engaged for a horse, and those who hear of it first rush to put down their money so as to get good odds, and the price shortens. There comes a rumor that the horse has been heard coughing. Down goes more money, to hedge on another horse. Some one else says the favorite has n't heart enough for the course. The odds lengthen. Ten minutes' racing and a month's hard thought about it. Ah, but it passes the dreary winter days!

Of the entry of thirty horses for the Dundrum handicap Miss Connaught O'Brien's (for she kept her maiden name as a racing name) Bard of Armagh was easily the best in the field. Aged, powerful, skilled in the timing of a jump, with the reputation gained by winning at Punchestown and Baldoyle, there seemed to be nothing to beat him on form. Near him was that excellent horse, Red Anarchist, from the Curragh stables. And Lady Jerry Kehoe's Shooting Star, a fast horse, a high jumper, but had he the heart? And Millicent Bradley's Connemara Breeze, a rogue horse, that never did his best. Mr. John Smith of Birmingham's Least Resistance, an unknown quantity but spoken of highly by the English book-makers. There were also entered the Sergeant Major, Johnny Moloney's gray gelding, and Sir Valentine McCarthy's sweet little mare, Munster Gentility, with the finest head had been seen on a horse since the famous Ormond. And there was also entered Mr. Richard Croker the American millionaire-statesman's animal, Civic Integrity. Against all others fifty to one would be laid.

Dermot was surprised to hear that fairly long odds were being laid against Connaught's horse, ten to one. The Bard should have started at fives. Against Red Anarchist and Shooting Star were the usual twelves. Connemara Breeze got no more than that, because one day the big black might turn honest and do his best, and if he did there were few horses in Ireland could catch him. Least Resistance was at thirty-three to one.

And then suddenly Least Resistance was at ten to one, and the Bard at fifteen.

Because he had ridden the Bard twice to victory as a gentleman rider, and because he was proud of the fine valiant horse, Dermot was hurt a little and worried. The Curragh entry, Red Anarchist, would probably not run, he heard. They were going to send him to England for the easy money, and Lady Jerry Kehoe was evidently placing no reliance on Shooting Star.

"Dermot," she told him, "if that animal were entered in a Farmers' Handicap, he would n't win it. He 's so damned polite he 'd wait until some

one came up and passed him.   The Bradley horse
has gone badly lame, I hear.   Dermot, why is
Bard of Armagh fifteen to one?"

Dermot did n't know.

"If you know anything, let me hear, will you?
We 're dreadfully poor now.   Father 's thinking
of looking for a job as a gamekeeper.   What
should we do if the worst comes to the worst, Dermot?   Emigrate!   Keep a saloon!   The Earl
of Clonroe, licensed to sell wine, beer and spirits.
The better sort of customers could call him
Paddy," she chattered on.   "And how would I
do for a barmaid, Dermot?   Not full enough in,
the croup, maybe.   Well, let 's have tea."

At Jammet's Restaurant, in the corridor, he met
the squat figure of Burton, biggest and squarest
of the book-makers.   Burton's hair was gray, his
features wrinkled.   He might have passed for a,
small struggling business man, but for the steely
eye.

"Mr. McDermot, may I have a word with
you?"

"Yes, Burton."

"What I have to say is private.   Would you
come this way with me?"   He led him to a sitting-
room and locked the door.

"Mr. McDermot, will the Bard run at Hannastown?"

"I should think so. Mrs.—Mrs. D'Arcy has turned over her stable to Robinson."

"I know. But I stand to lose a lot of money on this race."

"Burton, I don't want to hear anything about it. I'm an amateur rider, and the money end of it does n't interest me, beyond my own small bets."

"Please, Mr. McDermot, hear me out. I offered thirty-three to one against Least Resistance. It was taken up in one large bet. I stand to lose nearly ten thousand pounds."

"I don't think you 'll lose it, Burton. Barring accidents the Bard will win."

"Mr. McDermot, the bet came through a broker, but I found out who laid it. It was Mr. John D'Arcy, Miss Connaught's husband."

"Burton—" Dermot rose, red with anger— "I 'm going to break every bone in your body if you are suggesting anything against Miss Connaught."

"Mr. McDermot," Burton answered calmly, "I know Miss Connaught for a straight owner, and I know you for a straight sportsman and her friend. If you want to tell her of the bet, tell her. It 'll never pass my lips again. I don't like Mr. D'Arcy or his crowd. I like her and I like you. Have I said enough?"

"Thanks, Burton."

As they went out a client came up to Burton.

"Will you lay twenties against Bard of Armagh, Burton?"

"Mr. Connors, I will not. I lay only fives. There are other places in town where you can get more. I'm sorry."

"Thanks again, Burton," Dermot said.

He decided to see Connaught as soon as possible, and talk about the Bard, but he would say nothing to her of John's bet. It might be just some piece of engineering on the gang's part, an attempt to lengthen the odds on the Bard. Funny, though; if the Curragh horse was out, and another gone lame, and Connemara Black was still a rogue, and Jerry Kehoe's Shooting Star as chicken-hearted as ever, then there were only two horses in the race. The Bard of Armagh and Mr. What-do-you-call-him of Birmingham's Least Resistance.

If anything were crooked about the race, it would kill another interest for her, Dermot knew. It was like spring coming to see the flush on her cheeks in the Tara Hunt, and it had died out so quickly. And if they spoiled racing for her. Ah, damn this John, anyway!

§ 3

When he got home to Dermotstown that evening, five of the clock, and darkness in it, and a little white frost creeping out, he recognized a high dog-cart and groom standing in front of the house, the lamps blinking yellowly and clearly in the keen air. And his heart jumped.

She was waiting in the drawing-room, standing by the fire. She had still her driving things on, the great-coat of black frieze like a man's, and a white muffler, and the low-crowned mannish hat on her sweet head.

"Well, Conn?"

"Well, Dermot?" And she gave him a little smile, as though there was a part of her heart that was not broken yet.

"Staying?"

"No, running home. Cousin from Kerry. Dermot, I want to ask you about the Bard."

"Anything wrong?"

"Nothing wrong; of course not. I saw him to-day and the old sweetheart's splendid. But I wanted to ask your advice about a jockey for the

race. You've won with him twice in races.
Whom would you suggest?"

"Mick Hogan."

"Engaged for Least Resistance."

"Joe Muldoon."

"He'll ride for the King."

"Donovan. Harry Brown."

"Donovan's riding somewhere in England that
day. And poor Harry Brown's down with pneu-
monia."

"Outside of that, there's Larry Mason in Liverpool. Get him, Conn; you won't go wrong."

"Thanks, Dermot." She picked up her gloves.
"I must go. How sweet the old room is!" she
looked around wistfully as though she wanted to
stay. "Your mother's in London?"

"She's buying Christmas presents for the
country-side."

"Will there be a present for me this year, Dermot?"

"Of course, Conn. Every year. Always.
And I've got a present for you, too."

"What is it, Dermot? Please tell me."

"It's just a grayhound, Conn. She's a sweet
little lady; Silver Birch is her name. She's got
race speed, and knows her work, and is immensely
keen. I want you to enter her for some courses,

and go and see them. You'll be out, Conn, and you'll like it. And the little lady will win for you, too. She's a daughter of Mah-a-far, out of Annie Laurie, who was herself a great racer."

She turned her head away to hide the tears in her eyes.

"Thanks, Dermot. I'll love her always." She bustled out into the hall.

"Conn," said Dermot, quietly.

She answered, "Yes, Dermot."

"I want nothing," he said, "I want nothing to deter you from sending the Bard out at Hannastown on St. Stephen's Day."

She said again, "Yes, Dermot."

"You see, Conn," he went ahead, "you don't know much about the money end. A lot of poor people in Dublin put money on horses who should not. They can't afford it. And, besides, it gives them something to look forward to. Workingmen, and grocers' boys—oh, and everybody bets."

"I know, Dermot."

"And lots of street bookies and rotten touts and that give long odds weeks and months before, and they bet, and if the horses are scratched, they lose; do you see?"

"I see, Dermot."

"So they want a run for their unfortunate money on Miss Connaught O'Brien's Bard of Armagh. Don't be persuaded not to send him to the post."

"I won't, Dermot."

They were coming through the lighted hall to the dim drive. She looked so small in her greatcoat, so queerly lonely, he put his arm around her shoulders.

"Are you all right, little sweetheart?" A sudden access of tenderness came to him. She put up one warm firm hand and caught his that was on her shoulder, and held it a moment.

"Yes," she said, "I 'm all right, Dermot."

Before the door she stopped an instant and turned to him.

"Dermot, please tell me something, will you?"

"What is it, Conn?"

"Did you ever ask my father for his permission to marry me?"

"Who told you that, Conn?"

"John told me that, Dermot, and he was very amused over it. Is it true?"

"It 's true, Conn."

"I 've often thought about it—" she looked away and began buttoning her gloves—"and wondered what I would have done had you come to me yourself. But I know," she said, "that I

would have sent you to my father, and have abided
by what he said."

"I know that too, Conn."

"When one is young," she said, "one knows
nothing even of themselves. One goes to sleep at
night, quiet as a bird on a bough. And then one
day comes, and in the night one keeps awake and
thinks and things are so different. Poor Father!
Poor Glenmalure! How little wise he was, after
all."

"He meant everything for the best."

"He did, Dermot. He did really." She
moved toward the dog-cart. "I'll hardly see you
until after Christmas, Dermot. I can't ask you
up. You'll send up the dog, though, won't you,
Dermot? And so many thanks for her! so many
thanks!"

"Will you be taking the ribbons, my Lady?"

"No, thanks, Shamusy; you drive." Dermot
wrapped the rug around her knees.

"Good-by, Dermot," she said, "and I'll remember what you told me about the poor people and
their money on the Bard. Dermot, may I give
you the Bard for a Christmas present? Please?"

"No, Conn," he said. "No!"

"Then what can I give you, my dear?" she
leaned down and kissed him. "All right, Shamusy. Good-by."

He stood still while the dog-cart bowled away. Where she had kissed him his face was wet. Poor Connaught! She had been crying all the time!

XI

§ 1

WHEN you are going to Hannastown on St. Stephen's Day, you will notice, a mile or more from the track, a singular phenomenon. The Dublin Metropolitan Police, those immense grave men, with the largest frames and, to be noted regretfully, the largest feet in the world, have relaxed their ominous decorum. There is even a little smile upon their sad flat features, as though they were saying: "Ah, well, play, gentlemen, and even ladies, play. We personally know that all flesh is grass. But you, dance joyously; sing, even. But take heed for the morrow —a month without the option of a fine for assaulting an officer." And the wren runs from the hedges, and the rabbit cowers in his burrow, wondering what is this new hurly-burly humans have taken it into their heads to make. And have they all got guns?

And little whitewashed and thatched saloons are passed on the way, open in case anybody should be taken faint on the way to the race-course, and

it is an extraordinary thing how many people are.
And sometimes outside one of them a man has
put down a barn door, and is dancing a hornpipe
on it for money, to the accompaniment of an accordion.   The accordion gives out its high piping
and tremulous bars, and the feet of the dancer
strike the board with the strokes of small firm
hammers.

"Come on, my lads, the Shuffle and Cut!   The
Quaker's Delight!"   And *Mah-a-boohal!*—which
is Gaelic for "splendid fellow."   And *Awbejasus!*
—which means "good man!"   And a pelting rain
of copper and small silver coins on the board when
the dance is finished.

And now one is assaulted by the sellers of race-
cards, girls and women with shawls over the shoulders and the finest heads of hair in the world, black
and auburn: "Race-card!   Race-card!   All the
races!"   And sellers of oranges: "Oranges, two
the penny!   Oranges, two the penny!"   Though
who buys them, and when he consumes them, and
where, and why—all this is mystery.   And an ancient woman from the Liberties of Dublin raises
up a remarkably resonant and raucous voice:

"She's a fine, strong, supple lump of an Irish agricul-
          tural girl.
  She neither paints nor powders and her figure is all her
          own.

When she gives you a slap on the jaw, sure you think
    it's the kick of a mule you've got—
The full of my arms of Irish love is pretty Kate
    Malone!"

and there is another diving into pockets for small
coins.

At the gate is a throng through which even the
immense police cannot move with ease, so there a
man places a table and with three greasy cards in-
vites the sports to test their acuteness. "The
quickness of the hand deceives the eye, bullies,"
he announces, "and the bravery of the mind in-
creases the purse. Come on! Who's first to
spot the lady?" There arises a little way from
him a figure in a black frock-coat, with the grim
and intelligent cast of features one associates with
a Rosicrucian, with longish gray hair. "Gentlemen!" he calls, and there is silence. "Gentlemen!" One feels he is about to blast the three-
card man with a torrent of righteousness. "Gentlemen, I have here three thimbles and a pea! . . ."

Within, on the race-course, is all manner and
condition of people. There is the small crowd in
the steward's inclosure. There is the mass of
great-coats and furs on the grand stand. But
these are dignified people. Outside in the great
ring are tinker and tinker's woman, tailor, labor-
ing-man. The bookies chalk their boards, giving

the odds of the race. Around them the backers
tear at one another to get close. Before them is
the oval of the race-course, green although mid-
winter. The terrifying jumps stand out like imperfections on the grassy track, and closely packed
bushes bound and sit upright, the high Irish banks,
and the treacherous ditches where a horse may
break his neck, and a man, too, for that matter.
From stand to stand the bookies' runners signal
the laying of heavy bets in the small ring, their
shrill piercing whistles, their epileptic gestures.
And a bell rings for saddles in the first race.
Clung-clung-clung, clung-clung! In the inclosure
the horses are paraded, sleek, glossy, mild. And
half a mile away a late train belches forth its passengers and they swarm out on the green field like
a sudden invasion of ants. The board with
the names of the jockeys goes into position
with a thud. And Paddy Talbot screams the
odds:

"Here! I'll give you two to one on the field!
I'll give four to one bar one. I'll give seven to
one bar two! Eights, Erin's Jester. Ten to
one, Florence Nightingale. A hundred to eight,
Pious Patrician. Twenty, Doctor Joe. Here,
twenty-five to you! . . ."

Who would not be at Hannastown on St. Stephen's Day?

§ 2

All this is going now, of course; slowly but surely dying. Progress, that grim ogre, must ever destroy beauty. Where once the thatched white cottage was is now a utility in shingle and slate, and the moon is done no justice there. And where is the thatcher gone, that cunning artisan; none knew better than he how to make a home snug for the winter months and cool for summer. Will the swallows build their nests in the eaves of shingled houses? I doubt it; they care nothing for progress, the swallows.

And Reynard the Fox—he too must go. For him the trap, poison, the gun. I think he would prefer to be extinct, that exotic animal, than not to be hunted with horn and hounds and horses. And the yacht with its delicate jibs, its snowy mainsail, its tiller by which one turns it easy as spinning a coin. An oily noisy impertinence replaces it on the sea. But one keeps it for sport? Ah, yes, but sailmakers and craftsmen die and their craft with them. And one can replace things that don't matter, but never men.

And the horse too—he is going, the sweet strong animal with the kindly eyes, he the great-hearted: "He saith among the trumpets, Ha, ha; and he smelleth the battle afar off, the thunder of the captains, and the shouting." The engine pushes him from the streets, the tractor from the fields. And there is no longer a crash as of the Earl of Lucan's cavalry at Fontenoy, or the charge of Cardigan's Hussars at Balaclava. A Richard Cœur de Lion in a motor-car—it is a difficult thing to see.

In the coming times of progress, they may have racing, too: the thunder and smell of cars on tracks, the meaningless buzzing of an aëroplane against the sky, the drive of motor-boats on lakes, a whir of foam. But, for all this progress, we too have seen things: the moonlight on thatched, whitewashed cottages; the great yachts heeling under a cloud of sail, the delicate white fabric fluttering gently as a butterfly's wing as they rounded the point. We have seen the wedge of the wild swans as they drove southward trumpeting, and we have known the thrill of the crowd when men raced on great-hearted horses.

§ 3

Dermot had missed the first race, a mile and a half hurdle, but on the board where the jockeys' names were he had n't noticed Larry Mason's and he wondered why the English lad had n't been picked up by some owner for the first two races. The Bard's number was down in the list of probable starters. The stewards had loaded him with top weight, one hundred and seventy-three pounds, but that would not bother him. As he went around the ring he saw the red beard and tweeds of John D'Arcy in the distance, talking to some of his friends. Against their flashiness his beard and tweeds stood out like a reproach.

And suddenly he saw Connaught. She was walking from the paddocks to the committee rooms. There was something a little stumbling in her walk. Dermot went straight toward her. He sensed trouble.

"Conn!"

And when she turned around he saw her face was set hard. There were frosty frustrated tears of anger in her eyes.

"Dermot," she called, "what do you think? Mason has n't turned up."

"Get some one else, Conn. Get Maguire or Reeves."

"I tried," she faltered, "but they 're engaged."

"Has n't the trainer some one?"

"He has nothing but apprentices, Dermot, young untried boys. And there 's only Mulcahy, and he's crooked, Dermot; I couldn't trust him. Oh, Dermot, what shall I do?"

From afar off D'Arcy must have seen them talking together. He strolled up with his friend Regan, both wearing looks of concern.

"Oh, hello, McDermot," he said casually. "No sign of Mason yet, Conn?" She just turned away.

"Bit of a lad for the liquor, that jock. Christmas in Dublin's pretty heavy going." Dermot was wondering how much D'Arcy knew of the boy's disappearance, and how it had been contrived. Regan the gambler was smiling a little.

"Look here, Conn," D'Arcy urged. "Why don't you take Chris Mulcahy? There's gossip of course, but there's gossip about all jockeys. Don't be foolish."

She said nothing still.

"Oh, well, it's nothing in my life," he laughed. "You can scratch him if you like."

The clamor of the bookies rose in a high brazen din. "Five to one, the field! Five to one the field! Five to one, Bard of Armagh! Five to one, Least Resistance. Here! six to one, Bard of Armagh. Fives, Least Resistance! Gi' me an offer. Gi' me an offer. Here! Eight to one, Shooting Star. Ten to one, Connemara Breeze! Ten to one, Red Anarchist. Here!

What do you want? What do you want? I'll
give a hundred t' eight, Civic Integrity! A hundred t'eight, Munster Gentility! Here, twenty
to one, Civic Integrity! Here, twenty-five to one,
Civic Integrity. What horse do you want?
Brown Bee? Forty to one. Put in your
money!"

And then, one instant later:

"Three to one, Least Resistance? Here, ten
to one, the Bard of Armagh! Bard of Armagh,
ten to one!"

A little knot of people had clustered apart,
watching the four of them, knowing well something was in the air. Connaught's face was white.
Regan's saturnine. D'Arcy was smiling like a
cat.

"Here," Dermot growled, "I'll ride the horse.
I've won with him twice before."

"Oh, Dermot, will you?"

"Look here," D'Arcy all but shouted, "you'll
not! You'll ride no horse of ours."

"The horse is mine, John," Connaught said
with dignity, "and if Dermot is kind enough—"

"God damn!" he was beginning again. Her
cool aloof look struck him like a shower.

"Connaught," he said, "I forbid you to let this
man ride the horse."

"You have no rights over me, John, to forbid

me anything. And will you please not make a scene! People are looking at us."

"Just a moment, if I may, Mr. McDermot," Regan broke in suavely. "You know this is n't a point-to-point hunt race. And riding with professional jockeys is n't what it is with gentlemen riders—"

"I don't know how you get into this conversation at all," Dermot cut in coldly, "but I 'll trouble you to mind your own business. Connaught, tell Robinson I 'll ride. I 'll go and dress. The colors inside? Good!"

He felt suddenly a little shaky as he got into breeches and boots and put the green blouse on, and the gold cap. No, steeplechasing with professionals was not the same thing as point-to-point racing, and he could imagine the dash at the first fence. Thirty horses jumping crazily, fired by the competition and the shouting and the gay silk. Pierce Moloney, the wizened old veteran jockey, recognized him.

"Is it yourself, Mr. Dermot? Oh, begor, that 's fine! And what are you riding? Miss Connaught's horse. Ah, grand! sure we 'll make a great race of it! Mine, is it? I 'm riding th' English horse, Least Resistance."

"Do you know what happened to Mason, Pierce?"

"I saw the lad yesterday, Mr. Dermot, and he had a drop taken on the quays. Not that it would matter much. But it's very easy to put something in a man's drink, down them parts."

The bell for saddles rang. They moved out to the paddock. As he threw his great-coat off, they pulled the cover from the big horse. The great hindquarters, the sweet perfect legs, the fine neck, the head. Ah, Bard of Armagh!

"Mind you don't push him now, Mr. Dermot and he'll carry you home a winner," Robinson whispered.

"Even money, Least Resistance. Three to one, Bard of Armagh!" the bookies called.

"It should be the other way round, by right," some one was saying.

Beneath him the great chestnut gelding moved with the powerful easy motion of a locomotive. He felt, sitting up in the light racing-saddle, as if he were part of mechanism as delicately balanced as the mechanism of a watch. He turned into the track through a little gate. Behind him the other mounts were walking. He loosed the great horse for a spin past the stands. Beneath him it began to stretch in great waves of speed. The chatter and shouting of the crowds seemed to be seething some place beside him like a pool where water is bubbling. There was a strange highness to his heart that was half fear, half exaltation.

He pulled at the Bard's mouth gently, wondering whether it would have any effect even. The Bard slowed down. He turned him to the right. Past him and behind him other mounts thudded, great speedy engines with silken marionettes crouched on their withers, with caps that put their faces into strange small dimension, their jackets queer bizarre admixtures of colors, jarring, some of them, terribly. Here was a roan jacket with staring green spots. Here was a harlequin red and yellow. Here a black with green sleeves. Here the splendid black and yellow of the wasp. They trotted, cantered, walked back to the post. The stands were mounds, peopled by men and women as by ants. The loud cries of the bookies came to them, now like the tearing whine of the sea-gull, now the hoarseness of the corn-crake, now a high mechanical chatter unlike any bird at all:

"Three to one, the field! Four to one bar one! Eight to one bar three. Three, Least Resistance! Four, Bard of Armagh—"

Dermot's heart rose. So the Bard had dropped a point in the betting. People were trusting him. And suddenly they were all a milling mass, falling into line, jostling. And before them stood an imperturbable man in a hard hat, with a white flag raised in his right hand. And his right hand was steady as a rock. Now they were in rough line, and Red Anarchist sprang forward. The rest broke in gallop behind him, but the white flag in the hand of the man with the hard hat remained steady as a rock. So with curses they turned again, the horses pulling like Titans, jockeys cursing like longshoremen. Again they formed. Before them stretched the long green lane to the first high jump, heavy with furze. Beside them the grand stand, the chatter of the people like the chatter of some parliament of birds. Ahead of them, the man with the hard hat, with the white flag in the hand that was steady as a rock. Unconsciously they were forming into an even line, the hands of the jockeys moving like the hands of drummers, quickly, nervously, guiding their horses' mouths, very quickly, very nervously, like drummers' hands.

The man with the hard hat dropped the flag.

On one side of them, as they swept forward swiftly as swallows, a great bell clanged. On the other side of them, from the grand stand and the large ring where all the people were, came an immensity of voices saying in the same time the same hoarse words; "They're off!" And the sound seemed to hit the air a great flat blow, that the riders and mounts could feel vibrate as they swept past. And then there was nothing in their ears all of a sudden but the thunder of hooves, a silence filled with the thunder of horses' hooves.

A horse ahead had taken on himself to set a pace that was terrific, a black horse with a rider in scarlet and gray, the horse Red Anarchist. Almost beside him was Connemara Breeze. And close to the rails rode Least Resistance with the cunning Moloney biding his time, biding his time, with the wisdom born of years of steeplechasing. Rode beside him the jockey of the great yellow horse, Shooting Star. And Dermot behind them, fighting the Bard until his forearms were all but pulled from their elbows. The great chaser had been driven frantic by the shouting, and the flashing of the silken colors, and the thunder of the other hooves beside him. The Bard cooled down little by little, hit his long swinging stride, then the first fence sprang at them.

There was a crash of dry furze and the earth seemed to sink beneath horse and rider. Dermot rose in his saddle to save the jar. All the first five were over easily. But behind was a crash, and before the next fence was reached a riderless horse dashed past madly. McLoughlin, on Red Anarchist, let a wild cry from him.

"God!" he said. "My poor brother Joe!"

But he hunched down on his saddle and rode

forward. Back of them the second flight seemed
to have weakened. None pressed the leaders
now. They eased to a sweet easy galloping.
Moloney on Least Resistance had n't moved a
muscle of face or hand since the dropping of the
flag. They hurdled the second fence easily.
Shooting Star jumped lazily, losing yards, but his
great stride brought him even again. He loomed
alongside like some yellow monster in a dream.
Moloney kept his position by the rails and played
the game little English horse as one plays the
violin. They swept onward down the crisp frozen
track, and the hooves thundered in unison, as
though the horses were galloping along in harmony, each in harmony with the others. They
popped over a little gate laced with thorn bushes.
Red Anarchist swerved a little as he jumped, but
recovered easily. Some winter bird, too amazed
to fly, scuttled across the track like a sandpiper.
His loud fearsome chirrup rose quaintly above the
thumping of hooves.

They had swung around the turn now, and a
cottage and a great clump of trees hid them from
sight of the people, and now the wind, which had
been at their backs, seemed to veer sidewise and
strike them. On the stand it had just been a gentle southwest wind, presaging rain, but now it
seemed to lay its hand on their left sides, like some

great Arctic paw. It pressed on their ribs through the gay silk with a prickle as of needles. The great yellow horse, Shooting Star, was tiring now, and passing him it seemed as if they were passing him on a parallel train—two trains, both fast but one faster. Now were visible his great saffron hindquarters, now his jockey's white breeches and black boots, now his wet yellow neck and the racing-snaffle, and now his head, and now he was invisible. The four other horses had gathered themselves for the next fence. They were rounding the oval, a little more slowly. The wind suddenly hit them on the cheek. Moloney on the English horse looked sidewise with his brown monkey's eyes out of his brown monkey's face. He seemed to decide something. He wouldn't go just yet.

They rushed together at the great Irish bank, a great high ditch with water on both sides of it. Under him Dermot felt the Bard steady himself, ask for his head a bit. Before him Red Anarchist topped the barrier like a flying cat, make a mistake somehow, tumble and crash. As the Bard leaped nimbly, changed feet, Dermot saw with horror the elder McLoughlin lying beneath him, a poor limp thing in gay colors. His cap was still on his head. He turned faint with horror as the Bard jumped forward, fearing that the flying racing-iron of the Bard might touch the poor head as it lay, and fearsomely he sensed the feel of the hind feet as the Bard came down. Ah, no! thank God! And suddenly as they raced forward the queer notion came to him that both McLoughlins were dead, Charley and Joe. They had been called elder and younger by courtesy; for they were twins. And Joe had come down at the first fence and Charley now. Ah, well! it must have been dreadfully quick for both.

A sudden sight of the grand stand in the distance brought his mind back with a jump to the business he was on. The black mass of people, the sun glinting on the leveled field-glasses and making queer little pin-pricks of light in the distance, as though they were glow-worms out by day. The wind was now directly in front of them. It crept through the silken jackets and ballooned them out behind. It numbed their hands, and seemed to pour like cold water beneath the peaks of their caps, and though they were bathed with perspiration it seemed to them they were being sprayed by a minute cold spray. And now Connemara Breeze was done. To the right of him Dermot could see the black horse blowing badly, a lather of sweat, and suddenly the jockey loosened the rein. He had given up. He would finish with a canter to save the horse.

knees and whole frame were trembling. He felt it difficult to dismount. He clambered into the scales with his saddle, got off. Some one helped him into a great-coat, and he was turning away. Every one was very silent.

He felt a hand plucking his sleeve. It was Connaught's. Her face was dull white, her lips were blue. Her eyes were so haggard that it all seemed like some tragic mask of the theater.

"Oh, Dermot! oh Dermot! will you forgive me? Please forgive me."

"What, Conn? What's wrong?"

"Oh, Dermot! I did n't know it was so terrible. The McLoughlin boys are dead!"

"I knew it," he said, "poor lads."

"And I sent you out to ride Bard of Armagh! Oh, Dermot! it might have been you!"

"Listen, Conn," he said simply. The red ball had been hoisted on the number board. The jockeys had weighed in all right, and no objections had been offered. Now rose the bookies' surly cry: "Pay now on the Bard of Armagh!"

In the outer ring the swarm of poor people were besieging the gamblers with tickets.

"So you see, Conn. And, besides, there was n't very much danger. The Bard won the race by himself."

"Oh, Dermot, my dear!"

He was moving along toward the members' stand to go and dress, and Connaught was walking with him. As they approached the wicket gate, they saw John D'Arcy. They both stood still with shock.

He was leaning up against the paling, his tweeds immaculate, his glasses slung around him. And great tears were running down his cheeks, and out of his throat, through the reddish beard, great sobs were coming. There was something grotesque and pathetic about it, like a child's toy broken. And there was something terrible about those sobs, against the dignity of the great beard. When he saw them he turned his leaden face away.

"John!" Connaught gave nearly a scream. "John. What 's wrong?"

No answer but sobs, sobs of a child.

"John!" She laid her hand on his shoulder. "Can't you tell me: what is wrong?"

"Between the two of you, between the two of you," he cried, "you 've lost me ten thousand pounds, and, my God! how I needed it!"

"John, have you lost ten thousand pounds?"

"No, but I would have won it, only for that damned horse of yours, and that damned Dermot."

"Hush, John," she said quietly. "Hush, my poor man. I have money." But he turned his face away. The terrible tragic look of him touched Dermot's heart. He was n't a villain, after all. He was a poor devil of a broken man.

"Look here, John," he broke in, "I 'm very sorry, but what could we do? Sport 's sport, damn it !"

But John only turned his face aside and again the great gulping sobs came.

"Please go away, Dermot," Conn asked. "Dermot, please go away."

So John was only a fool, Dermot thought, as he dressed. And he had been posing as a villain, a great heavy-bearded slashing villain, like Captain Kidd, or Bluebeard, and he was only a chicken-hearted fool. But what did he want the money for? Was it some old intrigue with a woman in France, he wondered, and she was blackmailing him, now she knew he was married and on the threshold of a career? He had heard of such things, and he shuddered at the sordidness of it. Connaught to be dragged into a thing like that— Perhaps that was why he was afraid of the French officer, afraid of disclosures, of gossip. And the poor fool had gone and told the police about the Frenchman. And he was afraid John had been mixed up in revolutionary politics. What a fool himself, Dermot, had been!

He went across to the grand stand to see the

last race, a two-mile flat race for gentleman riders; there was a little mare called Jonquil entered, and she had taken his eye in the stalls. A friend of his, Patsy Ward, a son of old Sir Patrick Ward d'Aughrim de Ward, was riding her. As he passed along he heard a whining Irish accent.

"Would you have e'er a sixpence, Mr. Mc-Dermot, sir, to spare for a poor dark man?"

The blind man wore the longest, quaintest, and oldest overcoat in Dublin. It was green and had great buttons on it, some gentleman's riding-coat of bygone days. A red and filthy knitted muffler was about his neck, and of the clothing of his body nothing else was visible, barring a foot of ancient trouser and great clubby boots. On his head was a round hard hat that might have fitted anybody else but him, and he wore blue spectacles and his face was blue with unshaven beard. The blind man's dog, that he held on a leash, was a small black cocker spaniel, with his tongue out on one side in eagerness and the kindest expression in the world. Dermot put his hand in his pocket. He took it out again.

"Dark man," he said, "how do you know my name?"

"Didn't I see you, with my two fine eyes, riding the prettiest race in the world, and beating the best jockey in England by five lengths?"

"You dirty scoundrel!"

"And 't is myself knows something about horses, too, Mr. McDermot. Do you mind the Tara Hunt?"

"Look here, what 's your name?"

"I 'm called the Citizen." The blind man was looking away with the relaxed receptive look of blind men.

"I don't know your business here," Dermot said, "and I don't think I want to know, but do you know the police are after you? Do you know the risks you 're running?"

"I like racing," the blind man said, "and the race you rode was a grand race. Look around you."

Dermot glanced around. Lolling, and yet keen eyed, alert, muscular, were four young men of the small-farmer type. Clean-shaven, dapper even, they seemed to be four corners of a geometrical design in which the blind man and his dog were the center.

"Would your Honour have sixpence for a poor dark man?"

"Would you go to blazes?"

But he was strangely elated, as he moved away, by the praise of the French officer.

XII

THEY were arising from dinner, Dermot and his mother, when Dermot turned to her.

"Mother—" he put his arm around her shoulder—"I broke a promise to you to-day."

"Thee broke a promise to me, Dermot? What promise, my son?"

"Mother," he said, "I rode a steeplechase at Hannastown."

"Dermot, thee should not have. I have one son who is dead, and a little daughter. And now thee is all I have."

They had gone into the old-fashioned low-raftered drawing-room, where were the treasures of the house—the ancient Irish silver, the old Irish glass, the harp that was reputed to be the harp of Carolan, last of the Irish bards, the pictures of the sweet McDermot women, their curling brown hair, their merry brown eyes, their hands graceful as flowers; the duelling pistols of Lord Edward Fitzgerald; a poem in the writing of Oliver Goldsmith; and this thing, and that thing. The dogs

rose from before the fire, apologetic, wagging
their tails.

"Look here, sweetheart." He made her sit
down. "The horse was Connaught's, the Bard
of Armagh, and there was no jockey to ride him,
so I did."

"Thee should not have broken thy promise,
Dermot."

"Again, little mother, all the poor people in
Dublin had money on him, laid weeks ago—"

"But thee knows gambling is wrong, Dermot."

"But their days are gray, little mother, not gray
like your little Quaker bonnet, but gray with the
grayness of cold mist. And a bet on a horse and
a drink, and a little sweethearting is all they have.
Ah, little mother, don't be hard!"

"Did thee—did thee win, Dermot?" She
asked the question that had been trembling on her
lips since first he had spoken.

There came the stopping of a horse and the
grinding of dog-cart wheels on the drive without.
They listened. A gray-haired maid came to the
door.

" 'T is Miss Connaught is in it, ma'am."

Connaught came into the room, heavy with furs.
The night air had brought a flush to her cheeks,
but her eyes were hard. Steely and hard.

"I 've come to say good-by," she announced, "and to ask a favor."

"Sit down, child, and open thy coat."

"I won't sit down, Aunt Anne. No, please, I won't sit down. To-night I go to Dublin, and to-morrow to England, America—I don't care where—"

"Connaught," Dermot asked quickly, "what 's wrong?"

"Dermot, do you remember how John was to-day?"

"He was very miserable."

"He hardened after that, Dermot. He met some of his friends, and he became bitter and hard. He brought a lot of them back with him. Regan and that sort. And Dermot, I wanted to give you a little present." The tears she had been holding back quivered in her eyes. She winked them angrily away.

"I wanted to give you Bard of Armagh, after the race to-day. It would have made me unhappy if you refused him. So I told Robinson to send him to Glenmalure to-night and I 'd bring him over in the morning. I was dressing for dinner when he arrived. And John heard the horse, and went out to see what it was."

"Yes, Conn."

"They must have told him. I don't know whether he had been drinking or not; I think he had, Dermot. But he rushes upstairs and comes down with a pistol, and he shoots the Bard."

"He killed him?"

"He killed the great horse, Dermot. I could hear the thud even in my rooms. He killed our friend, yours and mine." She gave a little rasping sob.

"Steady there, Conn!" he said brusquely. In his own mind he was saying: "Well, to-night I kill John D'Arcy, and that's all there is to that. And he'll never bother her any more, and that's all there is to that." He would bring a revolver with him, but he rather thought he would do it with his hands, under that auburn beard. His mother noted his eyes, his outspread fingers, his nervous thumbs. She went over to Connaught and took her hands.

"And what is the favor Dermot can do for thee, Connaught, my dear?"

"I—I—took the liberty—" she was quivering with an attempt at control—"of asking the stable-boys to bring him over here. He will come in a cart, Dermot, who was so strong and swift and fearless to-day—"

She moved away from Anne and around the

He killed the great horse. I could hear the thud in my rooms. He killed our friend, yours and mine

room, picking up little things, laying them down. "He was such a gentleman," she said. "So strong and fearless and such a great racer. And when I went out hunting with him, he was so gentle and restrained. And I couldn't hold him if he ever tried to go, but he never did bother me, Dermot, such a gentleman he was. And he whinnied when I came near his stall—"

She turned around suddenly.

"Dermot, what I want of you is this. Is there a corner of Dermotstown where you could—put him down, Dermot? Some little place where the grass grows green, and the birds come, and primroses and bluebells. And the colts scamper in spring. And put a little stone there, just this: 'The Steeplechaser Bard of Armagh,' and the races he won. There will be none to see it—make it a very little stone—except the birds, and they will understand, and the young colts may. And it will be good for the colts, Dermot, for where he is buried, there must be strength and fire and gentleness. Am I very silly, Dermot? Am I very silly, Aunt Anne?"

"Thee is not silly, Connaught, my dear."

"And, Dermot, put on the little stone, too, perhaps, 'A heaven without horses and dogs must be a poor heaven. We give so much of our heart to

them.   And when I die and meet you all, maybe
I shall hear the Bard whinny.'   Is that very bad
religion, Aunt Anne?"

"God is very kindly, Connaught, my dear."

"Will you do this for me, Dermot?"

"Yes, Conn," he said harshly.

She turned to look at him, wondering why he
didn't say more, wondering why the curt harsh-
ness of his voice.   She looked at him, and as she
looked, the great amber eyes dilated, the mouth
trembled with fear.

"Dermot!   Dermot!"

"What is it, Conn?"

"Dermot, I know what's in your mind.   I
know what's in your mind.   Oh, Dermot, no!
He is only a poor crazy man."

"I don't know what you're talking about,
Conn."

"Oh, Dermot!" she nearly screamed.   "Don't
do it, Dermot!   Don't do it, Dermot; they'd
hang you, or they'd put you in jail forever.
Forever, Dermot.   Oh, Aunt Anne, for God's
sake," she called, "say something!   Stop him!
Don't you see what he means to do?"

"He shall not do it, Connaught, my dear."

She went up to her son.

"Give me thy hands.   Loosen them, my son.
Look at my eyes, Dermot; look in my eyes.

"Dermot, thee is all I have, and, I think, thee is all Connaught has, too. Thee was a little black-haired baby against my breast, and I loved thee better than my eldest-born, and even thy little sister. And that was a fault in me. Will thee not do something for me?"

"Please, Dermot, please!" Connaught's teeth were chattering.

"Hell's blazes!" He swore violently. "Must this man go free?"

"This man shall not go free, my son. Night, noon, no time will any one be free of a cruel thing done. Son, thee must not."

The dogs had arisen again. The little terrier looked at him and whined uneasily. The red setter moved around nervously. The deerhound rose and stood by him.

"Look at me, Dermot, my son. See what thee has never seen before. There are tears in my eyes."

"Dermot, dear Dermot!" Connaught pleaded.

"All right," he said. "All right," he sank down in a chair. "All right," was all he could say. The terrier looked pathetically up at him. The setter licked his hand. The big deerhound drew near, pushed out its black sympathetic muzzle, and gently touched the tragic face.

XIII

§ 1

SHE was over in England now—cold England,
she had called it—and out of Ireland, it
seemed to Dermot, the heart had gone. The
harsh winter the wealth of hawthorn had promised had not been realized. And even now, long
before spring, the birds were singing, the thrush
and the blackbird, and the wood-dove that will
never be silent. Still in the greenhouses of Dermotstown the chrysanthemums flaunted their gay
proud heads. Without, the early primroses were
showing modestly, and here and there were snow-
drops delicate as jewels, and out of the earth the
crocuses peeped up, like queer shy animals. And
she in cold England! Ah, God!

He could not find it in his heart to go hunting
the fox any more, though there was never such
good weather, the scent breast-high in the moist
air. He would go into Dublin, and wander
around there, and, queer fancies taking him, he
would go where he would not be bothered by
friends, down to St. Patrick's Cathedral, where

the great dean is buried, and Earl Strongbow lies
with his sword by his side, or down the Quays by
gray Anna Liffey, where the book-stalls are as
numerous as in Paris, and out of the windows of
strange dingy shops flash jewels that once adorned
Irish beauties of old Georgian days, and great
pieces of silver with arms on them that had once
been great and are now forgotten. Or he would
lean against the Leeson or Baggot Street Bridges
and watch the long canal that led to Athlone, the
other side of Ireland. Down the canal would
come great barges drawn by ponderous Percheron
horses, and loaded with grain and potatoes, and
stacked high with turf—the turf that burns with
the deep red of rubies, and has a terrible nostalgic
scent to it, of the crisp grass of the marshes, and
of white bog flowers, and of great forests forgotten thousands of years before. And the folk of
the barges were strange independent folk, with
tanned faces and surly Western eyes. And he
often thought, watching them, that he would like
to make friends with them, and go westward with
them when they returned, having exchanged fine
grain and bursting potatoes and the magic turf
for whisky and stout and biscuits and other in-
equalities. They would slip out of Dublin, down
the long path to the West, through Kildare and
Meath. The willow branches would dip into the

water, and the wild duck and goose rise before
them. And they would go through the great Bog
of Allen, where were digged up still the frame of
the great Irish elk, noblest of ancient deer, and
ornaments of red native gold which once old
queens might have worn, and here and there the
great swords and spears of some antique romantic
battle. And the bittern would boom on the way,
and the snipe utter his small sharp cry. And
there would be nights of moonlight over the
strange wide country. And days of soft gentle
rain, and days golden with glory. And as the
barge slipped through the black canal water,
maybe, too, this care would slip from his heart.
Ah, but below in his soul he knew it would n't.

He had thought of going to Paris for a month;
he would have to bring his mother, and what
would the poor lady do there? Or on the Riviera? She would be only looking for the sick
and unfortunate, as she did here. Or he thought
of a month in America, but she would be worried,
away from her husband's and her daughter's
graves in Kill o' the Grange. And might not
America be a shock to her, she having been away
now these thirty years? Poor little Quaker lady!

He went into the club once to which he belonged
in Dublin, and of which Glenmalure had been pres-
ident. And the first thing that met his eyes was

a portrait of the old Lord Chief Justice, the great jowl, the keen but weary eyes, the long fine hands.

"Ah, sir!" he said. "Ah, sir!"

And he came away.

The sight of the picture made him think of Glenmalure now. Strange stories were going the rounds, of the doings of John. His friends had gone. Not even Regan the bookie nor the Dirty Doctor, as de Lacey was called, would go to a house whose owner or occupier had killed a horse in a fit of rage. That was anathema to even their lax code. Had he killed a man, or a woman even, it would not have mattered. But to kill a horse or a hound wantonly puts a man outside all human society in Ireland, or anywhere else, for that matter. And to have killed the Bard of Armagh! Even such friends as he had, cut him in the street. The matter had been hushed up for the newspapers. Miss Connaught O'Brien's Bard of Armagh, so had gone the report, injured himself so severely in winning the Dundrum Plate that he had to be destroyed. But every one knew.

So he was reduced now for society to the pot-boys and barmaids and hangers-on of the small local saloons. Queer dingy places where the light of day hardly ever penetrates and where he grew so fuddled with whisky that he had to be driven home in a cab. And oftentimes he would bring home some strange local character for dinner who amused him with his conversation—some book-maker's tout, or some habitué of the saloon, who would go so as to be able to tell of the glories of the Hangman's House. The old servants had all left now, and a new careless set engaged who were ruining Glenmalure, and despised D'Arcy all but to his face.

Dermot did not mind Glenmalure so much, be-cause it was a new house, not more than forty years old, if that, and it never had quite settled into the Irish hills. There was a queer thing about a house, he thought: you never knew on what it was builded. There was Mr. Richard Crok-er's house, the American millionaire-statesman's, builded on the graves of King Parthelon and his Phœnician men, dead of the plague—their slim bronze bodies, their slim bronze swords, so far from Africa. They were such a proud ancient people. . . . One hoped there would be luck on the house. And Glenmalure! If Fiach McHugh O'Byrne, Chief of Clan Ranall, and his subaltern, Brian Donn O'Moore, rode the mountains at night, as old men said, in their ancient armor and on their high Norman horses, might they not re-sent this entry into their old stronghold? And nostrils a-quiver they might curse it with the dreadful curses of the dead. But if Connaught were asleep there, the ancient chivalry would arise in them, and light their scarred furrowed faces. Sleep well, little dark lady!—and they would gallop on. . . . Ah, but that was only his damned Irish superstition, Dermot said.

Still and all, a house was a queer thing, Dermot thought, something of your life and the life of your people went into the stones and rafters of it. And you could tell when you went into a house, whether the house loved or hated its people. And a child who was brought up in a house had a love for, a sweetness toward it, so that when he went away for good, or to foreign places for a time, the place tugged at his heart. There was the well with the great green frog in it. There was the great beech-tree around which he played. And an ancient picture intrigued a child so much, that in later days he clung to it, and would not have it down. And all things seemed so familiar, so friendly, or even so grotesque, so much entirely did one read into familiar things. And thoughts peopled rooms and made them fragrant, the shy virginal thoughts of young women, the romantic ambitious thoughts of boys. And here are the stairs down which one fell as a child, and here Uncle Alastair stood laughing before he went away to the wars, whence he never came back. And sitting by one's own fireside one dreams

dreams, and on the chair opposite, for an instant, appears the filmy seeming of some one, loved so long ago, dead so long ago. An instant only, and that only imagination, but maybe the life in our head is the real life, and the life of our hands and bodies a shadowy pantomime. Ah, be damned to that, Dermot said suddenly; it was getting too deep for him.

But one thing was certain, and that was this: that Connaught must come back to her home, her own house. Cold England, she had said. Cold anywhere! He thought of her life around the world, the hotel bedroom and sitting-room, the strange artificial atmosphere. The bed where God knows who had slept, with horrible thoughts and horrible dreams, and no longer her own sweet room, with her pictures and treasures about, the familiar place for her clothes, the sunshine coming from the same point every morning, and the birds singing in the trees. Nor a garden to sit in when the sun went down or to wander into on a night of the moon. And the chilly dining-rooms where one is constrained to speak low, and the servants with the ready-made manners. And in her own house had been huffy maids who would lay down their lives for her, and smash the dinner-drum in a rage that one smiled at, knowing how soon the trivial passion would pass. And if she looked poorly they were worried and if she looked well they stinted not their admiration. All this she had, her own familiar house, her garden, the servants who loved her. And now all she had was a bedroom and sitting-room in some cold hotel, and a maid, and the little Scotty terrier, who wondered at and hated being dragged around the world, and was thinking long for Glenmalure, and of the rabbits that he tried so futilely to catch, on his bowed stumpy legs. Ah no! Connaught must come back to her home.

§ 2

"Mother," he said to Anne one evening, "what is this marriage?"

She laid down the needlework she was doing, and looked into the fire and was a long time before she answered:

"If a man and a woman love each other, Dermot, it is the sweetest thing in the world. There is nothing sweeter, not flowers or big trees, even, or the singing of the birds. The heart of each of them is in the bosom of the other, and all their joy is doubled, Dermot, and their sorrows made nothing of, unless it be the loss of a little baby, and then

they know they will see it again, and tenderness
springs up between them, like water in a sweet cool
well.   And nothing can bother them, Dermot, not
loss of wealth when they have each other, nor per-
secution when they have love between them.   And
the imperfections of each are welcome, even, because they are something to be understanding of,
gentle toward.   And when one dies, the other dies
a little, too, and is purified and has little body.
And the other is often near the remaining one, telling him, or telling her, that just a few springs, a
few winters, a little revolving of the stars, and
they shall both know the cool untroubled eternity
of God.   Is that what thee wants to know, Dermot?" she asked.

He was silent for a little space.

"Dearest," he asked, "if people don't know
each other before they are married, will they get
on?"

"I have seen them be happy, Dermot, happy
and fond of each other.   But they were kindly
people."

"If, say, one hated the other."

"Before marriage, Dermot? Oh, Dermot,
that would be a terrible sin!"

"No, but after."

She rose and stood above him.   Her sweet

ivory hands caressed the dark head. She noted the silver hairs that were becoming more frequent in the curly locks. A tear dropped unnoticed on them.

"Was thee thinking of Connaught, dear lad?"

"Yes."

"And John?"

"Yes."

"Son, I am a poor mother for thee. I have no worldly wisdom at all. I do not know. Dermot, must thee go out to-night?"

"Yes, dearest, I must."

With the early spring had come somehow an early lambing, and for nights now he had gone up to Fifty-Acre on the mountain to be there with the shepherds and the farm-hands at night. Some thought came to him that it would be wrong to be absent from the piteous bleating ewes. It would have been somehow callous. The lambs came like pale petals of snow, so weak, so helpless, fragile as newly hatched birds, and in a few days they would be gamboling like lusty colts, their smiling gay heads, their inadequate legs, the tiny black feet. And they were sickly this year; many of them had to be wrapped up and fed from bottles. The darkness of the night with its great immensity of stars, so that all the world seemed a mysterious

dark blue.   And the candles and lanterns of the
men; the queer hushed activity; the pitiful bleating
of the ewes.

When things were quiet he would wander from
the folds, out on the short crisp grass of the mountain, and think of the problem of Connaught and
how to solve it.   High in starlight the mountains
rose like dim blue shadows, and one could imagine
one saw the three great stones of Three-Rock
against the sky, where the Crone of Three-Rock
sat and mumbled dread spells through her tooth-
less gums.   And little flaws of cold wind came
down the mountains and struck with cold buffets,
and a little distance off the candles of the men
and the hushed voices of the men seemed like a
pantomime in dreams.

The thought pursued him that if he were married to Connaught she would love to come up here
with him on a night of stars when the ewes were
lambing, and she might dress as he was dressed,
in riding-breeches and high laced boots and flannel
shirt and sweater.   She would love the soft night
feel of the turf, and the wind rustling in the
mountain-ash, and rippling over the heather, and
in the darkness she, thinking of the Crone of the
Three-Rock Mountain, she would put out her hand
to him, who would protect her against all ghosts

and evil spirits. And later she would fall asleep against his shoulder, her dark head, her dear dark head, her dear dark perfumed head. And he would bring her to a shelter, and wrap her in coats and rugs and leave her sleeping there until he called her at dawn, bringing tea the shepherds would make. And show her the lambs that had come during the night, and she would greet them with little cries of joy and pity, of joy because they were such sweet wisps of life, and pity because they were so weak and young. "Damn you, Dermot!" he suddenly told himself, "quit that, do you hear me? quit!"

He pulled himself together and thought, "What is to be done now?" She must n't be allowed to roam the world, away from the trees and mountains and the familiar things of the house. Of marriage he knew nothing, but he thought, "Cannot all this thing be fixed?" If John were all right, now, might she not come back and be content, or be resigned? It is so cold a thing to be blown about like a leaf. And could not John be made all right? He had come to the conclusion that John was not really bad, but crazed. He was a poor weak sort of fool who had got himself into a dreadful mess somehow. A man who cried and sobbed as he had done at Hannastown

could not be a villain, though in reaction to that
he had done that terrible shooting of the poor gallant horse. Ah, well! forget that, Dermot, for a
minute! What is wrong with him? It must be
fear of some kind. Wanting money: afraid of
the French officer. It was some kind of fear.
Fear was a nasty thing. Dermot had known it
three times. Once in steeplechasing and once on
the hunting-field, and once on board ship, coming
from Fishguard to Waterford and there was a col-
lision. A little trembling of the knees and a queer
sense that the blood had left his face, and there
was difficulty in lighting a cigarette for a moment.
But those things had passed in a minute. But
the fear John had was a fear that crazed him,
drove him to whisky, hunted him night and day.

Dermot had promised Connaught and Connaught's father to be a friend to her. Supposing
it was a money matter was wrong, he could help.
Supposing it was a matter of the French officer
who called himself the Citizen, could n't he talk to
him and try to straighten things out? One grew
afraid and ran away from things, and perhaps
they were n't so terrible at all. Supposing he
talked to John. And if he straightened things up,
John might n't be so bad at all. And Connaught
would come back to Glenmalure, to the trees and
flowers and her own sweet rooms, back to hounds

and horses and the friends she knew. He would talk to John and try to take this fear out of his life.

And himself, then—what would he do? Well, he knew. It would no longer do for him to be looking toward Glenmalure—no longer, no longer. He thought, in the queer cold starlight, with the men in the distance going about with candles, and speaking in hushed voices as in some strange mystical play, that the best thing for him to do would be to marry, and anchor a loyalty to some decent girl. Heart, he knew, he had none to give her, but he would give her kindness and courtesy, and all he possessed, and because of chivalry to her would look no longer toward Connaught's house. And the house where he and his mother lived now so quietly would become gay again, and there would be little children in the old low-raftered rooms, and a son to whom he could bequeath Dermotstown. Some jolly girl who loved dogs and horses and would not be oversensitive in emotion. And he would be kind to her, and courteous to her, and give her all but his charred heart. And a time might come when he would love her, thanking her, thinking of the hardship of women, and her laughing kindly ways. There was Jonquil McClellan, the sweet yellow-headed girl from the North, and Lady Betty

Boyle, with her hair like a copper beech, and merry brown eyes, and Angela, black Updike's daughter. He thought none of them would mind marrying him. Whom would he ask? Ah, it did n't matter. And Connaught would fade, become a ghost, become a dream, maybe. And she, too, might learn to love John, and one day he would meet her and find all the old passion dead, and they would smile at each other, and be friends. Connaught and her children—a great gulp took him in the throat, and he covered his eyes.

"I 've brought you a tin of tea, Master Dermot, and a piece of the buttered bread. It 's three of the morning, Master Dermot."

It was Shawn Dempsey, the tall old shepherd, with a beard like an ancient prophet's, and kindly eyes.

"Anything more, Shawn?"

"A few Kentish Downs, your Honor, queer sickly wee things. Ah, 't is a bad year, I 'm fearing.

"Master Dermot," he said, "my dear child, let you go home to your bed now. Sure you can trust old Shawn and the men, and sure the mountains at night are no place for you."

"Why not, old Shawn?"

" 'T is the queer high thoughts come to you here, and wisdom clean as water. And what would young lads have to do with wisdom, that should be in their warm beds, dreaming of pleasant worldly things?"

"Are the thoughts that come to you here wise thoughts, old Shawn?"

"They're so wise and powerful, Master Dermot, that myself, an old shepherd of the mountains, do be pitying the kings in their cities, and them making mistakes the livelong day. Will you go home now, my darling boy?"

XIV

§ 1

THE opportunity of seeing and meeting John came to him much sooner than he expected, and sooner, indeed, than he was ready for. He met him in Dawson Street on a dreary Dublin afternoon. In the distance the mountains carried great clouds on their shoulders tumid with rain. And the lethargy of spring was in the air. The sea-gulls swooped in the city streets, and from the Kish came the dull thud of the fog-gun, like distant crashes of thunder.

He saw him coming along as from Trinity, a great frieze coat about him, a slouch hat over his eyes. Only the broad reddish beard betrayed him. He slouched along as though not wishing to be seen. A sudden surge of hatred rose in Dermot, but he fought it down.

"John," he called. D'Arcy heard him and turned. His eyes were haggard and baleful. He recognized Dermot, and his face hardened.

"Well?"

"Look here, John, I want to speak to you."

244

"Is it about the horse?" And Dermot understood now why he slouched along as though not
wishing to be recognized. The desertion of him
by his cheap friends even, had hurt terribly. He
was the man who had shot the horse.

"No, it isn't about the horse. Look here, man,
it's nothing very unpleasant at all. Just let me
talk to you for a while. Will you come into the
club?"

John shook his head. He was the man who
had shot the horse.

"Will you come into Jammet's?"

He shook his head again. In Jammet's, where
sportsmen gather—he was there, too, the man
who had shot the horse.

"Is there any place we could go?"

John looked at him queerly for a minute.
Turned down a side street, and into a queer dingy-
looking bar. Dermot followed him. The proprietor from behind the counter caught John's eye
and hurried forward.

"Is the back room empty?"

"'T is, sir."

"See that it's kept empty. And bring me a
bottle of whisky."

"And glasses and water, sir?"

"And be quick, damn you!"

The room into which they went was a queer old-feeling room. The boards of the floor rose in waves. A fire was in the grate, and on the walls, one opposite to the other, were prints in crude black and green of Robert Emmet with his gallant head held high, which was so soon to fall, and of Parnell, his heavy beard, his outstretched orator's hand. Except for these, and a table and chairs, the room was bare. A gaslight sang over the fireplace. There was an air about the room of mean sordidness that had been done there, of cheating at cards, and fixing of races, and fighters of the ring bought to betray their backers, and political schemes hatched that would never bear the light of day. And yet the room was clean as a pin.

The heavy landlord hustled in with his tray, withdrew discreetly. John pushed the bottle toward Dermot. Dermot shook his head. John gave a "huh" of a sneer. He poured himself out a great dose, and took it quickly as one takes a drug.

"Well?" he said.

"Look here, John." Dermot leaned forward, his arms on the table. "You wanted money very badly that day at Hannastown, did n't you?"

"Well?"

"And you 're under some great strain at present, are n't you?"

"Well?"

"John, I want to help out on that money thing and try to take that strain from you."

John took another great dose of the yellow, acridly fragrant drink.

"I suppose what you 're going to do," he said, "is to offer me money to go away so that you and Connaught can be together."

A sudden impulse came into Dermot's mind: "I can't stand this man any longer. I think I 'll kill him now." He curbed himself viciously.

"You 're in love with Connaught, are n't you?" D'Arcy went on.

"I 'll tell you, John." Dermot lowered his head. "I 'm going to be married in a little while. So that should answer you."

D'Arcy threw back his head and gave a great laugh.

"God!" he said, "and I thought you were in love with Connaught!"

The whisky poured into the glass again with a great splash.

"John," Dermot asked quietly, "are you fond of Connaught?"

"Am I fond of Connaught, man! Am I mad about her!"

"Can't you pull up and cut this stuff out?"

"Of course I can."

"And drop all these ragged people?"

"I hate them."

"John, why did you want that money?"

"Dermot, it's a funny thing for us to be sitting here!" The whisky was beginning to relax him. "Do you know," he said, "that I always hated the sight of you? You're a cousin of mine, but I never liked you, Dermot. And now you're the only person in Dublin who'll talk to me."

"Why do you want the money, John? Tell me; I'll see if we can't raise it."

"I'll tell you, Dermot, and I'll tell nobody else, why I wanted that money. I wanted to go away for good. I wanted to go to Florida or California and buy a farm there, and forget there had ever been such a person as John D'Arcy or Connaught in the world. I said I was mad about Connaught, cousin, but do you know, I've only kissed that girl once—the day of our marriage. The telegram about the poor old duck dying came to us at Waterford, and then there was coming home and burying him, and she mournful about him, and there was no chance of making love to her—"

It seemed to Dermot that his heart was singing, but the moment after he remembered what he was there for, to reconcile these two. He drove himself onward furiously.

"And after a while," John went on, "it seemed

to me it was n't reasonable to act like that. But she seemed to take a dislike to me. And she would shut herself away and threatened to shoot herself. And I was mad about her. God! the slim little legs, the sweet arms of her——"

"I don't want to hear about that!" Dermot snapped. He felt like shouting at him.

"You rotten little Puritan!" John sneered.

"Here, go easy on that whisky. We want to talk. Tell me about this French officer, and what you 're afraid of. We 'll see if we can't straighten that out."

"What French officer?" John asked suspiciously.

"The man at the Tara Hunt."

"That swipe!"

"If you don't tell me about it, John, I can't do anything. If you do I 'll do my best."

"Do you know, Dermot, I never knew you were as nice a fellow. I always thought you were a damned little stuck-up prig, and in love with Conn. And now you 're going to get married, and you 're the only person in Dublin who 'll speak to me. Do you know, it 's funny."

"Come on, John. About this man?"

"Look! I 've got to have another drink.

"This man across here," he said, "is the son of old Dinny Hogan the Rebel—the Incorruptible, they used to call him. There was a big price on his head in the Fenian days, but he got across to Paris. And he got married there. And he had two children. Do you see, Dermot?"

"This man 's one of them."

"You 're right, Dermot. This man 's one of them. This lad went to a military academy— Ecole St. Cyr or some of them. Got commissioned in the cavalry and went to Algeria and made a big reputation. He 's a commandant, and is going to be a colonel soon. And this man 's a Fenian. The old boy just made him lap up Fenianism with his milk. And there was another child."

"Go ahead."

"This other child was a girl, or a woman when I got to Paris. She was a wonderful singer. She was n't an opera singer, Dermot, but she was a star at her own sort of lyric singing. She was a star all over Europe. Maeve Hogan was her name. Did you ever hear of Augusta Holmes? Of course you did n't, you ignorant swipe! Well, Augusta Holmes wrote the 'Chanson des Gars d'Irlande' for Maeve Hogan. There 's more passion and power in that song than in any song in the world. And to hear Maeve Hogan singing the 'Song of the Irish Boys,' and the drums rolling and the fifes shrilling, and the tears running down her cheeks and her arms out like a cross—God! Dermot, it would make a corpse claw his way out of the grave to fight!"

"Well?"

"So when I came along I was Ireland to her. Her old father used to call Dad every name he could think: 'Tricky Micky D'Arcy.' But she and I got along all right. I used to tell her about Ireland. About the rivers of Dublin, the Dodder and the Tolka and the big Liffey, and the mysterious river that vanishes in the streets of Dublin— what is it they call it? Hell! I forget. And the Wicklow Mountains. And Connemara. And the Aran Islands, and Killarney. The tears would run down her cheeks, right there on the boulevards in front of everybody. And she would say: 'My country! my dear country!' And mind you she 'd never seen the blasted place!"

He became silent, moody. Perhaps it was the drink. Perhaps it was regrets. Perhaps ghosts.

"This woman, Dermot, was a wonderful woman. She was a big woman. She would make two of Conn. She had red hair—my God! red! It was like a copper beech in summer. And her eyes were sometimes gray and sometimes black. And sometimes she would be merry as a bird, and sometimes she would be grave and dreaming, and both times she was beautiful. She was like an old Irish queen. And yet she was Parisienne. There was never such a fragrant woman in the world."

His fine hand was in his beard. His head was lowered.

"So we fell in love with each other," said he, and he went on talking to himself more than to Dermot, beginning a sentence, stopping the words in mid-course, finishing it in his head.

"I had no blasted money—not enough, anyway —so she would have to go on singing—managers don't like husbands around—I suppose it's because the audience is in love with the star—God! that woman was in love with me, Dermot! When I think of her love, and I think of the little wild-cat, Conn, who, if I put a finger near her—"

"Go on, John. Go on with the story."

"So we went to Madrid together. We went to Rome—there's a city, Dermot—*chic;* Paris is vulgar compared with it. And Maeve was going to have a baby. And we went to the Pyrenees until the baby was born. And from there we went to Vienna and up into Russia.

"I tell you, Dermot, it's a rotten life for a man. The artist is the whole thing, and you're nothing. And the blasted baby! And all the big people patronize the woman and despise you. And my place was with the big people, patronizing the art-

ist, too. After all, damn it, my mother was one
of the McDermots of Coolavin, and I'm as good
as any archduke—

"She was going to Irkutsk, where all the Si-
berian millionaires are, on a tour. So I got sick
of it. So I said, 'Look here, Maeve, I'm
through.' And she said, 'Are you?' And I said,
'Yes, and I'm going to quit.' And she said,
'Well, good-by, John.' Just cool as that.
Was n't that a nice way to be treated, after you've
cared for a woman, and you've had a baby together? I tell you, Dermot, that rankled, so I
got out."

"And left her, and the baby?"

"You did n't think I was going to drag a baby
around Europe with me, did you?" John sneered.
"So I had a year more around, in my right position. I went everywhere, and I was at my last
ebb as to money when I got a letter from Connaught's damned old fool of a father—"

Dermot's hand shot out and caught John's by
the wrist.

"Look out, John!" he said quietly and coldly;
"look out!"

"That's all right." John's tone was apologetic. "If you've got a respect for him, I've
got a respect for you. And I respect your respect,
so that's all right. Well, Connaught's father

wrote me he was at death's door, and proposed I should come home and marry Conn, and start a political career. And, do you know, Dermot, I was sick of the life I was leading. And I said, 'A good home, a nice Irish wife, a career ahead of me, and nobody will ever know about this singer woman.' I said, 'I'm going to live cleanly and honestly.' And the moment I saw Conn I fell in love with her. And you know how I've been treated. You've seen it. I've told you." He poured himself another drink.

"John," Dermot asked abruptly, "would you be decent to Connaught? kind to her? Could you drop all this mean sordidness? These wretched friends?"

"If I could ever get the chance, Dermot!"

"You'll get the chance. Tell me: is this lady bothering you for money?"

"Money?" John laughed. "She makes so much money she doesn't know what to do with it."

"Is it the baby, then? Listen, John. I'll tell you what I'll do. I'll go and find and see this lady. And if she likes, I'll take the baby myself. Our house at Dermotstown is lonely with just my mother and me, and I'll tell you, John, I'll adopt the little thing—if you'll only be decent to Connaught and be straight. And she will never know."

"Dermot, you're a friend. You're a good lad. Why—why did n't I know you better in the old days! I would n't have been the way I was, if you'd been my friend, Dermot. But, Dermot, you need n't worry about the baby. She would n't give it up."

"Then is it about the French officer? Look here, John, I'll talk with him. All he could want you to do is marry his sister, and you can't now—"

"Marry his sister?" John looked at him stupidly with his haggard eyes. "You damned fool, I did marry her."

§ 2

And then, as he looked at Dermot's face, he sobered suddenly, he came to himself. His face was white, white as the whitewashed walls of the mean room. His eyes dilated. He pushed back his chair. He stood up uncertainly.

"Don't!" he whispered. "For God's sake, don't!"

Very quietly, very coolly, Dermot pushed the table aside, and then all his control vanished. He sprang through the air like an unleashed hound. A sudden horrible fury took him. It seemed to explode within him like a bomb. He was conscious of swinging John from side to side of the room. Of throwing him savagely against the walls. Of lifting him up like a sack of corn and hurling him on the floor. The man's limp terror and drunkenness saved him from broken bones or death. He lay on the floor, looking at Dermot with conscious, terrified eyes. Dermot stood above him, panting with baffled fury.

The door broke open. The landlord rushed in.

"Oh, gentlemen! gentlemen!" he wailed. "Get up, sir. Get up." He pulled John to his feet, and stood between them.

"Don't hit him, sir," he appealed to Dermot. "Sure he's got drink taken. He's not fit to be struck. Ah, now, sir! Ah, now! you'll have the police in on me!"

"Don't kill me, Dermot; you can't!" John whispered. His voice seemed to have gone. A queer cry came from his lips. "It would all come out. Think of Conn."

"Leave us alone," Dermot told the landlord.

"Ah, how can I, sir?"

"I won't touch him again."

"Is it Mr. McDermot of Dermotstown is in it?" the landlord asked. "Sir, if you give me your promise I'll leave you be."

"All right!"

"Ah, sir, don't play me false! 'T is a bad enough name the house has, without murder in it."

"Get out!"

The door closed and they were alone together again, Dermot and John. Dermot paced the room with short quick steps, baffled, furious, his eyes red with sudden effusion of blood, a terrific drumming in his ears. John had fallen into a chair with weakness. His face was still white and fearful, but he watched Dermot with quiet, intelligent eyes.

"Look here." Dermot stopped and spoke. "You've got to clear out. Clear out of all of our lives, do you understand? Clear out of our country."

"Where will I go?"

"Blast you! What the blazes do I care where you go?"

"I can't go. I have no money."

"Walk it. Swim it. But get out."

"I won't," said John, suddenly.

"You can't do a thing," he said, "you can't expose me. It will make your friend Connaught no

more than a betrayed girl.   And there's none will
believe I wasn't a husband to her."

Dermot swung around with a terrible oath;
something ripped up from the subconsciousness of
him, words he had n't known he knew. Once more
the murderous look came into his eyes.

"You can't kill me.   You can't kill me," John
warned him.   "There's your mother and Conn
and all your people and Dermotstown."

Dermot stopped suddenly, and groaned. He
leaned against the mantel of the little fire, and
all but burst into sobs of rage.

"So I'll stay at Glenmalure."   John had sal-
vaged a drink out of the overturned bottle.   "So
I'll stay at Glenmalure, and be damned to you!"

Dermot turned around slowly from the mantel.

"No," he said, "I can't kill you.   But I know
one who can and will."

"And who is that?"

"The Commandant Hogan."

"That fool's in Africa, with his regiment.   I
had him chased out of Ireland."

"I have seen him twice since.   Once at Dundalk
and once at the Hannastown races."

"You're mistaken. He would n't dare show
himself."

"At Dundalk he was a Franciscan Monk.   At

Hannastown he was the blind man led by a little dog."

John's face was worse than white now. It was gray, ash-colored. His mouth opened, in sudden helplessness. He tried to rise, and sank back in the chair.

"I 'll go," he said; "I 'll go, Dermot. But you 've got to give me some money, Dermot. I can't travel like a pauper. I don't know how. I 'm not used to that." A queer whining note came into his voice. "I 'll go, Dermot. I 'll go."

"I 'll give you money," Dermot said. "But get out." His voice rasped like a saw. "Get out, and get quickly, and listen: get far!"

XV

§ 1

AND Connaught she was back, back in her own house, thank God! And once more the sunshine spread over the hills. And spring, that had turned heavy, grew bright again. The cleansed rain-washed fields shone a soft and velvety green. The shrill song of the birds, the shrill green of the trees. Primroses on the banks, like gaudy carpets, and daffodils with gay yellow heads, like young girls dancing. And in the woods were everywhere violets, sweet, timid as little children.

She had returned when Anne McDermot had written her, telling her that John had gone to America with the intention of never coming back. She had returned to take over Glenmalure. The old servants had been tracked down and brought home, and John's crew sent off. And the gardeners had set to work, and the women of the house set to scrubbing, and all the windows and doors opened, so that the breeze from Three-Rock Mountain could sweep through every nook and cranny of Glenmalure, and cleanse it as with blessed water. And in a little while none would ever know that John D'Arcy had been there, or any evil dark person of devious ways, such as his associates had been. And the little terrier was glad to be home again, chasing the rabbits on his stumpy little legs, and whining as he nosed after them, and giving his short peremptory bark.

And everywhere the news spread that the Foxy One, as D'Arcy had been named, had left the country. And they told in whispers how the ghost of the great horse he had shot had thundered into the room he slept in, each night, and awakened him with tossing mane and angry eyes, until he had to flee over the water, which shades must not pass. And Miss Connaught was in her home again.

"I heard this day," a blind beggarman said in an inn, "a sound that raised my heart."

"And what was that, Meehaul?"

"Every day now I do be passing the Hangman's House, coming down from my wee cabin on the hills, to ask the charity of kindly people. And my ear does be cocked, listening for the sounds of the road, the wee songs of the birds in summer or the gallop of a fine horse, and in winter maybe the slipping of a hare through the grass or the rustle of a weasel in the hedge. I do have great interest

in what I hear with my ears, the eyes not being
at me."

"Poor Meehaul!"

"And every time I pass Hangman's House, I
take my hat from my head and I say this: 'God
let you not be too hard on Jimmy the Hangman!
He was a hard man, and a cruel man, but there
was no meanness in him. And God be kind to
little Miss Connaught, for 't was she was always
kind to God's poor people. And when sleep
comes to her, let her forget.'

"And as I was standing there, I heard a sound
I had n't heard since the Hangman died, and I
never expected to hear again. And the tears
came into my poor empty eyes and the heart rose
within me."

"What sound was in it, Meehaul?"

" 'T was little Miss Connaught," he said, "and
she singing."

§ 2

They were timid when they first met, timid and
strange. She went forward to meet him, shy as
a doe, and his brusque air of comradeship deserted him, leaving him strange and awkward.

"Is he gone for good, Dermot?"

"Yes, Conn."

"And shall I never see him again?"

"Never again, Conn."

"Oh, Dermot," she said, "it is so good to be home again! And to see the Wicklow Mountains blue against the sky, and Dublin, the old gray city, and the Dodder tumbling down the weirs toward the sea. And your own house and your trees, and your own room, and your—your friend." She looked at him with a strange shy sweetness. "You are still my friend, Dermot?"

"Always and forever, Conn."

"Come into the house, Dermot. It is a long time since you 've been in Glenmalure."

About it was a strange clean brightness. And everywhere were great greenhouse flowers. In the days of the old baron it had been like some heavy conservative club, and he would have nothing moved, nothing touched.

But Connaught had changed things. A table shifted here, the great grandfather clock at a new angle, and somehow the hall was rejuvenated, welcoming. She threw open the door of the library, but there nothing had been touched. Still the great legal tomes, the portraits of Edmund Burke and the great orator John Philpot Curran. And there was the old baron's work-table still, with a great clean blotter on it, and new pens cut, the gray-goose quills the Lord Chief Justice used, and his chair turned at the accustomed angle, as though he might come into the room at any moment and work, who was dead. There was a sweet deep thought in it, and Dermot turned to look at her. In his eyes she read he understood.

"Yes, Dermot," she smiled.

And the drawing-room that Glenmalure had de-lighted in, with its long French windows looking out on the green tennis-courts, its heavy furniture of the period of placid good Victoria. The in-laid tables, the great carved mantel, the cabinets full of little objects such as Victorians loved, ivory chessmen from China, curved little men from Ja-pan, shells from Oceana, seals, fans, daggers from Damascus, and Indian brass-work, things that evoked placid dispassionate Victorian romance. Taborets with marble tops around, and small use-less tables. And prints of Meissonnier etchings on the walls, of cavaliers of the Three-Musketeers period, and of gentlemen playing chess, wearing swords and knee-breeches, and of Napoleon, surly and victorious, at Jena, at Austerlitz, and keen and proud at a review of the Old Guard. New standards of beauty, new standards of decoration had arrived, but this room of the period of placid good Victoria had something friendly and pathetic and familiar about it, like an old dog one loves.

Only Connaught's great piano was modern and
all the sweetness of flowers that colored the room,
the vases of high daffodils, and the great flowering
shrubs the gardeners had brought in, staggering
under their weight.

"Come, Dermot," she said.

The little terrier had joined them now, and lar-
ruped after them up the great broad stairs. She
turned down a corridor, and opened the door of
a room he had n't known before.

It was a long sweet room with two great windows to it, and the sharp virginal scent of verbena
everywhere. He looked around stupidly, not understanding. There was the small high bed with
the starched muslin canopy. There was the
dressing-table with array of silver brushes and
combs, and little things he did not know the use of.
His heart went suddenly thumping, and he felt
like dropping on his knees and covering his face
with his hands, as in a sanctuary. It was Connaught's room.

"Here is what I missed most in England, Dermot, the room I have had so long. And everything where I know it is. And see, Dermot," she
brought him to a window, "there in the distance
is the Hill of Howth, and the soft glimmer of the
Irish Sea. And look below you, Dermot, and see
the gardens, the great ash-trees and the little yew-

trees, and the green space where the sun-dial is.

"And when the candles and the fire are lit at night, there is a soft blue hush about the room, and I used to sit at the fire and dream. And the rooms abroad were so hard and glaring and there were no dreams, only sad gray thoughts. And when it is moonlight, I sit at the window and look out at the world, and everything has lost its body and is a sweet ghost. One would think the world had died, and was gentle and happy.

"And sometimes at dawn I used wake with the twitter of the birds, and go to the window and there was a queer half-light over everything, and a funny secret little life then. Do you know, Dermot, that the birds are on the ground at dawn, hopping around, hunting their breakfast? And rabbits with great lop ears, nibbling daintily. And I can never help a little laugh then, and the birds run and the rabbits scuttle away.

"Last night there was a moon, Dermot, and I sat at the window. But the little girl is gone forever, Dermot, and I am strong and a woman. I was n't unhappy, Dermot, but there was a tug at my heart."

"The little girl is not gone, Connaught. You are the dreaming little girl still."

"Ah, no, Dermot. She is gone, the little girl, but I don't mind, Dermot; I don't really mind.

There was so much in the world I was blind to, when I was only a little girl.

"Do you know, Dermot, that last night was the first night I have looked out into the moonlight since—since John came to the house, since—since my father went away. There has always been a woman friend in the room with me, and the little terrier sleeping at the door. And I brought you up here to do something for me, Dermot."

She went to the stand beside the small high bed, and opening the drawer, took a small revolver out. She handled it clumsily and fearfully.

"Please take this, Dermot, and throw it away. Throw it very far away, please Dermot. Put it away, Dermot; put it in your pocket. I'm afraid of it."

He took the heavy blue ugliness from her and shoved it in his pocket. They moved toward the door. On the landing he stopped and looked at her.

"My poor Connaught!" he said. "My poor little friend!"

She put her hand up on his shoulder. She assured him with her eyes.

"Please don't be worried, Dermot. It's all right now. Don't look so miserable, my dear. There is peace on me, Dermot; there is peace on me now."

XVI

§ 1

NOW she was almost settled in her house, and John had gone away forever, it seemed to Dermot that there was one thing to do before she could rest easy. He must see the Commandant Hogan and appeal to him to keep the story hushed. If it would come to Connaught's ears that she had been betrayed in this manner, she would never hold her head high again. If Hogan were anything like the sister John had described, he would be chivalrous and silent. And from what he himself had seen of the Citizen, he was a dashing daring man, who would not hurt a woman for anything. He felt sure an appeal there would be heard. If he didn't see him soon the commandant might say or do something, and he on John's track, that would unveil the whole miserable affair to the world.

But the question was how to get hold of Hogan. Where would he be now, who was here and there like a will-o'-the-wisp, and disguised and hunted? Dermot questioned himself as to who would be likely to know of his movements. Who among old Fenian men would trust him with information about the French commandant? He decided he would go and see McMurrough O'Reilly, the old chief who was supposed to have had so much to do with the '48 and the '65, and who had known his father and Smith O'Brien and Meagher of the Sword. The old chief would help him.

He journeyed down to Glendhu on a fine April day, and come to Abbeyreilly as the dusk was falling. Dusk was falling on the land, and a greater dusk was falling on the ancient house, for with McMurrough O'Reilly the great line of Miles the Slasher died. The one son of the chief was dead in far Tibet. Some greasy aborigine had finished the line that had held fast to their own against Norman baron and Elizabethan cavalier and grim Cromwellian Ironside. The ancient house itself was crumbling, and the manservant who opened the door was old, very old and poor. But the old chief, for all his eighty-five years, had the eagle face and the eagle eye of his ancestors, and the awesome courtesy of great old-time noblemen.

"I remember your late, very gallant father," he said. "If in any way I can assist his son, please command me."

And he motioned Dermot to one of the aged torn chairs, as though he were asking him to sit in some high place beside a throne. Nor would he be seated, for all his many troubled years, until his guest was.

"Sir," Dermot said, "I come to you on a very delicate mission. I know you have been associated with all the movements inaugurated to give Ireland her freedom."

"I have had that honor," said the old gentleman.

"Sir, there is a man in this country whom I wish to see and speak to on a most private matter. He is Commandant Hogan of the French Army, a son of Dennis Hogan, of Cork and Paris."

"I shall give you a letter to those who can bring or send you to him."

"Sir, I shall tell you to prove good faith, some reasons why I should see this gentleman—"

"Your name and family are sufficient good faith."

"Sir," said Dermot, "thank you!"

The letter the old chief gave him in his ancient spidery writing brought Dermot up again to Dublin, and sent him to an English peer who wore kilts, and an Irish baronet who spoke with an Oxford accent, and a Quaker merchant from Belfast who was so benign and wise that Dermot all but laughed in his face, so far removed did he seem from the atmosphere of revolution and battle on

the hills.   And they sent him to another man who
was proprietor of a little jewelry shop on the
quays, and who had the whitest hair and the most
hurt eyes Dermot had ever seen in a human head.
And thence he went to a saloon in the Liberties,
and saw the landlord, who had a great powerful
face and a great powerful frame and the hardest
eyes Dermot had ever looked into.   They were
not cruel, not bad eyes, but just hard, concentrated,
wary eyes.

"If you 're looking for fighting, you 'll be disappointed.   There 's to be none."

"I 'm not looking for fighting," Dermot said,
"and I 'm glad there 's to be none."

"Look, now," the man said.   "If you had n't
brought me this card, and you 'd said that, I 'd
have broken your back."

"You mean you 'd have tried to," Dermot said
quietly.   "But why?"

The man looked hard at him.

"Ah, I suppose it 's the hearty way you said it.
But you mean no harm."

He moved out around his customers for a minute.   Dermot saw him talking to a railroad porter.   The porter had the dreamy face of a student
and soft small immaculate hands.   He came back.

"The man you want," he said, "has left Galway and will be in Tory Island off the coast of

Donegal now. You'll have to hurry if you want
to catch him, for he has some private business to
transact before his year's leave is up. You'll
find him at Red Rory O'Donnell's. It's a sort of
Hotel called the *Ree na Spanya,* the King of
Spain. To get to see him, you'll have to say the
word 'Fontenoy.' Can I do anything more for
you? No. Then good luck, but hurry!"

He left Dublin on a fine April morning with
the sun laughing through the breaks in white fleecy
clouds, and journeying northward the train crossed
the great bridge over the Boyne where William the King and Duke Schomberg scattered the
gallant Jacobite clans, and passed through Dundalk where Edward de Bruce had been crowned
King of Ireland, and outside of which he lies, in
Fonghart, in an unmarked grave, he who was as
gallant as Robert his brother, and fought as well.
And thence the train swept into Armagh of the
apple orchards, and the sweet dreamy mountains.
And the train puffed into Portadown, which is the
bitterest town in Ireland. Going westward
thence, Dermot passed through Tyrone, which was
the country of the great O'Neill's, Shane, who had
been Queen Elizabeth's enemy and darling, and
Owen the Red, who achieved the great victory of
the Yellow Ford. And he came to Derry of the

great Siege, where the Apprentice Boys defied the might of James II.

And leaving Derry now he went into the wild and bitter sweet country of Donegal, and the train he now took was not like a train at all, exact, mechanical, but a friendly ambling sort of thing like a horse jogging home from market. And high purple mountains now came, through the gaps in which the train ambled genially. And now were left all townspeople, their wary eyes, their clipped Northern accents. And barefoot gentle women came into or got off the train at little wayside stations, shawls over their heads, and peace in their eyes. And little easy-stepping men with black slouch hats and white flannel coats. Their voices were gentle. And now the Gaelic was heard everywhere. There was no "good day" or "how are you?" with the quaint gentle people, but *"Go mbeannuighidh Dia dhuit!"*—"May God bless you!"—and the answer, *"Go mbeannuighidh Dia agas Muire dhuit!"*—"May God and Mary bless you!" Nor any "good-by" but *"Beannacht leat!"* —"A blessing go with you!"—and *"Beannacht De agot!"*—"The blessing of God at you!" Thus the soft-toned folk of Donegal.

And at Cloghaneely he descended, and making his way toward Ballyness he got a fishing-boat to

take him to Tory.   The wind blew eastward from
Labrador, keen as a knife, and within the North
Atlantic drift the waves rose green, curling, ponderous, infuriated at the first resistance of the
Eastern world.   They slid down some with a
breath-taking speed; they pitched into others with
a shattering crash that wet the mainsail with showers of spray.   They slid under the lee of Innis-
boffin.   Gulls whined and cormorants flew about
on black lazy wings.   In the dusk the fisherman
landed Dermot on the shores of Tory, and returned—as they phrased it, to Ireland.   And *"go
neirighidh ant adh leat!"* they wished in their very
soft voices, "May your luck rise with you!"

§ 2

He went up the roughly made fisherman's road,
leaning to the heavy Atlantic wind, past the
stunted distorted oak-trees that had somehow
found footing there and that the westerly gales
had trained into grotesque shapes; like sphinxes
they seemed in the dusk, or like women's hair flying in the wind, or like immense strange birds.
Above him and about him was the eerie whining
of the gulls.   He felt on this island, with Ireland

in the distance, as on some small helpless boat in
mid-Atlantic that had broken away from a large
secure vessel. And turning a hummock he came
upon a long straggling house with a sign-board on
the outside: *"Do Ree na Spanya,"* "Dedicated
to the King of Spain." It had probably been the
traditional name of an inn on Tory Island since
the great Armada perished on British shores, and
some shrewd islander had set up in business with
the loot of a great galleon and recorded the origin of the trade gratefully or cynically—such
queer folk island people are!

He entered the house. There was a big room
lit here and there with oil-lamps, that were more
points of light than light-giving devices. Everywhere were beams of yellow light and soft dark
shadows. In the corner was a bar, a small bar,
with a great red man leaning on it. His face was
red, his hands were red, his hair was flaming.
Dermot decided this would be Red Rory O'Donnell. At the other end of the room was a great
fire of turf and sea-timbers, and sitting about it
were five or six islanders in frieze trousers and
white-flannel coats. They were listening to an
old man, fattish, his face a thousand wrinkles,
telling a story. Beneath Dermot's feet fine sea
sand crunched. Above his head, hanging from
the rafters, were great flitches of bacon and ham.

Dermot advanced toward the red man behind the bar.

"Good evening," he said.

"Good evening yourself, mister." Red Rory never moved his eyes from him.

"Is there a gentleman staying here," Dermot asked, "whose name is—" he hesitated—"the Citizen?"

"Citizen," said Red Rory, "is a word that is not known to me."

"Is this word known to you: 'Fontenoy'?"

"The Citizen is here," Red Rory answered. "Is it on Irish business you come to see the Citizen?"

"It is on private business."

"Then you must wait, mister," Red Rory said regretfully, "because the Citizen is in counsel now with the men of Donegal.   But when it is through I shall tell you, mister.   And now," he said, "for entertainment, there is wine and brandy of France, and sherry wine of Spain, and Portugal wine from Oporto, and potheen of the Donegal hills, and if you are a friend of the Citizen's, young mister, you are the guest of me and this island."

"Could I have something to eat, too?"

"There is eggs from the fowls, and fish from the nets, and there is soda farls and strong tea.   I shall go and see about them. And if you would like to sit by the fire—"

Dermot moved toward the great fire, red of the turf and yellow and green of the salt in the sea-timber—fragrance of the turf, and clear clean fragrance of the sea. The islanders and the story-teller rose courteously at his approach and named themselves.

"This gentleman," an islander explained, "is a poet and a story-teller of Connemara, and he is telling us a story of Dan Hoyser, the great Irish poet, and how he met Venus in the mountains of High Germany."

Dermot puzzled an instant. Dan Hoyser and Venus. Wasn't there an opera about it? And hadn't Conn played some of the music from it? Deep-sea stuff he could n't get the hang of. But he did n't know the man was an Irish poet. He had thought he was some sort of a German religious chap.

"If it is not agreeable to you—" the old story-teller saw the puzzled look on Dermot's face— "we will talk about other things. About the weather that is in it, and about the crops, and about the news from Ireland and from foreign parts, but if it is agreeable to you, I will go on with the story, now that I have begun." There was something pathetic about the shy eyes and the myriad wrinkles of the traveling poet.

"It would be very agreeable to me," Dermot said, and they sat down.

"Now, the fuss they made over Dan Hoyser at the Court of England was nothing to the fuss they made over him at the court of the King of France. The Englishwomen were great fair-haired women with a shy way to them, and they would try to hide their love for him, but he could see it in their eyes. But did the women of France hide it? They did not. There were all kinds of women there; brown merry women with a languor in their eyes, dark women with dark eyes and white slim hands, and small fair women, deli-cate as flowers. And when he made a poem and chanted it while the apprentice boy played the harp, it was 'Dan Hoyser, Dan Hoyser!' they cried. 'Oh God! I die!' And they unwound all the fragrance of their hair and their eyes were moist with the tears of love and their lips were moist for kissing. So that the fighting-men of the king's court grew jealous, and said, 'It is a great shame to waste all this on a poet.' But Dan Hoyser was an Irish poet and the sword he car-ried was longer and heavier and sharper than most of the fighting-men's. And there was a look in his eye that said, 'Ah, well, if you want it you'll get it, but what about your poor old mother when you're gone?' So that the fighting-men were very polite to Dan Hoyser.

"But after a while he got tired of it all, and he said to himself: 'It's a queer thing,' said he, 'but when I withdrew to the mountains of Kerry to write my great poems, I could think of nothing but women, their sweet hidden ears, their shy feet, and how their ears would grow deep as they looked into the fire in the evenings. And my heart used beat in my breast like a wild bird in a fowler's net. And now for a year I've had nothing but women, and I'm sick of them.

" 'Where is the great itch was on me a year ago? The wandering eye and the wandering foot and the adventurous mind. A little more of this,' he said, 'and my body will be getting fat, and my face satisfied-looking, and there'll be a rust on my sword,' he said, 'and the roar and fire of my verse will become a cat's purring. What life is this for me,' he shouts at himself, 'taking presents from kings and love from a pack of women?' and he rings for the apprentice boy.

" 'Put new strings on the harp, and a new edge on my sword,' he says. 'Bring quills and parchment and crush out some more ink. And get ready the horses. We're off.'

" 'And where are we off to, your Eminence?'
said the apprentice.

" 'We 're going to climb the highest Alps,' said
Dan Hoyser, 'and find a monastery somewhere,
with quiet monks, and there we 'll stay the rest
of our lives,' he says, 'singing songs about the
glory of God, and the clean joy of Paradise, and
against the lure of women and the pomposity of
kings.'

" 'Good enough,' said the apprentice boy, and
he thought to himself: 'In a little while Dan 'll
get tired of that, and we 'll be off to the wars, setting the soldier men fighting mad with the power
of verse. Oh, 't is a great life, the life of an apprentice poet!' And he gets ready the gear, and
brings around the horses, and the women begin to
wail.

" 'Ah, Dan, Dan Hoyser! why are you leaving
us? Why do you go?'

" 'Well,' he said from the back of his horse,
'there 's no lie I could think up would satisfy ye,
so I 'll tell you the truth. I 'm sick of you. I 'm
sick of women. I can't bear the look of you, even.
I 'm sick of your languorous eyes, I 'm sick of your
red mouths and your pale hands.''

"And then one of them, that Dan had recently
a great love for, came forward: 'Dan, look at
me,' she pleaded. 'How can you leave my hazel

eyes, my eyebrows like the young moon?' And
she sprang on the mounting-block and laid her
hand on his cheek. And reining the horse away
from her, he turned and said a great poem:

> "*A bhean lan do stuaim,*
> *Connig uaim do lamh—*

> "'O Woman of the evil wiles,
> Keep your velvet hand from me—'

"But that," said one of the islanders, "is not a
poem of Dan Hoyser's. That is a poem of the
Reverend Doctor Sharoon Keating's."

"It is not a poem of the Reverend Doctor Sharoon Keating's. It is a poem of Dan Hoyser's.
What in God's name," asked the story-teller, impatiently, "would Doctor Geoffrey Keating, a
clergyman and a historian, know about the wiles
of women, and their velvet hands?"

"That," pondered the islander, "is very true,
and now I know it could not be a poem of Sharoon
Keating's, and I am very sorry to have interrupted
you. I have no manners at all."

"It is nothing," waved the old man, magnani-
mously.

"So Dan Hoyser left them, and went on his
way, and in every town before him was welcome
and jubilee, for the great Irish poet was in it, who

spoke so highly of women, but there was disappointment on every one, for all Dan Hoyser would write now were hymns, and what they wanted were songs about women. 'Let me tell you something,' says Dan Hoyser, 'when you're listening to my hymns you're listening to the finest in the world, better even than the psalms of David that you do be singing on Sundays. Give ear, now.' And they gave ear, and they agreed that they were better than the psalms of David, but they were disappointed all the same.

"And never a word did he speak to a woman, barring a poor ugly wee girl he met by the Rhine, and her tending a flock of geese on a desolate common. Barefoot she was, with thinnish colorless hair, and washed-out blue eyes.

" 'Horseman,' she asked, 'did you hear word on the way of the great Dan Hoyser?'

" 'What about Dan Hoyser?' says he.

" ' 'T is how I heard that Dan Hoyser, the great Irish poet was on his way to become a monk in the Alps,' she said. 'And a queer thought came to me minding the geese, and keeping the ganders from fighting. I'll never get a man,' says she, 'I'm that poor and I'm that ugly, and not strong itself, but only good for minding the geese. I'll ask Dan Hoyser to kiss me, and I'll be the last

woman he kissed before he entered the silent
monks. And there 'll be a queer fragrant flowering thought to me, and I in my poor ugly old age.
I 'll never tell it to any one, for none would believe
me, but keep it to myself, or at most tell it to the
trees and they whispering with the winds of summer.'

"And Dan Hoyser slung his leg over his horse's
head.

" 'Come here, my little girl,' said he.

"And she noticed then the apprentice boy behind him with the harp slung on his back. And
she understood. And a faintness took her so
she nearly fell.

" 'Oh, my lord!' she whispered.

"And Dan Hoyser put his arm about her, and
kissed her fair on the mouth. And he took from
his hand a diamond ring, and put it on her finger.
And from his arm he took a great bracelet that
had been given him by a daughter of the King of
Spain.

" 'Go and get yourself a husband, little lassie,
and be kissed by a better man.' And he rode on.

" 'Am I dreaming, your Eminence? or did I
see you kiss the ugly barefoot girl?' asked the apprentice boy.

" 'You saw me,' said Dan Hoyser.

" 'And did I hear your Eminence, with my personal ears, refuse a kiss to the Queen of the Lowlands of Holland?'

" 'You heard me.'

" ' 'T is a conundrum!' said the apprentice boy.

" 'A great poet you 'll make when you grow up,' sneered Dan Hoyser, 'when you can't see that a kiss to a queen would have been a flip to her vanity, and the kiss to the ugly wee girl was the glory of a great dawn.'

" 'Oh, right enough,' said the apprentice boy.

"And Dan Hoyser rode on, thinking in his mind how after a life of piety he would arrive in the parlors of heaven, and have great discussing with the other chief poets—with King Solomon, for instance, who wrote a poem he called the Song of Songs. And they would talk about their different methods of work. 'And how did you ever come to think of that likeness or this rime?' they would ask each other. And Solomon would talk of his battles and the temple, and Dan Hoyser would tell of the days when he was apprentice poet to Francis the Villain in Paris—a great thief, that fellow, and a great poet—poems about women and fighting-men, and poems about the Queen of Heaven, and poems about his friends who were hanged, and them written in thieves' jargon, and he made his will in poetry, a great rascal that lad, but Dan Hoyser could n't have served his time under a better man.

"And as the horse was walking up-hill, and Dan thinking high thoughts of heaven, there came to his nostrils the sweet scent of woman, of a lady and a sweet woman. Dan never lifted his head.

" 'Stand aside, cow,' he ordered.

"The horse under him stopped and lowered its great noble head. And there came a little laughter to Dan's ears, that was like the thrumming of the deeper strings of the harp.

" 'Dan Hoyser! Dan Hoyser!' came a voice. And Dan Hoyser lifted his head, and before him was a small sweet brown woman, with golden eyes and brownish hair. And in her arms were flowers of the mountain, and the fragrance of herself was greater than the fragrance of the flowers.

" 'I could not let you pass without thanking you for the poems you made about me, Dan Hoyser, and the sweet things you said of me.'

" 'Ma'am,' said he, and he was trembling from he knew not what. 'I never made a poem about you, for I never saw you in my life before.'

" 'But you did, Dan Hoyser.'

"A queer dreaminess was coming on the poet, and there were thoughts in his mind of the time when he was young, and the arms of women were a sweet secret dream of sanctity, and later a swirl of thunderous feeling, and later a pleasant thing, the pleasantest thing in the world, maybe, but only a pleasant thing. And he was troubled.

" 'Ma'am,' he said, 'what name is on you, that I wrote poems to you?'

" 'The name that is on me is Venus.'

" 'But, dear ma'am,' he said, thinking of Greece. 'This is High Germany.'

" 'They have exiled me from the summer sea, Dan Hoyser, and banished me from the sunny lands, and imprisoned me among the mountains in barren High Germany. There is a new people in the world, Dan Hoyser, who want to suffer and to make others suffer. And you too are going from me.'

" 'I am, ma'am,' he said. 'I must save my soul.'

"Come with me into my prison, Dan, for just a little moment.'

" 'I 'm on my way to a monastery,' he said, though he was trembling from head to foot.

" 'For a little moment, Dan Hoyser, my lost poet?' she asked.

" 'Well, I 'll come in for a little refreshment, ma'am, but I must be on my way.'

"He looked at the great cleft in the mountain, and looking behind, saw the boy with the harp coming up the hill after him.

" 'Ah, but the little lad?' he said.

"She put out her soft fragrant hand: 'Sleep, darling, sleep!' she cooed. And on the back of his horse the boy fell asleep. And following Venus, Dan Hoyser led the horses into the cleft in the mountains.

"And it was twenty years from that day to the day he came out. He went in on a pleasant afternoon, and he came out on a cold foggy morning. And he led the horses with him, and carried the sleeping boy. And behind him the mountain closed. And the twenty years had not aged Dan Hoyser one day, except to put a terrible look in his eyes, and the little boy was not aged either, but the horses were old and weak, and the strings of the great harp had snapped, and some hung loose and jagged, and some were curled about the woodwork. But broken was each string.

"And the little boy awoke, and said: 'Master, I have been sleeping.' And Dan Hoyser dropped a tear on his curly head, and said, 'Thank God, dear little lad, you have.'

"And the boy saw the horses and the harp, and a great cry came out of him: 'O master, let us get away from this place. There is a curse on this place. See the horses, master, and the harp! O master, the great harp! Master, let us go away. I am afraid.'

" 'Come, little lad!'

"And Dan Hoyser brought him into a great city, where new horses were had, and the old ones were killed quickly, for Dan Hoyser would not sell them to the foreign people, for fear of their being ill-treated.   And he had the harp re-strung, to please the little lad.   But he made no more songs.   They passed the Alps.

" 'Where are we bound for, master?' asked the boy.   'I thought we were going to a monastery on a high Alp.'

" 'We're going to Rome, little lad, and there we shall see the Pope.'

" 'Good enough!' said the boy.   'I've heard a lot about him in Ireland.   I'd like to see him.'

"So they rode through Italy and into Rome, and they clattered up the streets, and drew rein before the Vatican.

" 'Which is it?' asked the Vatican people, 'a great prince or a great poet?'

" 'A great poet,' said Dan Hoyser, 'and a very great sinner.   Bring me,' he demanded, 'where the Holiness is.'

"And they brought him to where the Pope was sitting on his throne, with the gold tiara on his head and the shepherd's staff in his hand.

" 'And who,' asked the Pope kindly, and held his hand, 'is the great poet is in it, whose face I don't know?—for I thought I knew the faces of all poets alive. Though I can see,' he said, 'that you 're a great poet on account of your brow and your hands.'

" 'I am Dan Hoyser,' said the poet.

" 'Dan Hoyser! Dan Hoyser!' said the Pope, delightedly. 'And where have you been, Dan Hoyser, these twenty years? Sure I 've often wondered at the mystery of your disappearance. Sure you were my favorite poet and me only a poor bishop, as you might say, many years ago. Did you retire from the world to write a great poem?'

" 'Holiness,' Dan Hoyser groaned, 'for twenty years I have been sinning, and I want forgiveness and absolution.'

" 'Well, you have it,' says the Pope. 'Wine and women and a throat cut here and there—don't bother yourself about that. Sure what fire or poetry would be in you if you were a mouse-like habitual man.'

" 'Holiness, it is worse.'

" 'Dan Hoyser,' the Pope said severely, 'don't go and tell me you 've sold your soul to the devil! Though if you have,' he said, 'I think we can get you clear. Send up the chief exorcist,' he ordered a cardinal. 'Sure what are we here for but to help a friend out of a scrape?'

" 'Holiness—' Dan Hoyser dropped on his knees—'I have been Venus's darling for twenty years, in the caves of the mountains of High Germany.'

"The Pope said nothing, but he turned pale.

" 'Absolution, Father, for the sake of Jesus, our dear, dear Lord!'

"But still the Pope was silent. And his face grew whiter.

" 'It is the one sin I can't absolve,' he whispered. 'For my god is the enemy of the old gods. You turned your back on the bitter cross of the dear Lord Jesus, for the lap of a foul pagan deity. Dan Hoyser, great poet,' he said, 'You are a damned man.'

"Then Dan Hoyser stood up, very white and erect.

" 'Then for me,' he said, 'there is no God's heaven.'

" 'There is as little chance, Dan Hoyser, of you getting into heaven as this staff in my hand has of bearing green leaves and flowers again, as it did when it was a branch on God's trees.'

" 'I am very sorry to have troubled your Holiness,' said Dan Hoyser.

" 'Ah, why did you do it? Dan, my poor boy, why did you do it?' the Pope mourned, but when he looked up, Dan Hoyser had gone.

"And that evening the Pope was taken with an illness that kept him to his bed for a month, and when he got a little better, he asked the cardinals to help him get up, 'For I would like to be on my feet again, and see the green of the olive trees, and the new moon in the west.' And they helped him up, put a great fur cloak about him. 'You'll find my staff in that cupboard,' said he. 'Give it me.' And they opened the cupboard and looked at one another in astonishment as they brought out the staff. For, from tip to shepherd's crook, it was covered with green leaves and white fragrant flowers, all blooming from the barren wood.

"And the Pope trembled from head to foot, and he sat down in a chair.

"'Where is Dan Hoyser?' he said. 'Send for him.'

"'Is it Dan Hoyser, your Holiness? Sure, Dan Hoyser's gone. He went from Rome to Genoa, and at Genoa he sent his apprentice home to Ireland. A ship he chartered for the lad, Father, and they say that Dan Hoyser gave him the great harp, and took the poet's gold chain from around his neck and hung it on the boy's. 'Brother and dear little lad,' he said, 'I have taught you all I can. Give all,' he said, 'take just reward, but sell nothing.' And they both cried, the people say. 'And tell them at home,' said Dan

Hoyser, 'that they will never see Dan Hoyser any more, and say to them this last poem from Dan Hoyser: 'There is an island in the Western seas, and there is an island in Dan Hoyser's heart—' And the cardinals recited to him the poem called *'In iarthar ta oilean san mhuir.'*

" 'And after he went North, and a strange tale came to us: that the shepherds saw him disappearing into a cleft in the mountains of High Germany.'

"And the Pope put aside the staff he was fingering, and then let the great cloak fall from his shoulders. 'Put me in my bed again,' he asked, 'for the little moon of God is not for me.'

"And they put him in his bed again, and there he lay for days, his face turned to the wall. And when they called him Holiness, he stopped them, saying, 'What sanctity have I, who am the greatest sinner on earth, having betrayed God?' And they asked him for the benefit of his wisdom, and he said, 'Ask the first fool in the streets, for he has more knowledge than I of the heart of God.' And they told him he must decide questions of faith and morals, because he was infallible, and he wept and said to them, 'Why do you mock a poor tired old man?'

"And one morning they found that the life had

gone from him, and turning him from the wall, they saw there was a great peace on his face, but that his cheeks had been furrowed by tears. And they took a little silver hammer and tapped him gently on the forehead, and called him by name. Three times they tapped and three times they called his name. But answer they had none. And they went out on the balconies and acquainted the people, saying, 'His Holiness, our dear father, is dead.' And they met in conclave, and chose a new Pope, and when he died they chose another, so that there were many popes since that time, but there was never another Dan Hoyser."

The islanders were silent, looking into the fire. The old man stirred himself, rummaged in the breast pocket of his greenish weather-worn coat. He produced a pair of cracked steel-rimmed spectacles. He placed them carefully on his nose.

He reached down for the old hat that was by his side. From the hat he took a red bandana handkerchief, wrapping a sort of parcel. He undid the handkerchief, and produced a sizable bundle of dog-eared manuscript. He looked at the company benignantly over the cracked steel-rimmed spectacles.

"I will now read a poem of my own," he announced, "in the Gaelic, which has been compared very favorably to those of the great Dan Hoyser."

§ 3

Dermot had expected to see the Citizen in islander's or fisherman's clothes, the white-flannel
jacket, the voluminous frieze trousers, red cowskin
boots, but through the door, into the quiet room
where he was finishing supper, sea-trout and golden
tea, came now the upright soldierly figure in a blue
double-breasted suit such as a ship's officer might
wear. He seemed very broad in the shoulders,
very light in the legs, walking with the knees giving a little, as a horseman walks. His face was
tanned to the color of leather, except for the white
of a great scar on the left temple. His blue eyes
were keen and steel-like, and in the curly black
hair were strands of white. Very much the soldier he was. Dermot could see the rim in the
hair where the kepi had rested. He could easily
imagine him in riding-boots and red breeches, and
belted blue tunic, and jaunty red kepi. The now
merry, now melancholy Irish eyes, the brown face,
grave and immobile as one of his own desert
horsemen's. Very much the soldier, this Citizen,
Commandant Hogan.

His greeting to Dermot was not cordial.

"How the devil did you follow me here," he

"How the devil did you follow me here?" he blazed, "and what do you want?"

blazed, "and what the devil do you want?"

"Count O'Reilly put me in touch with those who knew where you were," Dermot told him, "and what I want is to ask a great favor of you."

The Citizen's frown relaxed, and he smiled. "I 'm an awful swine," he said, "to greet you like that, but I don't like being followed. And if Count O'Reilly— Sit down," he said. "What favor can I do?"

He threw a few sods of turf on the fire, and drew an island-built chair before it. Outside the great velvet night of the Atlantic had set in, and from the shores of the island came the moaning roar of tumbling waves. A little shower flew overhead, pattered a moment or two on the thatch and panes, and blew eastward toward Scotland. In the distance, from the bar, came the sound of a reel being played by accordion and fiddle:

Ma'am dear, did you ever hear, of pretty Molly Bran-
     nagan
In troth, then, she 's left me and I 'll never be a man
     again—

and tapping on a board came the tapping of the light feet of a dancer, light as the feet of goats.

"Sit down." The Citizen put him in the chair; leaned against the mantel, looking into the red turf fire. "Lad, what favor can I do you?"

"Citizen," Dermot began, "do you remember the day I first met you, at the Tara Hunt?"

"I do."

"Do you remember, Citizen, a red-bearded man and a little dark lady, and myself, being together, and you came up and asked the red-bearded man if he was the John D'Arcy who had been in Paris, and he said he had never been in Paris in his life?"

"I do."

"Well, he lied, Citizen."

"I know that," Hogan said, "and, what's more, he put the hue and cry after me."

"Citizen, John D'Arcy is a cousin of mine, and the little dark lady, whom he married, has been my little friend all my days."

"And you are here," Hogan rasped, "to ask for mercy for John D'Arcy."

"To ask you to do nothing, Citizen, against him—that is, against her."

"My lad," the soldier's voice warned, "stand clear of this. You don't know what you're talking about."

"But I do, Citizen. I know it all. Hear my story, and then judge if I haven't as great a quarrel with John D'Arcy as you. But my hands are tied, Citizen, and so must yours be. John D'Arcy came out of Europe and went through the marriage ceremony with Connaught O'Brien, Lord Glenmalure's daughter—"

"James O'Brien's? Is it the daughter of James O'Brien, the rebel poet, who swore the oath of rebellion with my father, and later became a traitor and hanged the Fenian men? Jimmy the Hangman, is it? His daughter and John D'Arcy! Living God!" he sneered. "What a well-matched pair!"

Dermot stood up.

"I know nothing," he said, "of oaths of rebellion and treason. Glenmalure was a hard man, I know, but he was good to me, and he was very good to Connaught, his daughter. And as for her—Citizen, you're Irish, for all your French commission, and I give you the word of an Irish gentleman that there never lived a sweeter or truer woman than the girl John D'Arcy married. Citizen, I know this lady, and I love this lady with all my heart and soul."

"Go ahead."

"D'Arcy broke Connaught's heart, nearly. She did n't love him. She hated him after he told on you to the authorities, and the house, her house, Citizen, he filled with the riffraff of Dublin, and after he killed the Bard—"

"The horse you rode at Hannastown?"

"Yes, Citizen, he killed that horse, and she ran away from him. I saw him then and talked to him. I thought he was just crazy with fear and I could do something."

The Citizen laughed, a horrible, sneering laugh.

"And then he told me, Citizen, about your sister whom he had married, and the little baby, and how they had parted, and how he had returned and married my friend, while your sister was still alive." They both stood still looking into the red fire.

"So he told you that, eh?"

"Citizen, believe me, I'm immensely sorry. From what he said, your sister must be a very sweet, very darling lady; and for the little baby, too, I'm sorry."

"I loved my sister very much," the Citizen said slowly. "My father was only a poor exile in a strange country, and Maeve and I were closer than most sisters and brothers. If your little lady is anything but Maeve— Go ahead," he said abruptly.

"Then I nearly killed John D'Arcy," Dermot went on. "And in the end I gave him money to get out of the country and never let us see his face again.

"Citizen," he said, "to whom was the greater wrong done, your sister, whom he married, or my little friend, whom he married falsely, and who is not married to him at all, but who bears his name?"

"But—"

"Ah, no, Citizen! let me speak! I 've been thinking this thing out. I 'm not very good at thinking, but it seems to me like this: that it 's not so bad this way. Your sister is well rid of him and he won't dare go back and bother her, having done this thing in Ireland, and he won't bother Connaught any more, having no rights over her."

"Then what do you want if everything 's all right?"

"This, Citizen: don't say anything about his being married before he married Connaught. She does n't know. She thinks she 's married to him, and that he 's just gone. If she knew she had been tricked and fooled, she would never raise her head again. And she would have to go away. She would choose to go away, and leave her home and friends and her country and everything and even then not have peace. Citizen, I can think of nothing now, but if ever I can help you in any way, I will. And don't tell."

"And how about your caring for her?"

"Well, I care. But for me she has only got a warm, a sweet friendship. Oh, that 's all right," he smiled. "I 'm not the first person to care for

a girl he could n't marry. But, Citizen, I want
to protect her in every way I can."

"Look!" The soldier stood away from the
fire. "When I meet John D'Arcy, in Ireland or
abroad, from that moment on, John D'Arcy is a
dead man. Nothing you say could alter that.
Nothing on earth, except my death or his, could
alter that. But as for your little lady, be at peace,
lad. There shall come out nothing to make her
blush or hide her head."

"Thanks, Citizen," Dermot said. "I thank
you for her, too, though she shall never know.
But I hate to hear you speak of killing John
D'Arcy, for though I could do it myself, and have
tried to do it myself, in the heat of anger, yet to
hear you speak of it gives me a chill."

"Does it so?" laughed the Citizen. "Then
you may be glad you 're not in my trade. Come
—" he put his hand on Dermot's shoulder—
"We 'll go down to Red Rory's bar, and see the
dancing and listen to the music, and have some of
Red Rory's wine, and get the old story-teller to
tell us the history of the Queen of Scotland and
the Hairy Sea-Captain. Leave brooding be."

XVII

§ 1

THOUGH all was settled now as far as things could be settled, Connaught in her home, John in America, and the lips of the Citizen closed as by a lock, yet somehow to Dermot it seemed as if it were only a lull in a storm. Everything was so artificial. Perhaps it was the straightness of him that rebelled against the lie on which all this was built, perhaps it was some intuition that all this could not last. But he was unhappy.

He had thought they would all be happy. That Connaught would be at peace in her house, with her home and her gardens, her dogs, her horses, and that she would be dreaming in her seat between the great Druid oaks, watching the brown bees go in and out of their houses of yellow straw. A queer nun-like existence he had imagined for her, a great convent with a community of one sweet nun. But after a while she became lonely there, in the house that her father had filled with his immense impressive personality. And his old friends, his real friends, not those of politics, were

dying fast, as at times a whole circle seems to van-
ish from the earth.   For the Citizen he was worried, too, for suddenly through the country ran the
vague rumor of trouble, as the Irish term for revolution is.   Bodies of men had been seen collecting
in the hills, and dispersing there.   And there were
rumors in Connemara, and in the Kingdom of
Kerry of battalions tramping the moonlit roads,
and an ancient song crashing in the air:

> And what color will be seen?
>   Says the *Shan Van Voght.*
> And what color will be seen?
>   Says the *Shan Van Voght.*
> What color should be seen
> Where our fathers' homes have been,
> But our own immortal Green!
>   Says the *Shan Van Voght.*
> Our own immortal Green,
>   Says the *Shan Van Voght.*

Gunboats were dropping casually into Irish
harbors, and the black-headed gray-eyed reckless
Irish troops were being moved around the empire,
fusilier and ranger, dragoon and hussar, they
marched off with the bands crashing "The Girl
I Left Behind Me."   One never knew how the
Irish soldiers would act in Ireland.   They might
mutiny during a rebellion, or if they did n't it
would be abominable to ask them to fire on their

countrymen. So they marched off to India and Africa, to Malta and Gibraltar, to Jamaica and Bermuda, and the streets of Dublin echoed to the scream of the pipes as the gaunt Scottish Highlanders took their places, and the shrill fifing of the British Grenadiers. Dermot knew there was to be no rebellion, but he was bothered about the Citizen. He was such a decent sportsman, such a gallant officer, and if he were taken he would fight until all hope of escape was gone, and then for the sake of his adopted France he must finish himself with his last shot, for a country must no more be compromised than a woman. Such is the unwritten law.

And John, too, in America. What new deviltry might he not be up to? What dreadful scandal might burst, the echo of which would reach Connaught in Ireland?

He had thought, planning beforehand, that when all was settled, there would be peace. And he in Dermotstown would love Connaught in Glenmalure, silently, devotedly. Though he would not see her, he would love her. He had seen himself going about the spring bustle of farming, quietly with love in his heart, and resignation. The plowmen would shear through the rich black soil, the great patient horses pulling, the glossy crows following the freshly turned furrow, sedate

as monks; the harrowing; the sowing of seed, the
sowers moving rhythmically forward, rhythmically dipping in the great sling about their shoulders, making the splendid rhythmic gesture of the
sowing of grain.　And all the new life there would
be to care for: the dark red calves, the colts with
their legs like withes, the farrows of young the
great grunting sows would have.　The fairs at
which he would have to match wits with the horse-
dealers of Waterford; and the Longford pig-
buyers, the shrewdest men in the world— The
dealers of Crossmaglen claim the palm for cunning, but that is not true. . . . He had expected
to be happy at his work, now all was settled, to
come home exhausted in the evening, to drowse in
the drawing-room while Anne his mother played
the music of her youth, the facile sensuous Chopin,
the pompous dignity of Mozart, and with him the
dogs would drowse, and he would read the
"Irish Field," and agricultural reports, and wonder whether he could n't introduce some of the
new Danish dairy methods into Ireland.　Or
some of the great Irish novels: Lever's "Tom
Burke of Ours," maybe, or Carleton's "Black
Prophet," or some other book from the library,
like the Memoirs of Buck Whaley, who wagered
he would walk from Dublin to Jerusalem, play
hand-ball against the walls of Solomon's Temple,

and walk back again, all in the space of two years.
And did.   There were giants in those days.   The
evening finished, he would look toward Glenmalure, with his heart in his eyes, and thoughts within
him he could not put into words, so high would
they be.   And then to sleep.

But the reality was different.   He could not
keep his thoughts on the business of the farm.
The plowing meant nothing to him, and at the
fairs of this spring he was no match for the dealers, and cared little whether he was or not.   And
when evening came, a dark head and golden eyes
would come between him and the page of print.
His eyes would wander from the book to the fire,
and the dogs would not drowse, knowing all was
not well with him, but nudged him with their
moist cold noses, uttering little whines.   And
when he stood outside looking at Glenmalure, a
weight pulled on his heart, and no words would
come to him.   And when he went up to sleep,
sleep was difficult, so that often he would lie awake
until day was gray against the blinds, and the
keen twitter of the birds announced the dawn.

And Anne, though she said nothing—her heart
was broken.   To see her boy suffering so, and not
to be able to help him, and to see no end in sight,
no solution.   Little Kathleen, her daughter, had
gone so quickly, so peacefully, and she knew where

the little one was, "which is far better," her religion told her.   And for all her Friend's faith, she was somehow glad how Desmond had gone, the young bright soldier.   A gallant death is such a good death, and the sure Boer bullet so much more merciful than disease in ancient days.   But Dermot, her serious young Dermot, who took things so much to heart, was wasting before her eyes.   And she could do nothing.   She his mother could do nothing!

And at nights when he was not there she would go out into the gardens, and going gently, hushedly to this nook, that bower, where her lover, her husband, had been with her so long ago, she would wait, listen.   For it seemed to her that in her and her son's need he must come, and she had leaned so much on his wisdom, his decision. A little breeze would rustle the trees, and her heart would stop still, but there was nothing. Overhead the bright inscrutable stars, and the little wisp of moon in the west, and she waiting in the dark trees, and wishing, and praying.   But not even in her or her son's need could he break the tremendous Law of Silence, to which dead men are bound.   Was that a step, or did she just imagine it?   Ah, it was nothing.   The fragrance of the flowers blew toward her, with kindness, and a bird murmured sympathetically in the trees.

And, weak from concentration and intensity, she would return to the brightness of the room that welcomed her and, sitting by the fire, slowly shake her head. Alas, poor lady!

§ 2

Because he was fearful to leave Connaught alone too much, he took her to the great race-meeting at Fairyhouse, where the Irish Grand National was battled for. They swept over the green Easter country dappled with yellow, yellow of gorse and primroses. They went to the park together to see the first racing of the two-year-olds—the bonny fillies, the fearful young colts, the diminutive jockeys perched on their necks like birds. They went to Punchestown, to see the Conyngham Cup Steeplechase, over the second stiffest country in the world. They passed through green fields and little towns, and little villages that had once been great fortresses—*Nas na Riogh,* Naas of the Kings; they passed the house where Stella, Swift's darling, had lived, secret as a mouse. He was silent, so that he did not notice she was silent, too. He was looking within himself, looking into himself as into a deep well, so that he did n't notice she was watching him, watching him all the time. At the races she was watching him, not the horses. It was she who had the energy, who made her way toward the book-makers, dragging him off for tea. And all of a sudden she seemed happy. A sweet low laughter came from her, like a song from a bird. He looked at her in surprise. He had never seen her so pretty before, he thought. A light seemed to come from her face. Her eyes had grown darker, wine-colored, and they smiled at him. There was a sweet flush to her cheek, the flush of roses, of delicate wild roses.

"You are happy, Conn," he smiled.

"Yes, Dermot, happy, very happy."

He was glad he had taken her to the races, because they had made her so happy.

She was silent, but happily silent, he thought, as they drove home through royal Meath, passing Tallaght and skirting Three-Rock Mountain, purple in the setting sun. At Glenmalure they had dinner together, alone, and she talked of the day —of how this horse might have won but for bad riding, and of how lucky this other winner was that the favorite came down at the stone wall.

"Let us go out, Dermot. There is a moon, and it is like summer in the garden."

She draped a great black shawl about her, so

that there was nothing of her visible but her face, the sweet face with the golden eyes under the snood of black hair. They went down the path into the orchard, where the trees threw great fantastic shadows on the grass. They went along the ivy-covered wall. At a corner where the shadows were deep she drew him to an old stone seat. They were all in shadow, while before them was the garden with the lightly whispering trees. They were like trees enchanted, under the glamour of the moonlight, like the silver and golden trees of the under-world of old Gaelic bards. Dermot felt grave, felt troubled. He could feel Connaught beside him, though they were apart. He turned to look at her, but her face was averted from him. There was only the slim figure in the great black shawl, the black hair, and the one white cheek.

"Why do you come to see me so seldom, Dermot?" she asked slowly. There was a scent of mignonette in the air, and he did n't know whether the sweet virginal odor came from her or from the garden. He became afraid of this moment, and this question. It seemed important, and he was unprepared. "It is lonely here, and you come very seldom now, Dermot. Why?"

"Do I come so seldom? I did n't think, Conn. There seems to be so much to do on the farms."

"Oh, Dermot," she said slowly, "why don't you say the truth? That you love me, Dermot. Is n't that so?"

He could answer nothing. He could answer nothing. He would not deny the truth when it was put before him face to face.

"Because—" her voice came tremulously from the shadows—"I love you too, Dermot."

"Yes, Conn."

"You do not understand me, Dermot. I mean I love you as you love me, with my whole heart and soul."

"Conn!" he cried. "Conn!"

"Yes, Dermot."

He took her hand, that he saw white against the black of the shawl. It was warm, but it was trembling. His was trembling, too.

"Conn," he said, "there 's so much I want to say, and that 's in me to say, but I can't speak it. I 'm dumb," he said piteously. "I 'm just dumb."

He thought he could hear the beating of her heart. He knew he could hear the beating of his. He let go her hand from his left hand and took it in his right. He put out his left arm to take her against his shoulder, so lonely she seemed, so trembling in the shadows. To give her peace against his shoulder, to give her protection.

"Just a moment, Dermot," she pleaded. "I must tell you something."

"Yes, Conn."

"There is a cloud passing over the moon in a moment, Dermot, and when it hides the moon I will tell you. Just a little thing, in the darkness, Dermot. Now, Dermot. Dermot," she whispered—her whisper was a queer little ghost of sound—"Dermot, I have never—you see, I have never been wife to John D'Arcy. Do you understand me, Dermot? I am not betraying him, or being just a selfish woman, when I say I know you love me, and I love you too. Please, Dermot, don't think that."

"I knew it, Connaught, I knew it. I knew it, my little love."

She came to his shoulder now, fluttering like a bird. Against him the dark head rested, dark, fragrant as night. And her shoulders were relaxed and soft, like the breast of a bird. She was so slim, so little, so perfect.

"I want to say so much, Conn, and I am dumb, dumb as a stone."

"My ear is over your heart, Dermot, and I can hear it beating. Say nothing, Dermot; I shall understand."

He put his hand gently on her sweet hair. His

fingers moved over her closed eyelids, the arches of her brows, over her cheek, and firm little chin, over her lips. As they passed over her lips, she kissed them.

"Do you want to kiss me, Dermot?" she looked up with her shining eyes. "Is that it? Do you want to kiss me, my dear?"

He nodded. He could say nothing.

"Of course, Dermot."

It seemed to him she was taking her heart, her warm heart, from her white breast and offering it to him on outstretched palms, and smiling gently, trustfully as she did it. And he was taking it reverently, with such humility. Her mouth was so soft, so warm, so trusting, and something so holy about it, like water from a well. Like clear water from some ancient blessed well. She lay still on his shoulder now, after a queer little peaceful flutter of breath. And suddenly something happened to him that had never happened in his life before. From his eyes came tears. They did not run, or trickle. They gushed from under his lashes, and fell on her face.

"And you told me you were dumb, Dermot," she said. She had understood.

"Lie still, dearest heart."

On his shoulder she seemed to go to sleep, so still was she, so softly came her breathing. He

"JUST A LITTLE THING IN THE DARKNESS, DERMOT. DO YOU UNDERSTAND ME?"

looked out into the night, and the lighted house, not two hundred yards away, seemed very far off, very unreal. Everything seemed to have withdrawn quietly so as to leave them alone. In the distance rose the mountains, the Sugar Loaves and Three-Rock and Two-Rock, but to-night their mysterious entities were gone. They were silent. They challenged nothing. They were silent as the moon. Not a dog barked into the night, nor a hare stirred in the long grass. Only the *husheen-husho* of the golden and silver trees. The turf dappled with moon shadows.

"Dermot," she asked quietly, "are you sure that —that John is gone away for good?"

"Yes, Conn."

"Did you send him away, Dermot?"

"He went away." Dermot laughed a little. "I have been such a fool, Conn."

"How, Dermot?"

"I saw John, thinking you could be made happy together. I tried to start a reconciliation."

"And if we had become reconciled, what about you, poor dear?"

"I had a plan, Conn, a foolish plan. I thought I would get married, and put you out of my life and head."

She started up. "Oh, Dermot! to whom?" she asked.

"Oh, anybody."

"But there must have been some one in your mind?"

"Nobody, Conn dear; the first decent girl who would have me."

"Oh, Dermot," she said, "what an awful thing to do! Poor boy! I did n't think it was ever as bad as that. Oh, my dear, I'm so glad I told you I loved you, to-night!" She put her hands up and drew down his head to her, and kissed him. It was she who was crying now.

"Never, never, never again think of that, Dermot."

"I had put it out of my head, Conn, when John went away."

A great sigh went forth from him, and his jaw tightened.

"Oh, Conn," he said, "if only last summer your father had let us marry!"

"If he had, Dermot," her voice came sure and grave, "it would not have been the same. We were boy and girl then, and we would have quarreled like boy and girl, and pulled against each other. And we would have hated each other sometimes, loving all the time. But the year of trouble has made a man of you, Dermot, strong and grave. And out of my heart the year has taken the useless, selfish things, and made me a woman, quiet-tongued and wise. I still have the dreams, Dermot," she said, "the dreams of far countries and strange places, but I want to see them with you. We might have been sweethearts a year ago, Dermot, but now we are lovers; do you see?"

"What are we going to do, Conn? My God! what are we going to do?"

"Leave that for the moment, Dermot. Leave that for a week, or a month maybe, or any time. There will never come again an evening like this evening. This is the first flower of the year, and later there are fairer, finer flowers, but with the first flower of the year spring has begun.

"I love to lie on your shoulder, Dermot. I am above the ground. The earth is spinning like a top beneath me, and above me the moon is sailing like a ship."

"I don't know, Conn," he said shyly, "but— I 've felt lately my heart was wrinkling like an old man's forehead, and to-night it 's smooth again, smooth and clear.

"I 've been thinking about you, Conn, all the time you were away."

"Tell me, Dermot. Tell me, dear."

"I was thinking, up on the mountain when the ewes were lambing, how I wished you were there in the cold, clean night—if you were sweetheart

and wife to me, Conn.   And when you were tired
and sleepy I would wrap you up, and lay you
gently down in the friendly mountain dark, and go
ahead working while you slept."

"One day, Dermot, we will go together."

"And in summer when the grass is high, we will
go down to the mowers," he told her, "and be by
them when the scythes bite into the fields of clover.   And we will come on the nest of the
meadow-lark, Conn, and I shall take it from the
mown hay, and give it to you."

"And I will warm the fledglings at my breast,"
she murmured.

"And the nest of the wild bees, Conn.   The
mowers will topple that, and I will beat away the
surly outlaw bees, and give you the honey of the
comb."

"Wild honey of wild bees, Dermot."

"Ah, but when, Conn?   When?" he asked bitterly.

"Soon, heart, soon."

She drowsed for a moment, then started up.

"Oh, Dermot! where are the shadows gone?
We are in the full light of the moon."

Time, that had stood still for them, had not for
earth or moon.   They had swung on their spheres.
And where had been shadows was light now, and
where had been light was shadow.

"Oh, Dermot, I must go in. You must go home."

"No, Conn."

"Yes, Dermot. The servants would soon be searching for me, and at Dermotstown they will be worrying. Come."

They went up the garden path together. Her great black shawl was thrown back, and there showed now her white shoulder, her apple-green frock.

"You will be cold, Conn. Put your shawl around you."

"Cold?" she said. "I shall never be cold any more. Nor lonely. Nor miserable any more."

He stopped her and wrapped her around in the long silky folds.

"You will do what I tell you," he said, in his old domineering way.

"Yes, Dermot," she said, with a new strange meekness.

They went into the house together. She ordered the dog-cart around for him. They stood by the great fire in the hall.

"Conn," he said, "are you sorry you told me?"

She kept looking at the fire. She said: "I am not properly dressed. I should be wearing, this moment, some great vestment of red and gold. Something magnificent, something proud."

There was a grinding of wheels, and the pawing of a horse on the gravel outside. She turned and raised her face to him, standing on the toes of her little feet.

"Good night, Dermot. Good night, my lover."

He bent and kissed the sweet dark mouth.

"God keep you, my little Conn."

He stepped into the dog-cart beside the groom. His heart was singing. His whole soul was singing, and into his mind grotesquely came the queer uninvited statement: "To-night I shall sleep."

§ 3

They went together up Three-Rock Mountain, to see the world beneath their feet. They went together to Bray and southward, listening to the chiming waves. Over his farm he went, giving necessary orders, conferences, and with him she came too. At times she was merry as a cricket, singing little snatches of song. At times she was withdrawn and grave. At times the snatched kiss was an apparent necessary joy to her, and at times she was coy, blushing like some child out of a school. And always she was beautiful. They had a faculty of being silent together, each aware of the other, in harmony, dreaming dreams. One would stop for a moment, looking at something, and the other would stop, too, and look, as at a house, or a tree, or a field, or children playing. Once at Blackrock, Dermot looked over the parapet, and underneath ran the little private path from Frascati to the sea, down which Lord Edward Fitzgerald and his wife Pamela, the King of France's niece and Philippe Egalité's daughter, used wander in the short days of their happiness. He so soon to die in Dublin Castle, and she to go into exile, and the King of France and Philippe Egalité, their royal heads to be sheared from their bodies and to drop into a basket such as might hold vegetables. There was the path, there the moss upon the wall. All these were dead now and history, and here was the path where once had trod, night and morning, the great Irish rebel, and the beautiful French lady with the Liberty cap. He came out of his dreams.

"It 's raining," he observed.

"It 's been raining for ten minutes," Connaught smiled at him, "Dermot, my dear!"

She seemed to be always looking at him, smiling at him. He would turn to find her gazing, with her very sweet smile.

"Do you mind me looking at you, Dermot? Do you mind me looking at you all the time?

Sometimes your face is like a boy's, a boy of eighteen. And then it changes, and gets keen. It gets the hard look of hawks. Then you look like your great ancestor, Dermot, who stole Grania from Fionn, the King of Ireland. Sometimes you have the face of a boy and other times you have a hero's face."

"And you, you are always beautiful, Conn."

"Am I beautiful, Dermot? No. I am just young, and pretty, maybe. If I look beautiful it is because you love me, and I know, and my heart shines in my face."

At times they would go into Dublin, because she wanted to buy something. She would disappear for a half-hour, while Dermot was attending to business of the estate. And when they met again, she would have bought a new frock or hat, or some useless lovely thing.

"But you 've got hundreds, Conn."

"Yes, I know, Dermot. But somehow—I want to celebrate.

"And Dermot," she said, "I want to be nicely dressed when I 'm out with you. I 'm not half nice enough when I come along with you."

"Conn, my sweetheart," he turned and said to her, "if you were on the top of the most barren mountain in the barren west, and wearing nothing but sackcloth, and your hair disheveled in the mountain wind, you would be most beautiful, Conn, always most beautiful."

"Hush, Dermot, hush! In the street, too, and so loud! You must n't say things like that," she rebuked him, and thanked him with her eyes.

And when that was done, they would wander aimlessly through Dublin, and find themselves in the slums perhaps, the worst slums in the world, tenements that once were peers' mansions, in one room of which a whole squalid family lived, in a room whose panels Angelica Kauffmann had painted, whose ceiling was of the brothers Adam, whose mantel was the equal for beauty of anything Europe could show—ah, the wasted city! Or they would go along the quays by the Custom-house and see the vessels from oversea, the French boats from Saint Malo, whose sailors wore red tam o'shanter caps, or great Norwegian vessels, bringing pine and seeking granite, or some Indiaman with slant-eyed lascars shivering in the Northern cold. Or passing northward through a gap in the streets, they would catch a glimpse of the eternal mountains, so near as to make the heart rise, while above them in the streets the seagulls piped their long querulous note. Or stopping by one of the canals they would see the great locks open.

The locks had always fascinated him, hypnotized him, and now, watching a barge come past, he waited, Connaught by his side, to see the first great gates open, and the water gush and roar, like a cataract. The traces of the horses had been cast loose, and the squat boat had entered the level, and now the lower gates were being opened and the upper shut, and the barge dropped on the emptying water, as in some device of melodrama. The man at the great tiller looked at Dermot silently, aloofly. His face had the strange Spanish look of Galway men. There was the odor of burning turf from the barge chimney, and somewhere the acrid perfume of the crushed berries of the mountain ash. The look of the man of Galway and the odors of the west country called up something deep in family and race within him, until he was no longer by a Dublin street, but on the moors of Galway whence his family sprang. It was thither that Dermot, the great founder of his tribe, had brought the stolen Grania, when he was flying from the vengeance of Fionn, and there he had fought the ancient pre-Christian Fenians, and conquered. And people sang of great Dermot and sweet Grania until this day. A wild family they had been, the children of the Prince of Coolavin, raiding the Spaniards of Galway City, and asking tribute of Norman knights, and hanging the enemy clans. And when they wanted anything they took it, paying the price in battle and bloodshed, were it a woman, even, and she married to another man. How of that old chief who had stolen the Norman baron's lady? He had been asked to return the lady for the sake of her honor, and his reply had been that it was more to this lady's honor to be loving friend to the Mc-Dermot than to be his Norman Lordship's wedded wife. As indeed it was, Dermot thought to himself, did he love her, and she him. And a great desire took him, to be back in ancient times, and he would have had Connaught from under John's nose, and carried her to the house of the head of his clan, and there would be welcome for him and her and protection, were he right or wrong, and men to fight beside him to the last broken sword, such was ancient loyalty.

It seemed to him unbearable that the world had grown so tame and cluttered, fearing the newspapers and one's neighbor's tongue, and the bitter laughter of envious people who are glad to see the great pulled down, as they think. All these conventions, rules, fears, how they obscured the fear of doing wrong and the clear face of God! And were he and Connaught to go off now, loving each other, and meaning to be loyal to each other all their days and after days, what was wrong in that? John D'Arcy was only an incident, a sordid trick

of circumstance. Why couldn't they? Why
shouldn't they go together to some purple lake
island of the West and be happy there? Ah, but
friends, relations, property! All the antique sim-
plicity had gone and with it the faculty of doing
right, freely. One had to do right according to
rule.

"Dermot—" Connaught touched his arm—
"what are you thinking of? Why is your face so
hard suddenly? You have got the hard look of
a hawk. Why, Dermot?"

But he wouldn't tell her.

§ 4

She had come over to Dermotstown to dinner,
and after dinner Anne had left them on an excuse
of letters to write. They had said nothing to her,
and had been circumspect as deacons before her,
but it is hard to deceive the eyes of old people,
especially when they, too, have loved. And
though Anne must have been disturbed, in her
sweet Quaker soul, at this new and fearsome problem presented to her, yet there was such a happiness in her boy's face—she would leave them together for a little while in their happiness, she

must have thought. Soon they would have trouble enough, God knows, and for the young to be happy—surely there could n't be much sin in it!

Because it was not yet dark without, and because it seemed a pity to go into the lighted drawing-room while it was yet the soft spring April day, they had gone down the long avenue of trees, all gallant in their bright new green. And while they were there the night came on them, and the stars came out, one by one in the spring sky. They turned to go back. Connaught was silent. She leaned down and plucked a blade of grass from alongside the avenue. She bit at it mechanically. Dermot could see the white of her young teeth. He knew her brow was dark, was heavy with thought. She turned suddenly. She was a dim sweet shape in the dusk, and her face was vague, like some dim sweet flower, some pure star flower.

"Dermot," she asked, "are you sure you love me?" She paused. Her voice was grave. She was not love-making. "Tell me—I must know— are you sure? Is there a great faith in you, Dermot," she asked seriously, piteously, "that you love me?"

"Before God, Connaught, I love you."

"And before God, Dermot," she whispered, because her voice seemed not enough to say it with, she must say it with the breathing of the soul,

"I love you. Where is your hand, Dermot? Give it me. See." She took it quickly and pressed it to her young breasts. "There has never been a hand there before, Dermot, nor ever will be again, Dermot, excepting yours only. So that I know you love me, and I love you."

He felt his knees weak. His head bowed. He seemed to have been admitted for an instant into some tremendous sanctuary. There were no words to say. No words were important enough to say.

"Dermot, shall we go away together, you and I?

"Listen, Dermot," she went on, "I am not John D'Arcy's. I am yours. And you are nobody's but mine. And we love each other, for good, forever. Where is the wrong?"

"I thought so, too, Conn," he managed to say.

"Dermot, shall we go away together, to far cities, where none will find us, none know us? And before we go, Dermot, we will go together to some old lonely church, and kneel down, and say, Dermot—" her voice grew husky—" 'God, this is Dermot and Connaught, and we can't have a priest, our Father, but we love each other truly, and will be true to each other for ever and ever.' Shall we, Dermot?

"And after years we can come back, Dermot,

and people will have forgotten us, and if we have no friends, my dear, we have each other. Oh, Dermot," she asked, "shall we go?

"Dermot, why don't you speak?" she said tremulously, "why don't you say something?"

He stood beside her, dumb, no words coming to him; heavy, oppressed; locked up, he seemed, impotent.

"Oh, Dermot!" she said, her voice trembling, and "Oh, Dermot!" with a little shudder of horror.

"Oh, Dermot!" she wailed. "You don't speak because you think I am a bad woman, a cheap woman, Dermot. Oh, God!" she cried suddenly, "where shall I hide my head?"

A choking little sob came from her. She turned and began running in the dark, running blindly down the dark tunnel of trees. Her feet ran piteously. Her sobs broke out piteously. With darkness and tears she could not see. She left the path and a tree struck her. She sobbed again. And suddenly Dermot was free. With swift light springs he was after her; caught her in his arms. She struggled to be loose.

"Oh, let me go, Dermot! let me go! I must go and hide, Dermot."

"I shall never let you go, Conn."

"Let me go, Dermot. You think I'm an evil

woman, a cheap reckless woman, because I asked should we go away? Oh, God! what a fool a woman is to let her heart out! Loose me, Dermot; let me go."

"Conn, if I were never to see you again, the last sweet and lovely thing I should remember was your saying what you said. If you let your heart out, you let it out to me, your own love. I pick up what you said, Conn, and I put it away in the deepest corner of my soul."

She sobbed against his breast, her slight small body shaking like a sapling in a great storm.

"And Conn, I was thinking of that too. That was what I was thinking yesterday at the locks, when my face was so hard. My face was hard, because it is impossible, little Conn. You see—"

She was so troubled, he so serious, that they had not heard the light step on the avenue. A voice came to them, sweet, a little alarmed.

"Where are you, children? Children, where are you?"

Connaught raised her tearful face in the dark.

"Yes," she gulped a sob, "yes. I see, dear heart."

"Connaught! Dermot!"

He left Connaught for an instant, and went up toward the figure coming through the green tunnel of trees.

"Is that thee, Dermot? Where is little Connaught?"

"Mother Anne," he said, "will you go into the house, please? Connaught can't go in for a moment. She has been crying."

"Dermot, my son!" and Dermot knew his mother was trembling.

"Mother Anne, will you trust me? And will you trust Connaught, Mother Anne?" He put his hands on her shoulders, and little by little the trembling ceased.

"There is no evil in thee, Dermot my son," she said at last. "And in little Connaught there is no evil, either. Yes. I will trust you." And she went back up the avenue to the lighted house.

XVIII

§ 1

HE walked up and down the avenue of Dermotstown, slapping his boot with his riding-
crop, his brow now puckered, now smiling. The
solution of the whole matter was so simple, so
obvious, and he had n't thought of it. Good
Lord! what good was he, anyhow! A little
straightness, and a little confidence, and all would
be solved. If he were a women he would have
danced, so pleased he was, but, following his own
kind, he cursed delightedly. Old Neddy Joe,
from the porch of the lodge, regarded him with
his shrewd ancient eye.

"Ah, sure, Master Dermot, 't is a grand thing
surely to hear you cursing the way you are. It
doubles the brightness of the spring day, for I
know the way of the McDermots. When they
curse they 're happy and when they smile they 're
dangerous, and when they 're calm, begad, everything 's lost. My dotey boy, what 's made you so
cheerful this April morning?"

" 'T is something that should n't, Neddy Joe,

and that's a discovery I made: that I've no brains."

"Brains," the old man pondered, "is overrated. Sure, what's the use of brains except to make money? And money clouds old age with suspicion. You never knew whether they're fond o' you, or fond o' your money. Look at that daughter o' mine. She comes and shouts at me: 'Are you all right, old man?' and there's kindness in it. But if I had money it would be a valet coming in to me, and saying, 'Good morning, Mr. Hoolihan,' out loud, and under his breath, 'you old devil, are n't you dead yet?' Sure, that's all the use brains is for, to make money."

"You're wrong, Neddy Joe. They must be useful for something."

"Master Dermot, when a man dies, he's summed up by this: Does he leave a hole in the world? 'T is many is the rich man I've seen going to his grave with one carriage, and many's the poor man with miles of funeral. A great heart and a daring mind are more than the brains of colleges. Who does the world feel lonely after? Soldiers and poets and an odd saint. The soldiers that do the great dashing things are not the soldiers with brains. Don't I remember, myself, at the Crimean War, when the Light Brigade charged the Russian guns? That was a foolish and crazy thing to do, but the memory of it will make men's blood tingle forever.   And as for the poets, that make you say, when you lay down their books, 'Is n't this the mean small existence I lead?' Sure, if they had the brains they would n't see life that way at all, but know it for the poor dirty affair it is.   And if the poets stopped writing they 'd be only cantankerous fellows, without a friend in the world, instead of people putting up with their tantrums and treating them like lord's daughters.   Now, as for saints, there was that fellow, Saint Francis, that had the birds following him, the friend of the birds he was, and if he had brains, sure it would be in a bank he 'd find himself, making money by the basketful.   And if a bird came near him to disturb him at his figures, it would be reaching for the blunderbus he 'd be. There was also that other saint, Saint Martin, that gave half his cloak to the beggar, though I 've heard it argued," Neddy Joe said, "that he was the mean kind of saint, for if he was the real gentleman of a saint he 'd have handed him the whole of it—"

A groom ran down with Ginger II, the fourteen-hand four-year-old pony Dermot had ordered saddled.   Neddy Joe looked up with pain.

"Is it off on your flippings and jollities you are,

Master Dermot, and leaving me and my wise discourse?"

"It is," said Dermot, and swung into the saddle. He pushed his riding-crop into his boot.

"Your Honor," said Neddy Joe tartly, "do you mind what you told me about your discovery in yourself?"

"That I had no brains, Neddy Joe?"

"To me," said Neddy Joe, "that is no discovery at all."

Dermot held the pony to a trot down the road for a little and then broke it into its sweet swinging canter. He turned up the road on the mountainside that led toward Three-Rock and the Lamb Doyle's, and thence to Rathfarnham. There were matters he wanted to think out, to decide. Connaught must be told, but she wouldn't care now, and his mother—she must be told. And he would have to find a clergyman who would understand. His old tutor at Trinity, the sweet white-haired old gentleman, the Greek scholar, who was so desolate over the gaps in Dermot's scholarship and so proud of his standing in sport. Yes, he would understand. But there would be formalities to be gone through, proofs needed. Would it not be better for them both to go to London, and say nothing of difficulties? Dermot wished he had a friend, some wise friend to discuss it with. But all his friends were like himself, he thought, a bit stupid, willing to plunge through difficulties, but unused to such a delicate matter as this. They could only say: "Well, I don't know much about things like this. This is deep-sea stuff. But I 'm with you, old son." And that was warming to the heart, but no use at all.

He passed the Leopardstown race-track, the golf-links of Foxrock, where benign old gentlemen in red coats were hacking bitterly at small white balls and saying very evil phrases, or moving with overpowering dignity down the fairway. He passed the Soldiers' Home. The road from the mountains into Dundrum crossed the highway to Rathfarnham.

> "And will Ireland then be free?
>   Says the *Shan Van Voght*.
> And will Ireland then be free?
>   Says the *Shan Van Voght*.
> Yes, Ireland will be free,
> From the centre to the sea—"

He reined in the pony sharply. The soft baritone, and the rebel song made him for an instant think that the Citizen was near. He looked forward and back of him. He glanced to the left. Between the trees of the road leading to Dundrum he saw the singer, a mountainy man in the slouch hat and coarse clothes of a mountainy man, leading a little brown donkey. The creels on the donkey were laden with turf, and piled high on its back were brooms of heather with handles of peeled ash, for sale probably among the cottages of Stillorgan. So that there seemed to be an immensity of load, and very little brown donkey. But the load was very light.

> "Yes, Ireland will be free,
> From the centre to the sea.
> And hurrah for liberty!
> Says the *Shan Van Voght*."

Ah, if it had only been the Citizen, Dermot thought, he could have advised him, helped him. Very unreasonably he silently damned the mountainy man as he prepared to ride on.

And then a small black dog trotted out of the hedge where he had been hunting and looked up genially at the mountainy man. Dermot had seen that dog before. Where? At the Hannastown races, he remembered. The dog that led the blind man. But he might be mistaken. He took another look at the mountainy singer, and he noticed he had n't the loose springing step of mountain folk. He was stiff at the knee, as horsemen are. He clapped his heels to the pony's side, and hurled him forward down the Dundrum road.

"Citizen!" he called. "Wait, Citizen."

The rush of the four-year-old brought him up to the mountainy man with a rush. The mountainy man turned softly around as on a pivot. And as Dermot reined up, he looked into a short blue barrel, sinister as a snake's head.

"Oh, young Dermot!" the Citizen said casually. He tossed the weapon into the air, caught it as it fell, slipped it into his pocket, barrel upward. It was like a conjuror's trick—now you see it, now you don't—but Dermot was white.

"Do you have to be like that all the time?" he asked. "Always on guard, always armed?"

"Ah, yes," the Citizen said. "But you get used to it, you don't mind. Still and all, this morning I'm rather sick of it."

Dermot slipped from the pony, walked alongside.

"I suppose all this—" the Citizen's eyes were troubled, dreamy. He waved an arm vaguely, "is nothing to you. These green fields, and heather mountains and little rivers, and the blue flowers and the yellow flowers and the white flowers. How would you like to live in a country where it's yellow sand, and ugly white houses and coarse palms? And in summer the wind is so hot it chokes you, and in winter it's sometimes so cold, you die."

"I thought Africa was always warm."

"Look here," the Citizen grumbled, "I've a good mind to resign my commission, and go to England and tell the king I'll be good, if he'll let me live in peace on Three-Rock Mountain, and cut turf and make heather brooms for a living. And now and again I'll put off my old clothes and dress and come down and have dinner with you. What do you think, young Dermot?"

"You won't," Dermot told him.

"Of course I won't! Don't I know that? When this job's through, I'll go back. And then I'm going across the desert to Timbuctu, with an expedition. I'll get there and back if some filthy Arab does n't plug me, and if all works out right, I'll be decorated and kissed on both cheeks by a fat general officer who smells of scented soap. That's glory!" he laughed. "And how are you getting along, young Dermot?"

"Citizen," Dermot said, "you're exactly the man I wanted to see. I want your advice."

"If it's anything about cavalry tactics," the Citizen told him, "you've come to the best man in the world. But if it's anything else, my advice is n't worth a tinker's curse.

"Look here, young Dermot," he said suddenly, "I'm in a rotten grumbling mood to-day. I don't mean it. Come, tell me what's wrong. Look, let's move off the road down the lane here, and we'll sit and smoke it over. Hobble and spancel the pony. If I can help you, I will."

The lane twisted from the road in a narrow angle, to avoid encroaching on some conical field. The grass was lush on it, and it led evidently to a house long unoccupied. Beside it, on each side the blackthorn bushes rose in proud standards of white foam, and along one edge of it ran a little rill down-hill clear as crystal. And under the blackthorn bushes were clusters of yellow primroses, and harebells, blue as the sky. It was like some sweet retiring-place of Springtime's. The hobbled pony moved along the lane. The little brown donkey followed as if to make friends. The small black dog rested on its haunches. Dermot and the Citizen found a granite boulder and sat on it.

"Well?" the Citizen asked. Dermot felt suddenly shy of unmasking his affairs before this sharp capable man. He passed him cigarettes. The Citizen eyed the large gold case with the Mc-Dermot crest in the corner. He eyed it with surprise. "A present from a lady," Dermot explained.

"Ah, I thought so." The Citizen seemed relieved.

"Citizen," Dermot ventured, "do you remember my telling you I had love for a certain lady?"

"Yes."

"Citizen, I have discovered that this lady is— well, is fond of me."

"John D'Arcy's wife?"

"The girl John D'Arcy pretended to marry," Dermot corrected. The Citizen was silent.

"Citizen," Dermot went on, "if John D'Arcy were n't alive now, this lady and I would marry. But you see the difficulty he has put us in. She is not married to him, and yet she is married. You know how sacred everything about marriage is in this country."

The Citizen nodded.

"Well, Citizen, I thought this: that I would tell her exactly how things were, about your sister, and the little baby, and the marriage in Paris. And that the marriage of herself and John D'Arcy was no marriage. And I thought, seeing how we —we love each other, and mean to be true to each other, we could slip away and be married and none know. Of course, Citizen, we could n't live in the house, but just seem friends. But it would bind us, do you see? Do you see what I mean, Citizen?"

The Citizen was silently studying the grass on the lane. He seemed all ears and brain.

"You see, it would give me rights to protect

this lady, if anything turned up. And if the scandal broke, it would break on my head, and my head is hard. Also, if I had the right, I could force John into a position when he would disappear, with some seeming of being dead, and we could marry in public, marry again. If I had the right, Citizen, do you see?

"I just thought, Citizen," he went on, finding the man did not answer, "that I would tell you of this, and act fair and aboveboard. Somehow I would like to have your consent, because of your sister and her baby. She might feel bad at thinking her husband had twisted up another life, and it might relieve her to know that it had all come right. You're at one end of the mess D'Arcy made, and we're at the other. We can fix this up between us, and none ever need be the wiser. Isn't it possible, Citizen? Isn't it all right?"

"I'm afraid," the Citizen said slowly, "it isn't possible."

"Look, Citizen, you don't understand. If John D'Arcy married my little lady while your sister was alive, the second marriage doesn't count. And this lady and I are legally free to marry, although it would be—oh, out of the question to let people know about D'Arcy and the trickery of him."

"You can't," said the Citizen.

"But why, Citizen? Surely your sister would n't mind?"

"My sister would not have minded. There was nothing my sister liked more than to see people happy. But, Dermot, my sister is dead."

Dermot looked at him, not understanding.

"D'Arcy does n't know it, and few but myself know it, but my sister died in a little Russian town on the twenty-third of May last. And D'Arcy and your little lady were married in July.

"I hate to tell you, but—you see."

Dermot was silent for a minute.

"I 'm very sorry about your sister, Citizen," he said at last. "And the little baby—where is it?"

"Dead, too."

"I 'm very sorry."

He rose from the boulder and went in a dazed fashion toward the pony, and, bending down, removed hobble and spancel and winding the ropes, returned them in a mechanical meticulous way to the donkey's creel from which he had taken them. He took the pony by the bridle and came to where Hogan still sat on the gray boulder.

"Citizen," he said, "you should have told me this that night on Tory Island. Things have happened since then that, had I known, might not have happened, or might have been avoided. And my heart was raised high. You should have told me, Citizen."

"I kept silent," Hogan said slowly, "because I thought to spare you pain. I didn't want you to know," he explained, "that D'Arcy had any rights over your little lady."

"It was kind of you, Citizen, I know." He paused for a minute. "Citizen," he began, "you said you were going on a long expedition when you got to Africa. You were going to Timbuctu across the desert. Could you take me with you, Citizen? I am tough and strong and a good horseman. And though I know nothing of soldiering, yet I don't think I am afraid of anything. I will try to make myself of use, Citizen. Will you take me?"

Hogan rose and, coming over, put a hand on Dermot's shoulder.

"I won't take you, Dermot," he said. "You will stay here by your little friend and by your mother and by your duty, and by your land. You will stay where you have been put, Dermot, and not break and run.

"And besides, there is a feeling within me that you and your little friend will be all right soon. I have a sense that before I leave I shall meet

D'Arcy, and the day on which I meet D'Arcy, D'Arcy will die."

"I don't think that will help us very much, Citizen. In the first place, you will not meet D'Arcy. And secondly, if you did you would find it a hard thing to kill a man in that manner. And, again, it would be a very wrong thing, because a punishment like that should not be inflicted privately and without terrible cause—"

"As to the right and wrong," the Citizen said sharply, "it is not for you to judge, who only know what D'Arcy and I have chosen to tell you. As to killing a man, though I am a soldier and have killed and caused many to be killed, it is a hard thing. It is a memory that sours many a night and many a morning. So you can understand how serious I am about D'Arcy. Besides, I am not sure I 'll be killing a man."

"Is he such a devil then, Citizen?"

"No," Hogan said, "he is not a devil. He is a queer strange being without a sense of right or justice. He is like a faun or some grotesque creature out of a book of magic. When a bad man dies he is punished, somehow. When a good man dies he achieves peace, but when John D'Arcy dies he will be just dead. It is as though he were no son of his father, but that his mother had fallen sometime asleep in a wood, and the soulless things—" Here he laughed suddenly. "I'd better get out of this damned country. I'm becoming as crazy and superstitious as any one in it. But one thing—" his face hardened— "anything I do against John D'Arcy I accept responsibility for. And neither you nor your friend have anything to do in it. The conduct of this man, Dermot, killed Maeve, my sister, and her death killed my father. There was such love between my sister and me that she in Russia and I in Africa would feel when all was not well with the other. And my father was the hero of my youth. And these two great people shall not die and John D'Arcy walk the earth.

"Look, Dermot, I put this out of my head now, until the appropriate time, and if I can, you can. Be on your way now, lad. I shall see you somewhere before I go. Jump into your saddle, lad, and be on your way!"

XIX

§ 1

IT occurred to Dermot now that when he met
Connaught again, to-morrow, or the day after,
that he would not be the same to her. There
would be a constraint of manner, a cloud somewhere that she would be quick to see. Though
he could argue and passionately feel that her
marriage to John made no difference, yet out
of some occult chamber of his being a voice came:
"It does make a difference, Dermot. Yes, it
does."

It was a queer thing, that while he thought she
was not married to John, the love-making between him and her was natural, and if there were
obstacles in the way, yet they were only obstacles.
But now that she was married to him, with bell
and book and candle, with formula of religion
and of law, now he felt it was wrong. He
would n't say wrong, but just not right. Ah,
that was n't the word, either. Something, something was wrong.

He thought: "Am I just a damned little prig,

345

who won't love the girl I love who loves me,
because she is, in the horrible vulgar phrase, a
married woman? Or am I a coward, afraid of
a scandal?" And he said to himself: "I don't
think I am a prig. And if I am a coward in this
thing, it's not for myself I fear. But the thing
is somewhere, somehow out of kilter, in the
country speech."

He wandered off into the gardens, to think this
matter out, and sitting under the big horse-
chestnut tree, the brown deerhound at his feet,
the soft April evening took hold of him, all the
natural sights and sounds of it. And with one
portion of his brain he found himself discovering
that nothing jarred. The sounds, the song of the
thrush, the blackbird's deeper note, the shrill
crooning of the wood-pigeons—they did not jar.
Nor the colors of the flowers, the blue of the
bluebells, the throng of little daisies, nor, in the
distance the bronze tulips, the yellow primroses—
they did not jar. And trees that one might think
were untrammeled majestic growths—yet about
them was an exact unity of design. Their center
was delicately balanced. If on one side was a
great weight of foliage yet that was counter-
poised by some heavy unobtrusive limb. All was
delicate as a mason's level. Nothing jarred.

He thought now, as the April sun went down,

and the birds hushed their soft eager singing, and
the daisies closed their shy pretty faces, that the
love between him and Connaught was as natural
as all these—the bird's singing, the blooming of
the flowers, and the tall, splendid trees. It was
not in any natural quality that it jarred. One
knew very well, Dermot thought, when a thing
was bad and when it was good. A false man, or
a bad woman or a mean action—one knew that.
Within you something said, "Stop." And with
Connaught, he felt, everything was so good—so
good for him. The warm firm hand that was so
soft and yet had so much life to it. Her eyes,
now golden as the little golden speckles on a
trout, now dark as dark wine—in them was no evil
or cunning, but just a sweet soft melody, like a
bird's singing. And her mouth like a berry, like
some cunningly divided flower, and the frank
white teeth of her, and her eyebrows, soft and
delicate as moss. And the rich black hair, so
soft, so full of life. All this was good. And
when she lay on his shoulder, so that he was aware
of her entire being, of her arms, her young bosom
—all this was good, good and reverenced. And
the soft drowsiness of kisses was not a drunkenness, but a sweet hushing of existence, so that one
could feel the trees growing and understand the
benign friendship of the moon. There was no

spot in that. In all of this, were they to adventure even to the uttermost of love, there would be no blot, no unbeauty.

"But naturalness and beauty are not enough, at least for us," he thought being human. "There is within me a higher destiny than a tree's, or a singing bird's. What do I give to this love, these arms, this heart warm on the mouth?" Ah, warm heart!

"I give it protection," he said.

"Very well, then, decide to give it protection. Let arms be closer, the lips turn, the hair fall in soft perfumed rills. Let the swooning of love come, like some sweet welcome death. And into the dark comes a presence, comes a hand on the shoulder. Comes, say, John!

"You! How this intimacy? By what right?"

"I love her, and she loves me."

"That may be true. But this lady, by the custom of peoples, by the law of the land, and by the rites of religion is sealed to me. I have made a contract with God and this lady. And to that instrument you are no party."

"But you have n't the contract."

"That is a matter for settlement between God and me and this lady. You are an outsider, a stranger. You have no standing.

"And you know it!"

Yes, one would know it, and be helpless before, ah, the horrible situation! The woman who looked for protection and strength, and the chill creeping over her heart slowly as she realized that it was n't all as easy as she had dreamed in her mad passionate dream. The broken hearts, the shamed faces, the tangled lives.

No, when love was given freely and taken, a man must be able to say: "This is my house. Come over the doorstep and God bless your little feet! Now are you in your own home, and here you will be at peace. Outside is the fighting world—leave that to me. Here you will live and have your children, dark-haired children and fair-haired ones. And here is a fire that burns for you, and here you will have your own familiar things, your pets and books, your sewing and writing and music. And this arm that grows from my shoulder will protect you and this head shall think for you. And you are protected from everything, except fate, against which there is no protection. This house which was my house is now ours, and we, who were two people, are now one. So help us God!" The house might be poor, the arm weak, the head stupid, but they had to be given, else one could not take love.

A woman might give her heart and her body,

forgetful of all their mortalities, but the man who took her heart and her body and could not give her a house and an arm and a head, he was a cheat.

He could n't give Connaught a home, now she was married. Another arm was pledged to her, another head.

Very well, then, he could n't take Connaught's love.

"I shall have to tell her everything," he thought. He pondered whether he had the right to tell her of Maeve Hogan, and how John had married her and left her. How would he get around that? Ah, well, he 'd puzzle it out. But tell her of all this he would, for it was impossible to go on as they had been doing. Better never to kiss again, or have any intimacies, but just a sweet friendship in the heart, a strong secret bond that only they two would know of and that would abide forever. For dreams of their living under the same roof must cease now. He must never think again of long evenings together, of the lighted candles and the broad stairs, the sweet intimacy of a common room—the glowing fire of sea-coal, her dim hair, her pale nightgown. Her hand holding his while she slept. Ah, God, no! Ah, well, there was always eternity, he remembered, but in eternity we are spirits, and there would be no breath from her, soft as a soft wind, nor a sweet head to nestle in his shoulder as a bird settles in its nest. This eternity, he thought, is a cold thing—

Well—he set his mouth and shoulders—there's an end to that. And thank God! he said, thank God, they had not become closer. "I don't know, though, I don't know," he rebelled and regretted. There was the straight road for him, and there was the dim nun-like life for Conn, and an end of strange fears for his mother, whom they both loved. "And after all," he thought, "we still love each other, don't we? can't we?"

If in her loneliness, in her troubles, at Glenmalure, it was any comfort to her to know that there was a heart in which she dwelt, well, the heart was always hers. If she knew she had a lover, who could not speak of love, except what his eyes would betray, but would go to the end of the world for her, would lay down his life for her, was there any help in that for her? If all the world were to crash around her ears, she would remember she still had Dermot. And when they met—they would meet in company—a touch of the hand, a smile.

And God knows about John! If it happened that he should die—

He put the thought from him angrily. It was

such a mean ungentlemanly thing to ponder over. Of the Citizen's threat he took little notice. John would keep out of Hogan's way. And besides, shooting John was like a situation out of a play. Still and all, in Ireland people were always thinking of a situation out of a play and making life fall in step with it, and human life was never held very highly in Ireland, a future world being so real and near—just over the hill. Killing people was all right in a good wholesome fight when you didn't know what you were doing and didn't care much. But to remove a man after due meditation, it was so undignified, so damned Italian.

Of course it was possible that John might die. But he found himself thinking: "I do not wish that John should die." To sit watching for John to die, so that he might marry Conn—it was a sort of vulturish, ghoulish position. And thoughts take strange intangible forms, like the shadows of bad ugly people, and who knows too, he thought superstitiously, that thoughts do not help to kill? However— If he and Conn were ever to marry, they must marry with no ugly memories, no shameful shadows.

He might be a fool; he was not sure he was not. Practical hard-headed people would say, "Take love when it is offered." Or they would say: "Won't you be glad when John is dead?

Of course you will, and why shouldn't you? Look at the birds; what do they care for marriage ties? Look at the game of the fields: they kill and slaughter. What is natural is not wrong."

"And yet," he thought, "if I thought these unworthy thoughts, and did these unworthy things, could Connaught love me? would I be the sort of person Connaught would love and trust? would this big deerhound care for me? would the great jumping horses trust me on their backs? Are these scruples just foolishness or are they the essence of right? Am I a fool or a gentleman?"

And something cynical within him said, "Where's the difference?"

But he put that quirk aside. "Your practical man," he thought, "may be satisfied, and self-satisfied, but does he never feel a little unclean?"

§ 2

Dermot sat late at dinner, and late with his mother in the drawing-room of Dermotstown. The annual meeting of the Society of Friends was to take place in Belfast soon, and Anne was preparing to go, and she was thinking of and talking of this one and that one. A great week it would be, the gentle Quaker folk coming from all parts of Ireland to visit and be together. They would stay at one another's houses, and this week in the Northern city would be great preparations of beds and victuals. Big linen magnate and poor farmer, they would gather as friends. And out of funny little nooks of villages in the North would come figures out of another century, men with old-time Quaker hats and coats and quiet-faced women in Friends' bonnets. And all the things to be discussed. The business and the schools and the marriages of young people. And very serious problems too, he gathered from his mother. A member of a great Friend family had arrived at a crisis in his life. He had joined the famous Yeomanry Regiment of the North Irish Horse, and had been seen in its gay uniform. And now two Friends must wait on him and talk with him about it, and if he persisted he must resign from the Society. Dermot smiled within himself at the thought of the serious men and the recalcitrant in the cavalry uniform talking solemnly over the reasons for and against war. Ah, but it was very gentle! And he wished for a moment for the Friends' sense of peace, for the quiet Friends' God.

"Will thee come with me, Dermot?"

"No, thanks, Mother Anne."

"There is peace there, Dermot, and the heart becomes quiet as a cricket, quiet and wise."

"Some day, Mother Anne," he evaded. "Not now." But she knew in her heart that quiet gray faith was not for him, that he was uttering a kindly lie.

"It is so queer," she said; "I often think of it, that I, a little Quaker woman from overseas, should have married into such a turbulent clan."

"Does it bother you, Mother Anne, that my father was a soldier, and that Desmond died in the war?"

"No, Dermot," she said; "they were good soldiers, thy father and thy brother. They do not bother me. But thee, thee bothers me, Dermot. It hurts me to see thee sad and thy heart troubled."

"It is a mood," he said a little abruptly. "It will pass."

"Yes, Dermot," she said meekly. Ah, this queer strong, troubled son of hers, who tried to keep his heart concealed from her, but which she saw—ah, God! she saw—cut and bleeding.

He rose to say good night as she went, to light her candle for her, to kiss her cheek, so curiously soft.

"Thee will take care of thyself, when I am North, Dermot. Dermot, thee is not well."

She laid her hand on his arm. He smiled and hunched the muscle under his sleeve.

"I know, Dermot," she said. "But still, thee is not well. I think I ought to get a doctor for thee, Dermot."

"If you do, Mother Anne, I shall call the hounds and get a horse and hunt him from here to his hutch in Dublin."

"Thy great-grandfather once hunted a bailiff with a horse and hounds," she laughed.

"Good night, dear Friendly heart."

"Good night, Dermot, my son."

She stopped and spoke from the wide stairs.

"Thee will go to bed soon, Dermot?"

"Soon."

There was a sense of uneasiness on him, that made the idea of his sleeping-room, of the house itself, seem a constrained prison. All day long he had kept in his breast what the Citizen had told him—that she was married to John, married truly, legally. All his plans had been shattered, and the skein of trouble had become more tangled than ever, so tangled that it seemed hopeless now, and what to think, what to say, what to do?

He shook his head as she disappeared, and his face grew tired now, tired and grim. All the things he had mapped out in the April evening seemed futile now that night had come. This

matter of Connaught and him—it had been easy
to think and decide. But with thought and
decision the course had been only begun. Where
did one get strength to follow it out? ·And what
did one do when one's heart began to cry, cry
with sobs like a child's sobs? This existence of
Abelard and Heloise he had pictured. It was
splendid and noble, he sneered to himself, but
there were only five miles between him and
Glenmalure, five miles of hill and dale, of road
and field. He felt within him the power to spring
it in three bounds. And if all the time he were
to feel that terrible compelling tug— No, he
must get to business and put it on a firm honest
basis.

He felt he wanted to get into the air and think.
He slipped out of the side way, through the servants' region, down the old stone flags. Rory, the
red setter, rose out of nowhere seemingly and followed him. He went through the cobbled stable-
yard under the ivied wall of the gardens, under
the houses of the pigeons. The waning moon was
rising in the east. Last moon at the full he had
been in the garden of Glenmalure and Connaught
in his arms, her head against his shoulder. The
moon was full then, full and silver. And this
moon was red and waning, and soon would die.

He skirted the dairy and went out on the broad

lawn. To-morrow he would tell Conn. He would take her hands in his and break her heart. But she would believe him and trust him. He could picture her head turned aside, to hide the tears that would steal down her face, and her voice would say, "Yes, Dermot, and—I see, Dermot." And in the end her clear eye would meet his and say, "Dermot, you are right." And thus would he, who loved her so much, break her heart and his. Break her heart, he repeated, break her heart and his.

Outside here, under the waning moon, all was cold and lonely. The soft April evening had turned into the chill April night, warning that not yet was summer. And nowhere in the country-side was a light to be seen. The front of his own house—no lights were there, and the face of it seemed blind, blind and empty like a blind man's face. "So after to-morrow," he thought, "will be over life." Chill, like this April night, Spring halted in her stride, and a waning moon. A swift impetuous thought came to him, to walk across to Glenmalure, and scale the wall, and be under her window while she slept, and to steal away with the first bird song of dawn. The last time he would be with her, though she would not know. And he would send his heart up to her through the air, and it would gain her room where she slept with her dear dark head on a snowy pillow. And it would watch over her and soothe her in her sleep, only his heart. And she would never know. He would arise and walk there. He would go now.

The setter beside him rose and stiffened.

"What is it, Rory?"

He listened an instant. Faintly, from down the avenue, there sounded a light, a tired footstep. One of the maids, he thought, who has a sweetheart and who has slipped out to him. He looked at his watch. A few minutes past midnight, the faint light told him. He would move away and let her go into the house unobserved.

The setter turned to him with a soft, all but silent, whine. It wasn't one of the maids, then. It was some one who didn't have to do with the house. The setter was troubled, but not angry or afraid. The step came nearer. Dermot's heart jumped suddenly.

"Is that you, Conn?"

And the answer came, easy and natural: "Yes, Dermot. It's I."

Something in the tone alarmed him. The voice was so matter-of-fact.

"Is anything wrong?" He went forward to meet her. She was suddenly beneath him, looking up. She had a short polo coat on, and a bright scarf under it about her neck. Her head was bare. "Conn," his voice insisted, "is anything wrong?"

"John's at Glenmalure." Her voice was steady. Her eye was steady. "Please, Dermot, take me in. I'm tired."

"Did you walk over, alone, in the dark?"

"Yes."

He brought her into the house, into the drawing-room he had just left. He put his hand on her shoulder and turned her toward the shaded lamps. Her eyes were calm. Her face was calm. Her head was high. No word of love came from her, or pretty affectionate gesture. She was calm, collected. Dermot sensed she was, had been in danger. Or that matters had reached some great crisis, so cool she was. His heart thumped with pride. Ah, the blood of her mother's people, the soldier blood! When danger was present they were cold as ice.

"When did he come?"

She sat down before the fire and opened her coat. She had a thin black dinner frock on. Her slim satin shoes were dusty and misshapen from the long walk, and the garnet buckles on them sparkled grotesquely from the glow of the sea-coals.

"He came just before dinner," she said; "we

had a few words, and I went and locked myself in my room, and later slipped away."

"And you had no dinner?"

"No," she smiled.

He left her and went foraging in the dining-room, returning with all he could find there—sherry and biscuits. She was still before the fire. She had kicked the pumps off, and put out her slim feet in her heavy silk stockings toward the blaze. She drew them under her, as he entered, but then, as though ashamed of being ashamed, she put them out again.

"Do you mind, Dermot?" she said. "It was a long walk."

They were small, slender feet, muscular, like boys' feet.

"This is all I could find, Conn." He dragged forward a small table for the wine and biscuits. He poured her out a glass of the pale sherry.

"Is Aunt Anne gone to bed?"

"Shall I call her?"

"No, Dermot. Let her be. I'll slip up to the guest-room by myself. I know my way."

He watched as she sat before him, her eyes calm, her brow calm, not a quiver in her eyelids, not a tremor in her hand. So many Connaughts he had seen, and yet here was a new Connaught. He knew the laughing girl with the merry eyes, and the dreaming brooding young woman whose ear was tuned to strange distant music. And the soft warm presence of the dark head, and the sweet kissing lips that came to shy secret life when the birds and trees were silent and the sun went down. And here was a new Connaught, keen and cool, keen and cool as a knife.

She passed her wisp of handkerchief over her mouth. She dusted her fingers delicately. She took the cigarette he offered her. He waited.

"Dermot," she said, "John is changed."

"How, Conn?"

"He has taken his beard off, and he swaggers. And Dermot, he is no longer afraid."

"Then he knows," Dermot told himself, "that Maeve Hogan is dead, and that when he married Connaught he was a free man. Curse him!" Dermot thought; "he never went to America. He has been hiding somewhere, on the Continent perhaps, all the time."

"And, Dermot," Conn went on, "of the old John I was not afraid, but of this one I am. His step is so assured, Dermot. He feels he is so safe. His smile is bland. And when he looks at me with his smile, Dermot," she said in a hushed sort of voice, "I—I felt naked, before a strange rotten man."

"Blast him!" Dermot rasped viciously. "I

thought I had got rid of him for good."

"It's all right, Dermot; I know you did everything you could, but, Dermot, it was such a matter of loose ends. It couldn't last, my dear. There was bound to be a crisis.

"And so I must go away again."

A groan was wrung from him. Again the cold lonely world for her.

"My lover," she said softly, "I would have had to go anyway, didn't you know?"

"Why, Conn?" he asked her. She put out her hand and touched his for an instant, a swift trusting gesture, not the relaxation of love, but the frank touch of friendship, of very gentle friendship.

"Dermot," she said, "you here and I in Glenmalure and nothing between us but a few fields and a little ditch to jump over, and your heart and my heart aching. No, Dermot. It couldn't be."

"I know, Conn," he said, "I know."

"It would wear us. It would wear us to shadows, Dermot, and maybe, God knows," she said a little fearfully, "it would kill love. And you have your wish here, my dear heart, and your people, and I have nothing, Dermot, so it must be I who'll go away."

"But, Conn, you'll be lonely and cold again—"

"Heart, I shall never be lonely again, never

cold. I shall have you to think about, and a warmth in my heart for you, so that I shall never be cold— Listen, Dermot, I shall be like some woman whose affianced is on a long sea-voyage, or at the wars, but who she knows will return safely. And you, my dear, you 'll know I love you; you 'll know it like some immense magic word.

"Listen, Dermot; don't look so miserable, my sweetheart. This is the right way. Dear, you and I are together now for ever and ever, and it is for you to be strong and me to be wise.

"And, Dermot, it is not so bad that John has returned, for now we are taut and keen, he being here, and we are fighting together. We are not weak to-night. To-morrow we will not be weak. But if he had n't come we would have been weak and tortured."

"Ah, Conn—" he stood up and looked into the fire—"This is a little like death, Conn, your going away. And when all will be right with us, God knows. God knows, if ever," he said bitterly.

"Soon, Dermot, soon." She rose and laid a hand upon his shoulder.

"How, in God's name?" he asked. "Must we wait for John to die? Must we wait like vultures waiting for stricken game to drop? And what, even after this undignified waiting, if he lives on, outlives us both, what then?"

"Dermot," she said, "you have nothing to do with John. You have only to do with me. I have to do with John. It was I who made a contract with John.

"See, Dermot." Her voice was suddenly lowly, as passionate as his. "My heart is my own. That I give to you. John's rights are these: over my property; and Dermot, he has rights over my body. My property he can have, but me he cannot have. Not that I cheat on the bargain, Dermot, but because of the look in his eyes. He doesn't want me for honest marriage, Dermot—I could even go through with that, Dermot, and love you with my heart, my whole heart —I would just be a legal amour.

"Dermot, John D'Arcy is spoiled. He is spoiled like a piece of fruit is spoiled; corrupt. Sooner or later when I go away, man Dermot, he is going to get tangled with a woman. And then," she said with a sort of dark fury, "I am going to call on the law to free me from this unjust outrageous thing.

"Put John out of your mind, out of your life, Dermot."

Suddenly the knocker on the hall door smashed

once, with a loud shallow explosive sound.

There was a pause. Again it called, three times, peremptorily, abominably, with the obscene sound of the discharges of a revolver in a closed room.

"Put on your slippers, Conn," Dermot told her quietly, and turned to go to open the door. Something in his face disturbed her. She caught his arm. There was terror in her eyes. She ran past him to the door of the drawing-room and put her back to it.

"If this is John," she said, "promise me, Dermot, you will do nothing rash. Dermot, remember, if you do, you will ruin everything." Her voice was hoarse with entreaty. "I won't let you pass. Not until you promise me." There was agony on her. "Promise me, by the Lord Jesus Christ, Dermot," she whispered solemnly, "that no matter what provocation you will do nothing rash. It's for our happiness, our life."

He looked at her a moment. "All right, Conn," he said quietly. "I promise."

Once more a great crash shattered the still air. He picked a lamp up. She stood aside. He went into the hall. He placed the lamp on a table. He undid the heavy chain; turned the key in the great lock; opened the oaken door.

There was a man without, in a burly black

traveling coat, with a soft black hat. There was a polo-cart there with a groom on the seat. The man advanced into the light. He had a youngish, dissipated, handsome face. Dermot looked at him in astonishment.

"I came over for my wife," said John.

Dermot looked at him as though he were playing some strange trick. His bare face seemed somehow indecent, flagrant.

"I said, I came over for my wife. She 's here, is n't she?"

"Yes," Dermot said surlily. "Connaught 's here."

"Ah, I thought she would be," John said pleasantly, and swaggered in.

The light of the drawing-room flowed into the hall in a broad golden shaft, and following it John went ahead. He was nonchalant, assured. Dermot wondered had he forgotten the last time they met in the mean room down a mean street, and Dermot's fingers at his throat. Ah, then he was afraid, had no standing, was a criminal. Now he was a man in the right, a citizen, asserting his rights.

Dermot followed him into the room, passed and faced him. Looked at him with new keen interest. Under the beard he had been burly, dignified. And now for all his new youthful look, he seemed mean and gross. The fattish jowl, the loose lips, the eyes that could be seen plain now. Ah, before all this had coarsened it had been a high weak face, now it was a sensual mean face, for all its regularity of feature. From him came an air of foreign foppiness, un-Irish, unwhite.

His eyes caught Dermot's, and read in Dermot's the accusation he could not put into words, on account of Conn's presence: "So you have found out, you swine! And you never went to America! You hid in France. You took my money and you played false."

The mean eyes met Dermot's smilingly, and answered, "Yes, and what can you do about it?" Dermot turned away. He looked at Conn standing by the fire, outwardly calm, outwardly possessed, but her heart inside her, he knew, was fluttering like a frightened bird.

"Well, Conn," John said pleasantly, "are n't you coming home?"

"No," she answered.

"It 's past two o'clock." He looked ostentatiously at his watch. "Time to be getting back."

"I'm not going," she said.

"Are you going to stay here?"

She answered nothing. Dermot thrust his clenched hands into his pockets.

"Look here," he told John, "Connaught 's not

going back to Glenmalure while you 're there. Now get out," he threatened, "or do I have to throw you out?"

"Dermot!" Conn warned, "Dermot!"

"You two—" John's tone was velvet, but his eyes began to glint as the black eyes of reptiles glint, narrowly, viciously—"you two seem to understand each other very well. Might I ask," he purred, "what you are to each other?"

Neither answered.

"Connaught," he said sharply, "are you in love with McDermot here?"

"Yes," she answered simply.

He took a short gasping breath. His face went white. His eyes were mean slits in a white mask. "Are you prepared to acknowledge that in public?"

She thought a moment, and raised her eyes. "Yes," she said.

"And you?" He turned to Dermot.

"Oh, I 'm in love with Conn, and I 'm prepared to acknowledge it, whenever and however and wherever you like," Dermot told him coolly.

A shadow of terrific baffled rage came over the man's white face. He had come here to be master, to be cruel, to be suavely cruel. He had been assured by himself that he would find them afraid of him, harassed by him. The man whom he hated and the woman he loved now and who hated him. And they were cool before him, safe and unafraid and so coldly contemptuous toward him. All the baffled cruelty rose in him, rose to his throat, his lips. And somewhere within him a vanity was wounded, wounded to death. He would never forgive these two. All his life would be a vengeance against these two.

"How far has this gone?" he asked in strained accents.

"It has not gone far," Connaught answered him quietly. "Dermot and I have told each other how that we cared for each other. And he has taken me in his arms, and he has kissed me, and I have kissed him. But that was in all honor, and that is how far it has gone."

His face became a queer bluish tint with the boiling anger and hurt in him.

"How do I know it has gone so far, and no further?" He advanced toward them, raging. "And how can you talk of honor——"

"Dermot," Conn said quietly, "watch the dog!"

Dermot turned around, puzzled, and just in time flung himself forward. The red setter had been watching unnoticed and now, seeing D'Arcy's movement forward, and hearing the truculent tones, had risen silently, and silently bared his strong white teeth. Every muscle was taut, ready to leap. Dermot caught him as he launched himself forward at John.

His right hand caught the loose skin at the back of the dog's head. His left arm closed around its throat. The furious strength of the dog brought him to the floor with a thud.

"Steady, Rory, steady!"

The dog struggled tremendously, madly in his grip. It seemed suddenly to possess the strength of a strong man. Its paws scratched wildly. Its jaws snapped, a sudden fear came on Dermot that the dog had gone mad. He shifted his grip. Slid his right hand up under the dog's throat, slipped it over the snapping jaws.

"Easy, Rory, easy!"

The dog became less violent, became all but calm. Whined a little with the pain of the gripped jaws. Dermot staggered to his feet.

"The window, Conn," he said. She opened the door of one of the garden windows. He threw the setter on the grass. "Outside, Rory!"

He came back calmly. John was weak from fear, weak and shaking.

"You were saying, John—"

"I was saying," John rallied, "that I have only your words for this."

"Our words are enough," Dermot told him. "Now get out!"

"One word more from me," John said coldly. "I come home. My wife slips out of the house. I find her in the middle of the night, toward morning, alone with you, in your house. A fire burning and wine on the table. And you tell me, both of you, that you love each other, when I find you together, in the middle of the night toward morning alone in the house."

"Well?"

"Well," he said. "I am going to publish this. I am going to publish this abroad and in a court of law. By God! you won't kick me out and sneer at me! I'll make the pair of you ashamed to hold up your heads."

They looked at each other aghast. This was a new unexpected treachery, sordidness, with which they could not cope.

"I will call Philips to bear witness to what I have seen." He moved to go and bring in the groom.

As he turned toward the door Anne McDermot came in, her sweet Quaker presence, her soft gray Quaker dress, her pleasant soft Quaker smile. The knocking at the door, and the struggle with the dog had awakened her, and she had dressed and come down.

"Where is thee going, John D'Arcy?"

Her mild eyes and sweet face brought him back

to courtesy, though there was rage in his face. There was a grace about him as he answered her, the grace that had procured him an entry everywhere, and made for him so many rapid short-lived friendships.

"Madam," he said, "I am sorry to have to tell you, but I come here in the middle of the night and find my wife and your son together alone in this room. And I must take action, madam, and am going to bring my groom in to bear witness."

"Thee is losing thy time, friend," her sweet voice told him.

"How, madam?"

"Thee knows me, John D'Arcy."

"Yes." His reply was in a puzzled tone.

"Look at me, John D'Arcy. Thee knows that I have never in my whole life told a lie. Thee knows that."

"Yes, madam," he agreed. "I know that."

"John D'Arcy, I tell thee this: that I have been in this room with Connaught and my son since she came here to-night, and left the room only when thee knocked at the door. I tell thee this, John D'Arcy. Is that enough for thee?" There was no falter in her voice, no weakness in her eyes. D'Arcy hesitated a moment.

"Madam," he said, "that is enough for me."

He turned and left the room without a word

more, left the house. They listened to the grinding of the wheels outside, the shuffle of hooves, the
slow trot, the fast distant trot. Connaught came
forward, her head bowed. There were tears in
her eyes.

"Oh, Aunt Anne," she said heartbrokenly, "you
should n't have! You should n't have. In all
your life you never told a lie, and to-night for us,
Aunt Anne!" Anne put her arms around the
drooping shoulders, caught the dark head to her
breast.

"Hush, heart," she said. "It was nothing."
She looked across to Dermot. There shone a
happiness in her eyes. There was a hymn in her
face.

"I am going to bring thee up to the guest's
room, little Connaught," she said gently, "and get
thee a nightgown and a comb, and make thee say
thy prayers, little Connaught," she soothed, "and
see that thee goes asleep. And thee will put out
the lights, Dermot, and lock the doors, and go to
thy bed too," she directed. "Will thee not, dear
lad?"

XX

§ 1

IT was a queer thing, but with Connaught's second going into England, there came a happiness to Dermot.   He had thought, a week before,
a day or so before, that the sun would have gone
out with her going, and that a great bitterness
would have come on him.   But with her depar-
ture, there arose in him a sense that the close unjust triangle of her life, and his life, and the life
of John had widened from its intense sulkiness to
a tenuous geometry into which a clean wind of
sanity might blow.   It was as though they had
all passed through a crisis that brought them
nearer solution, though bodily apart.

And where she had gone secretly, this time, was
not cold, alien, but to the sweet West Country of
England, King Arthur's Cornwall, place of purple heaths and great cliffs, of little whitewashed
thatched cottages in the moonlight, and soft ancient memories—of the Phœnicians, who had their
great tin-mines there; they came northward from

Africa in their carven galleys with square purple sails; of the Jewish colony who had been there so long ago that of them naught remains but the name they gave to the place of their abiding, Marazion, in the Hebrew tongue "Bitterness of Israel," a name like a pathetic heartbroken wail. God rest you, little colony, and all poor exiles! And past Land's End where the little islands, the Scillies that had strange names like the names of Irish islands, Corregeen and Resveor, Ganniley and Innisoones. There would not be the little showers of Ireland there, nor the soft Irish mountains, but there would be always a salt sea-breeze.

He could see her there, in the evenings when the sun went down, sitting on some Cornish cliff, watching for the soft green ray that comes in the sky when the sun drops into the Atlantic. Her head would be bare, and there would be a dream in her golden eyes, and her little chin would be resting on the cupped palms of her white capable hands. Beneath her about the cliff the white gulls would be swooping, soaring, spinning, and their soft *kui-kui* would be like a mournful anthem of the wind. And the waves striking the cliff would send up showers of silver spray. And when the sun went down, a little wind would rise and breathe upon her forehead and ruffle the edges of her hair, and her eyes would turn from the great

golden west, and they would turn northward, to
where Ireland is. And a little song would come
to her lips, in her sweet small voice, a song of
loneliness, but that was not a song of loneliness at
all, but a song of happiness, that there existed Ireland, and a man of Ireland.

Though May was here, the thin sickle of the
May moon in the high air, and by field and by
river the couples courting, as though nothing mattered but love—as perhaps nothing does, but this
is not clear—though May had come in all her
beauty, yet it did not bother him that Connaught
was not here. The showers that should have
been done in April still spattered weakly—now an
impish flight of hail like small shot, now a dash
of cold pure rain, and after them the scent of the
bluebells rose in the air. And here and there the
hawthorn began to open in shy white stars. She
loved May and she was not here. Ah! but she
was safe!

A horrible vision of the three of them had been
in his mind for a long time now, some remnant of
a half-remembered horrible dream. That she
and he and John were in some dim half-lit place,
and that Connaught, who seemed a spirit with dark
hair and haggard eyes, was beating at the walls
to be free and appealing to him. But on his
hands were great manacles of some white metal,

and he could do nothing for her, the handcuffs were so close, so heavy. And in a corner John sat, a heavy amorphous shadow, half alive, half dead, baleful, watching them both out of strained red animal eyes. And Dermot knew that even could he get the gyves off, yet he could produce no effect on that squat terrible figure by beating it with bare hands. Though he throttled it to death, it would not die. And Connaught, distraught, wild-eyed in the half-darkness. Eh, God! horrible.

Now that she was safe, the morbidness had left him, and when he thought of her now, he thought of her sweetness on the Cornish cliffs, of the trust in her golden eyes. And John was just a cheap vulgar cad. Not a good scoundrel, not even a good lunatic, but a cad, a vulgar treacherous cad.

§ 2

He found himself thinking, once or twice, that his love for Connaught and her love for him had brought him wisdom. Only for John they would not have loved each other keenly, intensely. Connaught, he remembered, had said that. This outrageous thing had made him and her man and woman, as battle turns an armed man in uniform into a soldier. Until he has known terror and bravery he will only be an armed man in uniform, and not a soldier. So without pain they would never have loved. They would have been only sweethearts. And love had brought him wisdom.

Now that Connaught was gone, and his mother up in Belfast at her annual meeting, he sat and thought silently. It seemed to him that the life he was leading, the thing he was trying to do, was incomplete without his marrying. More incomplete for a man in his position than for another man. Here he was, master of Dermotstown, its house, its farms, the lambs on the hills, the cattle grazing in the fields that were milked night and morning so the city children might get their sustenance. And of the flowers that grew, and of the trees that bore fruit. And of the potatoes that would be digged and sent abroad, and of the oats that would be ground into meal, and of the flax that would be scutched and woven into linen. Why did he do it? God knows he had money enough, and he worked as hard as any one, and yet it wasn't for money he worked. He often tried to work out his status in the world, but he knew very little of the dry science of economics. He figured out to himself that he was the natural man. Others might go to war, create great businesses, bring social reforms to fruition, but without him they would be nowhere. They were dependent for the food they ate on his fields, for the clothing they wore on his linen and sheep.

While he served one group, he was bound to another. In a place like Dermotstown, every laborer on the field, the shepherd on the hills, the maids in the kitchen were not employees, they were members of a family. Though the laborers would work until they dropped, yet they did n't consider themselves servants. They worked at Dermotstown, they would say. And the shepherd had the right to be paternal toward him. And the maids had the right to talk politics to him while they worked. Passing strictures on some bitterness of Timothy Healy's, or encomiums on some statement of Mr. John Redmond, or puzzling over some deep-sea dictum of Mr. Joseph Chamberlain:

"An orchid in his buttonhole and a monocle in his eye, letting on 't is a fool he is, and him leaping with brains. Foolish, *moreya!* foolish like a fox!"

There was something more due to them than his protection. They needed "the woman of the house." His mother, dear lady! was not that any more to them. She had become a sweet lavender presence, a saint. They gave her love, but it was a reverential love. They were in awe of her. When she visited the laborers' wives, they were in a flutter, as though royalty entered. And it was not to her that a girl of the house could unburden her heart, crying over some handsome soldier or policeman who had jilted her. "Ma'am, my dear, when I was out walking with him there was roses under my feet. And he told me I was the star of Wicklow. And my heart's gone out!" No, they would sooner utter blasphemy than to speak to his mother of love, though none understood its depths better. Nor could they come into her soft Quaker presence in some abominable hat to ask did she think it suited them, now! Nor could the beggars of the road pour out their gratitude to her as they would to a young woman. " 'T is a great credit to God the way he made you, my lady. And when you die the saints will make room before the fire of Heaven for you to warm your pretty shins. Ah, heart o' corn!" And down the drive they would go chanting. "There is not her equal in the Irish nation, nor in the human world itself. I am telling you there is nowhere her beating for beauty—not the Queen of England, nor ancient Venus, no! nor Mrs. Patrick Hennessy of Dublin!"

They wanted, all the train of Dermotstown, a young mistress to adore, babies to spoil. They

wanted to see the tradition carried on—the be-
nevolent patriarchate of the gentleman farmers,
whose independence put a brake on the prices of
the business farmers. And the house would be a
sort of example to the world, of how happy people were when they abode close to the earth, drawing life and sustenance from brown earth and
golden sunshine.

When the young woman of the house came,
there would be completion. His mother, Anne,
could withdraw into her soft and gentle world,
thinking, as he knew she wished to be thinking, of
a world into which she must soon go, and where
her husband was, and her soldier son, and the little daughter of the smiling eyes. She would wish
to give over to a young comely daughter all the
cares of the house: the silver, the Waterford
glass, the ancient Belleek china, the linen from the
looms of Ulster. All the maids of the house, and
the gardens: pear-trees and apple-trees and strawberry beds, and the frames where the cucumbers
ripened in the sun. Dermot could imagine Conn
overseeing her gardens, a cigarette in one hand
and a strawberry in the other, listening seriously
while the head gardener urged her to enter some
promising colt for the English Derby.

"They'll have to wait," Dermot said, "for

there 'll be no woman come into this house barring Connaught O'Brien."

§ 3

Of the Citizen, from the day he met him on the Dundrum road, he had seen or heard nothing. And he reproached himself with not having thought of him, for the French-Irish officer had seemed such a friend. And also there was an occult intangible bond between them, on account of John. There had been that morning in the newspapers an account of a rowdy scene in the House of Commons. The journals had passed it over as being rather funny, remarking on the peculiar sensitiveness of the Irish people, but an undercurrent in it had chilled Dermot.

"In the House of Commons to-day," went the reports, "Horatio Blythe, Liberal, Member for Lancashire University, asked the Chief Secretary for Ireland whether he had any information as to military officers or a military officer of a foreign power, spreading disaffection and incitement of revolution among the aborigines in Ireland.

"Colonel Sir Hugh O'Neill, Unionist for Mid-Oriel, on a point of personal explanation, said that

his family had been in Ireland as far back as history
or tradition went, and that since Elizabethan times
his family had been supporters of the Crown.   It
required no military officer of a foreign power to
incite Ireland to rebellion.   It only required a few
members, like the honorable member for Lancashire University, to refer to the Irish by the nause-
ous term aborigine to make the whole country, in-
cluding himself, leap to arms.

"Mr. Blythe said he had been unfortunate as to
terms.   He meant the pastoral and agricultural
Milesians.

"Mr. Pat Lockey, Labor Member for the
Coombe, Dublin, rose to a point of order.   He
represented a manufacturing and transport dis-
trict, but he objected to the term Milesian in referring to the finest peasantry on any sod.   It was
well for the honorable member that the filthy
epithet had been used in the British House of
Commons and not in his own constituency of the
Coombe, where the honorable member would have
been torn limb from limb.   (Cries of "Order!
Order!")

"Mr. Lockey went on to say that when he met
the honorable gentleman outside, he intended to
break his damned neck.   (Cries of "Withdraw!
Withdraw!")

"The Speaker called for an apology from the member for the Coombe to the member for Lancashire University. The term Milesian had only been used in a scientific sense.

"Mr. Lockey said that English science was the ruin of Ireland. Since the Board of Agriculture had been founded, Irish farming had entered on a decline. However, that was beside the question. (Ironical cheers.) But by adding insult to injury by referring to his countrymen as Milesians—

"Mr. Horatio Blythe said that when he referred to the Irish as Milesians, he meant descendants of Milesius. Indeed, he knew no other meaning for the phrase. It was very far from his intention, he said, to hurt the feelings of a brave and generous people. He would say 'inhabitants.'

"Mr. Pat Lockey said he wished to withdraw anything he had said against the honorable gentleman. He had just heard the most sportsmanlike and courteous apology it had ever been his good fortune to listen to. In the name of the people of Ireland, whom he represented (Cries of "No! No!" from the Nationalist and Unionist Members) whom, he insisted, he represented, he thanked the honorable gentleman. He invited the member for Lancashire University to address his constituents in the Coombe.

"Order having been restored, and the question put, with the alteration of 'aborigines' to 'inhabitants.'

"The Chief Secretary for Ireland said he had no information on the subject."

Poor Pat Lockey! Dermot thought. What a fool he had appeared, who was really so wise, so generous! He had been friends with the big labor leader in Dublin, and he knew the story of his life: how he had sold papers on the streets when he was five years old, and mined in Scotland, and could not read or write until he was thirty, and little even then or now. How the Coombe loved him! He had probably thought there was some connection between Milesian and militia. And Sir Hugh O'Neill, who had brought his battalion into battle for the king, with the fifes shrilling the "Wearing of the Green," and how the battalion had withstood the mad charges of the Sudanese. How far apart these two, the big Tory soldier, descendant of great Shane, Prince of Ulster, and Lockey, the laborer of the Dublin docks, and yet when a word was said against the most beloved country, they closed shoulder to shoulder. How little the outside world understood!

The question had been passed over in the "unseemly Irish row" as the papers put it, but who was the military officer of a foreign power? Of course it must mean the Citizen. Whom else? And though Government knew, must know by now, that his mission was to disperse the gathering men, yet might he not be taken? Soldiers, officers would connive at his escape, such freemasonry is there between military men. But if some wretched police spy blundered on his trail, or some political tout, what then? Capture or suicide? And such an end for the gallant rebel, a cell for him who was so much at home in the Irish hills or the African deserts, free and terrible as an eagle! Or suicide, he who should die—if such a warm heart and high courageous mind could ever die!—fittingly on a field of battle! Dermot pondered, wondered if he could n't help. Perhaps the Citizen found it hard to get out of Ireland. To go across through England might be too risky, and was there a fishing-boat or French vessel he could trust, that was n't watched? He thought of his first love, the sea. There was a fifty-ton sloop-rigged boat he knew he could get— it was more a racer than a cruiser, but that did n't matter—and three or four men he could trust. And the Citizen might be glad to get out that way. They would slip down St. George's Channel in the dawn, the jib and mainsail drawing, the keen wind, the slap of water at the bows, and as they went to Brest, passing Cornwall, he might see, through his glasses, a sweet figure on the cliffs. He smiled to himself, thinking how many miles of cliffs. Ah, but he would see the cliffs where, high in the keen air, her little boyish foot had trodden! And he would be near her, ah, within twenty miles of her at any rate, and she would never know he was there. He could tell her later in secret. "And Dermot, to think I never knew!"

Another thought was troubling him. If by any chance John and the Citizen met, then in spite of Dermot's feeling that it was impossible, the Citizen might kill him. A storm rises in the mind like a black whirlwind, and a man shoots. And killing John was murder. A man might escape, might be allowed to escape, in a matter of revolution, but where murder was concerned English law was implacable. And implacable and certain were the men sent out to get a killer, the hard matter-of-fact men from Scotland Yard. They didn't look like detectives of romance. They were just very keen officers in civilian clothes, and their calling was stamped on them as plain as an inscription on a coin. But with uncanny certainty they brought in their man. Sooner or later they brought in their man.

And then the sordid vulgar end of it all—a greased rope and pinioned arms, and a black hood over the head. And the executioner was not a figure of majesty, but a barber from some distant town who had journeyed there for his expenses and a moderate fee, hardly the price of five hundred shaves.

And this might be the end of the gallant gentleman who had fought the Arab tribes on their native desert, and who ordered back to their homes revolutionaries who had dreamed of battle for the third of a century. For the killing of a cad, of a coward like John D'Arcy! "Ah, no, Citizen!" Dermot thought.

§ 4

It was a queer thing, but somehow now the thought of John did not worry him, was no longer a hated sinister being to him. Some vague intuition told him that John would pass from their lives, whether by death or by his own actions Dermot did not know. Unless it happened by the hand of the Citizen, John's death was not important to him. When a faun or a centaur died, there would be no human mourning. Some mistake of nature had been rectified, that was all. One felt more the death of a horse, or of a dog.

It seemed to him this way: things were right or

they were not right. There were shapes that were right, colors that were right. What was wrong could not exist for any time—a wrong shape, a wrong color, a wrong line of action. For this reason, that all the forces of nature, tending toward what nature thought right, would bear on and rectify that which was wrong. Or if it could not rectify it, would destroy it. In his own experience of farm life he had seen these mistakes of nature—a calf that had two heads, and a horror a mare had foaled—and these things were wrong and had died. Slowly, implacably, what was wrong nature destroyed.

It was right for him to love Connaught. It was right for Connaught to flee from her house when she could n't live in it. But it was wrong for John to be there, to live there, to live in it. This was wrong, and this action would die. John would assuredly pass out of their lives. When John had been in trouble, with the possibility of death before him, with the lesser possibility of discovery, disgrace and prison, he had feared him. But now that John was free, was assured, was safe to act as he thought fit, he did not fear him at all.

And John was acting all right, Dermot thought with a wry smile. All Connaught's servants had gone from Glenmalure, now, and John had done a strange unheard-of thing. Instead of engaging new servants, he had taken in two of the tinker people of the road, the Irish gipsies, to tend him and cook for him. He had most likely found them at some country fair, but there they were, he had heard, installed now in Connaught's home, a dark little man with great curls of black hair, and golden ear-rings, and a brown-faced woman with piercing eyes and a haughty tilt to her head and an impudent bosom. And now none of the peasant people went near the place, such a horror they have of the rambling tinker folk, who do not know God and whom God does not know. But the man had been seen lolling at the wicket-gate—the big gates were closed now—watching the mountains, with the immobility of a cat, as though he were afraid they would move away and disappear whilst he was within at the unaccustomed domestic work. And the tinkerwoman had been seen sitting on the grass and laying out a deck of cards, and the man of keen eyes who had seen her had said that these cards were not the honest cards of games but had strange devices on them. One card had a naked boy who held an apple in his outstretched palm, and another had a serpent standing erect through a ring that seemed a wedding-ring, and a third had a tree on it, and among the leaves of the tree were the heads of human beings—heads of kings with crowns on them and heads of bishops with miters on them and heads with ropes about their necks—and the woman was talking in a language that was neither Gaelic nor English, "as I have knowledge," he said he of the keen eyes, "because being a Raghery man, both tongues are at me." It was also rumored that the tinker people slept outside the house, on the grass. A great mystery was made of this in the country-side; a popular and conservative explanation was that John had sold himself to the devil, and that these two were acolytes in diabolic ritual.

But mystery there was none for Dermot. John wanted secrecy about the house, and had seduced the tinker people from their wandering life for a while, by promise of sufficient money to buy a caravan, or to send them overseas. Also, the man would be a good guard, if necessary, for the tinker people love fighting, and have a secret system of offense and defense very like the subtle methods of the Japanese. Why John needed secrecy he was soon to know.

A man from Sewell's auction rooms came to Dermotstown, an honest horsey-looking lad whose face was familiar to Dermot.

"Would you be on for buying some horses, Mr. Dermot?"

"Would I be on for selling some?"

"There's horses on the market," the coper went on doggedly, "you might be willing to buy." Dermot laughed.

"There's a horse called now Flying Scotsman, but will be sold under another name, is great in a dog-cart, so. There's a five-year old hunter you would n't like to miss. There's a lady's hack with a canter as sweet as honey. Symmetrical is the name he's known by, but to-morrow 't will be a new name, so. And there's a Welsh pony is fourteen hands high and goes bravely in a polo-cart. It does, so."

"Did Mr. John D'Arcy send you to me?" Dermot asked coldly.

"I'd hate to see the day when I'd go an errand for the like of Mr. John D'Arcy," the man disclaimed. "But there's friends of yours, sir, know about this, and would like to know do you want those horses bought in."

"Thanks," said Dermot, "and thanks to my friends, and I'd like those horses bought in."

"They'll be in your stables to-morrow, sir, and you won't be cheated."

So that was John's little game, eh? What was to be done? He could think of nothing but to buy what John offered. Would John stop then? he wondered. It was not likely. Dermot went into Dublin. He sought out Pat Lockey's lieutenant at Labor headquarters. The lieutenant was six foot four of brawny red-haired Dubliner who went by the name of Wee Joe Delaney.

"You know the quays?" Dermot asked.

"If I don't," said Wee Joe, "who does?"

Dermot knew vaguely that in the underground politics of Dublin were societies whose activities were vague and masked. They might mean corporation politics. They might mean national revolution.

"Joe," he asked, "is there any organization on the quays that embraces the second-hand furniture shops, antique shops, book-stores and the like?"

"There does be clubs," Joe answered guardedly. "Literary and historical societies and them things."

"Joe," Dermot said, "the matter is this: if Mr. D'Arcy from Glenmalure offers for sale furniture, books, pictures, or anything like that, I want to know so that I can buy them."

"Is it a matter where the police is concerned?"

Dermot thought for an instant. "No," he decided. "It is not."

"That's easy," Wee Joe nodded. "I'll see to it you're told if anything's offered from that quarter, and the stuff held for you." He paused a minute. "About them spuds during the black strike, and all the things from Dermotstown," he labored embarrassedly, "and the childers' milk, we don't forget it."

"That was my mother," Dermot said quietly.

"Ay, oh, ay!" Wee Joe smiled. He laid an immense hairy paw on Dermot's knee. "Mr. Mc-Dermot, there won't be a cat's basket sold out of Glenmalure without your knowing it."

§ 5

Old Neddy Joe was at his favorite occupation for the time of the year, sitting outside his lodge in the summer afternoon, making trout and salmon flies for fishing. Out of a silk handkerchief, tied carefully at the four corners, came an assortment of feathers—the feathers of woodcock and pigeons and partridge, and here and there the keen blue of the kingfisher's feather. And there were strands of very fine red and brown and white yarn. Dermot loved to see the cunning of the gnarled fingers, and the trueness of the ancient eye.

"For to say," said Neddy Joe, "for to say that my flies are the greatest flies in the world is but a poor compliment to them. But if you were to say now: 'Endow a salmon with the wisdom of

Sullivan, but Neddy Joe will make a fly would fool him,' you would not only be paying a compliment but telling the truth.

" 'T is a great lack in my collection, Master Dermot, not to have the breast feathers of eagles, for there 's no gold in the world like the gold of that feather. But 't is many 's the long year and day since I climbed the cliffs for them. Ah, sixty, seventy years. Master Dermot, did I ever tell you how the great eagle of Achill caught me and me at his nest?"

"No, Neddy Joe."

"I was coming down, with the feathers in the breast of my shirt, when I heard a thumping of wings and felt the wind in my face, and there he was before me, fluttering like a hawk in the air. The great talons of him and the eye, and I thought the air darkened, so big he was. Ah, Master Dermot, to have looked in the eye that looks the sun in the eye—is there any but one in the world?"

"Were you afraid, Neddy Joe?"

"I felt worse than afraid, my sweet lad; I felt mean. And I put a hand in my breast and took the feathers out. 'Before God,' I cried out to him, 'that made me and you, all I 've been doing is gathering a wheen of feathers to make flies for the inveigling of fish, and there 's ne'er a twig of your nest that's touched, nor any harm or malice done.' He let me pass, the great noble bird. And, Master Dermot, I felt like some mean fellow feels when he's caught trespassing on land, and the owner pays no attention to him, so small does he think him. I've thanked God for my life many a time, but I thanked the great eagle that day.

" 'T is what they say, Master Dermot—" the old man came out suddenly. He went ahead with his fly-making, neither raising his head, nor changing his tone—" 'T is what they say, the Hangman walks."

A sudden chill swept over Dermot's heart, as the meaning of the words came to him. A terror roughened the skin of his face. He could feel his scalp prickle. And then he was passionately angry.

"It's a lie," he said. "And people don't come back."

" 'T is what they say," the old man insisted, "and people do."

"Neddy Joe," he rose to his feet, white with rage, "I've a mind to have you pitched out on the road, for all your service with me and my people."

"Why shouldn't he come back, Master Dermot, with the stranger in the house he built, and his white darling over the sea, and yourself, the friend of her heart, kept from her?" the old man said quietly.

"Neddy Joe, who is it telling this monstrous lie?"

"Bridgeen Roe of the Mountain, it is, saw—himself."

"That crazy old woman!"

"She is not a crazy old woman, Master Dermot, She is a wise woman."

"What did she see?"

"She saw a great shadow on the wall, of himself in his wig and gown."

" 'T was a tree in the moonlight."

"There is no tree opposite Glenmalure. There is a bare lawn. The trees are back of it, and to the sides."

"This old fool of a crazed witch saw something once—"

"She saw it three times, Master Dermot."

"Neddy Joe," he said, "don't you see there 's no meaning to this—"

"There may be no meaning in it for you, Master Dermot, nor for little Miss Connaught even, but for John D'Arcy is meaning."

"Let me hear no more of this," Dermot threatened angrily. "Your crazy old tales—"

" 'T is not my tale, Master Dermot. 'T is just

what they do be saying, that the Hangman walks."

"It is a monstrous lie. A silly old woman's lie, and I want to hear no more of it." He walked away, but there was still the coldness of terror on him, and that silly feeling about his scalp.

XXI

§ 1

FOR all that he had told old Neddy Joe his disbelief in that people walked, as the Irish locution is, yet down in his heart he knew that whatever Glenmalure was, the great fighting spirit of the man must concentrate in anger against the spoiler of his house. Ghosts existed, he felt, as all Irish feel. But that they took shape and appeared either in the habits they wore in life, or in the abominable cerements of death—that he could not conceive. It would be, after all, a vulgar thing to do, and when we die we drop vulgarity. Intuitions, sensations translate themselves into images before the mind's eye and ear. Thus the banshee. Thus the ghostly pipers of the North Country.

And when one dies in Ireland, one does not leave the queer romantic land for a charitable heaven. One does not turn his back on friends and kinsmen for the glory of paradise. One is not so selfish. One is always around in the shadows or starlight to share their joys or try to help in their sorrows. One stays around until the friends and kinsmen come over too. Also, perhaps one stays by one's enemies, but this is a deep point. However, to the Gael the next world is over the next hill, and—this is a secret—hence heroism, hence the utter contempt for death that makes great soldiers, great poets, great men. Ghosts are, but these are not seen, except by horses and dogs and little children, and they see only the pleasant beloved spirits. . . .

And the chill leaving Dermot, he sat down to think of it reasonably. Glenmalure was not an old house. It had been built only a handful of years when the Lord Chief Justice bought it. But the folk who had built it, and lived there a little while were completely forgotten, so much did the great justice make it his own. Glenmalure had been the fulfilment of an ambition to him. All his work, all his life, all his politics had culminated in a position where he was a peer of the Irish Kingdom—Baron Glenmalure. And Glenmalure itself had become a symbol. In Cork once he had been a barefooted boy, and now Baron Glenmalure of Glenmalure.

Out of the fortune he had made as an advocate before he had been attorney-general, solicitor-general, or justice even, he had bought the big gray house. Immense fees had come to him in the days when he fought for men's lives against the law, and contested great will cases. And these had only been important to him in that with them he could found a house, and have a home for the little daughter of the black hair and the honey-colored eyes. What thought must have gone from him into the furnishing of the house of his dreams, the baronial residence he had achieved! Every book on the shelves, every picture on the walls, every chair before the fire, had been bought by his money, caressed by his thought. The great grim heart that had been like granite when he put the black cap of justice on his head—there must have been a tenderness in it for the making of a house. Here was the picture of himself he was so proud of, the picture young Orpen had painted; ah, that lad would go far! Here the water-colors he had bought in Italy, and thought so highly of; it had made him angry to hear them referred to so slightingly, so patronizingly, by the young whipper-snappers of Dublin. And the fine flowery rich furniture, such as Albert, Queen Victoria's husband, would have liked! And the cabinets full of curios, strange coins, little Chinese fans, what not. Damned interesting, all of them. He had liked them, every one.

And to Glenmalure had come his friends, to partake of the unstinted hospitality, this big soldier, that Chief Secretary of Ireland, this poet, that great advocate. And occasionally a bishop in apron and gaiters, before whom one must be careful not to curse. And more than occasionally some ancient friend, whose ways had not been gainful ways, and with whom great tact must be exercised so as not to hurt his feelings.

All this house, each stone and rafter, each picture, chair, and room was electric with the personality of the grim old man, though for nearly a year now his dwelling had been where neither stone nor rafter is. Here he had sat, looking over the great house and grounds which bore the name of his peerage, Glenmalure, and what a great pride to him it was, who once had been a barefoot boy of Cork! And the only regret was that the little mother of Ballingeary, who had no English, had not lived to see it all. Only at the thought of two people would the face, massive and granite as a sphinx's, relax and smile tenderly—at the thought of the young daughter in the riding clothes, and of the ancient dim woman in the long blue Irish cloak.

And now the house he had furnished for himself with his strange love and ambition, the house he had worked toward, was being looted by a stranger he had invited in. And the daughter he was so fond of was a fugitive from her home. How could he rest in peace, the fierce and terrible old man?

Everything now, surreptitiously, was being sold out of the house. John would have Dublin dealers up and the tinker fellow would drive into the city with cart-load after cart-load of valuables. The silver plate Dermot had rescued, and the books and pictures, and the furniture was coming to him little by little. What right John had to sell these things Dermot didn't know. He supposed when a woman married a man her property became his. Perhaps it didn't. Perhaps John was committing a criminal act in selling these things. But at any rate Dermot knew this, and John knew it too: that Connaught would rather lose every penny she had than make a fuss, take legal proceedings that would proclaim to the world how her private affairs were. Dermot thanked heaven he was not a poor man. To see the chattels of Glenmalure pass into strangers' hands would have been agony.

He wondered to himself how John could have nerves good enough to do as he was doing, apart even from the simple wrong of the matter. Did he not feel that the great law tomes he was selling had been pored over by the old baron's eyes? There had gone so much of the essence of the old man into these things. Was there no sense of

guilt in him as he took down this picture, had his
strange tinkerman wrap up that salver? Did he
feel nothing inimical in the house? Surely the
house itself must rebel against this! How did he
sleep of nights?

Dermot had ridden past Glenmalure in the
evening recently, and for a moment, as he looked
over the high walls at the trees and roof, in his
mind he thought of it not as Glenmalure, but, in
the peasant's phrase, Hangman's House. The
country-side called it Glenmalure when Connaught
was there, but once she left they went to the other
name. Dermot had never noticed it before when
Connaught was absent, and it seemed to him this
evening that although the sun was still in the sky,
and the birds singing, and all the sweetness of
May in the air, yet about the house, about the
trees there was a mournful, a somehow doomed
air. He wondered if what had made it cheerful,
vital, had been Connaught herself, and the life
she had put into everything, into servants, horses,
dogs. He found something within himself saying:
"This house will not last. This will go. Its real
name will be forgotten and there will remain only
the phrase by which country people know it."
And that was the Lord Chief Justice's monument.
If he had gone ahead on his path as rebel poet,
might he not have left a greater remembrance

behind him than this gloomy hollow house?

From it there emanated some spirit of ill-luck that made Dermot shudder, and he could imagine how Bridgeen Roe, the half-crazed mountain woman, was affected by it, so that she thought she saw the ghastly funeral shadow on the wall. Good God! Could it have been there that Connaught had smiled, Connaught had been married, Connaught and he told each other of their love? Or had that gloom only come on it recently? He felt himself thinking superstitiously: "If John has any brains, any wisdom, he will get out of there at once."

He sensed he was being watched from the house somewhere, and, looking up, he saw against a window a pale face. John's, he was sure. He felt embarrassed to be discovered looking at the place —spying as it might seem to John. He touched the cob with his heel and cantered off.

As he rode forward his heart rose. It seemed to have been compressed, as in a cold mist. He had ridden into a cold mist, and was now riding out of it. It was as though some pool of gloom were sending forth dark exhalations into the warm May air. Now he was in it, now he was out of its orbit.

Eh! he thought, Hangman's House! Hangman's House!

§ 2

There came a letter from her in Cornwall to his mother, back now from Belfast. She had grown brown, she said, brown as a gipsy woman, from the wind and the sun, and she had fallen very much in love with the sea. "It is not like our Irish Sea at all, this Atlantic," she had discovered. "Our Irish Sea has her ancient ghosts—Manannan Mac Lir, with his sad face and sad beard, and the three children of Lir, who were turned into white swans —but this Atlantic is so masculine, Aunt Anne, and the spirits of it are great full-blooded Neptune, and gnarled Triton." And she spoke of the rabbits scuttling around the cliffs, and the flare of the sea-pinks, "Ah," she said, "but I do be thinking long!"

She hazarded whether she could be over for the races at Baldoyle on Whit Monday. "Sure there isn't a person in the world would recognize me, and the brown way my face is, and Robinson might run Moon of Israel [this was a filly the trainer had bought in England for her, by Wandering Jew out of Honeymoon, by Lunatic out of Queen Bee—a great strain!] for the Viceroy's Cup. And I could stay in some quiet hotel, if you

could n't put me up, Aunt Anne. [As though
Aunt Anne McDermot would let her go to a cold
lodging, while warm Dermotstown was there!]
And Dermot, if he would, could take me down to
Baldoyle. For I 'm thinking long," she wrote,
"for the shouting of the bookies on an Irish track,
and the sight of the miles of jaunting-cars larrup-
ing along the strand. And the Liffey, itself, Aunt
Anne, I do be thinking of it. Aunt Anne, I 'm
thinking long for Ireland. I 'm thinking long.
Would it be possible for me to come over for a
night and a day? Ask Dermot."

Of John she said nothing, but she mentioned she
had heard that things were going queerly about
the house. The servants had probably written
her that they had left, and that pictures and books
were being sold, hearing of all this in some underground Irish way. "What worries me," she
wrote, "is about the gardens. They were always
so beautifully kept, and now, I suppose, they 're
going to wrack and ruin. And at this time of
year, too. My own roses, that I was so proud of
—they 'll miss me," she said. "It 's a queer thing
to think, Aunt Anne, that the roses are out in
Glenmalure, and I am not there.

"About the races at Baldoyle, Aunt Anne?
Don't you think I could come?" And again:
"Ask Dermot!"

§ 3

The question of Baldoyle was easily decided; she could come. He was as thirsty to see her as she to see Ireland. It was over a month, now, since she had gone, and surely they deserved a day together. The adventure of meeting her by the morning boat, that came with sunrise: of the drive to Dermotstown, there in time for breakfast, the brown tea and the small brown eggs, the golden butter and golden honey, and the flowers of early summer on the table. And her face, that had become tanned, she had said, her face like a flower—

She had once told him, speaking of flowers, that the flowers in other folks' gardens one admired, but the flowers in one's own one loved. And she had always been so fond of her roses. "I love roses, Dermot," she had once said. "I know I ought to love violets and modest flowers, as a lady should. But I am not so much of a lady, Dermot," she smiled. "I have n't got your pedigree, Dermot, that begins with history. My father was once a Cork jackeen, and my mother was of simple soldiering people. My great-grandfather looted a temple in Burma, and, what was worse, was caught doing it. So I can be as vulgar, Dermot, as I damned well like," she laughed, "and love roses."

A thought came to him in the dusk, that he would get her roses from her own garden and send them across to her in Cornwall. If he got them to-night, and had them off by the boat in the morning she would have them at the dinner table to-morrow evening. Fraser, his own gardener, was a wonder at packing things, and keeping life in them. To-morrow she would have her own roses from her own garden.

"Bring around a rig," he told the groom. "Put the mare in the dog-cart; she needs work."

He would stop the trap short of Glenmalure, he decided, and, crossing the fields, slip into the garden in the half-light, and gather from the rose-trees a great bundle of early roses. John he would not be likely to meet. The only person who might interfere would be the tinkerman. Stealing Connaught's roses for her out of her own garden—there was a sense of pleasure about it. And if he and the tinkerman came together? The tinkerman might show fight. And if he did? Well, a good stiff jolt on the jaw would do that greasy swipe all the good in the world, jingle his ear-rings for him. He wondered, as he bowled along the road, whether all that was said of these tinkers' fighting ability was true. He would n't mind trading a few clouts with him.

"Pull up," he told the groom. They were nearing MacInerney's public house. "Stay here, O'Hagan, till I come back, and remember this: if you go drinking any of the methylated spirits the MacInerney's sell for whisky, by the living Moses, I'll take the skin off your back with the whip."

"Oh, begor, you would, sir, I know," O'Hagan agreed. "But is it dry I'm to remain, or would stout be suitable?"

"All right," Dermot said. He got down and walked up the road. White dust rose as he walked. The dry spell had lasted three weeks now, but for an occasional insufficient shower, and the farmers were complaining of ruin facing them, as farmers do. There had not been such a spell since the night of the big wind, so old men said.

The creaking of a small cart came to his ears, and making a turn in the road, he saw, heading evidently for the Wicklow Mountains, a small donkey and a little red cart. A woman walked beside the little brown beast, a woman with a dark shawl, and a red blouse, and a yellow-patterned skirt. Her feet were bare. Behind her lolled a tall thin man. His corduroy trousers were full, his corduroy coat was narrow, his hat was wide and flaring, his feet were bare. There were gold ear-rings in his ears. Dermot looked at the red cart, filled, he thought, with something or other. Over it was a cover of sacking.

"Hold on a minute," Dermot said.

They all stopped and looked at him. The donkey with brown humble eyes. The woman with black level ones. The man with soft dreaming eyes.

"Are n't you two the pair who are at Glenmalure?"

"We are the pair who were at Glenmalure," the man said slowly.

"Where are you off to?"

"We are off," the man answered, "over the Wicklow Mountains, to the town of Gorey in Wexford, where there is to be a fair on Friday. And after that we are off to Waterford. And from Waterford to Cork City, and from there to the Reeks in Kerry, and that is as far as we can say at this time." And again they all looked at Dermot.

"Take the cover off your cart," Dermot ordered. If the tinker people were off again on the tinker trail it was probable that they were laden with booty from Glenmalure, he thought. The man with the ear-rings removed the sacking and stood aside. There were a couple of bags of potatoes in the cart, a dead hare, a small bag that seemed to contain flour, a kettle and a saucepan or two, and a couple of mugs, and some small packages, as of tea and sugar and the like, a fishing-rod, a milking-pail, and three ducks, tied separately by the flat yellow feet, that set up a loud un-dignified quacking. The man put the cover over the cart again. Dermot felt a little bit of a fool.

"I 'm sorry," he apologized, "I thought—"

"I know what you thought, Squire," the tinker-man said with dignity. "You thought you would find things there from the house we left. Squire, there is no dog I can't steal from its master, and there is no colt I can't steal from its mother's side, and sell under the eye of the owner," he went on in his soft, melancholy voice, "and herself, this woman, could take the watch from your vest and the money from your pocket while you are talking with her. There is science in all that. But we do not pilfer houses, Squire. We are robbers, we tinker people, not thieves." And he, and she, and the brown donkey waited patiently.

"Why are you leaving Glenmalure?"

"Because, Squire, life near a house, or with walls around us, is not life at all. Water from pipes is not good, nor butcher's meat; no, nor baker's bread. That is the way they live in houses. A badger in a barrel is the same as a man in a house. In a house there is no fairs to attend, to buy and sell horses to the ignorant people, nor the trick of three cards to play on the drunken farmers of the fair, or races to see. And going around, herself, this woman, might find a man she likes better than me, and I might find a woman I like better than this woman. So it is not fair to us to be in one place."

"Also," said the woman in a hoarse, not unmusical voice, "of all houses that is not a good house."

"There is this, too, Squire. There is a man looking around that house, seeking, we think, the man who is in that house. And tinker people will fight against tinker people or against house people, but will not meddle with fights between house people and house people. If anything happened to the man of that house, it would go ill with us of the roads."

"Also," the woman persevered, "that is a bad house."

"What do you mean?" Dermot asked sharply. "Ghosts?"

She laughed.

"Ghosts are for children," she answered. "There is worse than ghosts. There is ill-luck, that is against man and beast and tree."

"Is that all, Squire?" the man asked.

"Yes. What is your name?"

"The name that is on me is *Gilla Na Glas*—in the English, the 'Lad of Deceits.' And the name that is on this woman she is under bond never to tell, so that she is known as *Ban Gan Ainm*—in the English, the 'Woman without a Name.'"

The little brown donkey moved on, the cart creaked, the woman's soft bare feet padded quietly as a dog's upon the dust. Dermot put his hand in his pocket, took out a gold coin.

"To soften the road," he offered.

"We thank you, no, Squire," *Gilla Na Glas* answered. "We have no need. If we had need," he said, "we would have taken it when you were looking into the cart."

§ 4

The tinkerman had said there was some one about the house looking for D'Arcy, and for a moment the phrase had not registered rightly in Dermot's brain. It might be a bailiff or process-server, or some detective, but suddenly Dermot thought, "Is it the Citizen?"

He considered for an instant going after the cart and owners, and questioning them as to this man's appearance, but the bushes and the dusk had swallowed them up, as natural things fade into a natural background. And besides they could tell him nothing, he figured, barring a suspicion. Also, it might be anybody. The idea of Hogan on the trail of vengeance put the gentle idea of the roses out of his head, so that he went ahead unthinkingly, not crossing the fields as he had planned, but walking until he was in the shadow of the great gate. A thousand people might pass and look into the house, he decided. It was a thousand to one against it being the Citizen.

He stood pondering. To his ear there came suddenly, softly the whistling of the *Shan Van Voght,* a crisp step. Some one was coming down the road. Dermot waited, dumb.

"On the Curragh of Kildare,"

the whistle changed to a low song.

"The boys will all be there,
With their pikes in good repair,
Says the *Shan Van Voght.*"

"Lord God!" Dermot prayed aloud. A tweed-clad figure swung toward the gate, big and lithe in the dusk. It stopped suddenly.

"Who's that?"

"It 's I, Citizen, Dermot McDermot."

"What are you doing here?"

"No, Citizen.   What are you doing here?"

Dermot stepped forward and laid a hand upon the tweed sleeve.   Yes, it was the Citizen.   He looked into the handsome daring face.   It was difficult to imagine that the figure in the Irish tweeds, with the gay scarf and gay handkerchief, and the jaunty tweed hat with the salmon flies in it, was on a desperate errand, but the eyes were hard, the mouth was hard, and the pocket of the coat bulged with what Dermot guessed at.

"Citizen," Dermot insisted, "what are you doing at Glenmalure?"

"My lad—" Hogan's voice was cold—"go on your way."

"I will go on my way," Dermot said, "if you will come with me."

Dusk ended suddenly.   Night came.   A star sprang out in the east, and a cluster of little stars blinked faintly after it.   A little wind came up and rustled the trees, and a faint uneasy sound came from them, not the cradle-song of evening, but a sort of restrained moaning, a sort of secret sobbing.   About the spot where they were standing there was a strange doomed feeling.   About the valleys and the hillsides the cottage lamps were being lighted, and the golden pin-points were com-

forting happy things. But where they were was
no comfort or happiness. They might have been
on an island in some cold sea, on some malignant
island in a cold benighted sea.

"Citizen," Dermot asked, "are you going into
Glenmalure?"

"I am."

"Is it—is it for what you said, Citizen?"

"Go on your ways home, lad." Hogan's voice
came cold, peremptory. "Don't meddle in this."

"Citizen," Dermot pleaded, "come with me and
leave John D'Arcy alone."

"Leave this man alone!" Hogan laughed.
"Do you know I've risked my liberty, and my life
as well, if you want to know, for the chance, the
certainty of this evening? And now leave him
alone? What do you take me for?"

"I take you," Dermot said, "for a gallant officer and an Irish gentleman. You can't murder
this man."

"I am not going to murder this man. I am just
going to kill him. By Heaven!" he swore suddenly, "you're wasting my time. Go home."

He went past Dermot, and taking a bunch of
keys from his pocket began to work at the lock of
the wicket-gate. It opened with a soft click.

"Are you determined to do this thing, Citizen?"

"I am."

"Then I am coming with you."

The Citizen turned on him. His face in the starlight was white with rage.

"If you make an attempt to follow me," he said, "or raise an outcry, you'll be sorry."

"I am coming."

Hogan was beside himself with anger. His feet shuffled. His teeth ground. He pulled something from his pocket.

"Take one step forward," he said, "and though I hate to do it, Dermot, I'll pole-ax you with the butt of this."

A little chill of fear entered Dermot. He saw the bluish mass against the white of Hogan's hand. The eery moaning of the trees continued. He was afraid. He was undoubtedly afraid.

"You won't, Citizen," he said quietly. He stepped forward on unsteady feet. Each second he waited for the stunning crash between his eyes. The Citizen lowered the weapon at last. He caught Dermot by the shoulder. His fingers bit into muscle and bone like steel hooks.

"Listen," he whispered fiercely. "What I'm doing to-night is removing somebody who is good for neither God, man, nor beast. Do you think I could live easily and know that my sister's heart and life were broken and my father brought to his grave by this man, and that he was still on earth?

I am not doing murder. I am doing justice."

"There is a hell for people like him, Citizen,"
Dermot pleaded unsteadily.

"If there is, then he goes there to-night," said
the Citizen. "Now go home."

"I will not leave you, Citizen. If it is a matter
of justice, I will see justice done."

"You will see the ugliest thing in the world,"
Hogan warned him; "you will see a man killed.
You will not be able to forget it, Dermot. It may
haunt you. Please go home."

"No, Citizen," he said steadily. "I'll come."

Hogan hesitated a moment, and Dermot
thought, with rising hope, that he would turn and
go away with him, giving up the whole thing in disgust. He released Dermot's shoulder.

"All right," he said, "damn you! Come!"

They walked up the drive together. They
walked up in the starlight beneath the moaning
trees. Under his feet Dermot felt the rough un-
raked gravel of the drive, and once leaving it, he
was all but knee high in rough grass. His heart
sank. So this was what Glenmalure had come to
in a short month. The smooth drive, the lawns
that was once fair as a bowling-green. Desolation! Desolation! He felt, with the occult sub-
liminal sense of one who has to do with the soil,
that the land of Glenmalure was surely hostile.

As though it resented having been groomed from its former hillside wildness into a tame estate, and then once more deserted. Hostility was beneath his feet. The trees on the drive rustled resentment, hostility. A deserted, injured, insulted place. The house loomed alone there in the cold starlight. No windows were lighted. It was like an immense blind thing. A wounded, blinded, immense thing. The small dank wind moaned among the trees. An acute fear, a sense of isolation in a perilous place, came on Dermot. The dead house and the ghostly moaning trees, and beside him, a little in front of him, the dark passionate man in whose heart was poison. A wild desire came on him to turn and run away. To shout for help and run away. But he trudged silently after and beside the silent figure.

Hogan went up to the oak door. He fiddled with no keys this time. He put out his hand and raised the great knocker on the door. He turned to Dermot.

"Are you still determined to come in?"

A cold nausea came over Dermot. He was afraid of what was coming. A desire was burning in him to turn and go away. To tell the Citizen that he had done all he could to stop it, and to go away. He had done all he could, and he could do no more. But—but he must stay.

"Yes, Citizen," he said, "I 'm coming in."

The Citizen brought down the knocker on the door.

Dermot thought for a wild moment that, after all, John might not be here. He might be away. Hogan knocked again peremptorily. There was a slow treading of steps inside. The door opened a little. There was the yellow of lamplight.

"Who 's there?" John asked. And, "You can't come in," he said.

The Citizen pushed the door open, and stepped inside. Dermot followed him. John was standing in the hall, a tall lamp in his hand. He was dressed carefully, as though ready to go out. His face turned white, grayish white, as he looked at them.

"Who are you?" he said. "What do you want?"

Hogan closed the door coolly.

"I am the Commandant Hogan," he said, "and the lad you know. And I want you," he said ominously. Down the hall a room was lighted. "Go ahead in there," he ordered.

John put down the lamp. His hand was shaking. He walked ahead. His step was not firm. He put out a hand to steady himself against the wall as he walked. Dermot's eyes wandered in a shock around the hall. He could not believe he was in Glenmalure—in Connaught's house.

The hall was empty and dark—ravished. In the great fireplace no fire was, and the mellow clock that had been made by Huguenot refugees from Nantes—that was gone. Gone were the pictures from the walls—white unseemly rectangles showed where they had been—and the big comfortable chairs were gone. Only a head or so of moose or chamois on the walls, that seemed to make the place appear more deserted, so deserted did they themselves appear. And everywhere was paper-littered, and the package-wrapping that is called excelsior. A queer odor came to Dermot's nostrils, an acrid and oleaginous taint in the air, that Dermot was perfectly acquainted with, but to which he could n't give a name for the moment. What the devil was it, anyway?

He followed the pair ahead to the drawing-room. On a chair in the hall was a light coat, and a soft gray hat, tackle such as one travels in. Beside the chair was a pigskin bag. John was going away. They had interrupted him just as he was going away. Why had n't the fool gone before? Dermot asked futilely.

His heart sank when he saw the drawing-room. How could Connaught ever come back here? he thought. God! what a wreck! Even the carpets had gone from the floor. All the walls were bare

of pictures, and the cabinets where Glenmalure
had kept the grotesque curiosities he loved—they
were gone or rifled. All the little ivory chessmen
some Persian craftsman had made; the snuff-boxes
of enamel and jewels; the cunningly painted fans;
the old Roman coins; the autographs of great ancient men—all, all were gone. A desk, a light
fragile thing some French artificer had made, and
that Connaught used and loved, had been prised
open with a poker. It was a pathetic little feminine thing, and to see it now, wrenched and splin-
tered—to Dermot it was the last straw.

"You filthy swindler!" he roared at John.
"I'll horsewhip you within an inch of your life."

"Is this John D'Arcy?" Hogan asked.

"Yes, of course." Dermot turned to the Citizen in wonder at the question. He was appalled
by the saturnine passion in the officer's face. A
purple flush suffused it, and a great vein was standing out between his brows. He had taken his
hat off and thrown it on a chair. The scar of his
left temple showed grotesquely white, like a
brand. His eyes were blazing. His speech came
calmly, reserved, and this made his face more terrible still, so contrasted was speech and appearance.

"I wanted to be sure," he said. "I've only

seen the man once before, and he wore a beard then." He looked at D'Arcy coolly, minutely, as though he were examining some interesting, repelling thing. "You know me, don't you?"

"What—what do you want?"

The Citizen looked around the room keenly. The odor again offended Dermot's nostrils. It was powerful, choking. He went across and opened a window. The wind blew in and bellied the curtains. The lamp on a side table flared a little. Dermot remembered what the smell was —the odor of kerosene-oil. A lamp had been broken somewhere.

"So you 've looted this place, too." The Citizen smiled wryly. "You 're getting to be quite good at that sort of thing. Did you make as good a hand here as when you deserted my sister, and bolted with her jewels and money to gamble at Nice and Monaco? Not so good a haul this time. No?"

"What are you going to do?" John's voice was shaky. "Kill me?"

Dermot looked at him. The man was terrified, yet about him somehow some dignity remained. He was making an effort to stand upright and face Hogan. The dark neat suit, the immaculate collar, the mellow russet brogues, even the early rosebud in the buttonhole, so jaunty, so ready for a journey—and above these the strained white terrified face.

"Are you going to kill me?" John asked hoarsely.

"Just that!" said the Citizen.

"I have done nothing for you to kill me."

"Listen." The Citizen's own voice was hoarse now. "When you left my sister, her heart was broken—not for love of you, but because she felt she was being cheapened, soiled. There are people who are walking, living flame, and when you degrade them, they die. My sister was one of them. And she had no vitality to give her little son, and he died. And my father, the great rebel —the Incorruptible, they called him—he could no longer live, and he died from grief. Before God! John D'Arcy," his voice vibrated, "I lay on you the death of these three who were dear to me. Even your son was dear to me, because it was my sister's child. You could go free in courts of law, I know, but from me you cannot escape alive."

There was a terrible heartrending sincerity in Hogan's voice. It seemed as if all his spirit were quivering with pain and anger. Even the horrible, indicting words were not so powerful as the naked quivering voice.

"Go out of the room, Dermot," Hogan directed. "And you, if you know any prayers, say them: for your life is done."

Dermot turned to go. There was nothing more he could do, nothing say. He could not sincerely even try any more, after hearing Hogan's terrible cry. No, John was done.

"Give me a chance," John whispered.

"What chance?".

"I'll fight you."

"You!" Hogan laughed with immense contempt. "Where? When?"

"Anywhere. Anytime."

"Citizen." Dermot stopped and spoke. "The man is right. Give him that chance. If you kill him as you propose, you will be just an executioner, and you will have taken that office. It has not been given you. The other way is the way of a gentleman, I think. It would seem right that way."

"But how?"

"Can't you meet him in Belgium?"

The Citizen laughed. "Do you think if I took my eyes off him, I would ever see him again? And how much would my liberty be worth, if I let him out of my sight to-night?"

"That's so," Dermot nodded.

"I—I have a gun in my bag," John said.

They looked at him. His eyes were shifting from side to side. There was a rictus on his face of strained determination. He was like a cornered rat, fighting in desperation.

"Yes, Citizen," Dermot said. There had appeared on the Citizen's face for an instant the question, "Shall I?" "Yes, Citizen," Dermot urged. John understood, too.

"I 'll get it," he said.

A look from Hogan, and D'Arcy stopped at the first step he took. "Go out and bring it in," the Citizen told Dermot.

Dermot went into the hall slowly. His heart was heavy. Never in his life had he thought his heart could be so heavy as it was now. He seemed to have brought up against a wall of inevitability, so high, so cold. This, he recognized, was the end of John, and—God help himself, he said—he could see no wrong in it.

The odor of the lamp-oil was powerful in the closed hall. There must have been more than one lamp spilled, he thought. He noticed as he walked a piece of paper wet. Mechanically he picked it up. He picked up another. There were hangings on the wall. He examined them.

"So that 's it," he said. Could it have been the tinker people? No, he was assured, it was n't the tinker people.

He took up the bag beside John's hat and coat and opened it. There were a sleeping-suit and shirts and a collar-box, and brushes. He rummaged down. A crisp sheaf of paper met his hand. He pulled it out. A great bundle of bank-notes met his eye. "So!" he thought. A little bag of wash leather came under his fingers. He brought it up and opened it. Connaught's rings and jewelry.

"So that's it!" John was ready to disappear with everything, eh? The money he had made from looting the house, and the jewelry Connaught had left behind her when she fled. And Glenmalure sprinkled with oil. A match as he went, eh? and all would be blamed on the tinker people. Ah, good man John!

"Have you found it?" Hogan called. Dermot's fingers came on chilled metal. "I think so," he said. He drew it from the bag. It was a silvered, slender weapon, with an inlaid butt, mother-of-pearl. He broke it, and snapped it to again. Every chamber filled. He put the bank-notes and the rings in his pocket, slowly. He came back to the drawing-room.

"All right. Give it to him," said the Citizen.

Dermot walked over to John, and held out the shining pretty weapon. "Believe me, John, I've done everything I could to save you, but now I

think you're getting a better chance than you de-
serve." John snarled at him. There were no
words to his answer. There was just a bestial
sound. Dermot walked back to the Citizen. He
noticed a blue gleam in Hogan's hand. It had a
threatening deadly look, like a snake's head, like
the head of a black and deadly snake.

"Go out now, Dermot," the Citizen said, "go
out now and close the door, and one of us will be
with you in a minute."

Dermot looked across the room to where John
was standing, nervous, paying no attention seemingly. What a fool the man was, Dermot
thought; he was standing right by the lamp, his
face and shoulders bathed with brilliance. Where
the Citizen stood by the fireplace were shadows.

"If John D'Arcy comes out," Dermot said, "he
will have a little matter to talk over with myself."

"If John D'Arcy goes out," Hogan turned to
Dermot, "he goes free. Do you understand?
You are not to stop him. He is to go free. But
he won't come out—"

And then the loud outrageous crack burst in the
room; an evil sulphuric odor in the air. The Citizen spun around, and clapped his left hand to his
right shoulder. His revolver clattered on the
floor.

"The cowardly swine!" he groaned.

Dermot had an instant's vision of John standing by the lamp. Then the lamp was lifted and thrown on the floor. A crash of glass, and darkness lit only by a little flame on the floor. The wick was still burning. John's feet rushed through the door into the hall. The second lamp was quenched. Dermot heard him groping in the hall.

"Citizen," Dermot called, "where are you? Are you all right?"

"I'm all right," Hogan grunted. "He's just nicked me in the shoulder. Get a light."

John was tugging at the front door. Dermot could hear him cursing bitterly. Then there was the rush of his feet up the stairs.

"A light!" Hogan's voice came painfully. "Damn it! lad, quick!"

A gust of wind in the room moved a sheet of paper against the rufous flame of the wick. The wind bellied a curtain. There was a flash of fire on the ground. There was a great banner of flame in the room.

"Quick, Citizen, for God's sake!"

The room was suddenly a sheet of yellow-and-blue flame, shallow flame, like grass afire. Dermot caught the man somehow and pushed him down the hall. Fire was creeping along the hangings, was racing along the floor. Dermot pulled

at the door.   It opened easily.   They were out in
the cool air.   Behind them the door crashed to
from the wind.

"How the blazes——?"

Dermot drew a great shuddering sigh of relief.
His arms were shaking, and his eyes were unsteady.   His heart was beating with great thumps
as of a drum.

"The house is on fire," Hogan said incredu-
lously.

"Sprinkled with oil it was," Dermot told him.

The flame inside had a very steady roar, like a
great wind, and the windows of the ground floor
began to show great orange whorls and curling
waves of fire.   Then a mantle of smoke would
belch against a window, and the flames be obscured
for an instant.   Then again the fire would come
curling, saffron and deep red.   Windows tinkled
as they broke.   A buffet of fiery air struck them
and drove them back.   Obscene heavy smoke
sagged forth slowly.   Flakes of soot flurried
through the air.   The Citizen was ghostly white
in the glare.

" 'T was lucky he just gashed you," Dermot
said.

"Ah, he did more," Hogan grunted.   "The
blasted thing 's in my shoulder."

THE ROOM WAS SUDDENLY A SHEET OF FLAME, SHALLOW FLAME, LIKE GRASS AFIRE

"I 'm sorry, Citizen. It was my fault."

"Ah, no. It was my own fault," Hogan denied. "I should have shot him when you were out of the room."

There was a lurid infernal light now on the lawn. Fire licked out of the windows and seemed to try to climb the walls. Within there was a crash as of something heavy falling. Great floods of smoke passed against them. They staggered back, choking, coughing. The trees were evident in the red darkness, black, immense trees, threatening shivering trees. More shallow crash of glass.

"My God! Citizen!" Dermot said. "The man 's inside!"

"John. He ran up the stairs."

"He 's not inside." Dermot jumped around in panic. He started toward the door. The Citizen caught him with his good left hand.

"He 's not inside, I tell you!" he shouted. "He 's got away. Do you think a fellow like that would get caught? He 's slipped out somewhere, and escaped. I tell you—I—I—I—" he ended weakly.

He was looking up at the highest windows. Dermot followed his glance. John had broken some panes and was clawing at a sill.

"Wait! Wait!" Dermot shouted. "I'll get a ladder. Stay where you are. I'll get a ladder."

He tore racing around to the stable-yard. The cobbled ground was lighted by the flame from the rear of the house. He tore open a shed door. The place was empty.

"There's no ladder there!" He was puzzled.

He blundered from shed to shed, lighting matches, dropping them. Everything empty, everything bare.

"He's sold the ladders. Oh, God!" he wailed, "he's sold the ladders."

He staggered back, stupefied.

"Citizen," he said, "the ladders are gone. What'll I do?"

John was standing on the window-sill.

"Can't you tie sheets together," Dermot shouted, "and let yourself down?" He ran forward. "Do you hear me?"

Then John jumped.

His heels must have caught as he sprang, for he turned a ludicrous somersault in the air, and shot forward head first, like a diver. Toward the ground he went, as a diver goes toward the water head first. And smoke and flame covered him, belching from the lower windows as from artillery.

"A great blackguard is dead this day," the Citizen said. "I say—do you hear me?—a great blackguard is dead this day!"

He went on muttering to himself as though drunk. Everything now appeared a horror of delirium to Dermot. Vast shadows and heavy clouds of smoke. Crash of timbers, tinkle of glass. A black cat whirled out of somewhere, and fled, its hair bristling, its tail rigid, its eyes baleful and green. And all the birds around were aroused and fluttered in the air with shrill cries of alarm and wonder. Rats crept from the cellars, and galloped, like grotesque diminutive horses, into the long grass. And a colony of wasps, that had built their mud nest against the eaves of Glenmalure, now hummed with savage anger in the air.

"I must get away," the Citizen was moaning. "I must get away." He was going around in little circles. He caught Dermot by the sleeve. His face was drawn with pain and weakness. His eyes were glassy. "I know you," he said, "but I can't tell who you are. Listen, Citizen," he implored earnestly, and with a great dignity, "I am wounded and in danger, and it is important that I get away."

"Give me your left arm," Dermot said.

He pulled Hogan's left arm over his shoulder, bending a little down, and then, straightening up, took the man's whole weight on his back. He went down the avenue quickly, breaking into a run nearly, so eager was he to escape from the sudden mad inferno behind him—the blazing roaring house, the fleeing rats, the shrill affrighted birds, and John lying somewhere, broken like a stick, and covered with smoke and flame. Before him as he went a queer blotchy shadow of himself and his burden traveled, a great bloated shadow as of some giant of the under-world carrying prey. And somewhere in the shadows he saw the green baleful eyes of the household cat, who had settled to examine the scene whence he had fled. And the wind snarled and keened in the trees as he went. It keened and moaned above him in the black, indignant trees.

He got out through the wicket-gate and into the road of high white hawthorn bushes, that were green and sane. On to the white dust of the road, soft, familiar. His face, as he put one hand to it, was wet with perspiration. He pulled his collar loose. The Citizen was limp as a bag. He lowered him from his shoulder, and carried him in his arms, until even his arms were tired. There was the chirrup of a little stream near at hand. He slid from the road down to it. He laid the Citizen on the grass. Yes, his heart was beating, slow and faint, but beating. He wet a handkerchief and passed it over the man's burning temples.

"Is that you, Dermot?" he opened his eyes. "Good lad!" And, "I'm glad I didn't shoot that fellow after all," he said. And his head fell forward again.

Along the road now, in single persons, in twos and threes, came the country people toward the flaming house. Now came two young men on bicycles, and now an old woman came along with shawl and stick, muttering to herself, talking aloud in gibberish, mad with loneliness and excitement. And a farmer tore along on a great white horse, half galloping, half shambling; a country policeman, buttoning his tunic as he ran. Afar off came the steady pacing of Minnaluishe, his own mare. He put his coat beneath Hogan's head and walked out to meet the trap.

"O'Hagan, stop!"

"Is it you, Master Dermot?" came the groom's voice. His tones were vibrating with excitement. "Let you get up sir, let you get up now. The Hangman's House is afire. The Hangman's House is on fire, and the devils are dancing in the flames."

"Get down, you damned fool!" Dermot ordered. "Stop your shouting, and bear a hand here. I've a hurt man."

The groom slipped down without a word, and followed Dermot into the shadow of the hedge. Between them they carried the Citizen toward the dog-cart. A yellow beam of light from the big-lamp flashed on the limp man's face. O'Hagan all but dropped him in the road.

"Jesus, Mary, and Joseph!" he said affrightedly. "It's the Citizen!"

"Do you know this man?" Dermot asked.

"I do, sir," O'Hagan rapped out.

"Are you one—one of his?"

It was queer to see the easy-going groom, whom Dermot would have associated only with the jovial way of horses, put on hardness and efficiency like a uniform.

"I am, sir."

"Let's get him up. Easy, now, easy!"

"Is there a doctor among you?"

"There is, sir."

"Then drive to Dermotstown, and after, go get a doctor."

"Not to Dermotstown, sir."

"Do what I tell you, blast you!"

"Master Dermot," O'Hagan said firmly, "I know what to do in a case like this. And I know where to bring this gentleman. I'm sorry to go contrary to you, Master Dermot, but I've got to do what I think right. You're my master, sir,

and a better and kinder one never lived. But the
Citizen—" his voice was awed with the name—
"he is my officer."

§ 7

They had pulled up on the slope of Three-Rock
so that O'Hagan could run back to a roadside bar,
and fetch some brandy. Dermot slipped his hand
inside Hogan's vest. The heart was beating
slowly and firmly. There was probably nothing
to worry about, unless the bare chance he had got
a puncture in the lungs.

"I'm all right." The Citizen came to for an
instant. "Don't worry. I'm all right."

"Hush, man. Quiet." He was in Dermot's
arms, with a rug about him. His head subsided
again on Dermot's shoulder.

The mare turned around, a little impatient at
being kept standing, and the dog-cart turned, and
in the distance Dermot could see the yellow blaze
of Glenmalure. It had subsided now into a steadi-
ness as of a bonfire. Possibility of extinguishing it
there was none. By the time firemen could arrive from Kingstown or Dublin, there would be
nothing to save. Even the birds would have be-

come quiet, and the homeless wasps sought some ancient hollow tree.

He thought to himself that he was exhausted from the night, so little emotion did he feel at the burning of Glenmalure. There it had been, a house, firm, mortised; ready to cope with rain or storm, with wind, with lightning. And now before his eyes, it was being eaten with fire, and in a little while would not be at all. Only charred stones, and lopsided dangerous walls, and a hearthstone where grass would grow to show what once had been a humorous happy house.

But had it ever been a humorous happy house? Dermot asked himself. And now that he thought of it, it had not. It had been a setting for this grim fierce Lord Justice, but when he was out of it, what of him remained in stone or rafter. Nothing. And even Connaught's sweet laughter and soft virginal life had failed, could not bend it to humor or gentleness. It had never known the soft quiet life of a house. It should never have been. It would soon not be.

Some vague English merchant had reared it, whose name was now forgotten—some buying or selling man, who was not sib to the soil. And solely because he had liked the soft green country, the purple mountains, the silver Irish Sea, he had built him a house in a country he had not known as a wide-eyed child, where ancestors of his were not buried, who would bring protection and luck, a country in which he himself had no traditions. A brand-new man in an ancient brooding country, he had picked a place he liked, and built a house to cover him. And that was not enough. He had not even fought for it, spilling his blood as Normans and Elizabethans, as Scots and Cromwellians had, to give them a lien on the Irish earth. He had just intended, good-naturedly, perhaps, but, after all, intended. So that now even his name was forgotten, his coming having been a casual worthless event, and where his children now abided, and even how many of them there had been, was not known, except to lawyers and auctioneers.

And now that he and his were gone, there had come into it the old Lord Chief Justice and his sweet child, and their coming had not sanctified it, brought it to life. For with them they had brought no struggle, no passion, that would make the fresh roof-tree vibrate with sympathy and life. Here there had been no tender marriage-bed, no little children born. And the house itself he had taken only as a monument to title and dignity, assuming it as some robe of office, gilded, showy, which one respects but does not love. He had worn the house as he had worn the red robe of justice, with pride and dignity. Ah, but the pride was in himself and the dignity, too. And the house and grounds had resented that this owner had no love in his heart for it, only pride as a possession. A queer thing, Dermot thought, how it had been difficult to keep bees there—the mysterious bees who will only grace a righteous happy place, so sensitive they are. And the grass was ever riotous, and such battle there had been in the gardens, between the soil and men, before flowers would come and the purple damson and black cherry. Only the apple-trees that are ever kind, ever patient, ever generous, had flourished there. All else rebelled. And if the place had ever given out kindly comfortable exhalations, had ever been an abode of gentleness and beauty, would the shrewd sensitive country folk have dared call it Hangman's House?

There is more to a house than stones and mortar, beams and wattles, golden thatch or blue slates, Dermot knew out of an ancient race wisdom, these things are but the crude material covering of a house. A house is within. A house is past. There must be kindly life to it, soft dreams by a fireside: love and protection, a hush as the old clock ticks: swept hearth and mellow candles. And sanctuary for friend and enemy as they cross the threshold. So abide peace and beauty. And a house has memory of ancestors gone by, shrewd and kindly, or heroic men, and women with great softness in their eyes. And the rafters grow mellow with age and mellow with the memories of little children who played upon the floor, and who are now—God help them!—big men and women, and who will soon be in the soft October of their years. Out of the kindly entity went a welcome into the soft air, so that swallows came and built their nests fearlessly in the eaves, and the bees favored the garden, bringing honey and blessings. And the flowers were proud of the house, the daffodils, and the proud tall holly-hocks. And on the lawn the peacocks strutted, calling their proud high scream. Even the little rain came gently and jovial was the bursting winter wind. And there was merriment when the sun shone, and with the moon came peace.

And now that Lord Glenmalure was dead, the house Glenmalure had no further reason for being, unless to shelter some other casual folk whose traditions were not with it. It seemed to Dermot that Connaught was always predestined to come to Dermotstown. Never had she seemed a stranger to the house of quiet. And the house mourned her, it seemed to him, missing her friendly calls. Glenmalure had only been a lodging to her. A lodging for years, certainly, but a lodging all the

same. It had no duties to her, it had not seen her
born. It was not necessary to her. Now that
the house was gone, she had Dermotstown for a
home. The old sweet place would enfold her.
And she would be welcome to the lawn of the sun-
dial and the peacocks, to the garden of the flowers
and the bees. The dove of the steel-blue breast
would call her with its soft crooning, and every
tree in the garden would incline to her, every
tree—

It was burning down. In yellow and red it was
burning. Soon there would be only smouldering
embers, and blackened stones. And not even that
soon, for the country people would take the granite blocks to build new cottages for the tillers of
the soil. And the mountain would sweep down,
the green lower slope of it. Grass would arise,
and the trim trees would burst into rugged splen-
dor, and over the courts where John D'Arcy had
played tennis the bell-wether would lead his docile
flock. And the hare lie in the long grass. And
nice nimble goats pass on their light feet. It was
burning down, it would soon be gone. And when
it was gone, the great Glenmalure would have
quitted the last of mortal things. His red robe
he had put off, his black cap he had put off. He
had put off his mortal body, and now his house was
gone. And gone with it, Dermot thought, was

the horrible name the people had given it: the Hangman's House. That would be forgotten. Of him nothing remained now but a thing he had valued least of all—a song young men would be singing in the hills of Kerry and the mountains of Donegal, the "Song of Defeat."

O'Hagan came racing through the shadows. He sprang into the gig. He held brandy to the Citizen's lips.

"Is that you, Dermot?" Hogan asked sleepily. "Who's this?" He saw the groom.

"'T is one of your own boys, my general," O'Hagan answered. "'T is all right, sir. O'Hagan is the name that's on me, and my station is a corporal in the Dublin Guards."

"Then I'm all right," Hogan said.

"Master Dermot," O'Hagan whispered, "'t is queer news I heard at Doyle's and me getting the brandy."

"What?"

"'T is what they say there: that John D'Arcy is dead. Outside the house they found him and his skull split from the height he fell. A policeman brought the word and him flying for the coroner."

"Did they say," Dermot asked strainedly, "how it happened?"

"There was a great argument about it, and

Bridgeen Roe of the mountain was there and she laughing.   And she said a strange deep thing."

"What—what was it?"

"She said he was a wronging man, Master Dermot.   He wronged men and women and dumb beasts, and he might have escaped.   But in the latter end he wronged a thing she had never known a man to wrong and die in a bed.

"She said he wronged a house, and the house destroyed him."

XXII

§ 1

ANNE had wired of the fire and of the death of John to Connaught in Cornwall, and by breakfast-time in the morning the reply had come. "I am crossing to-night. Please meet me." "You cannot come," Dermot had answered. "I must come," fluttered back. "You shall not come," he insisted. "But what shall I do?" The quality of a little helpless wail crept to him over the wires. "Mother goes to you to-night," he decided. And the little Quaker lady unquestioningly crossed the Irish Sea.

For Dermot was afraid of what might happen at the inquest. Some one might have seen him and Hogan enter or leave the grounds, or the harsh crack of John's revolver-shot might have struck some inquisitive ear. So that it were better she were away in case anything happened.

But nothing of the kind arose. The coroner, an official all red beard and silk hat and unfolded umbrella, gathered the jury into the main room in

MacInerney's public house. A police constable reported to seeing the blaze, and discovering what remained of John, and this was corroborated by the country people. The only question arising was whether it was suicide or accident. Evidence was brought forward as to the eccentricity of the deceased, as John was now called respectfully. He was a passionate queer man, it was averred, and the shooting of the horse was remembered. Also the fact that he had discharged all the servants and taken a tinker couple to tend him.

"And why are these two not here?" the coroner asked.

"And how would they be here, and they gone God knows where in the Wicklow Mountains?" the constable asked back.

The coroner admitted the justice of this. A juryman with a Northern accent queried as to whether they might not have murdered the deceased.

The coroner replied that it was a well-known fact that while these nomads were admittedly a race of thieves and rogues, yet murder was a crime never imputed to them. A man now and then had been killed in a faction fight at a fair, by their hands, but that could not be called murder. He had no hesitation in exonerating the tinker people, he said magnificently, and he drew attention to the juryman's being a Northerner and a townsman and unacquainted with the habits of the rural people. No, in his mind, the coroner said, the matter had narrowed to this: Had the deceased committed suicide while of unsound mind, or had it all been an accident?

A second juryman asked impatiently who ever heard of a man setting fire to a house and going to a top window and giving a leap the like of a goat. There would be no man as mad as all that; no, not in all the asylums of Ireland. If it was a thing a man wanted to do away with himself, what was all the water in the sea for? Or could he not find a convenient tree?

The coroner said, "True for him!" There had never been a doubt in his mind, the coroner said, but that the whole thing was an accident. The deceased had overturned an oil-lamp and the house blazed up, and finding himself trapped, he had sought safety in jumping, with disastrous results. He went on to deprecate the extensive use of oil-lamps in Ireland. In a country so furnished with water-power, he said, it was a dying shame that electricity was not availed of. In the Liffey alone there was power enough to light by electricity three counties, and when one considered the Shannon, the Nore, the Suir, the Lagan, the Bann—

A juryman said they would have electricity when they got Home Rule.

The coroner deprecated the discussion of political issues on such a sad occasion, but while on this subject, there were a few remarks he felt he might venture to make—

Outside, the country people were discussing in hushed awed tones the burning of the house and the death of John.   And there were many who inclined to the mystic belief that the house had killed him.   For was it not a known thing that there were lucky and unlucky houses?   And stone and wood were not the dumb cold things that people imagined them, but partially torn from the earth, and holding part of the earth's vitality. And if a house could shelter, could a house not kill?   And an old man said in a whisper that he had heard there was a mark on John, the mark of a horse's hoof.   And had John not shot the Bard of Armagh?   And some one else said that above the roar of the fire and the keening of the wind there had been heard the triumphant neighing of a horse.   These were terrifying things.

But in a casual way, after a casual discussion the jury brought in a more tremendous decision than any mad country theory.   They gave the enormous, terrifying verdict of the Act of God.

§ 2

His mother wrote: "Connaught is ill, Dermot. She has been so brave all this year, and now when the strain is over, she is just a little shaking child. But that is only for the present, dear son, and was to be expected, and will pass. And she will be all right again, thy Connaught. And thee must look after thyself for a while, son, for I cannot leave her. My love for thee and love from Connaught, too." And she said further in a postscript that she and Connaught were for going to France for a little while.

He was not sorry they would be gone, for there had come into his mind a scheme: that he would raze to the ground Glenmalure, with all its sad unnecessary memories. The gaunt walls with their blind windows stood up against the June sky, hideously rectangular against the curve of the hill and sky, blackened with smoke, foul with charred timbers. And slates were lying in the drive, and broken glass. He went to see Connaught's attorneys. They were not sympathetic, but they wrote her. They would not understand, but she did. She wired: "Yes, Dermot. Thanks!"

With a fury of work on him, he engaged con-
tractors, masons, stone-cutters. And stone by
stone the gaunt walls came down. The broken
greenhouses were taken away. All the remains of
the fire disappeared. And on the site of Glenmalure, there rose a long low farm-house, that would
be whitewashed when finished, and thatched with
golden thatch. And the lawns were let go, so
that a great crop of hay could grow on them, that
later would be cut down and piled into a great
stack. And where the flower beds had been,
there would grow the humble things of the field—
potatoes of the gentle white or purple flower, and
yellow wheat, and the coarse stalk of the bean.
The orchard he let stand, with the patient apple-
trees. But until the low golden-covered whitewashed farm-house stood there he would not be
satisfied, until it stood there with the blue turf
smoke curling from the chimney and little children
playing around the door. He would find a tenant
for the farm, some mountainy man with sturdy
mountainy woman, who would raise a sturdy brood
of children. Some person from near by who was
starving for land, and to whom the mountain
would be kindly. He thought he would even
change the name of the place.

"Neddy Joe," he asked, "do you remember

before the English man built Glenmalure?"

"Master Dermot, your Honor, I do."

"Was it always called Glenmalure?"

" 'T was not, then. Glenmalure was the name the Englishman put on it, for that Glenmalure was a wicked ancient place, the headquarters of the raiding Wicklow men. And him a quiet old fellow with side whiskers and romantic notions, he liked a fierce warlike name."

"Was there ever any other name on it?"

"There was so, Master Dermot. *Teekewn* was the name was on it."

"What does *Teekewn* mean?"

"It means the quiet house, Master Dermot, though even I am not old enough to remember a house there before the Englishman built Glenmalure."

Quiethouse Farm he decided he would call it. And already in fancy he could see it nestle against brown mountain and green field—the low whitewashed house with the roof of golden straw, and the blue turf smoke rising in the still air. Skips of honey-bees, and brown and white milch-cows. Ricks of hay and straw in the haggard, and stacks of black turf. Who would remember then there had ever been Hangman's House?

§ 3

So tired was he now, of evenings, that there was no time for reading or dreaming. Summer sped along. The wheat and barley turned from green to gold in the fields. The whinge of the scythe cut through the clover-laden hay. He was here, there, and everywhere, now at the pulling and steeping of the flax, now where the potatoes were being dug from the warm brown earth. And every day he found time to go up the glen to where the new sweet farm-house was arising out of the ruins of Glenmalure. So that at night when the corn-crake was calling in its measured musical rasp to the summer moon, sleep would come on him and it would seem no more than an hour until the thrushes woke singing outside the window, brown thrush and mistletoe thrush of the white breast, and he would rise while the foggy dew was on the grass, and snatching breakfast before the sun was up, be out around byre and stable.

His mother and Connaught had gone from the Channel Islands to Deauville, from Deauville to Ostend, thence into Holland. "I am coming home soon, Dermot," she wrote. "Connaught is well now; when I speak of thee, she reddens,

Dermot, like a wild rose of the hedge. Thee must n't expect to see the Connaught thee knew in all the trouble, Dermot, the brave little lady. Thee will find a sweet shy girl."

She went on to speak of how small the world was: "We met Sir Brian Maguire in Deauville, where he lost a great deal at the gaming-tables. He and I had a talk about it, and he promised to reform, but next night he went and broke the bank. Professor Mahaffy passed through. And thy friend Aloysius Corrigan, the Bird as thee calls him, was arrested in Ostend for impersonating King Leopold. He was kissing some girl in a café when his false beard slipped. I managed to get him out of gaol, and reasoned with him, and he cried, and said it was all due to his losing his mother at an early age. He borrowed a hundred pounds from Connaught, and went on to Baden-Baden.

"I shall be home within a week, Dermot, but will leave Connaught in England for a little while. There are some relatives whom she ought visit. Love to thee from Connaught, which she has asked me to send, and from thy Mother Anne.

"P.S. Aloysius has been arrested in Amsterdam, charged with intoxication and injuring seven policemen. Connaught is rocking with laughter and can only say, 'Good old Bird!' I have tele-

graphed an ambassador to use his offices to get
the poor boy out of prison. Thy Mother, Anne.

"It is the first time in a year," she added a
further postscriptum, "that I have heard little
Connaught laugh. Love from thy Mother
Anne."

He had come in from the mountain, after an
interview with the shepherds—he had bought a
pair of blue English sheep-dogs, sire and puppy,
and he had been eager to see how far their train-
ing had gone—and he was settling down in the
study to answer the letter. The short summer
night was setting in. The birds were quiet except for the loud corn-crake, and the soft blue
dusk was over the land like some peaceful dream.
A maid came with lamps.

"O'Hagan would like to be having a word with
you, sir."

"All right," Dermot said. "Come in,
O'Hagan. What is it?"

"'T is a gentleman," O'Hagan said, "would
like to say good-by to your Honor."

"Where is he?   Bring him in."

"'T is on his way he is," O'Hagan explained,
"to the foreign lands, and no time at him." And
Dermot understood it was the Citizen.

He went out and followed O'Hagan down the
drive. They turned into the road past the

lodge gate. A dog-cart was standing in the shadows, with a groom in front and a groom behind. Ahead of it a man leaned over the bars of a bicycle. Back down the road were two others. A man came forward out of the shadows toward Dermot. His step was familiar. He had a crisp black beard.

"Well, Dermot?" he said.

"Well, Citizen?"

"Go ahead," Hogan told the grooms. "I'll walk a bit down the road." The trap, and the bicycle men, moved forward.

"Are you going away, Citizen?"

"Yes, Dermot, I'm going away for good." He put his arm on Dermot's shoulder. "Are you coming with me to Timbuctu?" he smiled. "You asked me once."

"No, Citizen."

"Are you going to stay and marry the little lady?"

"I am, Citizen," he answered. There was a catch in his breath.

"You have changed, Dermot." Hogan smiled in the dusk. "You have changed since the day I met you at the Tara Hunt. You were a great boy that day, Dermot, but now there is no man I would sooner have back to back with me in a fight." He paused. "Dermot, what's this I hear you are doing to Glenmalure?"

"It was an evil house, Citizen, and I am tearing it down for the lady who owns it. And I am building a happy farm-house on the site. I shall find tenants—Citizen," he suggested, "why don't you stay? Take over the farm there, Citizen. Trout in the river in summer, Citizen, and grouse on the hills in the autumn, and in winter the Tara Hunt. And always racing, that you love. And you would have a thousand friends here, and your quiet farm. Make peace with the Government. Resign your commission. Don't go back to Africa, Citizen!"

They stopped in the blue soft dusk for a minute. A little wind moved and from the upland meadows brought the keen high scent of the mown clover. In the distance the light of Bailey's Strand winked white from the Hill of Howth. The corn-crake sounded in the distant field, and a trout jumped and splashed in a near-by stream.

"When I die in Africa, Dermot," Hogan said, "or wherever I die, there will be before my eyes Three-Rock Mountain, and in my nostrils the Irish clover, and in my ears the music of the Irish birds—"

"Stay here, then, Citizen."

"I am too much a soldier, Dermot—" he shook

his head—"to settle down. My father, the Incorruptible, would have been a great soldier, too, if there had been an Irish nation. It's a big job, too, this African thing, Dermot, for one never knows what will arise out of Africa. There are always men of the desert ready to preach the Holy War. Once the Crescent floated over Southern Europe, and that it may never again, we keep patrol."

"Then you are not coming back, Citizen?"

"I am coming back when I can, on leave and to see the land I love."

"But not as—"

"But not to raise troubles; is that what you mean, Dermot? Ah, no," he said; "the days of the Frenchmen on the seas are over. I am the last. Saint-Remy, General Hoche, General Humbert at Castlebar. Even the Great Emperor had it in his mind to come. And I, a poor major of horse, am the last."

They passed out of the fields to a bend of the road that ran past the brow of the mountain. Lonely, dim, mysterious, the mountain raised its purple bulk to the left of them. A little wind crooned down it from the three great boulders.

"I am the last, Dermot. There will be no longer sense to the song of the *Shan Van Voght*. The Poor Old Woman need no longer sing of the French upon the sea. For I am the last, Dermot, and I am going now."

Shrill and clear against the broad rasp of the corn-crake's call, high and thin above the wind came a sound as of keening. Some trick of tunnels, or of the breeze in the branches of the mountain ash, Dermot thought. But it persisted strangely. A muted heartbroken wail that chilled Dermot with awe. The men ahead had heard it, for they had stopped, and the Citizen too, for he called.

"See what that is," he directed.

A groom jumped from the dog-cart and ran up the heather slope. The wailing ceased, in a thin whisper of sound. For minutes they could hear the groom stumbling against tussocks. He returned.

"There was nothing, sir. There was nothing I could find."

"It was queer," said the Citizen.

" 'T was a queer thing—" hesitated the groom.

"Yes?"

"Your Honor, I thought I saw a poor old woman in it, with a long cloak and gray scattered hair, and her wringing her hands. But when I went up to her, your Honor—"

"Yes!"

"When I went up to her, sir, where I thought she was standing, sure there was no poor old woman in it at all. Only the heather, your Honor, the heather and the empty mountainy wind."

§ 4

In the white soft dawn the little town of Kingstown was sleeping. For three hours now there had been no night. Night had only been a shadow like a bird's wing. At eleven of the clock it had come, and at two of the morning was gone again. And now at five the sun had not risen, but for three hours it had been day. And every one slept; even the dogs, even the wind was sleeping. A shred of waning moon was cutting its short arc across the sky; it had hardly risen in the east. It would soon go down.

Dermot walked up and down the pier, waiting, for this morning Connaught was to come home. She would stay at Dermotstown all day and night, and to-morrow she would be for Kildare, where some of her mother's people lived, and thence she would come in a week to marry him quietly. In a week she would marry him, but this morning she would come.

For all that it was day now, the Bailey light blinked whitely, white as the fading moon. Howth slumbered in a soft blue peace. And back of him the ring of mountains—the Sugar Loaves and the Scalp and Three-Rock Mountain —were like drowsy sentinels guarding an enchanted land. The water *lap-lapped* gently against the bulkheads of the pier, and now and again came to his ears the sea-gull's soft cry. From the open part of the pier to the covered wharf he walked, and he stopped to watch the train that stood motionless and lifeless there; waiting to carry the people of the boat to Dublin town. How queerly domestic the train was, like some shabby sleeping man.

A faint flutter of wind rose. Came the sharp iodine smell of seaweed, and the nostalgic odor of the sea. Kingstown woke. A horse galloped. There was a banging of tin, the milkman was on his gentle household rounds. Porters shuffled sleepily out of nowhere on to the pier, talking in quiet hissing Welsh, men from over the water. A bulky Irish seaman appeared and cursed them heartily. The eastern sea-line had a faint flush of rose. The sails of trawlers appeared against it. The moon faded in the sky.

And then, over the edge of the water, climbed the Holyhead boat.

It forged over the pearly Irish Sea like some black monster out of a fairy-tale, its squat bows, its funnels with their two banneroles of smoke. Behind it the sun leaped into the air through a foam of white cloud. There was no more moon, and Bailey's light went out like a snuffed candle. A red-headed longshoreman came lumbering down the pier and sniffed the morning air.

"Well, glory be to God!" he announced, "and His Holy and Blessed Mother, but of all the days I ever knew, this is the grandest day!" He turned and addressed Dermot. "I've a wife and ten childer, mister, and my poor old father has been out of his mind now for nearly three years and 't is poorly I am myself," he said, "with the favorites losing all races, and my brother Joe leaping with the horrors of drink, but—would you believe it, mister?—I'm glad to be alive this day!"

"My bully man!"

It seemed so intolerably long to Dermot, waiting for the boat to come in, that he made his way up the pier again, and out to the promenade, where O'Hàgan was waiting with the horse and trap. He rubbed Minnaluishe's nose, and pulled her soft silky ears.

"Master Dermot," O'Hagan pondered, "did your Honor give e'er a thought to Miss Connaught's trunks and boxes?"

Dermot felt stunned.

"Suppose now your Honor drives home yourself with Miss Connaught, and leaves me to do the arguing with the sailormen. And let your Honor be sending back the Monk Magennis with a cart, and Miss Connaught can be taking with her a bag for small convenience.

"Ah," he said, " 't is well for your Honor!—to be driving up sweet Three-Rock Mountain on a summer morning, with a grand mare between the shafts, and a grand road under you, and with—" he was venturing, but Dermot's eye turned coldly on him—" with your breakfast," he concluded magnificently, "at the latter end."

An engine puffed noisily toward the pier. The boat swept through the opening of the breakwater. A long wave murmured before it, as it came. Swish of water beneath the pier. Shouting of longshoremen. Clanging of the engine-room bell.

The rails were laden with people, sleepy in the dawn. White wondering faces, black bodies, and great-coats buttoned in the fresh cool air. Dermot searched rapidly, but the face he wanted to see was not there. He walked alongside, up and down feverishly. No Connaught there. A sudden enormous fear came on him. She had not come. She would not come. She had changed her mind. She did not want him. She was not there.

§ 5

The sailors were rasping down the gang-plank to the pier. It had barely touched the structure when he was on it.

"Wait a minute!"

"Get out of my way!" He charged through to the deck. He walked around quickly. He dashed here and there in panic. He watched the white-faced heavy-coated passengers land. He trudged aft with a sick heart.

Near the taffrail he found her. A soft perfume came toward him like a perfume of the sea and morning. All of him tingled. He turned and saw a great white coat, a small hat. His heart bounded. Ah, the little heart-shaped face, the golden eyes!

"Connaught!"

She said nothing. In her eyes was a soft shy look, and there was flight in her pose.

"Connaught," he said, "I looked for you everywhere."

"I was looking for you, Dermot—" the soft low voice came hesitatingly—"but when the boat came near shore, Dermot, I got shy and frightened and slipped away back here. I am shy still." There was a little catch in her voice.

"Connaught!" He put his hands forward to her. She took them. He felt she was fluttering, like a bird one catches in the hand.

"Yes, Dermot."

"Connaught!" he said again. He let her hands go, and took her small shoulders.

"Yes, Dermot." Her eyes went down toward the deck.

"Connaught!"

She raised her head. Her cheeks flushed as now the eastern sky was flushing. She looked swiftly to the right of her, and to the left. She lifted the small heart-shaped face toward him. She had to stand on the toes of her little feet.

—THE END OF—
HANGMAN'S HOUSE.

Augsburg College
George Sverdrup Library
Minneapolis, Minnesota 55404